Dear Denise,

Enjoy!

Mark Sanford-Wood

GODFORSAKEN

by

Mark Sanford-Wood

Ardea Publishing

ARDEA

First Edition

Mark Sanford-Wood is hereby identified as author of this work in
accordance with Section 77 of the Copyright, Designs and
Patents Act 1988

Published by Ardea Publishing
ardeapublishing.com

Edited by Kate Finlayson

ISBN: 978-0-9931338-0-0

ARDEA

About The Author

Mark Sanford-Wood read medicine at Cambridge University and St. Bartholomew's Hospital before embarking on a career in General Practice. His early specialist training brought him into contact with holocaust survivors in London's East End where he developed a keen interest in the psychology of survival.

His work in General Practice led to him counselling many survivors of World War II from multiple theatres of war, extermination camps and gulags.

He now works in a variety of diverse roles in medicine, both nationally and in his adopted Devon.

Author's Note

Godforsaken is a story of loss and redemption, of despair and salvation. At times it is not an easy read. It has certainly not been an easy book to write, but is a story that demands to be told.

I have had the great honour in my professional life of working with many remarkable men and women. People who have triumphed over adversity that we in the comfort of our modern lives can barely begin to imagine. As this generation of heroes and heroines passes into the pages of history their personal stories stand as an inspiration, but also a salutary lesson to those who believe that society could never again descend to such depths.

Some passages in the book are distressing, but while Godforsaken is a work of fiction it reflects first-hand experiences and accounts that haunted many of those with whom I worked. Their constant optimism and determination to endure, whatever the price, was a lesson to me in the human spirit. To have avoided writing of the true horror they endured would have been to fail them.

Godforsaken is dedicated to all those who suffered for a greater cause and who bore the scars of that struggle. If I was in some limited way able to help those few I met to come to terms with their past then I hope that I repaid some small measure of the debt that we all owe to them.

Mark Sanford-Wood
Devon

November 2014

Acknowledgements

There are so many people without whom this book could not have been written.

To my parents, June and Robin, whose unswerving love and affection has been my lifelong rock.

To my father, whose passion for writing has been the motivation for my own work.

To my wife, Caroline, for her patience over countless weekends and evenings lost to writing.

To my friends for their enthusiasm in this as in so much else.

To my editor, Kate Finlayson, whose expertise, attention to detail and boundless enthusiasm has been a constant source of support. Without her wise words, guidance, cajoling and unerring dedication this book would not have been possible.

To Rosemary Goad, whose advice and interest has been vital in shaping this work.

To the hundreds of unheralded contributors to internet and other archives, whose selfless work has lightened the load in researching Godforsaken's historical background.

And finally, to all those survivors whose courage to give voice to their darkest memories has been my inspiration. I hope I have done you justice.

I - Genesis

Freddie Zamoyski died before I met him.

Resuscitation can be a violent business. The kick of adrenaline on an unresponsive heart. The body convulsing grotesquely under electric assault. And ribs snapping like twigs. Sometimes it works. It did for Freddie that morning. On those rare occasions, doctors celebrate their success. But more often they reflect on how the poor soul was beyond help and had succumbed to the inevitable. They see the body before them as an inanimate object, their success or failure dictated by the mechanistic laws of physiology.

But what gives life to those mechanics, I ask? What is it that makes the atoms swerve? Back then I doubted. I began to think that perhaps science had explained everything. That there was no room for anything else. That there was no room for God. It was a bleak time. Nothing can compare to the torment of a priest losing his faith. A writer can lose inspiration, a painter can lose his steady hand and both will be devastated by the loss of their vocation. But when a priest loses his faith he loses far more than his calling. He loses his soul.

That was me in that long, hot summer of 1990. In that season when a nation lost a little of its heart to the tears of a young and passionate footballer, my passion seemed dead. As Paul Gascoigne emoted and dazzled his way across Britain's television screens on a quest for World Cup glory, I was a lonely thirty-two year old priest clinging to the margins of a belief I no longer held. I contemplated my life and the void thereafter. I was so adrift that I no longer searched my soul for something lost but simply searched for my lost soul.

And then the atoms swerved. That was His work, and in answer to my desperate prayers, my pleas and my challenges to show Himself, He sent Freddie Zamoyski back to save me. As the Catholic chaplain to Whipps Cross Hospital in London's

Walthamstow I had seen many resuscitations and, in most cases, had dealt with the grieving families, but I knew the scene on those rare occasions of success. It was never like the movies. The blind panic of the monitor's flat line before the soothing bip bip as the ECG fires back into life. Reality was different. The machine made no noise and any success was completely overshadowed by the ever present anxiety that the reprieve was only temporary.

And so it must have been for Freddie Zamoyski. Young, terrified doctors, half crazed with sleep deprivation clattering along the long Victorian corridors of the hospital as the first laser rays of the rising sun cut through the galleried windows. Every strike of their shoes on the austere chequerboard tiles echoing uncompromisingly as their signature white coats flapped in their wake. Then to work. To pound, inject and shock. They told me as I wandered onto the newly opened Coronary Care Unit that it had been a miracle that Zamoyski had survived. But they said it in that casual way that betrays an altogether different meaning. They did not believe in miracles. They believed in mechanics and calculus and cardiac electrophysiology. But who was I to condemn? For nor did I believe in miracles. And then my life changed.

Zamoyski was hooked up to so many machines it was difficult to see where the man ended and the technology began. He looked like some grotesque cyborg in a cheap science fiction movie. The efficient ward sister in her powder blue clinical fatigues explained the situation to me. She told me that Freddie, as I came to know him, had been rushed to casualty after collapsing in the street. It always amused me, and still does, that the verb meaning to go to hospital is "rush". You never hear of someone ambling to hospital, or sauntering or walking or simply going, although in Freddie's case rushing was probably appropriate. He had been fortunate. No one really knew why he was walking around Walthamstow at five o'clock on a Sunday morning or what he was doing on the Lea Bridge Road, but collapsing on such a busy route meant, even at that unlikely hour, that an ambulance was with him in minutes and shortly afterwards he was in the side room on this ward, having been one of those medical successes.

"He's very weak," the sister warned me, her gaze lingering long enough to tell me the significance of what she was saying. I considered asking if I should come back later, but understood there may not be a later.

It seems strange to me now, but at the time Freddie Zamoyski meant nothing to me. He was just another name. Perhaps a believer, or semi-believer, or non-believer hedging his bets. It was common enough. Even the most hardened atheist will call for a priest when he wakes up in intensive care. People are capricious. But then so was I. I was peddling a salvation I did not myself believe, and the slowly growing guilt of that lie was weighing heavier on my heart with every smiling, expectant face turning to me for hope, child-like in their desire for absolution. That was what struck me most vividly as I entered. Freddie's face did not look up with blind trust. Despite his weakness and dependence on all those machines his gaze was hard, penetrating, searching. I was transfixed.

"You are the priest?" he said after the long pause had exceeded convention. It was not a question, but a kindly way of defusing what had become a slightly awkward silence. I had frozen, not knowing what to say or do as I looked into those self assured blue eyes of his. And something in them disturbed my complacency. They were so deep I felt myself falling into their grip, but this blue was no lazy, tropical azure but a keen, arctic ice, deadly with life. I was there to offer him comfort, guidance and wisdom and yet he appeared somehow to possess those in abundance, and my lies seemed to have finally found me out. No superficial platitudes would suffice here. It was as if my lack of faith shone like a beacon under his probing scrutiny.

I blurted out some kind of response, but in truth I do not

recall what it was. It is strange that I remember so little of that first meeting. It still troubles me even though I now know it is so common. Since then, I have heard the confessions of thousands, and counselled hundreds. I have heard men talk of women they have loved so much they would have gladly died for them, and yet they cannot remember the time they met. One woman told me of the physical, visceral jolt she felt every time her husband was near, yet how he teased her for her lack of any recollection of their first meeting. For some people, it seems, that first startling exposure to the remarkable is so intense it defies capture.

I do remember him telling me something of his background. He was Polish and had settled here in Britain after World War Two. He was a linguist by training and his English was impeccable. In fact it was quite disconcerting. There is generally some trace of accent or affectation in a second or third tongue. Something to give away the speaker as non-native. There is always some little hint, a cue, a slightly rolled consonant or twisted vowel to suggest a foreign origin. With Freddie there was nothing. To listen to him I was talking to the cream of the English aristocracy. Every phrase, every nuance and idiom oozed centuries old roots on this insular island, and yet he talked of Poles, Germans, Ukrainians and Russians as we would talk about our neighbours. In subsequent conversations he mentioned nationalities I had never even heard of, and all in a voice that spoke of Eton, Cambridge or the Household Cavalry.

He was not married and had no family here. His relatives in Poland had died in the war. After he had settled on these shores he had made a living as a freelance translator, although he was modestly evasive when I asked how many languages he spoke. I did drag out of him that English was probably his fifth language, maybe his sixth. The one thing I do remember vividly from that first meeting was the reason he gave for wanting to see me.

"I would like to make my last confession," he said rather formally. There was something in the delivery of that statement that left no room for doubt that there would ever be another later confession. He was stating that this was his death bed and waived away my protestations to the contrary.

"Of course," I replied. "When did you last confess?"

His answer shocked me. The conversation so far, his whole countenance and demeanour, suggested a deep faith. To hear that he had not confessed for forty-five years troubled me, and it was in that moment that I appreciated that perhaps my own faith was not entirely lost, for if it was then why would it have so concerned me that the man before me had been lost to the communion? I cannot say whether it was on that morning in that room that I began to see His design in sending Freddie back to me, or whether that realisation dawned in the days following. But dawn it did.

Freddie's must have been a special soul to have been granted the chance to come back and confess his sins. For him just to die on a trunk road in north-east London, unloved and unmarked, was not part of His plan. So what Freddie had to say must be of importance, maybe to him, perhaps to Him or maybe even to me.

I think it was Freddie's unfolding story that made me understand that at least part of His purpose had been to show me the meaning of faith. But it may be that I am getting ahead of myself. On that first morning Freddie told me his confession would take some while, and he asked that I recorded it on tape. At the time I did not understand the importance of this, and at first I resisted. To record a man's last confession ran against every instinct. Freddie heard my reticence and yet this dying man soothed my concerns. "I absolve you," he said, and in that moment I felt a calming power in his words that wholly disarmed me.

This was to be no exercise in the guidance of a simple soul ready to cross over to the care of the Lord. We both understood that Freddie's confession would be an instruction for me and a release for him. He saw my doubt, my wavering faith, and I think he recognised that in saving me he might find salvation for himself.

"I am glad that it is you here, Tom." He smiled a deep, knowing smile and emphasised the word "you". His gentle face, assured poise and steady voice calmed me, but when he said "Tom" it was as if I had been kicked. I do not remember telling him my name, but I assume I must have done earlier in that conversation I cannot recollect. "I feel tired now. Come back tomorrow with your tape recorder and let us talk of days long gone and terrible deeds long buried."

The fan in the corner of the room continued to whir away, sweeping unremittingly from side to side. The window, opened a few inches, allowed the sounds of normality to drift in from the stifled city. The harsh beat of the pulsating capital was softened to a reassuring drone by the humidity. Freddie closed his eyes, his presence receded and I was alone. For a moment I felt an overwhelming urge to wake him so he could fill the room for me once more, but I resisted the inappropriate impulse and left.

I arrived early the next day after a disturbed night's sleep. It was not troubled, but strange dreams and visions had woken me constantly. Most were incoherent snippets of biblical scenes and voices talking of religious philosophy. It was as if something within was performing some sort of religious mind-dump, although I wondered if I had simply drunk too much coffee. I was armed with my tape recorder which attracted some odd looks that only then made me realise that it probably looked slightly incongruous with my black cassock.

Freddie seemed pleased to see me, and I felt myself light up once more in his presence. He had managed a small breakfast, and a kind orderly had shaved him so that his close grey pointed beard regained its precise Romanov poise. His white hospital gown gave him an unexpected air of informal nobility that I had not seen before in others.

"Pull up a chair," he beckoned with a small movement of his

hand. The fan whirred away as I sat by his bed. His face was pale in his weakness, but his full-bodied silver hair was close cut and the sympathetic lines that mapped his wisdom spoke of a gentleness of soul. High bones topped slightly hollowed cheeks, framing an angular intelligent nose, and those eyes again saw straight to my core.

"You are troubled, Tom," he began disarmingly. He paused long enough for his words to register before moving on in a kind of informal inconsequential manner. "But we're all troubled in one way or another. I haven't met a man yet who was not troubled by something. Big, small, simple, complicated. It makes no difference in the end. The troubles we face expand to occupy the space in our minds." His gaze drifted to the open window and for a moment he was lost in thought. "Some troubles persist though," he muttered, while his mind seemed to remain elsewhere. "They stay forever." His eyes focused, and he smiled at me. It was an uncertain smile, and for the first time he looked vulnerable. I put my hand on his and gave a slight squeeze as I returned his timid gaze.

For a few moments we sat there acknowledging our vulnerability with no sound but for the circular hum of the fan. And in that silence we spoke of trust and care and salvation. As I held his hand I felt the roughness of a scar under my palm which I lifted just enough to see the thick faded cheloid disfiguring the back of his hand. I looked at Freddie, and the question in my frown could not restrain itself. Without a word he lifted his other hand so that I could clearly see the stigmata on both palms. I looked back into his eyes.

"Why now?" I found myself breaking the silence unexpectedly. "After all these years?"

Freddie's answer was slow in coming. "I saw Him." He looked me straight in the eye. "Yesterday. He sent me back."

"To confess?" Freddie nodded unconvincingly, and I sensed he had felt some other purpose to his reprieve but did not ask further. "Shall we get started?" I asked, waving the microphone at him. He smiled more broadly, took and deep breath, and then nodded decisively. And so began the last confession of Freddie Zamoyski. The most remarkable man I have ever met.

II - Exodus

The furnace of a continental sun baked the rooftops of Krakow. Those last days of abundance rolled into each other so completely that it felt they would never end. The heat seemed to melt the city into the surrounding landscape as all of the usual barriers erected by man to keep nature out were cast aside. And it was not just windows, shutters and doors that were flung wide open. There was an increasing openness of minds and hearts. A coming together of a people.

It was a romantic notion, but in truth that increasing unity probably had little to do with the weather, and everything to do with the storm clouds that were gathering in the west. Europe in those days had fostered a madness that had taken us to the eve of Armageddon. We often look back from the safety of our haven in a new millennium and label that madness "Fascism", but Freddie explained to me that the sickness ran much deeper than a set of incoherent and hateful political policies.

For almost a century, he told me, European science had nurtured the idea that it held the key to paradise. Through science we would tame nature and build a utopia of our own design, and in the white heat of enlightenment we would free ourselves of the threats and constraints placed on us by the sullen cosmos. But we would go further even than that. We would wield our new found knowledge to change our very beings as completely as we remoulded our environment. No longer would mankind roil with the other species in the dark pit of biological chaos and imperfection. We would liberate ourselves from disease and disfigurement. We would create a future of super humans.

The logic was impeccable, but like Swift's Modest Proposal such flawless logic resulted in grotesque conclusions. These scientific notions took root in the popular psyche and soon a whole clutch of social and political movements grew, offering utopian visions to masses brutalised by trench war. And in 1939 we were about to learn just how far humanity would debase itself in pursuit of its new religion. For there are no limits to the insanity we will embrace in the name of progress.

This madness had twisted itself into a doctrine of hate and conquest, giving birth to a regime bent on delivering it with industrial efficiency. By the end of July the coil was sprung so tight it could no longer be contained. Austria, Czechoslovakia and Memel had all been swallowed to appease the snarling beast that was Hitler's Germany, but it was all in vain. The Poles knew they could not avoid invasion, and the spectre of that onslaught was what drove this flowering of brotherly empathy in the baking heat of that last long summer.

Freddie walked briskly along Grodzka. Behind him parts of the Wawel Cathedral glinted in the sun. The rays playing off the golden flourishes of the Baroque additions to the structure only served to highlight the grim austerity of the main edifice whose construction had been ordered by Casimir the Great. But the ancient seat of the Archbishops of Krakow was of no interest to Freddie. Like a hound with the scent of the stag in his nostrils he strode purposefully towards the city's main square, Rynek Glowny.

His stylish brogues marked out his purposeful strides and, despite the heat, he sported an expensive but informal suit and waistcoat, with a red patterned cravat. His self-assurance, poise and stylish attire marked him out as a young man of means and breeding.

As Grodzka opened out into the huge space at the heart of the city Freddie headed right and skirted the ornate buildings that crowded around this most hallowed place. The square had been constructed in the aftermath of the Mongol destruction of the city centuries earlier, and had witnessed the many victory parades of the great age of Polish domination over central Europe. On that day when little Poland stood against the might of renewed

German expansionism it was disconcerting to recall that Krakow had once been the capital of an empire that stretched from the Baltic to the Black Sea. And this site had mapped that rise.

The square was dominated by the imposing and beautifully appointed Drapers' Hall which sat as the proud centrepiece in an ocean of paving while on all sides the shores of that sea were formed by scores of houses, shops, cafes and chapels. And half way along the eastern fringe Freddie reached his destination.

The Cafe Sobieski was a favourite meeting place for Freddie and his vibrant group of confident, young intellectuals. Its high ceilings and fin de siècle grandeur provided the perfect setting for their earnest discussions. The dozen or so members of the self-styled "Sobieski Group" would meet on the last Wednesday of each month to discuss a vast range of subjects in the light and energy of this place that was so conducive to good-natured argument. Many a heated philosophical debate had been won or lost in its warm echoing hall and Freddie was savouring the prospect of this month's meeting, despite knowing that over half of their number would be absent.

It was a bittersweet moment. Some instinct deep inside him warned that the Sobieski Group, like so many other great things, was about to end before its time. He turned to look over his left shoulder at the bloated sun as it slid behind the ornate adornments of the Drapers' Guild. He looked around the square and felt an unexpected surge of national pride at the culture around him. Despite invasions, defeats and partitions Poland had maintained its identity. Like a cork after the storm it had always bobbed back up again, and that image brought a smile to his face. And with that thought he took one last deep breath of the warm air and stepped into Sobieski's.

It was busier than usual, but all the cafes had been like that for some weeks. People read the newspapers avidly, and many sat at home glued to their new wireless sets desperate for news of international manoeuvrings in the great capitals of the continent.

But the oral tradition was strong. People wanted to discuss and debate the latest developments in foreign affairs. Events were moving rapidly and everyone was an expert. Just a few days earlier the Germans had signed the Molotov-Ribbentrop pact with the Russians, guaranteeing each other mutual neutrality. It had been greeted with incredulity and horror throughout Europe, and was as good as an open invitation by Russia for Germany to invade Poland. That had been swiftly countered by a British announcement to guarantee Poland's sovereignty and spirits had risen across the country. But the buzz of anxious expectation remained everywhere.

Freddie walked confidently through the busy hall to the table where the group normally met and smiled at the three men sitting there. "No Gregor?" he asked, looking quizzically between the three.

"His call up came today," answered Theodore, a solid, bearded young man of aristocratic bearing. "Another casualty in our dwindling numbers. We didn't really expect to see you to be honest, Freddie." He shook the remnants of the ice and emptied his whisky glass.

"My last night of freedom, Teddy. I'm to report in the morning," The expectant pause around the table created a silence that was heightened by the energy of the many background conversations that echoed through Sobieski's. Freddie sat as he carefully assessed the mood at the table. "You all right, Karol?" he asked the morosely truculent nineteen year old sitting on his right. Karol stared at the table and refused to meet Freddie's gaze.

"He didn't know you were a reservist," answered Karl, the young man opposite, by way of explanation. "Come on Karol," he turned to the emotional youth. "You know Freddie's background. His father. The Hero of Lwow. The Scourge of Galicia. Call him what you like, but the son of General Zamoyski can hardly stand by and not fight at a time like this."

"To General Zamoyski," interjected Theodore, as he raised

his glass, the just perceptible slurring of his words suggesting he had been at the cafe longer than the others. He looked at the empty receptacle in his hand, and signalled to the barman to bring another round.

Freddie's father had gained an almost mythical status for his actions in the 1919 war with the Ukraine. The collapse of the eastern front at the end of the Great War and the fragmentation of the old empires of Russia, Germany and Austria had unleashed centuries of suppressed ethnic aspirations and the chaos that had ensued had fostered a patchwork of territorial wars from Estonia to Moldova. Poland and the Ukraine had emerged reborn, and fighting over the contested regions of Galicia and Ruthenia had been intense. The Poles had finally won victory when Freddie's father had repulsed the last Ukrainian attack on Lwow and driven the enemy back half way to Kiev.

The victory had ensured that Poland found itself the most ethnically diverse nation in Europe with large numbers of Germans in their western lands, while in the east a Polish elite ruled over a peasantry of mixed ethnicity including Lithuanians, Ruthenians, Hungarians, Romanians and Ukrainians. Such complex social structures were not uncommon in those lands where culture and geography blurred combustibly, but not for three centuries had Poland extended its borders so far eastwards.

"To General Zamoyski," repeated Karl raising his glass. Karol responded half-heartedly, his unhappiness at the news of Freddie's imminent departure tangible.

"Don't be cross Karol." There was a playfully cajoling tone in Freddie's voice. "I was a cadet all the way through school and I've been a reservist ever since. I thought you knew." He waited for a response before going on. "In any event, reservist or not, we know what is coming and we have to do something. Not you and Karl, obviously. You're still studying, but the rest of us who've graduated have to defend our homeland."

"He isn't," argued Karol, nodding at Theodore whose

attention was drawn to the business of ensuring that more drinks were on the way.

"Well, that's not fair, Karol. You know there's an unofficial policy against Jews. The army's no different to the civil service. Marshall Ridz and his cronies might not make them wear armbands like they do in Germany, but we all know the way the tide is running. He may not join the army, but he'll do his bit."

Freddie's honesty and readiness to talk of the darker forces that had stirred in Poland caused a troubled silence to descend on the table of enlightened thinkers. It had been easy to forget over the preceding weeks, so full of brotherly unity, that a strand of institutionalised anti-Semitism had grown at the core of Polish society, and Freddie's timely reminder injected a reality that was not entirely welcomed.

"Exactly," concurred Theodore. "Thank you Freddie," he smiled, while turning a theatrical scowl to Karol.

"No, I didn't mean..." he began in his defence, but Theodore waved away his awkwardness and interrupted to change the subject.

"How's your drama going, Karol?"

"Sorry?"

"Your theatre group? Do you have any more productions planned? You're very good." Theodore was putting space between them and Karol's faux pas, in the deft way practised by those used to deflecting such situations.

I have often wondered whether it was those higher instincts that led so many Jews in Hitler's Germany to ignore the writing on the wall so obvious to others. I remember talking once to the son of Jewish doctors from Hanover who was sure that the genteel respect paid to them by their patients and their need to believe they belonged had completely blinded them to the ugliness unfolding all around. Those higher minded beliefs in the inexorable progress of man were ultimately the cause of their deaths in the camps, and Theodore was instinctively doing the same, as he had all of his life.

"What was that play you put on last year?" he continued. "Twardowski's Wand?"

"Twardowski's Magic," smiled Karol.

"Twardowski's Magic. That's it." Theodore's open hand went up to demonstrate the memory recalled. "You were excellent, Karol. Really stole the show in my opinion."

Karol smiled sheepishly. "I'm sorry, Teddy, I didn't mean anything by what I said. Sometimes I'm so wrapped up in people I don't see the labels that others stick on them. You know my darling Ginka is Jewish?"

"Ah, now, Ginka," laughed Freddie. "The fair Ginka! Have you popped the question yet?"

Karol blushed and bowed his head. "Not yet. We're not sure what her parents will think, which is why I need to get a good degree and then maybe a job as a teacher. That would help, I'm sure." The words fell out so automatically that they had the ring of a jointly agreed mantra, and Freddie hoped that the lovers' dreams would be fulfilled.

"Quite right, too," pronounced Theodore ironically. "Proper parental discretion. A good Jewish girl, and you a gentile. Can't start diluting the blood with inferior types." The four smiled at his mischievous retort as the barman set their drinks down on the table. Theodore prompted them all to take their glasses and stood to propose his toast. "To Ginka and Karol, to Captain Zamoyski, and to Poland!" The glasses clashed as the others stood to affirm his words.

"Actually chaps, it's Lieutenant Zamoyski," muttered Freddie to the scraping of chairs on the hard floor as they all sat down.

"Lieutenant, Captain, General, Private. It's all the same in the defence of the motherland," smiled Theodore as he dismissed this irrelevant detail. "Now, if you will excuse me gentlemen, I must respond to my own summons to the grand army of the call of nature."

The others watched as he walked slightly unsteadily towards the facilities at the back of the cafe, before Karl broke the silence. "Why hasn't he left? We know what he has to put up with. And his family. In fact the only reason he's been allowed to graduate is probably because his father owns half of the chemical factories in Poland. They must be worth millions. Why haven't they gone?"

"I know," agreed Karol earnestly.

"Because he's Polish," smiled Freddie ruefully. "Why haven't we left?" He paused to allow the others to reflect. "Because Poland is worth believing in. Regardless of the government, regardless of what a war might bring, we are all Poles. And we stand together." Karl and Karol looked at him in silence, pondering his words. "Think about it. Teddy and his family have more to lose than any of us if Hitler attacks. We know that Jews across Germany have been dispossessed, and there's no reason to think if they are victorious here that Teddy's family will fare any better."

"How bad do you think it might be?" The anxiety in Karol's voice betrayed a worry for his beloved Ginka.

"Appropriation of their business. Seizure of their assets. And a life of menial work at the bottom of the pile. That would be my guess."

"And armbands?"

Freddie nodded dolefully. "So, you see, for Teddy to stay marks him as more patriotic than any of us. Of course they could have gone, but they haven't, and we should show them the same solidarity regardless of how they pray."

Silence descended once again, confirming their agreement with Freddie's lead. The buzz of activity and conversation in the cafe continued unabated. The ceilings echoed to a range of opinions and debates. On the next table two old men were deliberating over the merits of Marshall Ridz's leadership, while opposite three suited office workers were arguing about the implications of the Molotov-Ribbentrop pact.

After a few absent-minded mouthfuls of the crisp, golden lager before him Karol asked the question forming slowly in his mind. "And what about our prayers? Why are they not heard?" He stared into his beer, deep in contemplation.

"You mean, why do bad things happen in a world created by a good God?" replied Freddie. He paused a second before delivering the answer. "Original Sin."

"Oh. Not that nonsense again," sighed Karl. He chose the rest of his words carefully, keen to argue his point respectfully. "You are so widely read, and often so wise Freddie, and then at times you come out with these Stone Age ideas about life and its meaning."

"First of all," replied Freddie, energised that at last they had begun a strand of conversation based on the abstract rather than the depressing realities of the day, "Original Sin is not a Stone Age idea. It was formulated by St. Augustine in the fourth century A.D. and is based on sound philosophical argument. And secondly, as a scientist you should accept a theory of inheritance that fits with Mr. Darwin's notions of evolution." They were back on mainstream Sobieski Group ground, and Freddie lit up.

"That's right," agreed Karol, keen to demonstrate his support of Freddie.

"Oh, shut up Karol," snapped Karl, much less respectfully of his junior. "I swear that if Freddie claimed that God was a frog you would agree in that misty eyed way you have when he's around." He carelessly flicked his finger at Freddie to emphasise his point. Karl was studying Mathematics and Physics, was a self-proclaimed atheist, and had often crossed intellectual swords with these men of faith.

Stung into his own defence of Original Sin, Karol argued back. "Adam sinned in the Garden of Eden, and so we all inherit that sin through the principles of heredity." He folded his arms and nodded his head to signify he had just settled the matter. Freddie looked on impassively, anticipating Karl's line of counterattack, and so it came swiftly.

"Don't be ridiculous. You're talking like that fool Lysenko." Karol's blank expression betrayed his ignorance of the pioneer of Soviet agricultural science who claimed that acquired traits could be inherited. Karl sighed and, talking slowly for effect, explained further as a teacher to a young child. "If I punch you in the face do you think your children will all be born with crooked noses? No, of course not. So, if Adam sinned by eating an apple, that has no more implications for heredity than you deciding to eat an apple today."

There was a long pause as Karol struggled to find a riposte. Just as the matter seemed decided, Freddie calmly asked "But what if Adam was created with an innate drive to sin?"

Karl looked at him intently for a few seconds, his scientific mind turning over the implications of this new perspective. "So his sinful behaviour was simply an expression of his fundamental nature?" he extrapolated.

"Yes."

There was another hiatus as Karl calculated the conclusion of this altered set of assumptions. "Then that trait would be inherited by us all," he answered, conceding defeat to this inexorable logic. Karol looked in awe at Freddie who always seemed to have worked out these arguments long in advance, and a warm smile came to his face. Karl saw the look of adulation and rolled his eyes despairingly. "It still doesn't make Original Sin necessary. Only possible."

"Spoken as a true scientist," agreed Freddie.

"I just don't understand your need to hold on to all this superstitious mumbo jumbo." Karl shook his head. "Dr. Schrödinger from Austria has published a set of equations that describe how the universe works. And he has shown there is no need for a God to explain all of this." He opened his hand to the expanse of the room.

Freddie smiled benignly. "This Dr. Schrödinger, is he the

chap that said that if you put a cat in a box it is both alive and dead at the same time?" Karl looked uneasy. "And you call our beliefs mumbo jumbo?" The benign smile grew a mischievous twist at its corner.

Karl had no reply, but Karol was keen to continue the discussion. "So Original Sin? Bad things happen to us because we are born sinful?"

Freddie smiled patiently. "I prefer to look at it the other way round. Those of us who are redeemed are saved by God's loving grace."

"I'm leaving you two to your mutual admiration," muttered Karl tartly. "Teddy's over there by the radio set, and he's waving. I'm going to see what's going on." They all turned to see that Theodore had joined a group of men listening intently to a small wireless set in the corner of the cafe, and was gesticulating urgently to them.

"So, you don't believe we can save ourselves through our own actions?" asked Karol as Karl walked away.

"That's Pelagianism," explained Freddie as he turned back, and the echoes of the name of that ancient heresy stopped Karol in his tracks. "Man cannot make himself perfect. Only God may bestow that upon us through His divine love. We cannot pick and choose which church teachings we will accept, Karol. We must love everyone, embrace everyone, but the word of God cannot flex to the fashion of the day." He took another sip of his beer.

"Love all. Embrace all. But stick to tradition." Karol uttered the words as if reinforcing some newly learned fact.

"The Christian tradition is to love all, Karol. It's nothing new."

Karol thought in silence for a few moments as the background hum reached an excited crescendo around the radio. Neither of them turned in response to this growing hubbub, happy in their private space. "You always talked of joining the priesthood,

Freddie. Has that dream been lost in your love of Poland?"

"It's part of my love of Poland!" Freddie looked shocked that Karol would see these two forces as opposites. "I can feel God, Karol. He works through us all, and I can feel Him calling me to do this for my countrymen. I believe we can repel the Germans. The English and the French will come to our aid. If we can hold them for long enough, they will have to back down. The French army is huge and will squash them. The English navy will blockade their ports. And Poland will remain free. The whole thing will be over within a month. Just you see."

"And then you'll return to become a priest?"

"Exactly." Freddie smiled again and raised his glass in invitation to Karol who reciprocated.

"Well, just you make sure you do," he ordered with mock belligerence. "Otherwise I'll have to do it for you!"

"Not once you're married to Ginka, you won't," Freddie laughed, before fixing Karol with a piercing gaze that signified the weight of his words. "You have many gifts, Karol. Lavish them on your family." A broad grin came to Karol's face for the first time that evening. Freddie's picture of a defeated Germany and his own future of domestic happiness lifted his heart. Once again Freddie had melted an icy uncertainty with his warmth of belief and optimism, and Karol loved him for it.

"I think it's over!" proclaimed Karl excitedly, breaking their private moment. He had rushed back to the tabled leaving Theodore in his wake.

"What?" replied Freddie. "What's over?"

"The Germans. They've offered peace talks. The British have insisted. And a minister is travelling to Berlin to sign a deal tomorrow."

"You're joking!" exclaimed Freddie.

"It's true," beamed Theodore, with his arm round Karl's shoulder. "Hitler is frightened of the French and the British, and he's backing down. The war is off!"

Freddie looked across at the men by the radio, and the relief and delight on their faces told him it was so. He could scarcely believe it, but the laughing and celebrating that grew around the cafe as the news spread was intoxicating, and he joined the swell of emotion. As the evening grew longer, a rapturous relief gave way to a swell of national pride and the inevitable singing that went with it.

It was late when Freddie began to stagger home. He bade his comrades farewell in a flurry of bonhomie and one last rendition of the national anthem, and made uncertain progress back to his comfortable lodgings before falling into a deep and happy sleep.

The following morning he woke with a start to the sound of his alarm clock. As he forced himself to an uncertain consciousness he was aware of a headache and a slowness of movement that marked the night's revelry. Truce or not, he still had to report to the muster point at seven o'clock to be sent to whatever unit he was to join. Fortunately, he had packed his bag a dozen times already, so casting aside his hang-over he freshened up, donned his smart green uniform with its distinctive square topped peaked hat and brown knee length boots and set off for the pick up point.

By the look of the other reservists Freddie had not been the only one celebrating the previous evening's news. As they collected by the convoy of tarpaulin covered trucks the conversation was jocular and relaxed. Cigarettes were shared freely as the men contemplated a week or two of menial army duties before a return to their homes and families. Some had even slipped out without waking their wives or sweethearts, in the belief that their return would be swift. A minority stood with countenances more grave, refusing to believe that peace could have been so easily achieved, and their sullen expressions made Freddie think more carefully about the announcements the previous day. Deep inside an unpleasant, disconcerting feeling welled up, and his mind was thrown back into doubt.

Hitler had traduced and bullied the whole of Europe for nearly two years. The British and French had consistently refused to stand up to him and his brinkmanship had always returned a profit. Why should this latest turn of events be any different? Freddie shook his head as if ridding himself of an annoying fly and returned to his habitual optimism.

With military precision, the convoy pulled out to the second and began its slow but steady journey southwards towards the distant Carpathian mountains. As the trucks climbed away from Krakow Freddie looked back at the city he had grown to love. The sun rising from his right cast an atmospheric light, picking out features that slowly softened in the haze of the dust raised behind the wheels of the vehicles, until finally the ancient seat of Polish power disappeared altogether. And in that moment Freddie wondered how long it would be before he would set his eyes on its beauty again.

-oOo-

"That was the last time I ever saw Krakow." Freddie gave a sad smile as his eyes looked through me, recalling once again that last glimpse of the city. The fan swivelled back and forth churning the heavy London air.

We sat in silence. There was so much I wanted to ask, and yet had no idea what to say. "What became of Theodore?" I heard myself asking.

Freddie turned and sat motionless staring at the foot of the bed. "He died." The sound of the fan did nothing to mask the anguish in his laboured silence. "Murdered. In Chelmno Concentration Camp." The fan droned on. "His name appears in the inventory. January 1943." Freddie turned to look at me. "They were very organised in their killing. All to the plan. Nothing improper."

It was difficult to absorb the human implications. Six million people killed by a hateful regime. The death statistics for the camps were chilling: Auschwitz - 1,100,000. Belzec - 600,000. Belsen - 35,000. Buchenwald - 60,000. Chelmno - 320,000. Dachau - 32,000. Majdanek - 360,000. Treblinka - 800,000. Flossenburg - 30,000. Sobibor - 250,000. Mauthausen - 120,000. And so the list went on. As I later delved into the records I found so many smaller camps that I lost track of them, but each took thousands of lives. Some taken quickly by bureaucrats fulfilling quotas. Others taken slowly in unimaginable pain by sadists given utterly free rein to their worst depravations.

The genocide was so grotesque in its scale that I found myself constantly groping for some perspective. It hit me hardest when I read of Stutthof, a place that I had never heard of. An insignificant addendum in the records. It was a small camp outside Danzig in East Prussia, and opened its doors the day after the Germans invaded Poland, its purpose to murder Polish Jews and dissidents. Eighty-five thousand men, women and children died there. The extermination of the equivalent of the entire population of the City of Chester, forgotten in the footnotes of genocidal excess.

The numbers became meaningless, more like football scores, until each and every one of those people had a life given to them as Freddie's testimony had done for Theodore. Only then did every single name on those lists come to life as a human being with hopes and loves, ambitions and fears.

"And the others?" I could scarcely ask. "Karl and Karol? Ginka?" Freddie shrugged his shoulders, his eyes fixed. He was spent. "Would you like me to stay?" I offered. There was no response, just an infinite stare into a dark past with painful memories.

Offering sympathy with an awkward pat on his arm, I left. The walk home seemed longer and bleaker than I had ever known it and, despite the heat wave, I felt chilled to the core of my soul.

III - Carpathian Retreat

The next day I arrived late at the hospital. I had not slept well and, paradoxically, had ended up rising late. Images of extermination camps and casual institutionalised slaughter had unsettled me as I drifted between sleep and wakefulness. In that state it was difficult to know which thoughts were willed and which were the product of my dream world. But then I wondered whether there was any difference between the two, until I questioned whether that notion had itself also been a dream.

Somewhere in that disorientating somnolent bocage vivid images swirled of wagons full of cattle herded into abattoirs. The slaughter men happy in their work. The mundane realities of the food chain never once demanding any reflection on their task. The animals turned to human, but try as I might I could not make those butchers see. They simply continued idly processing the meat, deaf to my screams, and blind to their crimes.

I remember waking with a start, troubled that even in my dreams my mind could begin constructing a justification for the actions of those murderers. As I slipped back into my hypnopompia a notion occurred to me that the deepest parts of my psyche might be tapping into some ancient instinct to tribalism. An unseen and malevolent racist rhizome. Were we all like that? Beneath a thin veneer of civilisation that could be stripped away as easily as fresh spring bark were we all careless killers of the outgroup?

And so my night progressed. Incoherent snippets of thoughts and visions. Hallucinations of death and murder. And, as if those ruminations were not bad enough, a storm had broken. The long days of heavy humid heat had generated a charge that nature could no longer contain. The air groaned under the weight it carried, until it finally dropped its load in large fat raindrops that splattered off the windowsill.

The downpour grew and the clouds unleashed their static on the city. The sky discharged its vengeance on the world with each forked jab, and the air was split as electrons fizzed like the Devil's whip. And then came thunder's reply, the anger of Thor that shook buildings and cowed men.

It was no wonder that I had slept poorly, but there was yet something else. Something that Freddie had said about God's grace had been nagging in the background although each time I tried to grasp it I found myself clutching at nothingness as the concept evaporated. Something about Pelagianism. But it had gone.

As I bustled into Freddie's room I apologised for my tardiness and for dripping small puddles of rainwater over the floor. I had been caught in a brief rainburst left over from the previous night's meteorological frenzy. In the couple of hundred yards it took me to walk from my moribund Morris Minor to the safety of the hospital's cover the skies had opened and I was soaked through.

Freddie looked much better than when I had left the previous afternoon. He was beaming, and his radiance filled the room.

"You look a lot happier," I smiled, rearranging my damp clothes into some semblance of comfort as I sat.

"It was hard for me yesterday. So many very dear friends. Painful memories. And regrets."

"Such as?" Something told me Freddie was asking for this prompt to expand on what was in his mind.

He gave a small laugh. "It's silly really, Tom. And yet I can't shake off the regret that those last moments with that wonderful group of dear comrades were not spent talking of our bond, I suppose you would say of our love. They were spent singing 'Poland Is Not Yet Lost'. And singing it badly." I must have looked slightly quizzical and it prompted him to an explanation. "Poland's national anthem, Tom."

I nodded understanding, but could not stop myself from commenting. "It's an odd title for a national anthem. Hardly rousing. Supremely anti-triumphalist. 'Poland is not lost'. Well, not yet, anyway."

Freddie laughed openly for the first time since I had met him. "You're so English, Tom. I envy you English your certainty. Your geographical certainty. Your historical certainty. And your cultural certainty. You must remember that when that song was written Poland had disappeared from the maps of Europe, carved up in the great partition. It was a song that appealed to the Polish people to stay true to themselves and to their heritage. To keep the torch alive. Your national anthem speaks to the world of your greatness. Ours speaks to ourselves of who we are. Of our brotherhood"

"Then, perhaps it was the best way for you to say goodbye to your friends." There was a silence, and for the first time I felt that I had actually said something that brought him comfort. He smiled at me, content in the reframing I had offered. "I was thinking about what you said yesterday, Freddie. The business about Original Sin and God's grace."

"Yes?" His reply filled the pause that had developed as I groped in the fog of my thoughts. He scrutinised me before continuing. "You're troubled, Tom. I can see it. You're a good man."

"I hope so."

"You are. Trust me. But you carry a burden. You doubt your faith." I felt suddenly naked. I had sensed strongly that Freddie saw my waning conviction, but for him to vocalise it so directly shocked me, and the impact of his words showed in my face. "Don't be alarmed," he reassured me as he laid his hand lightly on mine.

I tried to explain what I was feeling as our gaze met, but all that came out was meaningless sound. "I...."

"You want to lead a perfect Christian life. You feel it is your responsibility. To God. To make yourself perfect." My silence spoke my agreement. Freddie's intense face broke once again into a broad smile. "You can't, Tom. That's the point. That's what Augustine was saying to us in his arguments around Original Sin."

"But I must try. Try to be perfect, I mean."

"Well, certainly you must." He gave a slight frown to indicate that this was obvious. "But you are human, and so you cannot perfect yourself. Only God can do that."

"And that's what you meant about Pelagianism? When you were talking to Karl and Karol?"

"Yes. Poor Pelagius. I feel sorry for him. In many ways I think he offered a far more pious brand of Christianity than Augustine ever dreamed of. But if you believe as he did that you can perfect yourself then who needs God?" He turned his gaze on me in challenge, and it suddenly struck me that all this time that was exactly what I had been doing. Trying to perfect myself. And failing. And that failure marked me as unworthy in my own mind, and had gnawed away at my faith. Freddie was offering me a way to redemption, and suddenly the burden of guilt that had come so close to breaking me lifted.

"So, it's God's job to perfect me."

"Well, I wouldn't express it in quite those terms, Tom. That makes it sound as if God owes you something, which He doesn't. But, to put it a little less crudely, if you are to be perfected then it will be through His grace."

The excitement of this realisation was so unexpected that Freddie's mild rebuke passed me by completely and for the first time in months I felt a kind of peace descend on me. The room was cooler, and the fan sat silent and motionlessness as Freddie picked up his story.

-oOo-

The convoy of trucks made its way south from Krakow through the rapidly warming morning air. The formation of over twenty vehicles progressed slowly but steadily along the metalled road that linked Krakow to Novy Targ, and continued onwards into the Tatras Mountains and ultimately to Czechoslovakia. As reservists drawn from Krakow, the men knew they would be assigned to local units, but this had taken on a greater significance since Germany's annexation the previous year of the Sudetenland.

Access to Czech territory allowed the Germans the opportunity to attack Poland from the south at the same time as launching offensives from German lands in the west and north. It was an opportunity they would not squander, so the imperative for the units of Army Group Krakow to hold their ground in their southern fastnesses was absolute. If they crumbled then not only would the German invaders descend on Krakow, but their forces could then sweep west into the rear of the main Polish forward defensive lines. Such an encirclement would spell disaster, and those with any military understanding knew the vital role they would play here in the deep south. The flank of an army was always the hinge on which any battle would turn, and the task of its defence fell to those men riding with Freddie that morning.

He looked about him at the twenty or so reservists crammed onto the bench seats of the lorry. They were fairly evenly divided between young enthusiasts like himself, products of school cadet groups, and older men who would all have been veterans of the Great War and the conflict that followed with Ukraine. That chaotic conflagration that was the crucible of Poland's rebirth.

He wondered how many had served under his father in that distant time. It set him thinking as the shadows of the trees lining the avenue strobed sunlight onto the tarpaulin and dazed his senses. He had only ever known Poland as it was then. Independent, proud and free. Freddie and Poland had been born almost simultaneously so everything around seemed commonplace. Polish institutions run by Poles for the good of Poland. Looking at the older men in the lorry he realised they remembered a darker past. A past of subservience.

Many were in their fifties, and it occurred to Freddie that only thirty years earlier they would have been young men growing up in a Habsburg Krakow looking southwards to the rule of Vienna. They had lived in the northern most bastion of an empire that stretched to the Adriatic and they would have fought on that empire's eastern front. Only when that collapsed did they break the chains of bondage that had shackled Poland for over a century, and fought their war of independence that had brought Freddie's father so much fame.

He looked at their grim faces as they stared in silent contemplation and reflected on the incredible changes they had witnessed. And now they looked south once again, but not this time to the neo-Baroque clutches of the Habsburgs. On this day they anticipated a German foe that would come at them through the mountains as had so many conquerors down the years. But these invaders would fail, Freddie reassured himself. The looks on the older faces around him seemed less certain.

As the convoy snaked its way further into the hinterland the landscape began to rise and the road twisted and turned as it followed the broken contours of the Carpathian foothills. After an hour the trucks growled through Myslenice, a small settlement about 20 miles south of Krakow, their low pitched diesel engines shaking the buildings from their rural slumber. Small boys ran beside the trucks excitedly waving to the troops. Some waved back cheerfully, while others remained absorbed in their own distant world of thoughts.

After another couple of miles the trucks pulled over onto a large expanse of flat ground between the road and the small river that meandered its way back towards Krakow. It was not yet nine o'clock and the morning dew still clung to the grass and flowers, glinting in the early sunlight. The place was alive in the clear morning light and as Freddie dismounted the truck he stretched his back and took a long deep breath of the fragrant country air.

He marvelled at the beauty of the land and the perfection that God had created.

The reason for their stop soon became apparent as they were joined by other smaller convoys, decanting their conscript and reservist booty from a variety of small towns across the region. Once they were all present a detachment of abrasive military policemen called them to order and divided them into new groups for onward transit to their forward positions.

They were told that they had been assigned to the newly formed First Mountain Brigade whose task would be to defend the river valleys that ran from the mountainous watershed down to the Krakow plain. They were divided into four contingents and dispatched without any further ceremony.

Freddie was in the group they called the Berezwecz battalion and along with his new comrades dutifully climbed aboard the ten trucks that had been assigned to them. The vehicles had progressed less than a mile when they turned right and continued for what seemed like an eternity with the rising sun streaming in through the back of the trucks. Freddie surmised from this that they must have been assigned to the western most corridor which from memory he guessed would be the Sola valley. His suspicions were confirmed as they eventually descended from the hills to join a river basin and met the small town of Zywiec. Southwards they pressed as Freddie saw the hills that corralled the valley closing to a pinch point. It was the perfect defensive position, and it was no surprise that here the convoy left the road and laboured its way up the slope to the left.

As the newly arrived contingent stretched its legs once more Freddie took a long look at the landscape to establish some familiarity with his new surroundings. He almost laughed at himself as he noticed what he was doing. Was this some standard military procedure that had been drummed into him through years of schoolboy cadet training or was it some hereditary instinct? Either way, he found he was drawing in the information from the scene around him. It was as if he could not stop himself.

The main Sola valley ran north south to his right as he looked southwards to the threatening mountains that harboured the menace they could all sense. Before him ran the valley of a small westbound tributary, giving him this wonderful vantage point on the prominent hill that marked the angle between the rivers. It also defined this as the ideal place to stand against whatever came down the valley.

The hills that bounded the river were not impressively high, but the ground underfoot was very difficult. It was covered in a mass of dense vegetation that the locals called the wilderness. These hills would form an effective barrier to the movement of any significant troop numbers. If a German advance was to come it would be funnelled through the mile wide gap where the rivers met. The village of Wegierska Gorka.

Freddie looked down on the settlement and could pick out people going about their daily business as they had for years. A small railway station nestled between the ramshackled collection of cottages and huts as its iron umbilical cord ran off into the distance to service the mines in the mountains. The scene had a timeless air of order and serenity and amid all of these preparations for war Freddie recalled the feeling from the night before. The hope and optimism at the British intervention. The previous evening now seemed a distant memory, but the news of the re-opening of talks and the prospect of peace was still real and tessellated with the rural idyll before him.

"Zamoyski!" Freddie was woken from his private reflections by the harsh crack of a commanding voice that came from behind. He turned as his back straightened automatically, to see an impressively large sergeant major walking towards him. Freddie was about to salute, when he remembered his rank. He may have been raw and inexperienced, but he was an officer and he found himself staring down the man with an instinctive, aristocratic air. The sergeant major's body language changed in response. "Lieutenant Zamoyski. Sir. You are wanted in the house, sir."

The sergeant major half turned to indicate the building behind him. Architecturally, it was somewhere between a well appointed home of one of the rural gentry and a small country retreat for the nobility. It was impressive without being imposing, and nestling on the south facing slopes with panoramic views of the valley and the mountains beyond it would have been the perfect Carpathian retreat from the machinations of the court in Vienna. Those same attributes now made it the ideal point from which to conduct a defence of the Sola valley.

"Thank you, Sergeant Major." The inflection in his voice rose, inviting a name.

"Raczynski, sir.' It was Raczynski's turn to stiffen to attention, as Freddie studied him with the kind of superior look that he had observed so often in his father. Even as he played his pecking order game with this far more experienced and accomplished warrior he observed the change in himself that shocked and pleased him simultaneously. He recognised the need to adopt a military demeanour, but the instinctive ease with which it had so suddenly happened was disconcerting. Perhaps he did not know himself quite as well as he had thought.

"Who do I ask for, Sergeant Major?"

"Colonel Galadyk, sir. Commanding Officer."

"Thank you, Sergeant Major. At ease." Freddie walked through the wrought iron gate of the walled garden to the house, and immediately stepped back a century in time. He was struck by the beauty of the building even as he recognised it as a projection of Austrian imperialism against which his family and nation had fought so hard.

He was directed by an adjutant to a large first floor room that was unmistakably the library. Shelves covered every available space save for the wall opposite, and were packed with books of all sorts. The far side of the room offered the most stunning panorama from generous windows that it seemed to Freddie to generate a tension. The books in the room pulling against the lure of the vista. How could anyone concentrate on reading in so beautiful a space with such a view as this? It was the logical place for Colonel Janusz Galadyk to establish his headquarters, and Freddie thought that the comfortable oak chair with its large improvised map table and strategic views over the battlefield must have been the most perfect command position in the whole of the Polish army.

"Zamoyski." Colonel Galadyk offered no smile, no warmth, no greeting. His ample frame remained firmly seated. "Sit down."

"Thank you, sir." Freddie sat at another chair by the large table in the centre of the room that was covered with maps and lists of troops and units.

"How old are you, Lieutenant?"

"Twenty-one, sir."

Galadyk scrutinised him closely. "Your file here says you are a student." His heavy face and bald head spoke of a man who was well past his physical best, but his eyes betrayed a keenness of thought that Freddie suspected he would need in the coming weeks.

"Graduated, sir. French and Russian at the Jagiellonian." There was a tone of pride in his voice at the mention of this most ancient seat of learning. The Jagiellonian University was the oldest in Poland and one of the oldest in the world, and this tradition mattered to Freddie.

Galadyk was unimpressed. "The works of Voltaire are hardly likely to help us here." He glared his challenge at Freddie. It was confusing. Why would a colonel, the commander of an entire brigade on the potential eve of battle with an overwhelming foe take time to deride the studies of a young reservist? It could only be a test, and one that Freddie intended to pass with distinction.

"How many men do you face, sir?" Galadyk's glare turned to a frown, inviting clarification. "The Germans? How many men are going to come down that valley?"

The impertinence of the question from such a junior officer intrigued Galadyk and interest sparked in his eyes. He decided to give Freddie some rope and waited to see if he would hang himself. "Intelligence suggests the whole of the German seventh infantry division along with other elements. Nearly 20,000 men in total."

"And we have?"

"Twelve hundred."

"In that case, sir, Voltaire has a great deal to say about our predicament." Galadyk stared impassively, waiting for Freddie's explanation. "God is not on the side of the big battalions, but of the best shots." Having defended Voltaire's honour, Freddie summarised what he had concluded from his brief view of the potential battlefield. "Concentrate all available firepower on that bottleneck," he continued pointing to the village. "Use the houses as strong points. Place skirmishers in the woods to prevent any flanking manoeuvres, and keep a reserve of 300 men to plug the gaps that will appear."

Galadyk's expression did not change. For the first time Freddie was aware of an old clock ticking in the corner of the room, the sound of its mechanism seeming to grow louder with every beat. Freddie stared back, refusing to be cowed. His battle plan was sound and he had no reason to apologise. Perhaps on reflection the colonel had not actually asked for his advice, but now it was given he would stand by it.

Galadyk made his decision. His face suddenly broke into a broad smile as he laughed. "You are George Zamoyski's son." It was a statement, and one clearly based on personal knowledge. It was Freddie's turn to frown quizzically. "I served under your father in Lemberg." Then he corrected himself. "I'm sorry. I mean Lwow." He looked slightly embarrassed at having used the old Habsburg name for that eastern bastion of Polish rule, but it was a common thing. Many places bore two or even three names in different languages depending on who ruled them, and Galadyk looked old enough to have known the city as Austrian Lemberg for much longer than it had been Polish Lwow, and would not have dreamed of using the Ukrainian Lviv.

"You knew my father?"

"A fine man. The finest. I was seconded from Supreme Command to liaise with his general staff during the campaign of 1919. I remember your mother well. She travelled with us on campaign. Through the shelling and the gunfire. The advances and the retreats. She never once complained, despite nursing a newborn. A scrawny thing it was." There was another long pause as Galadyk confirmed to himself his decision. "Astonishing then, that I should now entrust the fulcrum of my defence to the man that babe has become."

"Sir?"

"Let me speak plainly, Zamoyski. Our position is good, but the men are either old or raw. This brigade was formed only two months ago. It is a scratch unit drawn from anything we can lay our hands on. Reservists, conscripts and border guards. And we defend the flank of the entire Polish army. I have few officers who can actually lead men. And I sense that the Hero of Lwow runs deep in your veins."

"But I..." Galadyk stopped Freddie's protest.

"There are five bunkers around the village, and they must hold." He stabbed his finger into the map on the table to indicate the strong points clustered around Wegierska Gorka below. They are manned by the 151st Company. Less than 80 men under Captain Semik. A good officer, but when the whirlwind hits he will need able subordinates. The bunkers are unfinished. They have no electricity. No radios. Nothing. When the fog of combat descends each will become an island. Each will need its own leader. A man of resolve, who can stiffen the men to dogged defence."

Freddie's opposition died as he understood the task that was being entrusted to him. "I will do my best, sir." He thought about the predicament for a moment. "Do they have tanks?"

"Of course. The second panzer division sits somewhere in those hills. This is the main valley south, so I'm sure we will have the pleasure of their company." Sensing Freddie's unease he went on. "Tanks are wonderful on open ground, but in confined spaces they are death traps. If they break out onto the plain then we are in trouble, but here in these closed spaces hemmed in by hills and rivers they are a liability."

"Really?"

"The Germans have developed a doctrine of mobile warfare. They tested it in Spain, and now they are ready to put it into action here. But remember that it was actually invented by your father and Marshal Pilsudski in those conflicts that saw the rebirth of our nation. There is nothing sweeter than to attack with speed across the supply lines of an advancing enemy. I was military attaché in Germany for two years and saw their rehearsals. On open ground they will be fearsome. But here? Here in these valleys we will have them."

"I understand, sir."

"Good man." The issue decided, Galadyk allowed himself a moment to turn to happier thoughts. He took two glasses from a small table by one of the windows and poured a generous shot of vodka into each.

"You believe this battle is coming, sir?"

Galadyk snorted. "Of course it's coming. You think this diplomatic offer from Germany is anything other than a tactic? A game? A ruse? Have you read Mein Kampf? No? Know your enemy, Zamoyski. It may be the ravings of a lunatic, but it is chillingly clear in its aims. Lebensraum is a neat little word given to a strategy of German conquest of the east. It is their destiny to attack us. The only question is when. My guess is within a week."

"That soon, sir?"

"Maybe sooner. And a few pill boxes are not going to even up odds of 20 to one. You know your military history, Zamoyski?" Freddie nodded. "This is our Battle of Thermophylae." The reference to the most famous conflict in the history of Ancient Greece caught Freddie's attention. For two days, 300 Spartan hoplites held back a force of tens of thousands of Persians in a defeat that has resounded down the centuries. Like Wegierska Gorka, Thermophylae was the narrow point of an overwhelming enemy's advance. Unlike here Thermophylae was defended by the cream of the greatest warrior caste ever known. "We don't even have enough ammunition let alone enough men. Our job is to hold these bastards back as long as we can to give our reserves a chance to man the defences further north. Don't kid yourself we can win. That's not our destiny." He offered a glass to Freddie. "How is your father?"

"Very well, sir." Freddie was still pondering on his commanding officer's candid statement of their chances. "His hips hurt, and he walks with a stick, but all things considered he's fine."

"Good. I have not seen him in 20 years." He paused for a moment in contemplation. "How old is he now? He must be over 70."

"He's 75, sir."

"Yes, he would be." Galadyk nodded to himself amazed at how the years had sneaked past. "We all thought he was quite the old dog when he appeared on campaign with this utterly gorgeous woman half his age." Galadyk was oblivious to the slight stiffening of Freddie's demeanour as he heard his parents spoken of in this way. "But she soon showed us. She had more fight in her heart than the rest put together, with the exception of your father." He pondered again, lost in memory. "A perfect match, despite the age difference."

"To me they are just my parents, sir." Freddie was trying subtly to suggest that Galadyk's reflections were less than appropriate, but nuance was plainly not his strongest attribute.

"It came as a shock when he talked to me late one night of his first wife." Freddie cleared his throat and thought of intervening, but Galadyk forged on oblivious. "We had been drinking, and he told me how she had died in childbirth not long after the turn of the century. The infant followed her shortly afterwards, and he was bereft for a decade. Terrible business. In fact he told me that he signed up for service in 1914 because he wanted to die. Despite his military background he was old enough to have sat it out if he wanted. But no. And it was that decision that led to him commanding our forces against Ukraine. Strange how fate plays with us." He paused again, and Freddie hoped his private reminiscences had come to an end. "Does he still run that estate of his?"

"He does, sir." There was relief in Freddie's reply as Galadyk moved away from comments on the private life of his family. The respite was short lived.

"No doubt those Ukrainian peasants try to give him the run around. That'll keep him busy chasing after that bunch of liars and cut-throats."

"Actually, sir, there is a great deal of mutual respect between them and him. And those liars and cut-throats were my childhood friends." It struck Freddie as strange that they were facing war against a foe who saw it was their right to take Polish land because of their belief in Polish inferiority and yet the Poles themselves could not see their own racial stereotyping when it was so obvious.

"Ah yes. I forgot. Your father was always very egalitarian when it came to the races. And very good too." Galadyk was typical of many within the Polish establishment who gave a nod to these enlightened attitudes, but who always seemed to slide casually into ingrained prejudice.

"To equality!" He raised his glass in an attempt to bring the conversation to a close.

"To your father. And to Poland. Poland is not lost!" The

glasses clashed and they drained their vodka in one go even as a voice in the back of Freddie's head completed the phrase. "Now take this to Captain Semik, Lieutenant." He stood, indicating their conversation was over, and handed Freddie a hastily written note.

Freddie saluted. "Of course. Thank you, sir."

As Freddie opened the door Galadyk called to him. "Good luck, Freddie my boy. Make your father proud." Freddie nodded solemnly and left.

He found Captain Tadeusz Semik in one of the bunkers across the railway track and the river. It was nestled in the hills that rose from the west bank of the Sola and gave a wonderful vantage point over the valley. Semik was a clean cut, powerfully built man around forty with an air of efficient authority that allowed a safe degree of informality of command. The men around him responded respectfully, as his orders came clearly and purposefully. He read the note from Galadyk and weighed up Freddie with a quick eye.

"Good to have you on board," he smiled. "Let me appraise you of the situation," and walking briskly out of the small command post he climbed the steps onto the roof from which he gave his briefing. "We have five bunkers. This is Mountain Cracker, and below us down the hill is Hobo." He pointed vaguely down the slope to another position. "In front of the village is Traveller, and over there in the valley of the tributary are Gorge and Dancer. We have only 70 men so Dancer is unoccupied."

The realisation that they had insufficient men to occupy even these few positions was chilling, but Freddie understood that further reflection on the woeful lack of troops was pointless. "Mountain Cracker, Hobo, Traveller and Gorge," he repeated.

Semik's energy seemed almost demonic as he pulled an apple from his pocket and continued his summary. "Our flanks and rear will be covered by the Berezwecz battalion under Major

Czarkowski." He bent down, slid a small knife from its concealed housing inside the lip of his right boot and cut the apple into rough pieces that he devoured as he spoke. "They will hold the woods and provide us with reinforcements. None of the bunkers is complete. They have no amenities but they are structurally sound. We have a couple of artillery pieces. One here," he pointed his knife at the muzzle of a large gun that protruded menacingly from the firing slit of the room below his feet," and another in Traveller. When they come, we shoot. And we keep shooting until they retreat or we are dead."

"Understood, sir." It was an unsophisticated plan. There would be no finesse. None of the brilliant sweeping manoeuvres that had so marked his father's campaigning. The men would fight or die. "Where would you like me?"

Semik thought for a few seconds before making what he knew would be a vital decision. "You take command here. The rock of our defence will be Traveller." He pointed to the valley floor to where the bunker sat defiantly beside the railway track as it left the village. "That's where I will be, but if they take this position then they will be straight in at my rear." He turned on Freddie. "You have my back, Lieutenant. Don't fail me!"

"No, sir."

"Right, I'd better introduce you to your men." Semik re-sheathed his knife, bounded down the steps and called the men of the bunker to order in front of the concrete monstrosity that they hoped would keep them alive. He announced Freddie's arrival and status as post commander, and gave a brief address to the mismatch of inexperience and infirmity before him. But Freddie was aware of a strange atmosphere. These men did not exude fear, or even blustering defiance. And Semik's brief speech did not exhort them to deeds of unlikely heroism. He spoke simply and plainly of their duty to hold their position whatever the cost, and their proud silence declared the grim fatalism Semik required of them.

"No retreat. No surrender." Semik finished, and his quoting of King Leonidas of Sparta pricked Freddie's ear in the echo of his conversation with Galadyk. "Come with me, Lieutenant," he ordered as he strode off down the hill, and the men returned to their business. "I'll introduce you to the commander of Hobo."

"That speech back there?" asked Freddie as he struggled to keep pace with Semik.

"Yes?"

"Leonidas."

"Yes?" There was an irritated edge in Semik's voice.

"It was something Colonel Galadyk said. Are we handing them a suicide mission?"

Semik stopped and turned to Freddie. "This is a suicide mission. Get that straight. The whole war is a suicide mission. We can't win this, but we can die like men and make those bastards pay heavily for taking our freedom." Semik's composure slipped as the strain of preparing this rag tag group showed in the ferocity of his speech. "Once you get the lads to realise that their aim is not to win, or even survive, but is to die well, that's when you free them of their fear. And that's what they are going to need." He looked Freddie up and down to add weight to his next question. "You ever been in combat, Lieutenant?" It was a ridiculous question. "No? Well, I have. I was sixteen when war broke out and I was conscripted to fight for Austria. I was a kid, and I shat myself for four years. It was only serving under your father that I learned that the way to steady your fear and fight more effectively was to assume you would die. The Spartans got that." He paused and spat on the floor. "And now the 151st get it!" He turned and continued his descent along the wooded path as he called over his shoulder. "And you'd better get it too."

They went another 50 yards or so along this corridor through the dense woodland. Freddie considered how difficult it would have been to veer off the path and realised that these woods really would protect their flanks. As they rounded a bend they came upon the rear of the bunker they had named Hobo. It was smaller than Mountain Cracker, and had no heavy gun, but the dozen or so men who laboured like ants had the same steely gaze of inevitability about them. Semik had done his work well.

"Sergeant!" He barked at a man directing work a distance away by the tree line. The man turned and as he walked up the slope Freddie could see it was Raczynski. The two men saluted and then embraced. "Sergeant Major Stanislav Raczynski." He turned to Freddie. "Lieutenant Freddie Zamoyski."

In the context of Semik's unit Raczynski was plainly free of certain aspects of military etiquette. This was not an environment in which rank was the sole determinant of authority. That would always be a factor, but charisma and strength of personality were clearly important drivers in the culture Semik had drilled into his makeshift unit in the short time it had existed.

"Lieutenant." Raczynski nodded politely. "You understand the code?"

"No retreat. No surrender." There was resolve in Freddie's tone.

Raczynski looked questioningly at Semik who nodded reassurance in reply. "Then I shall be proud to call you brother." He gave Freddie an unexpected hug, and in that moment the pact was sealed. Raczynski looked back at the track Freddie and Semik had taken and impressed the trust he was placing in his new comrade. "You have my back."

Freddie understood that each fortification's strength was in its forward face, and that each would be vulnerable to a rear assault. Mountain Cracker was the key. If that fell then the others would be exposed and would fall like dominoes. Hobo would be overrun, then Traveller, and finally Gorge.

"I have work to do," announced Freddie.

"Good," confirmed Semik. "Eat a hearty breakfast, for tonight we dine in Hades."

Freddie watched him as he walked away and disappeared

down a lower rat run that he assumed led to Traveller on the valley floor. He reflected that only a day earlier such self-conscious allusions to Spartan war culture would have seemed comical, and yet here and now in the frantic preparation of their makeshift redoubts it made grim sense. Galadyk had been right. Enlightenment thinking was of little use here, and rarified Augustinian theories on the nature of a Just War meant nothing. If the Germans came these men would kill or be killed. The rationalist had gone. The nationalist had emerged. Semik's approach may have lacked finesse, but in many ways it was an inspired solution to forging a unity without which they would all surely die in the first assault.

He spent the rest of the afternoon reconnoitring the area around Mountain Cracker and satisfied himself of the disposition of units of the supporting Berezwecz battalion. They were dug in at strategic points in the wilderness, covering his flank, and there was nothing more he could do but trust in their resolve.

The situation in the bunker itself was a concern. They had two heavy machine guns covering the forward ground with arcs of fire that made the 50 yards to the tree line a killing zone, but the ammunition store in the rear of the post was barely half full and that concerned him. He sent a runner to Hobo to ask for supplies, but he returned with the news that Raczynski's men were in an even worse situation.

There was a food store in the rear of the building, but there was no food. There was a toilet with no plumbing, and electric lights without electricity. There were some kerosene lamps that might be of some use, but Freddie pondered on how safe they might be given that the back half of the bunker stored the ammunition.

One piece of good news was that he found the large gun well stocked with its 75mm shells, and manned by an experienced crew. They would at least be able to maintain concerted fire on the valley floor which would be a huge help to those holding out in Traveller. Corporal Tomanek, the crew leader, explained to him that their effective range was well over 4,000 metres, while the best developed German tanks had guns with a realistic combat range of less than a kilometre. If the Germans did come with armour then Tomanek and his men could be relied upon to set the battle ground alight, which would give Traveller a fighting chance against the inevitable infantry.

As dusk settled on their fortified island on the wooded slopes two of the men served up a stew. And the increasingly tightly knit family of fifteen talked and joked and sang as the night fell.

-oOo-

"It was amazing how quickly I slid into the warrior code," commented Freddie as a nurse replaced his water jug. "We faced adversity, and that drove us together. I understood who I had to be, and I was determined not to fail them."

"Did you feel no fear at all?" I asked.

Freddie smiled wistfully. "Semik was right. Once you acclimatise to your inevitable death then what is there to fear?"

I was pleased to see Freddie recovering from his ordeal the day before. He was tired, and we agreed to end for the day. We both knew that the following morning would hear his account of the Battle of Wegierska Gorka, and no doubt that would be painful. But we also both knew that death in battle was in the natural order of things and somehow that made it safe.

IV - Careless Cerberus

The day dawned to a fanfare of footballing chaos that was impossible to avoid. It was Wednesday, but you would scarcely have known that. England was in the semi-final of the World Cup, and the nation had lost its senses to a light-hearted nationalism that spawned what seemed like a public holiday. Little work would be done that day. People who hardly knew the rules of soccer and could name perhaps two English players at most, were driving around in cars that trailed scarves and flags. It was moronic and wonderful in equal measure, and I felt a twinge of sympathy for the true supporter whose decades' long wait for this moment had been hijacked by these sporting journeymen. Their passing fancy would be short-lived, while the true believers would live a genuine ecstasy or agony that would turn on the outcome in Italy that night. England's rivals were to be the Germans, an irony not lost on Freddie as I entered.

"I'm sorry I'm late, Freddie. The traffic is terrible."

"That's okay. I have no other engagements. At least not yet," he finished, dramatically raising his eyes to the heavens.

I could not help but laugh. "We'd best get cracking then!" I plugged the tape recorder into the socket in the wall. It had struck me the night before that we had already filled five full tapes, each of 90 minutes, and yet the time had passed in a flash and Freddie's story seemed only just to have begun.

The respite of the previous day's coolness had gone, and the oppressive summer humidity pressed in again. The fan stirred once more as an unexpectedly chirpy Freddie drifted back in time to relive the horror of the Sola Valley.

"That night news began to filter through that the diplomatic mission had stalled," he explained. "Galadyk and the others were right. Hitler's ministers gave the Polish delegation the runaround, as telegrams and ultimata flew around Berlin, Warsaw, London and Paris. But to no effect."

-oOo-

The first rays of the morning sun were accompanied by distant thunder. The men of Mountain Cracker hurried to the roof and looked up the valley from their vantage point. The tranquil scene was as peaceful as it had always been, but from high in the mountains the ominous sound of artillery filtered through the dawn mists. It was almost beautiful, as if those craggy peaks were calling down to the plain below. But the men understood the hell that was being unleashed at the border where the high passes clung precariously to the rock face.

"Poor buggers." Sambor was an elderly reservist whose eyes held a distant fear born of the trenches. He knew what it was to be shelled incessantly. Shelled to breaking. Shelled to madness. The irony was that he came from the deep east, well beyond Lwow, and had a strong Ukrainian accent. In the Great War he had been pressed into service by the Russians and so the shells that had fallen on him might have been fired by any of his current comrades. Such jumbled suzerainty had been the price of Poland's subjugation.

"Who's up there?" asked Freddie.

"My brothers," replied Tomanek, his granite face hardening further. "Both of them. A single company against a whole division." There was a silence as the men glanced at their comrade respectfully, sharing his anguish. "Crew! Present! We have work to do." The five artillery men jumped to his order and scuttled back inside the bunker to prepare their weapon for the day's business.

"At ease," ordered Freddie to his expectant platoon. "They're a way off yet, and we need to prepare this ground." He cast his hand over the rough earth between the bunker and the tree line. To the far left the dense vegetation gave way to the opening that led to the track to Hobo, while on the right some 50 yards away was another gap that led into the maze of paths through the wilderness that were guarded by the Berezwecz battalion.

Freddie ordered the men to collect the supplies of barbed wire and wooden stakes that were piled up behind the strongpoint. Along with sandbags, they were commodities they possessed in abundance, and he intended to use them to the best possible effect. He knew that any frontal attack was likely to come from the right. For it to come from the left would mean that Hobo had already fallen to a frontal assault, so trusting in Raczynski's resolve he quickly decided the right portal was the key.

He was eager to ensure that no attackers would be able to come from the right to skirt the edge of the foliage and attack the fortress lower down the hill so the platoon got to work laying a dense barrier of wire that was firmly anchored in the undergrowth and extended towards the bunker, dividing the ground in two. He then ordered the stakes and wire to be erected running back and forth in a zig-zag pattern across the ground between the right opening and their concrete strongpoint. These improvised fortifications left an open channel inviting the attackers to run left then right then left and right again to avoid the razor edges of the barbs on the densely packed wire.

"Won't they be able to get through this, sir?" asked a young private. "We're giving them an open route."

"You ever shot rabbits as they run across in front of you, Wozny?"

"Yes sir."

"You ever done that with a Browning heavy machine gun?"

Wozny thought for a moment, and then a broad smile of understanding lit up his face. "No sir."

The other men laughed as the simple Wozny delighted in Freddie's deadly plan. They were happy in their work in the knowledge that each barrier they erected would allow them to kill more Germans. The artillery in the distance seemed to provide a soothing melody to their labours and they almost forgot the death it heralded.

After a while Freddie felt the fullness of his bladder and, remembering that there were no facilities in the outpost, decided to relieve himself where he stood. It was an action that would have been unthinkable just two days earlier, but already he was living a different life. His men looked at him with amused surprise.

"Just marking our territory," he quipped, and before long they were all sharing in his joke that tapped into something primeval as they joined in the ritual marking of their range.

Satisfied that his instructions were being followed efficiently, he returned to the command room in the bunker. It was a small office in the back of the blockhouse that was accessed directly from the main firing room and, making a show of wishing to check some maps he entered and closed the flimsy door. He noted that if it came to fighting inside the strongpoint this would be no barrier at all. There was a table on which stood a lit kerosene lamp, two chairs and an array of maps, but this was not Freddie's purpose. In the men's jocular urinating he had suddenly been overcome by the enormity of what lay ahead. He sat and unbuttoned the top of his tunic. He reached inside and pulled out the simple wooden crucifix which he kissed and then held tightly as he muttered a brief prayer asking for strength.

The men were quickly growing to trust him, and in that moment he was acutely aware of the responsibility he carried. His mind floated back to a time when he was only eight or nine years old, recalling a conversation with his father. He had been competing in a school wrestling competition and had just beaten a much heavier boy. He was flushed with the joy of the victory and his father had taken him to one side.

"Do you know why you won?" his father had asked.

"Because I was better," Freddie had replied triumphantly.

"No, Freddie. You won because you showed no fear. He

didn't expect you to fight. He thought you would be afraid of him. Of his size. When you attacked you showed him you were fearless. Despite his advantage he was actually the one with the doubt. The one with the fear." There was unmistakable pride in his father's voice.

"Is that what it was like in the war, Papa? Did you win because you were fearless?"

"No Freddie. I was very afraid. But only ever before a battle. A battle makes you reckless, and anyone can fight when their blood is up. The trick is not to let the fear of the battle defeat you before it starts. And then to control your recklessness after it begins."

"I won't be afraid."

"Maybe not. But one day you may have to fight for Poland. You might lead men and, if you do, your job is to make sure that they don't let fear beat them before they can fight. That is what leaders do. They inspire their men to be greater than they thought they could be."

Freddie squeezed the crucifix and wondered for a moment where that memory had come from. He had never recalled it before and yet now it was as vivid as the day it had happened. Freddie began to realise the strange effect that anticipation can have on the mind, and kissing the crucifix once more and thanking God for giving him that recollection, he pondered on the remarkable way in which Semik had freed his troops of their fear in so short a time. He rebuttoned his tunic and rejoined his men.

"This is a nice little chicken run", announced Freddie, admiring the completed defences. "I can't wait to see those Germans try and take us." It was midday and as they looked to the valley there were still no signs of any enemy advance. "The boys in the pass must be putting up one almighty fight."

"They volunteered for the job, sir," replied Podolski. The sergeant was a calm man who held the respect of the men, but who understood he did not possess the charisma to lead. He was not a Raczynski, and was happy to support Freddie in his new role.

"Brave men."

"Brave. And dogged. Hotheads. But they will fight to the last man to buy us the time we need."

The work done on their killing ground, Freddie ordered another weapons check. The two Ckm wz 30 heavy machine guns that were based on the American Browning design were readied as the men methodically checked the anatomy of each. The feed, the firing mechanism, the ejection port, the coolant system, the firing stand. Their lives would depend on these machines performing, potentially for hours at a stretch, and nothing could be left to chance.

The ammunition boxes were fetched from the store and lined up for quick loading. Each belt held 250 fat rounds that would carve through wood and flesh alike, but these monsters could throw out 500 bullets a minute, and in the heat of battle they knew that survival would depend on their skill in reloading quickly. It was a process they had practised until they were sick of it, but they all knew that enemy fire would dull their senses and rob them of the precision that was so vital and each of them silently feared the tremor that panic might induce.

They checked their sight lines from the firing slit in the thick blockhouse wall to ensure complete coverage of the ground before them. To their left the eastern end of the firing room was separated by a wall with a small archway, making it into an independent bay that housed the big gun. The walls of the structure were six feet thick and would withstand anything the Germans could throw at them short of engineers laying static charges. At each end of the building there was a single, armoured door, which when closed cut out all light from the firing room save for that which streamed in through the firing slit. Electricity would have solved that, but they had none.

Their rifles were checked and cleaned one final time, and Freddie examined the single grenade launcher and the dozen or so rounds that came with it. He contemplated the battle ahead, turning over the options in his mind and thinking how he might respond to each eventuality. His main worry was the track that led out of the wilderness to the western flank of the bunker. It opened onto the ground about 20 yards from the western door of the firing room and Freddie shuddered to think how easily an entry could be forced from there. If the Germans managed to push through the wilderness then their only defence would be small arms fire, and the hastily erected barricades they had placed earlier in the day to block that entrance would be of only very limited benefit to them.

And there they waited, scanning the horizon, their eyes straining for the first movements in the valley or the sound of approaching gunfire. A silence had enveloped them all as they struggled against the numbing effects of the adrenaline that pumped through their limbs. The tiniest sounds were magnified a thousand fold in this awful anticipation as a fog seemed to close in around their minds. Heightened senses. Dulled sensibility.

The artillery crew had spent most of the day practising their loading routine and had even fired three rounds at a makeshift target that had been placed on the valley floor half a mile or so in front of Traveller. The first landed short by 20 yards. Tomanek ensured they corrected for this and the next two rounds were direct hits. But none of this made him feel any better about his brothers as the distant guns taunted him.

And so their waiting continued for hour after endless hour. The resistance of the volunteers ahead of them was remarkable, and the sun was low in the western sky before the few survivors trickled back down the valley pursued by the German vanguard. Tomanek spotted the danger and dropped four shots on the enemy, forcing them to pull back and allowing the mauled remnants of the volunteer force to escape.

Just a single company of 100 men had held 20,000 at bay for a whole day. Their fortitude had blunted the German attack so that their heavy support was not sufficiently advanced for them to mount a full scale assault that night. This minor reprieve did not help the men in Mountain Cracker to sleep any better, but it did reassure Freddie that his first action would at least be in daylight. Leading men for the first time was daunting enough, but to do so at night would have been an unwelcomed additional burden. In front of them they were aware of intense small arms fire in the wilderness, and guessed that the Berezwecz men were suffering steady losses. The Germans could afford to play an attritional game given their overwhelming superiority in numbers. And that was their grim plan. Eventually, simple pressure of numbers told, and the route to the right opening in front of the bunker was forced by the Teutonic wave.

It was eight o'clock on the morning of Saturday 2nd September when the forward elements of a great blue grey mass issued onto the killing ground in front of Freddie's men. The tortuous narrow route through the undergrowth made it difficult for the men at the back to know what was happening ahead, and the human surge in the crowded rat run forced men forward onto the wire as non-commissioned officers barked their orders to halt. Freddie's Brownings took their first lives. A dozen corpses adorned the wire.

There was overt confusion in the German ranks generated mainly by their own weight of numbers. Freddie had anticipated this moment, and calmly took the grenade launcher. In easy earshot of the curses and shouts of the chaotic crush he placed a round in the breech. Deliberately and coldly he held the weapon out at arm's length, aiming for the mouth of the opening. Mechanically, and with murderous intent, he raised his arm a little to give the projectile some elevation and then fired. There was a hollow popping noise and the grenade flew through the air and over the heads of the front ranks who had dropped to the

52

ground to escape the machine gun fire.

The grenade disappeared from sight, lost in the darkness of the crowded trail. After a couple of seconds there was a flash some way down the track and a moment later a loud crack split the air. Dust rose from the ground and for a few seconds there was a strange silence. Then came the screams of agony. It was not a large charge, but detonated in the midst of tightly packed flesh its force was magnified as it ripped through organs and limbs and blew holes in bodies.

Wozny looked on with a grin. "Well done, sir," he beamed, and with excited encouragement pressed Freddie to fire again.

"Use your head Wozny."

"Sir?"

"What's happening in the undergrowth over there right now?"

Wozny looked puzzled. "They're dead."

"All of them?"

"No. We can hear loads of them screaming."

"Exactly! So what are the others trying to do right now? What would you be doing? A conscript, your first action, and your friends dying in front of you."

"I'd help them."

Freddie smiled knowingly, and turned to Podolski. "And what would you be doing, Sergeant?"

Podolski knew the answer, and looked at Freddie admiringly. His leader was a cold-hearted bastard, and that was exactly what they needed. "I would be pulling young conscripts away from the wounded."

"What! Why?" Wozny was indignant.

"Because the shit in the bunker is about to fire another grenade and kill everyone trying to help the fallen. And soon the path will be blocked with dead bodies. It's tough but they have to leave them and pull back while they decide on a proper strategy."

"So you see, Wozny. Down there right now a conflict of

hatred is being played out between the men and their commanders. The NCOs are right, but the men don't know that, so why would I fire again and demonstrate the point for them?"

"There will be guns raised," commented Podolski. "Some might even be fired."

"Who do you think will win?" asked Wozny naively.

Podolski looked at Freddie with despair. He in turn explained by means of a question. "You and the boys against Podolski and Raczynski? Who would you back?" No answer was needed.

A single shot sounded in the undergrowth, and was replied by a burst of automatic fire from several weapons. "Confrontation over," commented Podolski. "One dead sergeant. One dead private. Command restored. One belligerent, hateful mass of men." He turned to look at Freddie with new found respect. Their gaze met, and the slightest nod from Podolski was all that was required to express his admiration.

Warfare is so rarely about simple brute force. It is a mysterious broth in which raw physicality is given life by guile, cunning, intelligence, bluff, psychology and luck. And Freddie was proving himself to be a ruthless leader.

There was no immediate response from the German column. Freddie could see little movement as they had retreated around the gentle bend in the rat run. The curve of the walkway through the wilderness and the slope of the hill that ran away along its arc gave the invaders a safe place to pause while they rethought their attack. Freddie considered sending another grenade skitting down the slope, but thought that with only eleven rounds left he probably should avoid anything speculative.

Battle was breaking out all around them. The crackle of small arms fire was everywhere, and as the sounds bounced off the trees and the walls of the bunker it was difficult to know exactly where the fight was. But one thing was plain. The majority of the sound came from the right, from the dense wilderness up the hill from Mountain Cracker. This was the battle that worried Freddie the most. The men he had pinned down to his front were not really the threat. Podolski and Lesniak, another dour, older reservist, had them bottled up with their machine guns. To the right though, God only knew what force was trying to push its way through the wilderness. Would the Berezwecz battalion hold?

Freddie went to the door to his right, unlocked the mechanism and swung the heavy barrier open. The threshold was protected by a concrete screen which he needed to peer round in order to see what was going on up the hill. In front of him sat the innocuous opening of the rat run that was the source of his anxiety. At the moment it was silent. Abandoned. But if Freddie's infantry support buckled then this would be the main line of attack. And he had little defence against it. He satisfied himself that for now the gunfire in the woods was a long way off, closed the door and returned to the firing slit to reassess the situation.

There was as a long period of inactivity as the Germans readied themselves for another assault. Freddie found himself feeling impatient in his battle lust. He wanted more contact, more confrontation, and he immediately recognised the wise words of his father. "A battle makes you reckless, and anyone can fight when their blood is up." Freddie was experiencing firsthand what that meant. If the Germans had waited much longer the impulse to attack them headlong would have been powerful. His father's words came again. "The trick is not to let the fear of the battle defeat you before it starts. And then to control your recklessness after it begins". It was strange, but he was satisfied that he no longer felt any fear and hoped that a similar feeling had descended on his men.

Eventually, driven on by their superiors, the German infantry came once more. A dozen or so men emerged from the track and threw stick grenades. All of them were cut down by Podolski's Browning as their projectiles fell short or overshot their target which was the slim firing slit from which protruded the Polish guns. The small explosions barely grazed the bunker as the pile of dead bodies grew. One grenade came close, but the long handle that gave the weapon a greater throwing range caught on the lips of the opening and the charge exploded harmlessly on the ground.

The gathering collection of dead bodies gave the hope of cover for those men following, but the heavy slugs from the bunker's guns cut through them like paper, dealing death to the hapless men sheltering in their shadow. Freddie was for a moment transfixed by the action of the bullets tearing through the dead flesh. The energy from each round caused the corpse to jerk slightly in a strangely fascinating Danse Macabre. He was lost momentarily in this ghoulish study until he forced himself to refocus on the matters in hand.

After a further pause to consider their predicament, a few hopeful Germans decided to run the zig-zagging wire alley provided by Freddie's directions, and were inevitably cut down. It was foolhardy beyond belief, but Freddie was beginning to see how combat could change a man's behaviour out of all recognition. One of the men was not dead, but lay on the ground behind the wire with his legs shattered, oozing his blood into the Polish earth. His pitiful cries cut through the morning air like the mewing of a wounded cat. Both Podolski and Lesniak watched on. Freddie waited for a moment and then called to Podolski to finish the poor man off. Podolski fixed Freddie's gaze and then slowly looked away, registering defiance for the first time.

Sensing their own moment of tension, Freddie hefted a rifle to his shoulder, took aim across the 40 yards of open ground, and sent the wretched man to his maker. It was a good shot to have hit his head dead centre and the men nodded their respect. Freddie patted Podolski on the shoulder. "I know you hate them Konrad. But we are not monsters."

Podolski shrugged ruefully and smiled to himself. The moment had passed.

In the midst of these close quarter exchanges Tomanek's men

began pouring shells into the valley where large formations of infantry were advancing under sparse cover against Traveller. There was another pause in the forward attack on Mountain Cracker, and Freddie took the opportunity to observe what was going on down by the river. Through his binoculars he could see little groups of men which, through the lenses, looked like a colony of ants foraging from some evil nest higher up the valley. As he watched, one of Tomanek's deadly rounds landed. Ants were thrown into the air, and dropped motionless to the ground. Other bodies further away staggered and fell, stunned by the blast. The view from Mountain Cracker seemed abstract and stylised, but there was no doubting the carnage that the artillery was inflicting below.

And so the battle continued into the afternoon. The gunfire from the wilderness above growing steadily nearer. The waves of frontal attacks repelled. The infantry on the small plain massacred by a combination of shelling and murderous fire from Traveller.

By mid afternoon the Germans had somehow managed to drag a large canon up the rat run and pushed it into a firing position. Its menacing barrel was protected by a large metal shield that provided cover for the crew, and Podolski's machine gun bullets bounced off harmlessly.

Freddie recognised the danger early and called to Tomanek to swing his gun to the right. Tomanek's shout echoed through the doorway from his firing bay, confirming the order. Moving the gun was a clumsy manoeuvre that was agonisingly slow, and to buy some time Freddie planted another grenade at the canon's foot. A fountain of blood, flesh and dirt spurted upwards more than ten feet as Freddie ordered the Brownings to slow the enemy's response. "Suppressing fire!" he shouted urgently, but Podolski and Lesniak had anticipated the command and were already laying down a hail of death.

Many attackers fell, but two made it to the cover of the canon's shield and began firing. In an instant the bunker was lit up as terrifying 20mm shells burst into the command post. The air boiled as canon rounds tore through the firing slit and smashed into the back wall, carving away large chunks of cement that crashed to the floor. Worse still were those shells that struck the edges of the firing slit where the concrete was thinnest. There the masonry disintegrated to powder that threw up a dense screen that blinded the Poles to anything outside the room.

As the men choked on the caustic dust Freddie knew the German infantry would be rushing their position. It was only a matter of seconds before multiple grenades would come clattering through the slit and they would all be dead. Podolski was half crouching behind the cover of the bunker wall, his hands above his head, firing his Browning aimlessly into the white fog. He was cursing and shouting at two of the men to keep the belt feeds running freely so the gun did not jam. Spent shell cases cascaded out of the gun's exit port, the musicality of their tinkling as they hit the floor strangely incongruous in the frenzy of battle.

Freddie hoped beyond hope that Tomanek's men could still see to fire. Their shot on the canon was what stood between the men and certain death. He grabbed a handful of grenades and threw six of them one after another through the slit, aiming from memory for the end of the meandering barbed wire avenue that he knew was on the right. The cacophony of noise so dulled his senses that he was not sure if they had detonated, when the ear-splitting sound of Tomanek's big gun cut through the air.

The Brownings continued to spew forth, but the canon fire that had shouted back was suddenly mute. As the smoke and dust cleared Freddie and his men cast their eyes over the results of those minutes of chaos and almost wept. Whether their suppressed tears were of joy or disgust even he did not know. Tomanek's gun had destroyed the German canon utterly, and Freddie could only conclude that its crew had been so eager to stop the Brownings that they had no freedom to swing its attention on the artillery piece. In an instant he saw the dilemma the Germans had faced. To turn the canon would have allowed the machine guns to tear them to pieces, and so all they could do was pour fire into the bunker and hope their grenadiers could run quickly enough to drop their sticks into Tomanek's placement before finishing off Freddie and his men.

There must have been an agonising panic for them as the large gun barrel fixed them, and then discharged its death. What must that have felt like? To look straight down the barrel of a 75mm gun at virtually point blank range in the knowledge that the end of everything was a heartbeat away.

The runners had not made it through. Before them, Freddie saw a clutch of small craters where his grenades had landed. It was a nauseating sight. Each looked like a shallow cauldron, filled with mangled body parts and sinew, and resounded with blood-curdling screams. It was a sticky slumgullion of human flesh cooked by the Devil himself. For a moment Freddie reflected on the terrible suffering he had inflicted in his quick thinking efficiency. But it was plain that it had been a close run thing. A moment later and some of those grenadiers would have been across the open ground and the men in the bunker would now be the ones ripped into unidentifiable pieces, their flesh mutilated by Nobel's gift to mankind.

Behind the craters a line of dead and dying men filled the chicken run, presumably victims of Podolski and Lesniak's blind fire. The many men still clinging to life writhed like maggots on the hard ground made slippery by human offal. Some cried for help. Some cried in pain. Some cried for their mothers. The men of the bunker did not need Freddie's fluent German to understand those cries.

"Shall we finish them off?" Podolski asked dubiously, deferring this time to Freddie.

He thought for a moment, wrestling with his conscience. He had a human responsibility to the wounded, but he owed far more to his own men. "No. There are too many. Save the ammo."

Podolski nodded, relieved.

"You fucking bastards!" came a visceral shout from the German position. Freddie immediately recognised a thick, uneducated Bavarian accent.

In his finest Hochdeutsch Freddie shouted back. "Are you enjoying Poland, Nazi?" He emphasised that last word for effect. The name Nazi was the diminutive form of Ignatz, a common Bavarian name, but the shortened version carried a deeply insulting connotation in Freddie's precise accent. It would have been like an English aristocrat calling an Irishman "Paddy" or a Scot "Jock". It reeked of condescension and Freddie calculated that it would rile the enemy. "You may retrieve your wounded, Nazi. We have no quarrel with them."

It is interesting that the label "Nazi" was used by Hitler's opponents precisely because it so strongly reeked of dull brutish asininity. The fascists themselves naturally hated the term, but here on this ground Freddie was stamping his superiority on his attackers.

A further exchange shouted across the killing field convinced the German he could send men to rescue the stricken, although the combination of a perfect Junker's accent and racial insult juxtaposed with this humane largesse was confusing. Freddie hoped that it would sow the seeds of further doubt in their minds. He knew that German society was still incredibly hierarchical, and the idea that the opposition was led by a warrior of superior birth might worm its way into their self-doubt and feed on their fears.

"You speak German?" Podolski was surprised at Freddie's ease with their enemy's tongue.

"Yes. I've just insulted them deeply, and then offered for them to collect their wounded."

"No sir!" exclaimed Romanowicz, another young reservist.

"Quiet!" barked Podolski.

"But..."

"But nothing!" Podolski took control of himself and explained patiently to the private the cold reasoning in Freddie's decision. "They'll reclaim twenty or so wounded that will clog up their column as they carry them back down the rat run. Their other men will see what awaits them, and they'll also know that we are honourable. And it's always more difficult to kill honourable men in cold blood." He turned to Freddie. "You're good, sir."

Freddie nodded. He wanted to thank Podolski for his compliment, but recognised that might tarnish his growing aura with the men. And he knew he would need to call on every scrap of their belief in him by the end.

The moment was broken by a muffled groan from the darkened recesses at the back of the room. In the chaos no one had noticed Wozny slumped on the floor. As they ran to his aid they saw the large hole blown in his chest below his right collar bone, and the growing pool of blood soaking his uniform and gathering on the floor. Freddie rolled him slightly to look for an exit wound. There was none, and he realised that the young enthusiast must have been hit by a ricocheting canon round that was now lodged in the back of his thorax. The whole of his upper lung and its blood vessels would have been liquified by the bullet's energy and he was now bleeding to death into the cavity. There was nothing they could do, but cradle his head and hold his hand as his life slowly slipped away.

He desperately tried to speak, but all he managed was to expel spattered lumps of rapidly congealing blood through his larynx. As the red treacle filled his airway he struggled to say something important, and groped clumsily at the middle of his chest. Freddie instinctively tore open the tunic to reveal a crucifix similar to his own. He looked around urgently, but seeing no oil or other sacramental fluid, he dipped his thumb into the pool of blood and used it to make the sign of the cross on Wozny's forehead. His eyes flickered and he gave a brief smile, finding comfort as Freddie whispered the last rites in his ear. "Per istam sanctan unctionem et suam piissimam misericordiam, indulgeat tibi Dominus quidquid....."

His eyes closed, his hand opened, and he was gone. The small group huddled around the corpse looked at Freddie in silence. "How did you know?" asked Lesniak.

"I didn't," he replied softly. "Man your posts!"

Their grief for Wozny would have to wait. This first loss had left them reeling, despite knowing that by the end of the battle death among them would be inevitable. But they wondered who had sent this young officer to their rescue. He knew instinctively what to do. He played mind games with the enemy. He slaughtered them in droves. He spoke perfect German, and yet in that most intimate moment of a man's life, the moment when he departs, he was his priest. He said those words that helped Wozny to cross over. The aura grew still further.

Podolski had been watching the Germans, his gun trained on them for the slightest false move, but none came. They had removed their wounded, were licking their wounds and were regrouping. The battle up the hill was becoming louder, and Freddie needed to know the level of the threat. He sent Romanowicz up the side rat run to get a progress report and ordered the men to replenish the ammunition from the stores. While this was being done he joined Tomanek once more.

The big gun had been trained again on the valley. As Freddie examined the plain he understood the importance of Tomanek's job. Across the ground moving toward Traveller was a formation of tanks firing rapidly as they came. There were ten Mark II Panzers whose armour would not be troubled by machine gun fire. They all carried the same 20mm canon that Freddie's men had just experienced, and he shuddered as he contemplated the appalling state that the inside of Traveller would soon be in as they opened up.

Somehow the big gun in Traveller managed to keep firing, and the Panzers advance halted temporarily as they tried to move to avoid its attentions. Tomanek's gun then joined the conversation with devastating effect. His crew was well practised and his leadership was grim and determined. He had a double score to settle with the invaders, a blood revenge, and three minutes later two more tanks were blazing wrecks.

To see a high explosive round hit one of those older, smaller tank types was both exhilarating and chilling. One shell scored a direct hit, and Freddie watched flame jetting out from every opening and rivetted seam. The machine simply imploded on the spot, the only saving grace for the crew being that they could not possibly have known anything about it before they were vaporised. The others, sensing the danger, began to withdraw rapidly, but their six cylinder Maybach engines laboured in reverse gear and Tomanek's men accounted for two more machines before they were able to retreat to the safety of the dead ground behind the shoulder of a hill.

There was another hiatus in combat as the Germans thought again. This was becoming frustrating. Their intelligence had told them this sector was guarded by a scratch unit formed of old men and boys. The High Command's plan had been to amass an unstoppable force to break the Polish flank. They had practised for years the newly developing art of mobile armoured warfare and now unleashed it on Poland. Their ideal opportunity had seemed to be to drive their outflanking pincers down from East Prussia, that isolated island of German territory on the Baltic coast. The problem with that plan was that northern Poland was heavily wooded, and the strategy required open country.

The pincers therefore had to follow a southern route, but before they could break onto the Krakow plain they had the small job of swatting aside this troublesome barrier. The plan had called for them to be in Zywiec by the end of the first day, and their generals were growing impatient at the unexpected delay caused by this bunch of reservists.

As the pressure from above came to drive on, the second panzer division formed up three squadrons of tanks, and attacked Traveller one more time. It was another attempt at brute force, which so rarely succeeds against wily and determined defence. The two main guns in Traveller and Mountain Cracker hit them hard with an uncompromising accuracy that forced another retreat. Before they left the scene they had managed to cleft a scar in the flank of Traveller, but by six o'clock the valley floor lay littered with the remnants of ten Panzers, two of them state of the art Mark IV designs that constituted Germany's sharpest blade. The Wehrmacht could not afford such losses. These machines would be vital once they had forced their way onto the easy terrain below the hills and throwing them away against mountain defences was profligate. The infantry would have to shoulder this burden, and that order came down the line very powerfully.

This was the reason that in the lengthening shadows of the day, Freddie's men faced another onslaught of almost insane intensity. The Germans had at last managed to bring their medium artillery into range, and they now called down a barrage on Mountain Cracker of such ferocity that it seemed that the world had ended and they were already in hell. The German guns dropped their own 75mm rounds about Freddie's position and it was only a matter of time before one scored a direct hit on the roof. As that happened dust fell on the men and the building gave a deep groan. Freddie wondered whether that low throated complaint signalled a structural failure, but the next two direct blasts made no greater impact. The men were growing to love this ugly, concrete monstrosity. It may not have had electricity or water but it was solid and it was keeping them alive.

The impatient attackers could see the artillery was having little effect and changed tactic. The next few rounds that came down were smoke canisters, and this time the whiteout was total. This was the most dangerous situation they had faced. The

Germans could keep this up for a very long time, which meant wave after wave of them would eventually overwhelm the position.

Freddie shouted to Podolski and Lesniak to fire short repeated bursts at the turning points at opposite ends of the chicken run. They could not see them, but they had poured fire onto this earth for the last ten hours and knew every feature. The rest of the men he ordered to take up rifles and spread themselves evenly across the firing slit. Their job would be to shoot any Germans that came out of the smoke and their reactions would need to be quick.

And so it proved. For 20 minutes or more this game of reflex action played itself out. The Brownings were probably accounting for much of the assault, but every few seconds a German would half emerge from the white smoke. The strange lighting effect it cast drained them of colour, and their wild eyes and battle face gave them the appearance of undead wraiths brought back from the grave. Each was shot down as Freddie realised that the smoke was even more disorientating to the attackers as they had to navigate the wire and then somehow find their bearings in this dense whiteout. Many of them seemed genuinely surprised to see the fortification and could not respond as quickly as the defenders.

The smoke cleared, and the men could see the real intention behind this assault. In the time they had been dealing with these sporadic attackers the German engineers had been hard at work on the wire and had cleared a direct path to the bunker.

"Oh shit." Podolski was not prone to expletives and the men understood the significance of what lay before them. The enemy's line of attack was not completely clear, in fact it was not at all easy, cluttered as it was with the corpses and body parts of nearly 200 men. It was a scene worthy of Dante himself. But the wire had been blown aside and the way for a mass assault prepared.

There was a loud banging on the locked entrance to the right, and anxious looks were exchanged. "Romanowicz," reassured Freddie calmly. He had forgotten he had earlier sent the youth to reconnoiter the hillside. A few words shouted through the door confirmed it was him, and Freddie swung it open to allow him in.

He was bleeding from a light wound on his upper arm, but proudly announced he had killed two Germans in return. Serendipity had brought him back from the wilderness just as the smoke had fallen and recognising the need to cover the entrance he had waited for any attackers that veered in his direction. Freddie realised he had not thought of that possibility and thanked God for sending Romanowicz back when he did. It was one of those strokes of luck that marks out the successful commander.

And then began the inevitable German onslaught. A charge of unparalleled bluntness. The open path through the wire was about 20 yards wide and easy for the machine guns to cover. Smoke was of no use, and more likely to confuse the attackers, and so they came on in broad daylight in the full glare of the Polish canons. Ten minutes later another hundred bodies had been added to the count, and the Germans ceased this futile madness.

As night crept in, the day had undeniably belonged to the Poles. Some were beginning to believe in their own invincibility, but Freddie knew different. The threat had always come from the wilderness up the hill, and Romanowicz's report was not encouraging. There had been hand to hand fighting in the undergrowth, but the 300 or so men that guarded their flank had become entangled in a death match with an estimated 5000 invaders and they were close to cracking. The Germans were also torching the vegetation to allow them through. It was only a matter of time.

The moon was waning, but was still almost full, and it cast a silvered glow over the mountains that denied the Germans any opportunity for guile. Eyes quickly accommodated to the lunar light and so the meagre store of flares would not be depleted. After their severe mauling at the hands of the crew of Mountain Cracker the Germans staged no assault that night. They had no need as the wilderness slowly succumbed.

In order to benefit from every possible sense in that strange new silvern world Freddie had opened the door and posted two men as guards. The gunfire in the wilderness had receded to the odd sporadic crackle, but the smell of charred and smouldering trees and bushes filled the still air.

Shortly before midnight the news that Freddie had dreaded came to them. A lieutenant of what remained of their flank defence arrived to deliver the message that they had been ordered to withdraw.

"The 21st division to our west has crumbled and the Germans are on the outskirts of Zywiec. We are about to be cut off. We've been ordered to fall back to new defensive positions near Wadowice. What's left of our battalion is on the move."

Freddie thanked the young officer who hurried on his way. "So," he began slowly, turning to his men.

"No retreat. No surrender." Podolski sensed Freddie needed the moral permission he gave. A murmur of approval rumbled through the platoon.

"Exactly," nodded Freddie. "We're not abandoning Hobo and Traveller. We stand and we fight." He took stock. There were four grenades and six boxes of machine gun belts. 12,000 rounds between them and the end. There were some sandbags in the rear store, and Tomanek still had nearly fifty of his big shells.

Freddie ordered the hasty construction of a wall of sandbags at the vulnerable western entrance and one of the Brownings was moved to cover the side rat run. More sandbags were placed in a defensive arc on the roof of the bunker to give a better firing position despite the knowledge that any men there would be much more exposed to enemy fire. Finally, Tomanek's gun was turned once again to the rat run at the front. Their heavy explosive rounds were not normally ideal against dispersed infantry, but in the tight confines here they would draw a heavy toll.

Lesniak remained at the firing slit with 3,000 rounds while Podolski manned the makeshift machine gun nest by the door with the other 9,000. There was nothing more they could do. Eventually they would run out of ammunition or be overwhelmed by artillery or mortar fire. And then they would die. If they fought well they would buy their comrades time to form a better defensive line around Wadowice, and for the first time in two days Freddie recalled his life before the Sola Valley. Karol came from Wadowice, so perhaps his action here would slow its fall and in some way allow him and Ginka to flee ahead of the Teutonic tsunami that was crashing against these Polish shores. The fleeting thought passed and his attention refocused on the job in hand.

Sunrise was at 5.30 and brought the full force of the Wehrmacht war machine crashing down on Mountain Cracker. As the pale golden crescent of light in the east grew, giving life once more to the colours of the landscape, the first mortar rounds began to fall like hailstones on the Poles. They were soon joined by more deadly artillery rounds that threw dirt high into the air. Freddie feared for the two men cowering in the cover of the sandbags on the roof, but they escaped a direct hit, and the blasts from the shells falling nearby were thankfully absorbed by the simple earth-filled sacks.

Before long the artillery barrage ceased and the ground attack began. It seemed as though the whole of the undergrowth was alive with gunfire as bullets streamed in from every conceivable angle. The frontal assault was easier to deal with as Tomanek's men jabbed explosive punches that carried awesome force at such close range. Men and trees were uprooted indiscriminately, and although these shots widened the mouth of the rat run, there was still no serious threat from the bunker's forward face.

The flank, however, was a different matter. Podolski fired the Browning as best he could back into the chaotic mass of densely packed trees and shrubs but still the deadly hail of incoming fire continued. The men on the roof lobbed a grenade blindly towards what seemed to be the epicentre of enemy forces, but the resultant lull lasted only seconds. Another grenade was launched, and another, but to no avail.

The venom of the attack was startling. After barely more than 30 minutes the end began. The tenacious Podolski, fighting to the last, gave up the defence when a bullet found his head. Freddie looked on in horror as the back of his skull exploded spewing out blood and brain, and this rock of a man fell to the ground. There was no time to register the shock of his loss. Romanowicz took his place, but the inexperienced private was less adept at firing while crouching and he made an easier target. A couple of minutes later his upper chest was riddled with heavy machine gun bullets that tore through him turning his back to a pulp. As he fell his place was taken in turn by the brave men of Mountain Cracker who seemed determined to feed themselves into this Hadean meat grinder in the defence of their comrades.

A tightly packed clutch of mortars fell on the roof and Freddie saw a forearm and a booted leg tumble down in front of the firing slit. The position on the roof was empty. The big gun continued to pour disproportionate death into the front rat run but was helpless to influence the only conflict that now mattered, the holding of the western door. Freddie gave his orders for the continuing defence of the doomed outpost and took Sambor with him to reoccupy the roof.

They collected as much ammunition as they could carry, left by the entrance at the opposite end of the bunker, and scrambled onto the top of the redoubt. The sandbags were scattered all around, impregnated with the scorched flesh of the two dead men. Freddie and Sambor hurriedly formed enough of a barrier to protect themselves as they lay down with their rifles and began to return fire.

The air was thick with smoke and dust as another German canon emerged from the wilderness. The game was over. As the gun's heavy teeth chewed the Browning's crew beyond recognition, Freddie ordered Sambor to run. "You have to warn Hobo", he yelled over the din. Just as he did, Sambor was hit in the leg by heavy machine gun fire that shattered his femur.

He made no sound. There was no cry of pain, just a grimace as he looked Freddie in the eye. "That's your job now, sir. I'll cover as best I can. Now go!" Freddie hesitated for the first time in the battle. He knew he must warn Hobo, but to leave his men was close to unthinkable. "Hobo depends on you, sir," came Sambor's justification. Freddie nodded and took a deep breath. Just as he was about to launch himself down the steps at the eastern end of the bunker Sambor grabbed his arm. "Thank you, sir." There were tears in his eyes. "For giving us victory."

Freddie nodded and ran. He ran as he had never run before, the hissing whine of bullets chasing him as he went. He was half way across the open ground to the left hand rat run when the onrushing German grenadiers coming from the wilderness under the cover of the canon's fire delivered their load of death. Close to a dozen stick grenades clattered into the bunker and detonated together.

The blast was searing and the heat flash that jetted from the firing slit lightly singed the back of Freddie's neck as he ran. The shock wave almost knocked him from his feet as he skidded down the rat run towards Hobo. Even as he ran he reflected on Sambor's words. Victory? What kind of victory was this? A calm voice in his head told him that for 15 men to hold up the German army for over a day and claim hundreds of the enemy as their price of capitulation was indeed a victory. Hobo would soon fall, and then Traveller, but these 80 or so scratch warriors had bloodied the nose of the Wehrmacht's finest, and if everybody fought like this then Poland might yet hold out.

Raczynski heard the news of the fall of Mountain Cracker with an impassive face. He too had been fighting intermittent waves of Germans to his front, but had also prepared sandbags on the roof of Hobo to provide another shooting position. The inside of Hobo was more intricately designed than Mountain Cracker with a complex system of rooms and fully armoured internal doors that would make the structure difficult to take room by room.

"Organise the defence here," Raczynski ordered Freddie, their ranks no longer holding any meaning. This was his bunker and these were his men. They would follow his plan. Freddie did not demur. "Salko. Gorski. Bakowski. With me!" His orders were clear. The four men would man the roof position. "The rest of you are under Lieutenant Zamoyski's command." Raczynski's authority was so absolute that Freddie knew these men would now follow his orders without question. He turned to Freddie to say goodbye. They hardly knew each other and yet somehow what was passing between them was stronger than the friendship of a lifetime. "No retreat. No surrender." They both nodded and in a second he was gone.

Freddie ordered the rapid construction of another machine gun emplacement from sandbags, and the installation of one of the two Hobo Brownings was completed urgently. Freddie grimaced when he saw that the total remaining ammunition for the machine guns was just four belts. He knew they would last only a few minutes and, giving three belts to the new makeshift position guarding the flank he left the forward gunner with a single belt and orders to fire sparingly.

The German whirlwind was on them in a matter of minutes. Raczynski and his men on the roof did what they could to suppress the German advance, but the brave Spartan was cut down by heavy machine gun fire, his body riddled with hot lead as he joined his brothers across the Styx.

The final belt of bullets ran through the Browning's

mechanism as the firing pin beat against the empty air of the breech and came slowly to rest. The crew were engulfed in the blast of a grenade, as Freddie hurled the last remaining defenders into the relative safety of the empty store rooms to the rear of the bunker. More grenades cleared the firing room and filled Hobo with dense, disorientating smoke.

The next minutes were a blur of blasts and shock waves as the Germans cleared the structure of any remaining threat. Effective command was now impossible and Freddie groped in the dark blindly seeking an escape route. He was crawling on the floor fumbling for anything that might signal an exit when his world shut down. His body was smashed by the compression wave of another explosion, and his battle was over.

The long darkness of his unconsciousness lifted hours later. His return to the living world was marked by a searing pain in his chest as he coughed out the remains of the acrid smoke.

"Steady, Lieutenant," he heard a familiar voice say.

The blurred image of Semik's grim face formed in Freddie's eyes as he regained his senses. "How many?" There was a stark utilitarianism to his question.

"Twelve." There had been no retreat and no surrender, and seventy dead was the price of their dogged defiance.

"What day is it?"

"Still Sunday." As Freddie slowly drew himself up on his elbows he could see the long shadows that told him it was late in the day.

"When did you fall?"

"We held out until five. We bought Galadyk another day. And between us we must have taken nearly a thousand of those fucking bastards."

Freddie smiled, even as his body screamed in pain. Every part of him hurt. Every movement was a reminder of the ordeal his frame had endured over the two days, but he was strangely content. "Where are we?"

"In the village. It looks like they've brought all the survivors here. I guess to be logged and sent to POW camps."

Freddie slowly sat upright and looked around. They were in a large barn that was piled high on three sides with bales of straw. "It's been a good harvest," he commented before reflecting that most of his men had been scythed down every bit as easily as those stalks of wheat. Around him were some forty men, their faces blackened and bloodied, but none of them broken. "Who survived?"

"You, two lads from Hobo, four of us from Traveller and five from Gorge."

"Dear God," murmured Freddie, reaching for his crucifix. It was missing.

"They've pretty much stripped us of everything other than the clothes we stand in. Even our dog tags. No doubt for the scribes to record the precision of their triumph."

There was a loud grunting coming from the side of the barn. "What's that noise?" asked Freddie, turning.

"Pigs. They've been squealing for hours. With the battle going on I don't think they've been fed for days. Anyway, the rest of the boys here are the Berezwecz lot. I'll introduce you."

Just as Freddie was getting to his feet the doors of the barn swung open and the blinding light of the low sun streamed in on them. The two German guards carried MP38 machine pistols which seemed to tweak Semik's curiosity. "That's odd," he said in a low voice.

"What?"

"Those troopers are both carrying Schmeissers."

"So?" It was an unusual sensation for Freddie to feel that he was not keeping up.

"Well, they only give them to squad leaders. So if both of these men have them then they must be some sort of special forces."

They both squinted at the guards, but it was difficult to make out any uniform insignia as the glare from the sun dulled their acuity. As they looked, a truck pulled up in front of the barn's open doors, its canvassed roof tightly trussed. The lorry pulled forward and then reversed in an arc bringing its rear to face the Poles.

"At last," sighed Semik. "Although it's an odd time of day to be carting off prisoners. I guess they want rid of us so they can advance."

Freddie was not so sure that this was what was being played out. A warning voice in his head suddenly called out to him and for the first time he felt fear and panic. As this mental alarm sounded, the lorry's tarpaulin was pulled open to reveal a heavy MG34 machine gun, fully loaded and cocked.

The wide-eyed, disbelieving Poles dived for the floor, but there was no escaping this killer's breath. Bullets tore into bodies, ripped organs open and sent a fine mist of tunic fabric, sinew, bone, skin and blood into the air of the barn. Where the shafts of sunlight had played in the fine dust of that summer evening they now frolicked in this mist of misery. Bodies fell all around as the venomous projectiles hissed passed Freddie. He found himself falling underneath Semik's large frame, but knew from his own observations the day before that Semik's body would offer him no protection. It would now be his body's turn to be mangled.

The bullets continued to fly, ripping up straw, earth and flesh in a tornado of death. The adrenaline rush was so intense Freddie could not feel any part of his body. He must have been hit, but he could feel nothing. The ground fizzed and boiled in the storm of bullets until eventually the firing stopped, and Freddie found himself lying on his front with Semik's heavy dead weight over his head and shoulders. He was acutely aware of a hot, sticky liquid soaking through the back of his uniform and dripping round his flanks. It was blood, but was it his?

There were heavy footsteps as the two troopers walked round the barn kicking corpses. Freddie could not see them and lay frozen, his face in the dirt under Semik. One of the soldiers said something brief to his companion, but Freddie could not make it out. There was a short burst from a Schmeisser.

"Done!" replied the other.

One of them stood over Freddie. He could hear him breathing heavily, and dared make no movement and no sound. He felt a drip of perspiration splash on the back of his hand and realised just how close death was. His potential executioner was near enough to share his sweat. A fly landed on Freddie's wrist and he resisted the reflex urge to flick it away. The blood over his tunic plainly deflected the man's attention away to other possible survivors and a moment later he seemed satisfied that their task was complete. He gave a long whistle and on that signal the truck pulled away.

The two soldiers were still standing by the door as Freddie heard one strike a match and smelled the cigarette smoke that wafted into the barn to mix with the ghastly death mist. After a few minutes another man joined them and struck up a conversation.

"Didn't see much of you SS boys in the fight today."

The smoker exhaled a chest full of smoke loudly. "Fuck off."

"No, I guess you're too good for real fighting."

"We'll be there, soldier boy. When there's a real fight to be had. It took you regulars long enough to deal with this bunch of grandads. You'll be shitting yourself when you face real troops."

"Yeh? Well it's easy to be brave when you've all got machine pistols. You try storming a strongpoint with a standard issue rifle."

"They give real weapons to real men, fuckwit."

"Shit! Are they..."

"The prisoners. Yeh. So?"

"But they're..."

"Dead. Yeh. You got a problem with that?" There was a pause, as Freddie strained to hear the conversation. "Now piss off."

"Twats!" Freddie heard his heavy boots walking away.

"Cunt!" shouted the smoker as the man stomped off. "I hate the fucking Wehrmacht," he said in a lower voice to his comrade. "No fucking balls to do what's needed." And so Freddie was treated to a prolonged discourse on the shortcomings of the average German infantryman from the perspective of these black-hearted fanatics. Two more cigarettes later, and with the day turning to twilight the troopers' conversation moved to other matters.

"We'd better finish up here, Kurt. The sergeant has rounded up some fillies from the village. They're down the road in that red house. We don't want to miss out."

"Huh! Fucking Polish whores. Still, it's been days." He took one last long drag, blew out the smoke and spat. "I'm gonna have myself a skinny little thing until she bleeds. And she can scream all she likes, 'cos no one's gonna save her. They're weak, and we'll take whatever we want from them." They both laughed, and in that moment Freddie understood the horror that was about to befall their whole nation.

"Shall we torch it?"

There was a pause as the other man thought. "No. There's too much straw. It'll burn too fiercely. Don't want a fire getting out of hand. We might be called back to deal with it, and I don't want anything getting between me and my little Polish arse. Let the pigs have them. They're starving."

There were sounds of latches lifted and gates opened, as the two Germans corralled a dozen swine into the barn and shut the door. There was now little light outside and in the growing gloom Freddie could hear the pigs sniffing around the bodies excitedly before the inevitable, nauseating sound of powerful teeth cutting flesh and grinding bone. He felt the snout of something large nudge the back of his thigh, and almost cried out. He managed to muffle his scream, conscious that his would be executioners might still be just outside the barn, and resisted the urge to lash out for as long as he could.

The pig stepped forward, both of its front legs on Freddie's back and began eating noisily. Saliva and blood trickled down beside Freddie's face that was still planted in the earth, and he realised that the hog was eating Semik. Freddie guessed it must have been feeding on the Captain's throat as sinew and cartilage crunched inside its powerful porcine jaws.

After another minute he could contain himself no longer. The weight of the pig was beginning to crush his lower ribs and he was finding it hard to breathe. He pushed all of his strength into rolling over, and although the beast's mass prevented any significant movement, the slight rolling action was enough to unbalance the boar which pulled back, releasing Freddie from its crushing weight.

With astonishing speed, he rolled Semik from his shoulders and jumped to his feet. The scene around him was diabolical, like some apocalyptic vision of a slaughterhouse reversed, as pigs fed on men. They had been fattening towards the end of the summer and were big beasts in excess of 200kg, but had starved for three days since their owner had fled before the oncoming army.

Freddie looked down and what he saw almost broke his heart. The proud Semik, the honourable Semik, had no face. Chewed off by the slobbering monster that now sensed the danger Freddie might represent. One of Semik's eyes hung out of what remained of its socket, while above his preserved jaw was an open cavity. The pig stared at Freddie with cold eyes that glinted in the meagre light and gave an urgent grunt. The others stopped their feasting and turned to Freddie as if following their leader's command, while Freddie stared defiantly into the boar's gaze. The challenge drove the beast to charge at him, its rudimentary tusks slashing the air as it came.

Freddie waited until the moment of impact was almost on him and then threw himself to his right, barely avoiding the animal's menacing jaws. He stumbled and found himself floundering on the earthen floor of the barn. He knew that was not good. On his feet he might still stand a chance of survival. On the floor he would be pinned and crushed by the weight of these monsters that would gore him and eat him as he still lived.

His head was next to Semik's boot, when a memory inexplicably forced its way into his mind. Yesterday. Semik. The apple. The boot. The knife. Before he had even thought consciously of what he was doing he had slipped his hand inside the lip of the boot. Miraculously the Germans had not found the captain's blade, and it was tight in Freddie's grasp as the pig bore down on him. A tusk flashed past his cheek and the jaws opened wide as the pig turned its thick neck to bite down on him. As it did Freddie plunged the savage metal deep into the pig's eye.

The beast's reaction was shocking. It gave out a deafening scream that stunned Freddie for a moment. The huge bulk of its body writhed uncontrollably as its limbs kicked out. The sudden convulsion of the massive animal crashed against Freddie's legs and the piercing shock that seared up his spine was agony. He could not feel his feet, and feared that in its spasm the pig had broken his back. The creature squealed deafeningly as blood poured from its face.

Freddie looked at the knife in his hand and realised that the five inch blade must have pierced the back of the orbit and skewered the boar's brain. Almost 300 kilograms of uncontrolled, screeching pig flesh thrashed wildly in a death dance before collapsing motionless on the ground.

The other pigs broke out in a cacophony of anxious noise, momentarily uncertain of how to respond. Freddie rolled onto his front and, feeling no pain, convinced himself that he had been only stunned. With great effort he managed to draw his knees up. He staggered uncertainly to his feet, all the time waving his small knife in a threatening arc to deter the other pigs. He need not have bothered. After their initial shouting, they seemed to care nothing for their fallen brother and continued to crunch into the dead bodies at a safe distance from Freddie.

Just as their threat receded, a greater one reared up. Freddie's legs were still responding only partially to his will as the heavy latch to the barn door was lifted. There was no talking, and he prayed that a single German had come to check on the commotion. He moved as quickly as he could, and managed to get behind the door just as it opened far enough to allow the soldier to look in.

His torch lit up as he half entered the barn to make a closer inspection. The beam of the bright light seemed to throw the rest of the space into greater contrasted darkness as he looked from corpse to pig to corpse.

"Oh, sweet Jesus!" he exclaimed to himself. His voice was thin, more like that of a boy. The torchlight moved to another pig whose evil eye shone in its beam as it continued to trough on the spilled abdomen of a dead Pole. "Dear God!" Freddie could not tell whether his disgust was at the men coldly executed or the ghoulish dining of these devilish creatures on the still warm human flesh. "What the fuck..." The light had stopped on the growing pool of black blood that oozed from the dead boar. The lamp was readjusted and the mutilated face of the dead pig was fully displayed.

As the soldier swung his lamp in a reflex action, Freddie leapt to the attack. His stunned legs did not provide the force he wanted or needed, and the element of surprise was squandered. The two men lurched across the barn as one, before clattering to the ground. The light went out, and the space was illuminated by nothing but the meagre remnants of the day seeping in through the barely open door.

In this strange light Freddie could not see his opponent, but he could feel his thin frame and short stature. He smelled his bad breath, edged with beer, and felt the thin stubble on his chin as Freddie's hand closed around his mouth to prevent the cry for help. He was lucky in the fall, and found himself on top of the German who was face down in the dirt trying to lift his head to shout through Freddie's left hand. The man began to shake and flail his arms as he sensed the end coming. Despite the man's lack of size, Freddie had difficulty holding him as he struggled in abject desperation.

Freddie pressed himself as hard as he could into the man's back, and pulled up on his face to keep the seal with his mouth. His right hand moved carefully and deliberately over his opponent's right shoulder, slid under his neck, turned to present the blade, and cut deeply into his throat as Freddie pulled his hand up with all his force. He felt the blade break the skin and then meet resistance as the cartilage of the German's larynx pushed back. The struggling intensified further before the knife slipped through softer tissues then more dense cartilage, before stopping altogether at a hard barrier. As Freddie pulled his hand to the right he knew he had reached the front of the man's spine. The knife sliced through the remnants of flesh and gristle and the body beneath him went limp.

Freddie lay there in silence for a few moments, shaking uncontrollably. He was suddenly aware that every fibre of his body was locked in a tetanus, struggling to hold the man and prevent him from crying out. He took a deep breath and consciously told his body to relax. As he did so he noticed that his face and arms were saturated with thick, hot blood. In the height of the conflict the pumping of the severed carotid arteries had not even registered in Freddie's drive to despatch his rival quietly, but now he needed to move quickly. This man would soon be missed.

His legs working again, Freddie took handfuls of straw to wipe as much blood from himself as he could manage. He stripped the German of his uniform which he threw hastily over his own despite the arms and legs being too short. The fit was tight, but it would at least help him pass as a German from a distance. The torch would be very useful, but he realised with dismay that the man had no gun. He dragged the body into the corner behind the door and, checking that his exit was clear, he slipped out of the barn and disappeared into the night.

-oOo-

"I thought of going to look for the red house," sighed Freddie ruefully as the fan droned on, "but I knew that would be futile. One half dead and unarmed man against a whole platoon of SS troopers. I felt for those poor girls. To be raped by anyone must be terrible, but to be abused by those men who revelled in the suffering of others must have been an unspeakable ordeal."

"There was nothing you could do," I offered.

"Yes, I know. But still it pricked my conscience for a long time." He shrugged his shoulders and sighed. "So that was the battle of Wegierska Gorka. So many fine young lives sacrificed in the defence of our motherland. Of the eighty men of the 151st I was the only survivor. There had been no retreat, and no surrender. We were good to our oath to the last."

"You were." Freddie's gaze was lost to me as it stared across a 50 year chasm. The memories of those men haunted him as if they had lived a lifetime together. Three days had delivered him an entire family of brothers and, just as carelessly, fate had snatched them away.

"I entered that valley still a boy. And with God's grace I slipped away a man".

V - Reunion

On Thursday morning Walthamstow looked like a wasteland. The German victory in Turin's Stadio delle Alpi had broken London's spirit more completely than Hitler's Luftwaffe ever managed in the dark days of the blitz. The game had been infused with passion, culminating in a penalty shoot out of agonising tension. The Germans had won.

The scarves and banners and flags disappeared as England mourned its loss and turned its attention away from football for another four years. The news reverted to its usual dull commentary on economic indices that were largely meaningless to the mass of people going about their daily business of trying to make ends meet. I was not in the least bit interested in football, but had enjoyed the holiday spirit the tournament had induced, and it was sad that it had evaporated so completely.

As I hurried onto the ward I nodded to a thin, grey-haired old lady that I thought I had passed on the hospital's interminably long corridor the day before. She returned a nervous half smile as she bustled away, deep in thought. No doubt she had been visiting a loved one or friend. She looked as though she carried the worries of the world on her slight frame. Perhaps she was wondering about talking to me. It was a look I had seen many times before in relatives who feared the end was approaching. But I knew it could take time for people to reach that decision, and there was a subtle line between intrusion and inviting that first contact.

"Bloody Jerries!" exclaimed Freddie in his finest, theatrical Queen's English as I entered. I marvelled at how he could remain cheerful and upbeat in spite of the story he was recounting, but perhaps that was a protective response. I have often found that we can cope with the enormity of some things only through black humour. I regularly frequented the doctors' mess, which was the only place in the hospital to get a decent cup of coffee, and the irreverent repartee in that sanctuary from the front line of life and death was simultaneously callous and touching.

I remember one registrar who had slowly lost a patient over a number of weeks, powerless to prevent the irresistible call of The Lord. She was distraught and had turned to me for counsel, and yet in that private space in the company of others who understood, she joked about it as they laughed, understanding her pain and anguish.

And so I thought it was with Freddie. Flippant quips about the race that had brought his homeland so low were his way of taking back some control. "Are you okay?"

"Yes, yes, yes." His nonchalant waving away of my question warned me not to puncture the bubble within which he coped.

"That battle was quite an experience."

"Yes. Yes it was." We sat in silence as I gave him the space to talk more. Eventually he went on. "The strange thing is that afterwards I found myself hating the pigs most. It's irrational of course. They were only doing what nature intends of them. But somewhere inside the malevolent stare of that boar I saw the eye of the Devil. To this day I still can't eat pork. It makes me feel sick."

"I didn't know they ate meat."

"They'll eat anything if they're hungry enough. They really are the creation of the dark one. Orwell got it right. A pig called Napoleon." There was another long pause. "I have never been able to forget the sight of Captain Semik, his face eaten away. No man should lose his identity like that. The remnants of his body were no doubt disposed of in a pit with the others, like the left over scraps from a dinner plate thrown into a bin."

"You respected him."

"I respected them all. But especially him. Somehow in the space of a few days he gave the men exactly what they needed. The resolve to repel the Germans time and time again. The courage to exact a heavy price for their capitulation. The belief to stand together."

-oOo-

Once the 1st Mountain Brigade crumbled the invaders faced no more serious opposition in the south. General List's 14th Army that had finally overrun the Sola Valley turned east and drove headlong towards Lwow. No battle plan ever survives first contact with the enemy, and Hitler's military planners had not envisaged the speed with which they advanced. The original strategy, named "Case White" by the German High Command, had assigned List's men the job of encirclement to the rear of Krakow. But that objective had changed within days. The Poles, hopelessly outgunned and outmanoeuvred, had a fall back plan to withdraw to the south-east. The idea was to form new defensive lines in the "Rumanian Bridgehead" and hold out until the French could attack Germany in the west.

The Germans anticipated this plan and the twelve divisions under List's command were ordered east to cut off this line of retreat. And so it was that as Freddie trudged determinedly eastwards he shadowed the German advance. Sleeping under the cover of hedgerows and thickets by day, and walking carefully by night he made his slow progress past Nowy Targ, Nowy Sacz and on towards Sanok.

Ahead of him the Teutonic war machine laid waste to the land he loved, as the wave of misery spread out across Poland. With no orders and no idea what to do he settled on the only course open to him. The Polish army was disintegrating around him, so somehow he would make his way back to his family and help them to escape these monsters. He thought of the conversation he had overheard between the executioners in the barn, and shuddered at the thought of his younger sister, Anna, being handed around those scum to be so hideously violated. He would die before allowing it, and that thought drove him forward in spite of his hunger and terrible fatigue.

Water was easy to come by. There were many agricultural buildings along his route that had abundant water supplies. A small, abandoned farmstead near Jelesnia even yielded a water bottle in a shed among the outbuildings. Caution was required, for in war every house looks vacated as civilians do everything possible to avoid attracting attention to themselves. The bark of a dog or the sudden illuminating of a window was always enough to warn Freddie away, and so he remained unseen and undetected on his journey.

He navigated by the stars that through the cloudless nights showed him the way home. But his constant companion was the moon. As the days passed it rose ever later, and each night its crescent slowly diminished. He had not quite reached Nowy Sacz when only half of his lunar companion remained, but still it spurred him on his flight home.

His progress was steady, but often punctuated by the need to find cover as convoys and the other paraphernalia of military supply lines trundled past. He estimated that he was managing 10, maybe 15 miles each night, and was alarmed that the German spearhead seemed always to be ahead of him. Such a speed of advance was unheard of in modern warfare, and at this rate the whole of Poland would be swallowed within a month.

Water was not an issue. Food was. After five nights Freddie was so hungry he could scarcely think of anything else. As the road he was walking meandered through a wood he noticed a small cottage a hundred yards or so down a side track. It looked deserted, and as he approached there was no warning bark and no light at a window. There was silence.

Cautiously, Freddie tried the door. It was locked. He assessed his options in the dim moonlight. The house was small. Tiny in fact. He judged there was space enough for only two rooms on each of the two floors. He opened his mouth wide and breathed slowly to minimise the sound of his own respiration and strained his ears for any other information. Half a mile away through the woods he could hear the faint trickling of a stream. Here and there an animal called and in the far distance the softened sounds of sporadic night fighting floated into this other world.

For a moment he was engulfed by the strange comfort of feeling he was the only person in this private existence. Then his stomach called and he answered. It took less than ten seconds for him to force the window into the dimly lit kitchen. In the silence around him his entry rang out so that he thought they must have heard it in Warsaw. But he knew it was only his senses playing tricks on him, and he fumbled to light the torch he had stolen from the German.

By torchlight he could see the kitchen was a meagre affair. There was a sink set in an uneven work surface, a wood burning stove, a small table with two chairs and a cupboard which he opened to reveal an equally scant supply of food. A loaf of stale bread, some butter, three tins of sardines and a jar of coffee. It was not much of a meal, but in the dead of night and having starved for five days to Freddie it was a feast.

The sardines were shovelled hastily between slices of bread and devoured. He swore that nothing had ever tasted so good in his life. The torch sat on the table casting a weird half illumination around the room and, as Freddie forced the last of the sardines into his mouth, his mind played with the shadows that danced on the walls. He was transfixed by them and by the way his own movement changed the faces of the shapes cast around the room. As he stared the darker patches seemed to swing to his right and he leaned forwards puzzling as to what movement he had made to induce the change.

As he did so he heard the unmistakable click of the cocking of a shotgun over his left shoulder. He froze. His heartbeat was deafening in his ears as he slowly lifted his hands in surrender.

"Don't shoot."

"What do you want?" asked a reedy, elderly female voice.

"I'm sorry," replied Freddie. "I mean you no harm. I thought the house was deserted."

"You speak Polish?"

"Yes. Yes. I am Polish."

"You look German to me."

Freddie realised in horror that he was still wearing the German uniform over his own. To the old lady of this house he must have looked like an invader. He began talking as quickly as he could to convince her otherwise. "My name is Freddie Zamoyski. I'm a lieutenant in the 1st Mountain Brigade. We were overrun near Zywiec. I managed to escape by killing a German. I stole his uniform to help evade them. I'm trying to get back to my family in Lwow. I have my Polish uniform on under this. Please don't shoot me. I'm Polish. I swear."

The long pause seemed to last forever. Every breath felt like his last until the woman broke the silence. "Do you always steal from people?"

"No ma'am. I am most sorry. I'm starving. I'll write you an I.O.U. I'm good for the damage. I promise." As the words passed his lips he recognised how ridiculous he sounded. He had broken into an old lady's house in the dead of night in a warzone and he was talking now as he would have addressed his old school mistress. In the height of the disintegration of his beloved Poland he actually felt embarrassed by what he had done. The feeling was almost reassuring to him, as if it were a link to a more civilised past that had ended abruptly a week earlier.

The woman laughed. "An I.O.U? We're not posh Warsaw folk here you know. All right, take off that German jacket. Let me see your real uniform." Freddie slowly obeyed, not wanting to make any sudden movements that might startle the woman. He set the Wehrmacht tunic on the back of a chair. "Now move back against the wall." As Freddie complied the woman stepped fully into the kitchen and took the torch, all the time her gun trained on him. She shone the light in his face and seemed to be scrutinising him. "Poland is not lost."

Freddie paused, considering his response in the blinding glare of the lamplight. "Not yet."

The woman let out a belly laugh that surprised him, and concluded, "All right. You're Polish. Sit down." Freddie breathed a deep sigh of relief and sat as the woman carefully released the hammer of the gun and placed it on the table. "Give me a chair," she ordered indignantly.

Once again Freddie's conscience was pricked by the elderly woman whose apparent self reliance gave her an air of authority. He apologetically moved his chair for her to sit and took the other for himself. "I'm terribly, terribly sorry," he repeated. "I thought your house was deserted. I'm starving."

"How far have you walked, Freddie Zamoyski?"

"I'm not sure, ma'am. From somewhere near Zywiec."

"That's quite a walk. And you haven't eaten?"

"No ma'am. I've been travelling by night to avoid the Germans."

"And the uniform?" She nodded at the German tunic.

"I took it from a German I killed."

In the strange shadow light of the kitchen Freddie began to make out the features of this proud woman. She was wiry and weathered, suggesting a life of labour, perhaps here in the woods. Her hair was silver grey and the piercing blue of her eyes caught even the meagre scraps of light that ricocheted off the walls.

"The 1st Mountain Brigade, you say?"

"Yes, ma'am."

"Oh, for heaven's sake. Stop using that word. My name is Milena." She looked at the remnants of the food Freddie had eaten. "So, you've had the sardines?"

"Yes, ma'am. Sorry. Milena."

"And you're starving?" Freddie nodded. "And you're trying to get to Lwow? Well, Freddie Zamoyski, you're going to have to

learn to forage much better than this or you won't last a week."
She stood, and with a quick strength she pushed the table to one
side. Rolling back a small rug she deftly grasped a sunken handle
and opened a small trap in the floor. "This hiding place has saved
more than one life. Now it hides my food."

Freddie peered into the hole in the ground. It was tiny, and
would have made a very cramped refuge, but Milena's story was
unfolding. "You were part of the resistance?"

"Both of us." She sat upright, and for a moment her
nationalist defiance lent her an almost regal poise. "My husband
and me." Freddie hesitated to ask, but she went on. "Before the
Great War we helped to hide resistance leaders on the run. The
Austrians were incompetent. Right up to the day that they
searched the place properly. They shot the man they found here.
And then they shot my husband as a collaborator." Her voice
carried the flat practical tone of one who has learned to live with
an eternal pain, and her clipped delivery did nothing to hide the
deep love she still held for her long dead soulmate.

"I'm very sorry to hear that."

"Thank you. Would you like some bread and jam?"

They continued their conversation as Milena offered various
things from her store, and Freddie ate. They talked of Milena's
involvement with the Polish nationalist movement and their
struggles to rid themselves of Austrian rule, and the conversation
inevitably moved to Freddie's father.

"I had a sneaking suspicion," she smiled. "A well-heeled
Zamoyski trying to get back home to Lwow. You don't know
much do you? I'd change your name if I were you. You stick out
like a sore thumb."

"Perhaps I will," reflected Freddie as he pondered on how this
woman's mindset had already shifted to that of an occupied
people. Perhaps it had never really changed. Perhaps she was still
stuck in 1910, and only now was the world catching up with her,
only this time with different invaders.

"Have you lived here alone since then?"

"You ask a lot of questions, Freddie Zamoyski."

"I'm sorry. I mean no offence."

She paused for a moment, contemplating how much of her story to tell. "I have a son. He would be about your age." Freddie did not respond, but understood immediately that the maths did not work, and wondered at the story behind that. "I was raped. As the old empires were crumbling in that chaos of 1917. God sends us some very strange tests. My husband and I were never blessed, despite all of our efforts. And how we tried." Milena's gaze drifted away for a second, and Freddie was aware of his embarrassment as she appeared to recall a sexuality that seemed so incongruous with the crone before him. Then she came back abruptly. "And then one day I was raped by a gang of soldiers and so I have a son."

"I'm sorry."

"Don't be. He's a good boy. A bit simple. And only rarely now does he remind me of those stinking brutes with their bad breath, and what they did to me." Now her distant gaze recalled a very different memory. "You know, Freddie, the worst thing was to know that my most sacred parts were swimming with a cocktail of strangers, like they were a public space. Who the father was no one could ever say." She shook her head is if purging the thought. "Anyway, I called him Bozydar."

"Divine gift."

Milena smiled approvingly. "You know your languages, Freddie."

He smiled. "And is that how you see him?"

"Of course! Are you a religious man, Freddie?"

"Very much Milena."

"Good." She continued to feed him. "You know, he was in your brigade."

"What, the 1st Mountain Brigade?"

"Yes. You were hit pretty hard?"

"Yes."

"Hmm." She paused again, and continued almost to herself. "I hope he is safe. How many were killed?"

"A few. Most of the brigade retreated towards Wadowice. I'm sure he's digging in there with the rest of the boys." There was a long pause as they shared the unspoken reality. "Do you know which company he was with?"

"No. He wrote a little to me, but he was never very good with his letters." She gave a deep sigh, slipped her hand inside her nightgown and pulled out her crucifix that hung around her neck on a slender silver chain. She kissed it in silent prayer. "God will decide. Now. Eat."

By now Freddie was so full that he could manage no more. They talked a little longer, but as the sky began to lighten outside Milena suggested he slept the day in the comfort and safety of her home. There was an obvious risk, but Freddie was so tired and so full, that the lure of a warm soft bed was overwhelming.

He slept like the dead. Here and there he dreamed of the battle, and called out orders, called to comrades, and cursed the pigs. But still he slept.

The sun was setting as Freddie prepared to leave. "You have been so good to me Milena. I really don't know how to repay you. You may have saved my life." Milena gave a thin smile. "Is everything okay?"

She looked at him with sad, fearful eyes. "How do you know my name?"

"You told me."

"No. My family name."

"I don't. What is it?"

"Wozny. You shouted it out in your sleep more than once. Clear as day." She stared at him as an awful realisation unfolded. "Did you know Bozydar, Freddie?"

He fought to hold back the tears. It could not be. Of all the deserted cottages in Poland how could God have brought him to the mother of that simple peasant he had cradled in his arms in his last moments. "I don't know," he murmured. "I mean, Wozny is a common name."

"He is dead?" Freddie could not reply. "Your Wozny. Did he die?" Freddie nodded. "Alone?" Freddie shook his head, and with a supreme effort he gave words to the simple private's last moments. He was in tears as he finished. The emotions of the last week had been held back by a damn of will and denial that cracked as the first tears flowed, and which was soon swept away by the torrent. Freddie wailed, and Milena wailed with him.

"I'm so sorry. I'm so sorry," he repeated over and over.

Milena hushed him. "You were there for him right at the end. You said his rites and gave him what he needed. He died in peace because of you." Milena stuffed his pockets with food in abject gratitude through Freddie's tearful apologies. She took his hands and kissed them. "Now go, Freddie Zamoyski, and find your family."

As he disappeared into the growing night he felt a hopeless despair descend on him. Each and every one of those fallen was a soldier, a comrade and a friend. But each was a beloved husband, a cherished son or an adored divine gift. War was brutal, but the human misery was unfathomably worse.

He trudged on through the nights. As the moon finally disappeared from the sky Freddie found himself east of Sanok, heading into the vast lands that had been seized by Poland in 1920. He had grown up in these eastern parts, but until now he had not really noticed just how different they were from the rest of Poland. The contrast he had always drawn was between the people on his family estate and those in Krakow. He had lazily assumed this was the difference between rustic country folk and those living in the city, but the last two weeks had shown him that life in these parts was very different to the rest of the country.

He continued his routine of travelling by road in the dead of night. Walking silently he was always assured of hearing and seeing the lights of any potential threat long before it arrived, and he was constantly alert to the nearest hiding point. The Germans were too busy trying desperately to keep up with their thrusting panzers to be able to hunt down every straggler and refugee, safe in the knowledge that there would be time enough to consolidate their gains. And so Freddie's progress was reasonably safe and made paradoxically easier by remaining in the wake of the advancing battle front.

When he reached sizeable villages or towns he headed off the roads and navigated with increasing skill around the settlements, eager not to attract attention. But now he was bypassing a town that held a strange sadness for him. Sambor stood on a small river at the head waters of the Dniester, the ancient artery that flowed south-east to the Black Sea. Freddie had crossed the watershed. Until now every river and stream had flowed ultimately north into the Baltic. All roads now led south and east, and with the change in watercourse came the noticeable change in culture and architecture that for the first time impressed itself on Freddie. Perhaps this was a colony after all. Perhaps Galadyk had been right.

But the town of Sambor reminded him of those last seconds on the roof of Mountain Cracker, and that moment of undeserved gratitude. Whether the man had actually come from the town, or from some other place in the region was irrelevant. The reminder of the men he had left behind could not be avoided even as he moved steadily and carefully around its limits.

Freddie was now in countryside that he recognised from his childhood, but the challenge presented by his trek rose as it became clear that the German advance had focused on Lwow. The effect of this was that the countryside to the south of the city was rapidly degenerating into chaos. Effective Polish rule was crumbling, and as Freddie picked his way towards Zydaczow he passed an increasing number of burning buildings and ravaged homesteads.

There were no signs of the German advance. These pockets of devastation were isolated and Freddie began to fear that they were the mark of the release of ethnic tensions. With the state collapsing around him came the chilling thought that the ruling Polish minority would reap the harvest of its two decades of rule, as revenge was taken by the Ukrainian peasantry. This fear was brought abruptly to life on the outskirts of Zydaczow when he saw the town's name sign ripped down, replaced with a makeshift placard declaring it to be Zhydachiv, its Ukrainian name.

His home was half way along the road to Rohatyn, and he hurried as quickly as prudence would allow in the desperate hope that his family's good relations with those who worked the estate would have protected them from the vengeance that he saw was unfolding around him.

The sun was just rising ahead of him as he broke the ridge of the hill that looked down on the house and fields in which he had played as a boy and grown to become a man. He almost wept with joy when he saw the house standing unmolested. There was no smoke, no sign of trouble. His weary body flew on a wave of elation as he discarded his caution and ran to the house. Still he kept a careful eye on the fields around but could see no movement.

His approach brought him in towards the side of the imposing main house that faced southwards over the land it commanded. As he reached the out buildings something struck him as odd. The peaceful tranquility was not how he remembered things. The bird song was uninterrupted by the sounds of industry that he recalled as normal. The mucking out of horses in the stable block to the rear of the property, the collection of the gangs of labourers ready to be assigned their tasks on the land. Did these not begin at daybreak? Or was his memory playing tricks through his terrible fatigue?

Running past the low-roofed agricultural stores that flanked his route, he opened the iron gate in the side entrance to the rear courtyard. The stillness continued. Where were the horses? The stables were a hundred yards away, but surely he should be able to hear them stirring. And where were Daedalus and Icarus? The two Great Danes were his father's favourite animals and were kennelled in this large enclosed space with the freedom to roam within its confines. They had known Freddie from their first day and had keen noses. Why were they not bounding excitedly to greet him?

Freddie's heart turned cold and a chill fear pierced his soul. He drew a deep breath and walked to the kennel by the back kitchen door. Many a time he had played here with the dogs, feeding them scraps, while the ever irascible cook had scolded him for spoiling them. But now each step towards their shelter brought him nearer to seeing the awful truth that had now dawned on him. He braced himself, glanced back at the iron gate as if taking one last look at a past that was already gone, and then swung his head to look inside.

The kennel was empty, and he gave a long sigh of relief. There was no explanation for their absence, but his worst fear had not been realised. He looked around quickly, trying to take in the scene and make sense of the deserted estate. His gaze fell on the wall of the large coach house that ran along the opposite side of the courtyard to the gate through which he had entered. A couple of traps were still kept there, but his father had had most of the building converted into a workshop and garage for the large black Mercedes that he had bought three years earlier just as Freddie was going to university.

The car was a rarity in those parts and one of the main obstacles to decent motoring was the lack of petrol stations. For that reason, his father had installed a huge tank by the back of the garage in which to store fuel. Freddie remembered his mother's objections, but in the end the Hero of Lwow had got his own way.

He suddenly found himself running towards the garage. Was

the car still there? It should not be. His parents were smart. The Germans were advancing. The countryside was erupting in revolt. They had a car and a thousand litres of gas. They would have left immediately and driven to the Rumanian border. "Please let the car be gone. Please let the car be gone."

The garage was empty. There was no car, and not even the horse carts remained. Freddie closed his eyes and thanked God for hearing his prayer. He smiled as he pictured the scene, his parents and sister disappearing with the dogs on their flight to the safety of the Rumanian border. His tension receded as he considered his next move. With his family safe where should he go? He sat down on a large box of tools by the garage door and took out the last of the bread and cold meat that Milena had given him. As he ate in the growing warmth of the climbing sun he took stock.

He was still a soldier, and Poland was still at war. He was needed, and could only guess that the fighting had moved to Lwow. The sound of artillery fire to the north confirmed his thoughts, but to head that way in broad daylight would be foolish. He may already have risked too much in approaching the house in the bright morning, but that was done. There should be food in the kitchen and he could spend the day hiding in one of the many places he knew from his youth.

He remembered fondly the games he played with Anna, who was two years younger. She had often complained that Freddie had known all the best hiding places, but her protests were always with the warmth of a girl who idolised her older brother. She had blossomed from an assertive tomboy into a self-assured, radiant debutante whose delicate beauty belied her formidable strength of will. The Zamoyski genes ran deep in her, and Freddie smiled as he considered how indomitably she would have led the men of Mountain Cracker. She had her mother's grace and disarming manner but her father's singular will, and Freddie knew how youths far and wide had dreamed of the impossibility of wooing his sister.

He finished his bread and rummaged through the tools in the garage. There was nothing that would really be of much use to him, and moving carefully, he returned to the courtyard. The kitchen door was unlocked and as it opened a sense of anxiety filled him.

It was a large room with a big central island that the cook and her staff had worked at for years, preparing food for the family and the many labourers that tended the estate. There were two large oil fired cooking ranges and cupboards and dressers all around that were always kept in immaculate condition. But the scene before Freddie was one of chaos. The cupboards were open, and the many glass fronts were smashed. Two dressers were overturned and broken crockery littered the floor mixed with the fine cutlery that cook was always so proud to keep ordered.

A feeling of foreboding immersed Freddie as he anxiously hurried to the door that led into the back of the serving hall from where the food had been laid out ready to be presented in the grand dining room. It was a functional space with few adornments and to his relief there were no signs of damage. He carried on into the dining room itself and looked around. The chairs were arranged haphazardly around the table as if an impromptu meeting had just ended, and the expensive curtains were half ripped from their rail. But the silverware had gone.

Freddie steadied himself and ran through the likely events. His family had flown. The villagers would have known soon enough that the house was unoccupied save for the handful of staff that lived with them. The temptation would have been too great, and free to do their worst the more unsavoury elements would have looted the place. The thought was reassuring.

He stepped into the grand hall. To his right a wide, ornate staircase ran up to a galleried landing, and he smiled at the memory of how he loved to slide down the polished wooden bannister, and how sometimes he would be caught and admonished by his mother. His smile turned to horror as he looked down and saw the large Persian rug that lay on the expanse of the wooden floor. It was soaked in blood. Then he noticed the blood on the walls by the main door to his left.

His heart suddenly pounding with fear, Freddie ran to the heavy double doors opposite and pushed them open into the drawing room. It looked like a bar room after a brawl. Empty bottles of spirits and wine were strewn everywhere. The sofas were ripped and covered in boot marks, and much of the furniture was smashed and overturned. The large ornate mirror over the fireplace was shattered into a thousand pieces, many of which still clung precariously in position, while broken glass was everywhere, ground into the floor.

At the back of the room a ramshackled dais had been erected, on top of which stood a high backed leather chair. And in that chair, soaked in the blood that had poured from a wide open abdominal wound sat his lifeless father. The body was held in place by rope, and on his head was a makeshift crown fashioned from an old piece of silverware. Around his neck was hung a small placard that announced in Ukrainian "King George, Hero of Lviv."

Crying out, Freddie ran to the parody of the throne and ripped the ghoulish adornments from his father's body. He was filled with hatred and revulsion for the men that had done this. They could only have been locals, peasants who had known his father personally, and who had delighted in such abject humiliation before taking his life. Freddie's mind conjured up unwelcomed visions of the mob breaking into the house and assaulting the lord of the manor in the hallway. He would have fought back, and Freddie could only guess at how many of these wretched animals his father had taken with him. But they had exacted their revenge and Freddie felt sick at the thought of the demonic revelry they had enjoyed as they scoffed at the dead king sitting in state over them.

As he pulled his father's body down from its contrived repose he saw by the dais the decapitated bodies of Daedalus and Icarus. He would have wept, but the rage that surged through him was too overpowering for tears. As he looked around the room he saw the dogs' heads nailed to the ornate frame of the doors through which he had come. Their faces drooped and their tongues hung in lifeless sadness as though mourning their powerlessness to prevent this invasion. As vengeance engulfed him, he realised he must find his mother and Anna. Had they managed to hide? Could they have escaped? Had his father bought them the time they had needed?

An instinct drew him upstairs, and running as fast as he could he rounded the top of the staircase. Sprawled out on the wide landing were the bodies of three men lying where they had been shot. And at the far end was the crumpled form of his mother. He ran to her and saw immediately that she was covered in knife wounds. Her forearms were slashed to the bone and the skin of her face hung in strands. The attack had been frenzied, and yet in her clawed hand there remained the revolver she had used to fend off these monsters. In its rigor her body still clung to the weapon that was her only defence.

Freddie was aware of his loud, rasping breaths as they echoed in the silence of this hallway of death. He was shaking uncontrollably with a malevolent rage that he had never known before. It felt like his body had been taken over by a dark power that could scarcely be contained, and for the first time he felt the transforming effect of genuine, visceral hatred.

The calculating beast that Freddie had experienced within him at Wegierska Gorka resurged, and his first instinct was to check the chambers of the gun. Empty. Nonetheless he prised the weapon from his mother's grasp and flinched at the cracking of her fingers as he pulled them open to release the handle. "Sorry Mama," he whispered, before leaning forward to kiss her head. He assessed the scene and realised that she had died in front of the door to Anna's room. That could be no coincidence. His mother was a society beauty, but inside she was a lioness who would have fought ferociously to protect her cubs. He looked at the closed door and hesitated for a moment. He had to see this with his own eyes. To turn away now would mean always to wonder the worst.

He grasped the handle and pushed the door open. His beautiful Anna was dead on her bed. The room was utterly destroyed. Furniture was broken, the windows were smashed, and blood was everywhere. Anna was laid out on her back across the double bed, the remnants of her ripped clothes hanging from her bruised and battered form. Her golden hair was matted and stuck to the bedding with blood and her quick blue eyes were still and lifeless.

Her wrists and ankles were bruised to a blackish hue and Freddie realised she had been held tight as she had been taken. That meant a pack of attackers. His stomach turned. There was no doubting the fight she had put up as these savages had taken their opportunity to have this beacon of womanhood of which they were ever unworthy. But the blood was everywhere. It surely could not have all come from his little sister. It was over the bed, pooled on the floor, and even sprayed across the walls.

As he looked down at her broken body, there remained something unbowed in her. Even in death she retained her defiance. As he was taking in the impact of what had passed here, he caught something out of the corner of his eye. A scrap of flesh lying on the floor. Bending down to take a closer look he saw it was the end of a finger. A thick finger. A thumb, perhaps. He looked back at Anna. Her thumbs were still intact and Freddie smiled a gruesome smile.

He crouched down to pick up the digit she had bitten off, but as he did he felt how soft it was. There was no bone within this scrap and he looked more closely. There was no nail, and as he peered again he suddenly realised this was not a thumb. It was the last inch or so of a penis, severed roughly from its owner. He dropped the thing in revulsion, and turned in admiration to look at Anna's proud face.

"Well done Anna," he murmured as he bent to kiss her forehead. He recoiled as he realised that her face was covered in dried semen.

Boiling with anger and his heart aching, he tenderly carried her to the bathroom across the landing, and washed away the signs of defilement from her still beautiful face. Her inner thighs were thick with dried blood and fluids, and Freddie paused. He felt uncomfortable about washing her there, but Milena's words came back to him, and he understood that Anna could not bear to spend all eternity covered in the seed of her tormentors. And so he washed and cleaned her body thoroughly. It was his last gift to his beautiful, radiant little sister.

The sun was high in the sky, but there was no question of Freddie leaving his family unburied. One by one he carefully carried his mother, father, Anna, Daedalus and Icarus to the small copse of trees that stood behind the garage. It was not the perfect resting place for the only people he had ever loved, but it was secluded and out of sight and he calculated that it represented his best chance of burying them without being detected or interrupted. As he dug furiously with the shovel he had taken from the garage he promised them he would return when all this mayhem was done, and would bury them properly.

The loamy soil broke easily under his impassioned onslaught, and it was still only early afternoon as he laid his family in their graves and said prayers for them. One by one he turned the earth back in on them, saying his last goodbye as he went. It struck him as strange that he felt an equal surge of emotion as he covered over the dogs' muscular bodies and severed heads. But they were ever part of his family. A family massacred. He was alone. The last Zamoyski.

As he struggled with his emotions he heard a sound he

recognised. It was the click of a gun being cocked behind him, only this time he knew this would be no benign, elderly woman. He stood upright and raised his arms.

"Don't move," ordered a rough Ukrainian voice. Freddie was sure he recognised it, but he could not place it. His mind raced to put a face to the voice. It was different. Older. But he was sure he knew this man. As he thought, a hood was placed clumsily over his head and his hands were bound roughly behind his back.

A group of voices exchanged humorous obscenities in vulgar, bucolic Ukrainian as he was prodded and dragged back into the house. A couple of times he stumbled, but quickly got back to his feet under a barrage of insults and boots. He was bundled back into the dining room and pushed forcefully onto a chair as the rabble debated his fate.

"We kill him now," growled a young man to a murmur of approval. Freddie felt a rope fall round his head and started as it was yanked tight to his neck. The coils bit into the base of the hood, drawing its fabric closer into Freddie's face so that he now forced his breath through the weft of the material.

"Wait!" ordered an older man. "He's military."

"So?"

"So, the Russians have ordered us to turn them over."

Freddie's mind was in overdrive. The young man, the one clamouring for his execution, was Wasyl Pavelko. He was sure. And what was this about the Russians? Why would they have any bearing on matters? "Is that you Wasyl?" he blurted out.

"Shut the fuck up!" shouted Pavelko just as Freddie was dazed by a blow from something heavy and solid. He reeled for a few moments as the pain stabbed through his left cheek.

"Ha!" laughed another man. "He's clocked you Wasyl. Shall we tell him you fucked his sister too?"

"Shut up Marko. At least I did it properly, instead of getting my dick bitten off like your brother!"

The room exploded into violence as Marko responded to

Pavelko's taunt. Freddie's chair was knocked over and he lay on the floor as a dozen men exchanged chaotic blows. The fighting went on until a gun sounded.

"Stand up, all of you." Freddie knew this voice immediately. This was Olek Lipko. He was a huge man in his fifties and was renowned locally as a hard operator that nobody crossed. Freddie's father had often spoken admiringly about him as a man who could fix things, a local enforcer among the peasantry. It was also rumoured that he was a communist. Through his blindfold it was obvious to Freddie that the others obeyed without question. "Remove his hood."

"But..."

The gun spoke again. "Remove his hood." This time there was no dissent, and Freddie breathed properly as his head was freed for its incarceration. "Freddie Zamoyski." Lipko's cold, calculating gaze bore into Freddie. "The Prodigal Son returns."

It was hardly the right analogy, but Freddie realised that now was not the time for a Bible lesson. He turned his head to the left to see Wasyl Pavelko, and another wave of hatred welled up within him. He and Wasyl had been the best of friends when they were seven. They had been inseparable for a whole summer, playing on the estate and getting up to childish mischief. Wasyl had even stolen a kiss from Anna in the innocent manner of childhood infatuation that seems to blossom through long, summer days.

"How could you?" said Freddie coldly.

Another younger man to Freddie's right struck him again with the butt of a hunting rifle, but as Freddie reeled from the blow he saw Lipko land a fearsome punch into the youth's face. He collapsed as if hit by Thor's hammer.

"Shut up Zamoyski," he ordered. His eyes shone like jet, their iridescence magnified by the glaring whiteness of his full head of thick hair and flowing beard. Then, turning to the other men, he made his pronouncement. "He belongs to the reds. Take him to the station."

-oOo-

Freddie pressed his call button as the fan droned on through the Walthamstow heat. A few moments later a nurse's head popped round the frame of the door. "You all right Mr Zamoyski?"

"Please may I have some more water?"

"Of course. I'll get the domestic to sort it out for you."

Freddie turned back to me with a drawn expression. "I don't really know what happened that morning. I didn't cry. I couldn't cry. I think I buried it all in some vault inside my mind and bricked up the door. It finally hit me one day in 1951. I was looking in a shop window in Pimlico when I found myself crying. I cried uncontrollably for a week as the walls of that vault finally came crashing down."

"It must have been awful for you."

"It was no worse than the suffering of millions of others."

"But to know that such unspeakable things had been done by your friends must have been hard to accept."

"Hmmm." He drew a deep breath. "They weren't really friends, Tom. That was a childhood fairy tale. The truth is that they were servile and resentful. The world we constructed for ourselves in which we were appreciated as good overlords was a fantasy. Deep down they loathed and resented us. We were a ruling class from a ruling race, forged in a war of conquest. And their pent up hatred was channelled into an orgy of destruction and revenge."

"Did you ever go back to rebury your family?"

Freddie stared into the distance once again. "No. I have never again set foot in Poland. It was Lipko who saved my life, and I have often pondered on the respect he must have held for my father to have done that. He could have let them lynch me, but he intervened and my story took a different turn."

"You were handed over to the Russians?"

He nodded. "I had no idea that they had invaded. Stalin and Hitler had done their deal. Two devils so ideologically opposed had signed a pact that defied belief, but by the time the Red Army came there was no one left to fight them. I was taken to the gaol in the town and was picked up by Russian military police two days later."

"For interrogation?"

Freddie shook his head with a wry smile. "No. Lipko stripped me of my uniform and dressed me in some stinking peasant's clothes. I hated him for it. But the night before the Russians arrived he came to me in my cell. He fixed me with that disconcerting stare of his and told me I was a Ukrainian fascist, and that he had denounced me. 'Remember that or die,' were his last words as he turned away and left me."

"That's odd."

"Not really." He smiled again. "He knew. He knew they were rounding up Polish officers. He knew how they worked. He decided to give me the chance to live."

"I don't understand."

"Read your history Tom." His eyes closed. "I'm tired."

And that was my cue to leave. He had a way of being gently direct. I had been dismissed without being insulted and I smiled my acknowledgement. "I'll see you tomorrow." And with a pat on the back of his hand, I left.

It was later that I read of the slaughter of Polish officers in the Katyn Forest. Thousands were killed in cold blood as Stalin crushed any will to resist within his newly acquired lands. Freddie ultimately understood what Lipko had done for him, and the risk he had run by consigning him to the labour camps. Things are rarely what they seem, and the extreme events of such a vicious conflagration can twist honour into the face of cruelty.

I slept heavily.

VI - Gulag Vacation

Friday was just like any other Friday. All memories of the football had faded to nothing and it was business as usual. I went into the hospital and spent an hour or so with the stricken widow of a man who had died during the penalty shoot out. For him the atoms swerved a different way.

After we had finished I thought I would visit the canteen. Their coffee was mediocre but they sold very good croissants, and I sat in quiet contemplation as I reflected on Freddie's story. The way a nation had disintegrated in so short a time was troubling, and I wondered how events would unfold.

A couple of tables away the grey-haired old lady I had seen the day before sat staring into space. I looked at her long enough to subtly catch her eye, but she was blind to the canteen and everything within it. She seemed to have the kind of outer strength that hides an inner softness, and I watched as she deftly wiped away a single tear from her cheek. I finished my drink and went up to the ward. Freddie was keen to get started.

"Come on, we don't have all day!"

"I'm sorry Freddie. Is everything all right?"

Freddie paused for a moment and then told me his news. "Things are not looking good, Tom. The doctors have told me the muscle of my heart is failing. Too much of it died and what's left isn't enough to do the job."

"That doesn't sound good."

Freddie laughed. "Ah, the art of English understatement. Thank you for that. Nothing ever seems too terrible when spoken by an Englishman. It'll all come out in the wash, eh?"

"I'm sorry. I didn't mean..."

"Don't be silly. I'm pulling your leg." He dismissed my apology as unnecessary. "That's not the worst of it, though. I had a scan this morning. They tell me that a large part of the wall of my ventricle is dead. Every time my heart beats it bulges out a fraction more, becoming ever thinner and thinner. Apparently, it's only a matter of time before it thins out enough to burst."

"And that means?" I think I knew the answer, but I had to ask.

"The end." He looked me square in the face. I did not need to ask the next question. "Five or six days. The only treatment is a transplant, but that's not going to happen."

"I see." I took in the enormity of his words. "If there's nothing they can do then are you going home?"

Freddie looked round at the machine by the bedside that slowly delivered its infusion with pharmaceutical precision. "Sadly, I can't. What power my heart has left is being driven by this stuff. I often wondered what my death bed would look like. Well, now I know." He opened his hands as if presenting it for the first time. "I must confess it is a strange feeling to know that my heart could go pop at any time. They tell me I'll know nothing of it. It will all be over in a moment. It could be now. It could be in a fortnight. Only He knows."

I took a deep breath through my nostrils and moved on. "We'd better get cracking then. We don't want this story ending half finished."

Freddie beamed a broad grin at my directness. "That's my boy!" The timer on the infusion made a noise as another small bolus of dopamine was pushed into Freddie's body and he picked up his narrative.

-oOo-

He had been herded into one of a dozen cattle wagons that collected their load from Lwow station. The commissars and soviet military had been busy in the days following Russia's annexation of eastern Poland and Freddie found himself in a large crowd of bewildered men and a few women pressed onto the platform. They had been identified as enemies of the Russian state. Undesirables ranging from fascist activists to intellectuals, rounded up and shipped off to work in Stalin's camps. Among them was a little known Ukrainian fascist called Fedir Shevchuk.

The train had spent days lurching and rocking along the tracks that seemed never to end. The stench in the wagons grew to an intolerable haze. The smell of bodies and excrement was so overpowering that Freddie could taste it. Twice a day the train would pull into sidings and the wagons would be cleaned under the scrutiny of the ever watchful guards. On the third day a group of three prisoners tried to escape, but were immediately cut down by rifle fire. The soldiers had dogs and could have captured the men and brought them back, but they seemed to delight in the fear their execution instilled. There were no other attempts.

Onward the train went, although Freddie suspected their progress was slow. They seemed to spend large amounts of time waiting for signals to change and even when they were rolling along they scarcely managed much more than running speed. After six days they climbed into hills and then on into heavily forested mountains. The landscape had changed dramatically, and Freddie guessed that they were crossing the Urals.

By day nine those gloriously wooded peaks were far behind them and the endless forest began to break up, first into small clearings then into open country with scattered copses and finally a barren tundra. By the tenth day not a single tree could be seen from one horizon to the other. The days were shortening rapidly and Freddie realised that with the drop in temperature they must be travelling north.

He smiled to himself as he recalled that it was Poland's own Nikolas Kopernicus who had explained the celestial movements that now led to this rapid change in the hours of daylight. Then Freddie remembered that he himself was not Polish. Not any more. He was Ukrainian. A pang of sadness hit him as he recognised that for the first time in his life he had denied his

Polish heritage. God's grace had twice delivered him from death, but the price he was paying was the betrayal of his roots.

On day twelve the train stopped and its cargo was unloaded onto a man made earth bank that served as a platform. The prisoners were herded into holding pens as if they were cattle on market day and there they stood or sat for what seemed like an age. Their captors kept a disinterested watch over the rabble, safe in the knowledge that there was nowhere for them to flee. But Freddie was aware that a new group of soldiers showed much more interest in the human livestock.

This handful of men in uniforms bearing the insignia of the 415th Rifle Regiment were sizing them up and making notes which they appeared to be taking back to a large lorry parked at the end of the platform. Standing on the flat bed of the truck behind the cab was an imposing figure. He must have stood two metres tall, and Freddie guessed that over 130 kilograms of muscle were strapped to his giant frame. The deference paid to him by the other men was chilling. As Freddie watched he saw it was nothing to do with rank, but an instinctive compliance offered through fear. He thought he could make out three stripes on the man's arm, but his authority came from a pervading aura of malevolence.

"Who's the Goliath?" Freddie overheard a young soldier asking one of the older guards from the train.

"That's Ivan Volkov." Even the tone of the older man's reply emanated fear. "Keep away from him. Don't ever cross him. If he wants something, let him have it."

"What's he doing?"

"He's buying stock. You'll get your cut. Just leave the talking to Sergei." He looked down and noticed Freddie sitting on the ground. Fearing he may have been overheard, he gave him a sharp boot in the back. "Fuck off scum!"

Freddie scuttled away and watched Volkov keenly as he issued instructions to his minions. It was obvious that he was selecting people from the lists that had been presented to him, and it was not long before a deal was being struck with the head guard. Hands were shaken, money exchanged, and six well built prisoners were roughly dragged from the pens and loaded onto the lorry. The men of the 415th stood over their purchases as the vehicle pulled away, leaving Freddie to ponder on the meaning of it all.

Their business concluded, the guards marched the prisoners towards the one physical feature in this barren, desolate place. Half a mile from the makeshift railway station a craggy mass rose from the tundra as if some huge, stone leviathan trapped beneath the ground was trying to force its way to freedom. As the column of prisoners neared this enormous rock, Freddie saw that its face was cleft in two by the mouth of what looked like a giant sink hole. Then he saw it was the entrance to a man made inferno that penetrated deep into the earth and pierced the heart of the flat-topped hill.

Around the entrance to this forbidding underworld nestled a collection of wooden huts enclosed by a wire perimeter, watched over by tall wooden guard towers. In time the whole world would come to know the meaning of the word "gulag", but on that day in the meagre warmth of the last dregs of a tundra summer every man and woman knew what their future held as they looked into the mouth of the monster that would swallow them.

The chill arctic winds came soon enough, biting at their flesh and gnawing at their fingers as they laboured endlessly to dig ore from the bowels of the mine. Their picks and hammers slowly consumed the hill from within like some parasitic plague, while in return the rock took its revenge as the death count rose. There could not have been more than three thousand inmates in the complex, but such was the rate of attrition that numbers were barely replenished by each load of new arrivals swapped for the piles of ore dug up by the dead. It was a death camp that consumed people through toil, cold and starvation. That was the mine's price for giving up its treasures. They dug. That was all they did.

The cold was terrible and the work back-breaking, but Freddie soon realised that what would kill him would be a lack of food. The gruel they were served by the few prisoners lucky enough to be assigned to kitchen duties was a paste whose substance seemed to be a combination of corn starch and sawdust. It tasted vile, although it fought off the hunger pangs for an hour or two. Freddie wondered if it had any nutritional value at all. And still they dug.

They slept in long rows on mats on the floors of the wooden huts, each man finding whatever he could to keep warm. For the new arrivals that meant the danger of freezing, and Freddie thanked God that he had come to the camp in the last of the mild weather which had given him a chance to claim the overcoat and blankets of the man on the next mat who died on Freddie's third day.

He would like to have said that the man had died of exhaustion. Indeed, that was what he told people for years afterwards. The truth was that driven by the mounting cold and the realisation that he would die without more to keep him warm, Freddie had helped the slowly dying man to a rendezvous with his God and, before anyone else knew he was gone, Freddie had taken everything of use.

The man had been mumbling incoherently and Freddie had initially tried to quieten him with a hand over his mouth. But something between the cold and the hunger took control of him, and in the dark of the night the man breathed his last.

"That was heartless," came the unexpected comment from over Freddie's shoulder as he snuggled into the filthy clothes and blankets he had stolen. The voice was steady and self-assured, almost menacing in its deep Ukrainian tone.

"He was going to die anyway." Freddie's reply was hardly self-justification, but more a weary statement of fact.

There was a long pause before the voice continued. "Heartless is good." Another hiatus. "Heartless survives." Curious to know where the conversation was heading Freddie turned over to face his neighbour. The man was thick set and, until that moment, had completely ignored Freddie's attempts at conversation over the preceding days. "It's a wasted opportunity, though."

"How so?"

"You think the most valuable thing he had was his clothes?" Freddie stared back, uncertain what the man was getting at. "You've been here three days. What's the worst thing already?"

"Hunger."

"So why waste food?" There was no evil in the man's eyes. Only cold, logical survival. "How long do you think you will live on the shit they feed us? Three months. That's how long most of you new boys last." He sized Freddie up. "I can't work you out. You sound like an intellectual, but you look like a kulak. The intellectuals always die first. Too high minded. So which are you?"

Freddie sensed potential danger, so evaded the classification on offer. "A bednyak, and proud of it." The defiance in his voice seemed to do nothing to convince the man that he was, indeed, one of the lowest class of surf.

"A genuine peasant, eh? Well, what difference does it make whether you had one cow or ten. You'll still die."

"How long have you been here?"

"Two years."

"Two years!" Freddie's whisper rose in surprise and the man in the next row stirred.

"Quieten down. Yes. Two years. You either adapt or you die." The freezing wind gave a low pitched howl as it whipped past the hut.

Freddie marvelled at this man's achievement. To survive here for a season would be outstanding, but two years seemed impossible. "How do you..." The answer to his question was now dawning on him.

"How do I overpower and kill people by myself so that I can eat them?"

The man's direct matter of fact manner was disarming. "Yes."

"You need a partner. Mine was Maxim. He slept where you are. He was shot a fortnight ago for stealing."

Freddie suddenly felt the projection of Maxim's ghost settle over him, and it was uncomfortable. Who was Maxim? What were his values? What unspeakable deeds had he performed? The conversation was beginning to sound like a job offer. And it was a job he was not sure he could stomach. "My name is Fedir Shevchuk," he offered changing the subject.

"Taras Bilyk."

"Very nice to meet you, Taras. I'm from the west. Just south of Lviv. How about you." He was careful to use the city's Ukrainian name. One slip here could mean death.

Bilyk's eyes bored into him. Eventually he answered. "I was a lecturer in German at Kiev University. I'll hand it to you, your accent is good, but you're about as Ukrainian as the Queen of Spain's tits. Polish?" Freddie could see little point in denying what Bilyk had so easily recognised, and nodded. "What a world." He spat out an ironic laugh. "I fought against your lot. I was a messenger. Fourteen years old, and being shot at by Polish bastards. And now here I am offering life to one of them." There was another long pause as Bilyk stared into Freddie's eyes as if probing for a weakness. "Think it over, Fedir." The pointed emphasis he placed on the name made it clear he knew it was made up. "Do you want to live or die?" With that he rolled over and seconds later the sound of light snoring began.

The next few days were an emotional torment for Freddie as he came to terms with the fact that he had murdered a man in cold blood. To kill in battle defending your home is one thing. To dispatch a sick, defenceless man in order to steal his clothes is something entirely different.

Freddie saw it as a blessed relief that he had so little time to reflect on his actions, as they were set to work by their pitiless guards. There were 50 of the large wooden huts laid out in a grid pattern to one side of the mine's entrance, each sleeping 50 to 60 workers. They were raised on short legs that just allowed a man to crawl under each on his belly, and the layer of air provided some insulation from the solid ground set in its permafrost. Freddie's hut was somewhere in the middle of the arrangement. Hut 27 was to be his home until he died.

In front of the entrance that led to the tunnels was a large open space that every now and then acted as a mustering ground where the prisoners were collected for the brief roll call that took place each week. Freddie wondered at the point of this exercise, as escape into the barren land beyond would have been futile. It was only after the second week that he understood the purpose of the counting was simply to establish the number of dead, in order to inform the request for deliveries of more workers.

The quarrying methods may have been from the Stone Age, but the organisation was precise and ruthless. By the second week over two hundred more workers were needed as the frail and exhausted fell, and another consignment of the damned arrived.

On the far side of the muster ground was the canteen that fed the inmates in shifts as they rotated from the rock face to their huts. The routine was constant with almost a thousand workers hacking at the rock at any time day or night. The gruel was served on a rota before they were locked back in their wooden boxes to sleep before the next cycle began.

Beyond the canteen and kitchens were the guards' barracks, where Freddie assumed the accommodation was somewhat less spartan. Even so, the posting must have been thoroughly resented despite the lorries that regularly took them away and returned them hours later rolling drunk. That told him there must have been some sort of settlement nearby where the soldiers no doubt drank or whored away their pay, but that place might just as well have been on another planet for all the relevance it held for him.

Freddie ruminated on the man he had killed. He prayed for forgiveness in those few moments that he could engineer to be by himself. But God's reply startled him. For some reason he did not feel anger. He felt God's forgiveness. It was difficult for him to describe, and for weeks he struggled with the notion that he was twisting God's word for his own self-serving needs. They dug more and the ore piled up.

As he wrestled with these internal conflicts and the weeks rolled on he could feel himself growing weaker. The work was inhuman. There was no respite. Anyone slowing in their labours was beaten by the nearest guard, all of whom carried large batons for that very purpose. Life was worthless, and anyone showing any defiance was dragged into a space big enough to allow three or four guards the freedom to wield their sticks properly. The death beating was frequent and public and served to terrify.

On Freddie's first day he had seen one man beaten mercilessly and left with a fractured shin, ribs and jaw. He had seen the teeth fly from the impact as the guards cheered their colleague's aim. The broken but still live body was left where it fell. Nobody dared help, and the man died in the night. A lingering death of unspeakable misery. The corpse was still there on day two as a warning. On Freddie's third day it had thankfully gone.

The food was as worthless as the lives in this place that was nothing more than hell's waiting room. After two months Freddie was feeling light headed and slightly sick. The teeth of a Siberian winter were biting, and despite his best efforts he was being hit more regularly with sticks as he inevitably slowed. His vision was becoming blurred at times and his movements lacked their usual coordination. Despite his terrible fatigue he could hardly sleep as the pain of savage hunger tore at his insides. He was slowly dying.

Bilyk still pushed him for an answer to his offer. "I don't know," was the reply. "It's wrong. It's disgusting."

"So you are an intellectual, eh? But I don't think you will die of high-mindedness. Not you. You're like me. In better times we can be civilised, even cultured. But here, in this hell, we survive."

"No. I'm not like that," protested Freddie, although he was already not sure.

"We'll see. What you did the night after you arrived was not cultured. Your base instinct will always defeat your intellect. It's already winning. I see it."

"Why me? Why not one of the others?"

Bilyk's logic was troubling. "They are mice." He glanced around at the other workers in their tortured sleep. "They are weak. They accept their fate. I need a partner who will do whatever it takes to live. Who will do anything." His intense stare redoubled. "I need you."

The cold grew deeper, and the days disappeared as the camp entered a perpetual cycle of darkness punctuated only by faint twilight. Freddie had lost count of their passing until the routine was broken abruptly. He woke to discover that they were not being herded to the mine, but instead were left to fester in the hut. From outside came the sounds of drunken revelry, and it seemed that all the guards were indulging in some sort of party.

"Happy Christmas," offered Bilyk glibly.

"Is that what this is?"

Bilyk snorted. "It's my third. Enjoy it. And if the door opens, pretend you're asleep." He stood, and looked down at Freddie's emaciated form. "I can't wait for you any longer Fedir. And after all, it's Christmas."

He gave a furtive glance to satisfy himself that he was not being watched and deftly pulled his mat to one side. In a moment he lifted two short planks from the floor to reveal an opening and reached into a recess. He smiled menacingly at Freddie as the small blade he had retrieved glinted. "Cover this up!" he ordered as he lowered himself quickly through the floor and was gone.

Without questioning his part in the enterprise, Freddie replaced the planks and covered them with the mat. He could only guess at the lengths to which Bilyk had gone to get his hands on a knife, but his musings were short lived, as the door to the hut was opened roughly. Freddie immediately lay down and followed Bilyk's advice to look asleep.

Two drunken guards staggered in and grabbed a prisoner with less sense who was sitting close by. The man struggled as he was dragged out onto the ground outside. The door was slammed shut, but there was no mistaking the sounds of a savage beating as the man's cries echoed between the timber buildings. Before long the shrieks of pain became a whimper and then stopped completely as the only sounds left were those of broken human pulp absorbing heavy wooden blows.

Bilyk was gone for what seemed like an age, and Freddie was beginning to worry that he had been caught. Just as he had given up hope of seeing the professor of German again, the mat moved and he heard a faint knocking. He scrambled to open the hole in the floor and within ten seconds Bilyk was lying on his mat as if he had never left. He looked around to satisfy himself that he had not been seen, and then with a warm smile of friendship reached inside his coat and pulled out a brown slippery mass.

"Happy Christmas, Fedir."

Freddie looked dubiously at the offering in Bilyk's hand. It was smooth and shiny, as it glistened a redolent brown. "What is it?"

"Food." Bilyk was already chewing into a second piece with a look of ecstasy.

Freddie held his Christmas present in his hand as he struggled against an overwhelming desire. "Liver?"

Bilyk smiled and nodded enthusiastically. "It's the best bit. Muscles get stringy and infested. Heart is just too tough and chewy. The liver is always pristine. You'll see."

A half congealed red liquid seeped between Freddie's fingers as his revulsion was overpowered by the smell of warm flesh. A voice in his head screamed to stop, but a drive more powerful than anything he could ever have imagined forced the meat to his mouth.

"We are just animals, Fedir," smiled Bilyk as he watched the inner struggle play itself out. Freddie felt his teeth bite into one edge of the meat and was consumed by the explosion of taste that filled his mouth. Nothing had ever tasted so good in his life, and in that moment he was lost in a primeval orgy of carnivorous desire.

"Slow down," warned Bilyk. "Chew each piece thoroughly. It's stringy, but the slime helps it slip down, and you can let your stomach do the rest."

Freddie was almost incapable of stopping himself from forcing the meat into his mouth whole, but managed to tear the flesh into pieces he could swallow. As each congealed bolus slid into his gullet the taste and smell tapped into some ancient drive he did not understand. It was glorious, and it seemed like only a moment before he found himself licking the bloody remnants clinging to his empty hands.

"Good, eh?" Bilyk beamed genuine happiness. "Now lie down, and keep still, or you'll be sick."

"Thank you Taras," whispered Freddie as he settled back and savoured the feeling of a full stomach for the first time he could remember.

As the liver infused his body he began to feel light-headed. He marvelled at the intoxicated feeling that washed over him as he slipped into a protein-fuelled drunkenness and his metabolism struggled with the sudden nutritional flood. Try as he might he could not keep his eyes open, and drifted into a deep satisfying sleep. The cold and the hut receded from his perceptions and he was floating on a bed a feathers. The air was warm, and the sounds of high summer from his childhood wafted through his consciousness.

He slowly opened his eyes and smiled at Anna who looked down on him lovingly from the end of his bed.

"You're safe," he muttered.

"Yes," she whispered. "And mama and papa. They're here too. They're safe."

"I'm glad. Can I join you?" She was suffused in a golden glow, and her serenity engulfed him.

"Darling Freddie." Her pure voice filled every part of him. "You have suffered so much." She stepped forward and knelt by his bed. Her hand reached out and stroked his forehead, washing away his pain. "But it's not time." Somehow he knew what she was about to say. "He has a greater plan for you."

"Why?" He so wanted to join his family, to hold them and rejoice in their togetherness.

"You must survive, Freddie. Your work is not complete. It's His will."

"But I'm tired."

"His will, Freddie." Her voice echoed slightly. "His will." She began to fade.

Freddie struggled, but he could not move his body. He wanted desperately to reach out and pull her back, but the air turned cold and the warm light evaporated to the darkness of the hut.

"You okay, Fedir?" asked Bilyk. Freddie turned in a daze to look at his friend. "You've been mumbling in your sleep for hours. You'd better ready yourself. They're about to take us back to the mine."

And so began the strangest, and in some ways the most contradictory relationship of Freddie's life. Bilyk was a man of learning, a university professor. His passion was for languages. In normal society he and Freddie would have had so much in common. Freddie may even have looked up to this older man. But in the crucible of eastern European nationalism and the tribal savagery it unleashed, the deeper currents of culture and history led them to be enemies. The Ukrainian and the Pole brought low.

And yet in a perverse switchback, history had been so cruel to them both in equal measure that it created yet a lower plane. One on which they became natural allies in the most basic quest. The quest for simple survival. And as the weeks passed into months which blurred into years their alliance grew to friendship. The friendship blossomed into affection, and ultimately to a deep brotherly love.

They would never be the same. They were cut from different cloth. But there was not a soul alive that Freddie would have trusted more than Bilyk. The phrase "Brothers In Arms" is so often applied to comrades in war. But this was profoundly true of Freddie and Bilyk. Before their time in the gulag was done they would gladly have laid down their lives for each other. It was the tightest bond that held them together. It was the bond that dictated their survival.

-oOo-

The machine delivered another dose of dopamine and Freddie sighed. "That was what kept me going. The belief that He had something higher planned for me."

"That was Christmas 1939?"

He nodded wearily. "That's right. I celebrated another three Christmases in that hell."

"Three more years?" It was almost inconceivable.

Freddie stared at the bedsheets deep in thought. "This is my confession. So I confess. Taras Bilyk and I survived by preying on others." I had no response, and could only sit in silence as he slowly recounted the roll of death they inflicted. "Every week or two we would slip out of the hut and find some poor victim. Even now I can't be sure whether Taras was sent to me by God. A gift to ensure that I survived the camp. Or whether he was at the Devil's temptation sent to test me. The guards were lax. Half of the time they were drunk, and didn't really miss the odd worker snatched as they were returned to their huts."

"Didn't they find the bodies?"

Freddie looked at me as he pursed his lips and drew a deep breath through his flared nostrils. "Yes. But they couldn't care less. After a year or so I think they knew the prisoners that were...." he thought for a moment to choose his words, "...supplementing their diet. We weren't the only ones. You could tell who they were. They were the ones who didn't lose weight. The ones who survived. We were good workers, and I think they figured they would rather have strong survivors who would dig."

"So, they just left you to it?"

He nodded in shame. "There was a team from hut 39, and another pair from hut 16. Two fellows from hut 4 were caught in the act and had to be shot, but as long as we kept out of their way the guards turned a blind eye."

"It must have been awful. Having to kill just to be able to eat."

"The worst of it, Tom, was that it wasn't. I used to look forward to it. Of course the hunger drove us, and the prospect of the feast was all-consuming. But, God help me, I know I enjoyed the thrill of the hunt. And I became very good at it. In time the roles changed. Taras became my assistant as the apprentice became the master, and I called the shots. He often joked that he had created the perfect gulag survivor, and he was happy for me to lead."

"And you were never caught?"

"No. The only time we were in real danger was the night we bumped into a successful two man team from hut 42. There was an unspoken rule that hunters kept out of each others' way, but the winter of 1941 was so terrible that we were all pretty desperate."

"What happened?"

"We accidentally ended up stalking the same prey, and when it came to it neither team was prepared to back down. The conditions were so harsh we just had to have the food."

"You won?"

Freddie nodded reflectively. "Hand to hand combat turned me into a monster. I never really understood what happened to me but every time I got myself into close quarters fighting it was like I was possessed. I told myself it was the strength of The Lord filling me." His tone gave the lie to the words. I looked at him and waited. "But it was really the Devil."

"You did what was necessary to survive."

"Perhaps. But in those moments of intense clarity that hit you in battle I could see deep into my own soul. And I know the calculating relish with which I killed all those people. May God forgive me."

There was silence as I allowed him the space to process what he was telling me. Eventually his infinite stare focused and he caught my gaze. "It's more difficult to say this than I thought it would be."

"You've never talked of this before?"

"Only once. To someone very dear." He could hardly get the words out, and he quickly turned away to conceal the rogue tear that had forced its way to the corner of his left eye. He deftly wiped it with his hand, feigning annoyance at a fly.

"You did what you had to to survive" I repeated. "God willed it."

Freddie turned on me with a passion I had not seen before. "Did He, Tom?" His intensity was undimmed by his age. "Did He really? Or was that my justification for committing those atrocities?" We sat in silence, which for the first time was awkwardly filled with Freddie's anger before, like a kettle removed from the heat, the boiling cauldron cooled. "You know, Tom, there is an awful lot of nonsense spoken about survivor guilt." His ire simmered to reflection. "Psychologists and their theories. Fitting the emotions conveniently into their pet theses." His contemplation drifted to the window. "I am not ashamed that I survived." His look quickened and he fixed me with those intense eyes. "I am ashamed at what I did to survive."

I nodded at the disarming truth of his insight. Stripped of analysis. Laid bare in its heartfelt simplicity. After a time I asked the obvious question. "When did you finally get out?"

"Spring 1943."

I stared at him with a mix of admiration and pity. "Three and a half years in a place like that. It's remarkable. It's unspeakable. It's more than any man should have to endure. It's no wonder you were driven to extremes. Driven to a form of madness. It's not your fault, Freddie."

After a while Freddie's mask of self loathing finally broke into a wry smile and the slightest nod. "Perhaps you are right, Tom. But in the eyes of God I'm still a murderer."

"I know He doesn't see it that way, Freddie." His face disagreed with me but he remained silent. Eventually, I could contain my curiosity no longer and the question that had been hanging in the air could be ignored no more. "How did you escape?"

Freddie smiled at me, weary in his mock contempt. "So clumsy and direct. You want tales of tunnel digging and derring do? Nobody escapes from the gulag. You are sent there to die."

"So how...." I did not know how to rephrase the question.

Freddie smiled and patted me on the back of the hand. "That, my dear Tom, is a whole new story, and I am tired. So very tired."

I nodded my understanding. "I'll see you tomorrow." Freddie grunted and nodded as his eyes closed. What demons he was battling behind his closed lids I could only guess at, but as I made my way home it struck me as truly awful that here in a vibrant, affluent democracy there were old men who knew from first hand experience things that no one should ever learn. That a dying man in London in 1990 could tell me the best cut of raw human meat seemed awful. And yet it was in the forming of experiences such as these that our democracy had been defended and assured.

People like Freddie had endured that kind of hell so that we could live our lives of ease and excess.

VII - Siberian Colosseum

The weekends at the hospital always had a slightly strange feel to them. The usual rhythm of focused medical activity was suspended as the junior skeleton staff did their best to keep things running. Senior figures were nowhere to be seen, and I always had the feeling that everyone was simply marking time until business as usual was resumed on the Monday morning.

Meanwhile, the wards and corridors were full of visitors who had been too busy to see their loved ones during the week. It all conspired to produce a kind of end of term feeling that was out of place where there were so many sick people fighting for their lives. And I was very conscious that Freddie had already lost his fight. The only question was when he would be taken. I knew it could be at any moment, and so the need to hear the rest of his story was all the more pressing. I prayed to God that he was given the chance to end his account before he died, and for the first time in two years I realised that my prayers had a substance to them. They were heartfelt and said in earnest to a real God. Some small part of me had already found my way back to Him, even if the rest of me presumed the right to ask for Freddie's survival in return.

I think that worry was why I slept badly, and by six o'clock I was dressed and ready, marking time until it was acceptable for me to go in to the ward. Inevitably my anxiety got the better of me and the ward sister frowned her disapproval at my early arrival. Freddie, on the other hand, was keen to start and his breakfast tray was already done with as I greeted him. For the first time I saw the signs of impatience as I set up the microphone and invited him to continue.

"I still can't believe you survived that kind of ordeal for three and a half years."

The guilt of the day before had transformed to muted

modesty like a disfigured lump of forged iron being beaten by the telling. "It was nothing really. Only the decision to abandon a civilised existence. Anyone could have made it. Taras was right. Intellectuals mostly clung to their high-mindedness and died as a result, but that is the measure of the stoic. Whether they had read Boethius or not, they lived that philosophy of the grey-eyed lady, and perhaps were better for it." I sat and nodded. I think I may even have given an affirming grunt to conceal my ignorance as I had scant idea what he was talking about. I made a mental note of the reference, and it was only later after yet more research that I recognised he was referring to a philosophical text written by a condemned Roman fifteen hundred years ago. Its Neoplatonist themes were of self reliance and inner peace transcending physical suffering, and as I read I understood just how deeply our culture ran in Freddie even as he doubted it himself. It was a text that I returned to many times in later years. It consoled me and fed my revitalised faith. Freddie had that power. A single phrase, one utterance from him in passing and a new vista opened up for me. That was another of his abundant gifts.

"But you survived," I replied.

"Yes, I survived." He looked out of the window. "I discovered there was much more of the street fighter in me than the philosopher." His infusion whined as it pushed more drug into his veins and he smiled ironically. "This is the one fight I will lose."

There was a pause as we both acknowledged what he had said before I continued. "How was it that you managed to escape? You said yourself that no one ever got out of the gulag."`

"Ah, well." Freddie's eyes opened wide, and the narrator came flooding back. This was his story, and while there were parts that were almost unbearable to speak aloud, he was going to make the most of the power of the story teller to keep his audience enthralled. "I didn't escape." I looked at him quizzically, as he returned a teasing half smile. "The guards opened the gates for me and gave me my own lorry."

My expression turned to exasperated disbelief, imploring him to the truth. "Come on Freddie."

His mischievous smile melted into something more sincere as he nodded his head. "It's true. Perhaps not in the way I've painted it," he conceded, "but they did open the gates and they did allow us to drive out. Or should I say, be driven." He knew he had hooked me, and paused before continuing. "I was sold, Tom. One morning the whole camp was called to muster. It was a sorry sight. Most of them were half dead, and the rest wished they were. A military truck drove into the compound and out stepped a small group of soldiers led by a man I recognised." He paused again, but this time I sensed it was not for dramatic effect but the genuine hesitation of the recollection of a deep fear. "Ivan Volkov."

"The man who had bought the prisoners from the train?" It was a distinctive name that had impressed itself on me the day before. Volkov. The Russian for wolf. John Wolf. For some reason I could not explain even the simple juxtaposition of "k"s and "v"s sounded menacing. The name seemed more than apt from Freddie's chilling description.

"Exactly." Freddie's grim face seemed to reflect Volkov's aura. "He and his men inspected us and quickly picked out the fitter specimens. Some of the newer arrivals who had not had a chance to lose too much weight, and the three remaining hunting teams that had made a success of survival."

"Had they bought men from the camp before?"

"No. Never. They had only ever dealt in the new intake from the trains. The ones that were fit and healthy. But the delivery of fresh inmates was waning. We didn't know it at the time, but the need for men to fight the Germans at the front was so pressing that the flow of victims to the camps had stemmed to just a trickle."

"And so they came looking for you?"

"Exactly. The Battle of Stalingrad was at its height that winter, and they needed fodder to throw before the German guns while the marshals prepared their counter attack. Then when the thrust came they needed to keep feeding men into the grinder to maintain its momentum. It was a matter of accountancy. The Russians sacrificed a million men. The Germans lost a quarter of a million. And then they did it all over again. And again. Except the Russians could afford the losses, and like an unimaginative poker player they just kept raising the stakes. The Germans couldn't afford to go all in, so they folded."

I turned over the dates in my head trying to fix a point on the timeline in my mind. He was talking about the spring of 1943, and I pondered the obvious question. "What on earth did a group of infantrymen want with you?"

A hollow, brooding stare crossed his face. "Entertainment."

-oOo-

The soldiers roughly manhandled their purchases into the lorry in a manner that suggested they were not worth much. Even as they were being loaded, Volkov remonstrated with the camp guard who seemed to have been deputed by the others to conduct negotiations. As Freddie was dragged past the increasingly heated exchange he saw Volkov up close for the first time and could almost feel the malevolent energy that exuded from him. His thick, heavy grey coat still bore the insignia of the 415th Rifle Regiment and a set of substantial stripes with the extra markings that denoted him as a sergeant major.

"They're fucking rotten," boomed Volkov.

"Maybe. But they're all we have. And there are six who've survived here for more than two years. They'll be exactly what you want. Fighters. Now pay up or the deal's off."

Volkov was still not happy, and Freddie wondered if the verbal confrontation would spark into something more dangerous. Eventually though, the posturing settled and money was exchanged before the hapless chattels were driven away to an unknown fate. Freddie and Bilyk were among them.

Freddie found himself feeling suddenly anxious, but wondering why. He knew that there would ordinarily be no escape from the camp, so this turn of events was one of the few ways in which they might have any possibility of avoiding inevitable death. Still though, he felt a profound unease. It was clear that Volkov's motives were focused and pitiless. Whatever it was that he had planned for the slaves he had bought, Freddie doubted it would be any better than the hell they were leaving.

After a couple of hours of being jostled painfully on the floor of the truck they came to a halt. The ten men were decanted and marched at gunpoint across a wide expanse of ground towards a large, brick building that looked like a warehouse. Above his head a carpet of thick grey cloud extended to infinity in three directions, giving an even greater impact to the bright sun that projected its low rays from the clear horizon before them.

Freddie found his mind pondering on the effects of permanent half light on a culture. They had lived for almost four years shrouded in unremitting cloud that robbed everything of all colour. The linguist in him recalled that the English word for the space above our heads was "sky", but that word itself came from the old Norse for cloud. To the English, sky and cloud were linguistically indivisible, and so it was here on the tundra which made the startling sun in their eyes the more stunning.

The group was prodded and cajoled across the ground and Freddie was at once struck by the contrast. The new arrivals were bigger, heavier and still walked with a relaxed stride. The six hunters were lean, tenaciously wiry in their thinness, and stalked the ground as if alert to some imperceptible threat. This sudden realisation showed him how much he had changed, and the civilised man within reflected on the feral beast he had become. It was an absolute necessity for sure, but he pondered on how the

Freddie of four years earlier would have reacted.

His military mind immediately began its automated programme of information gathering. The sun, low in the sky ahead of them, marked south while on his left to the east were rows of huts that looked significantly better appointed than those they had been forced to endure in the camp. Freddie swayed slightly as he walked to allow himself to sneak a look over his left shoulder. Another substantial brick building framed itself in a snapshot within his photographic memory. As they trudged across what he now realised was a large concrete parade ground he studied the memory of that brief glance. It was some sort of brick built hall sporting a large regimental banner, and the picture was complete. They had been brought to the barracks of the 415th Rifle Regiment.

There were no guard towers and no wire. There was no need for any out here in this desolate, barren place. To his right the road by which they had arrived simply tracked off into the far distance and the open expanse of nothing seemed to invite the wind to swirl in and lash around them. Freddie was used to the close confined spaces of the prison camp and found himself feeling wary of the wide vista and the suffocatingly big sky. He pushed those agoraphobic thoughts to the back of his mind as he weighed up the situation.

This was an infantry barracks. The architecture suggested late nineteenth century, so perhaps it had been one of those Tsarist military centres that enforced the yasak, or fur tribute. It was a form of economic exploitation that stretched back centuries. The word itself derived from the Turkic language of Genghis Khan's conquering horde that set the pattern for the extraction of the soft gold of animal pelts. The Tsars turned that protection racket into an art form.

Freddie had read about the appalling treatment of the Siberian natives by government forces and how they were forced to pay taxes in the form of furs taken from the forest and tundra.

Failure to comply invited raids by Cossacks stationed in centres like this, and Freddie wondered whether they might be close to the forest. That might provide sustenance and shelter if he could escape and his mind began to permute the possibilities.

But Volkov's purpose was still opaque. As they walked closer to the warehouse he was struck by its size. Close to five stories high, the wall facing them must have run for nearly a hundred yards. The yasak must have been big. High up, large windows overlooked the parade ground as if keeping a watchful eye on the discipline of the troops stationed in this wretched, forgotten outpost of the empire. Freddie stole surreptitious glances at the structure before they were bundled into its bowels through an inconspicuous and ordinary looking door that seemed lost in the far right of the expanse of brick. He hoped to steal a glimpse around the corner to estimate the depth of the building but failed.

Once inside they found themselves in a large stairwell that was generously lit by cascading light, Freddie assumed from some of those large windows. From the floors above came sounds of clerical industry, and Freddie pondered further on the nature of the place that he assumed had once been a storage building for those tribute furs awaiting shipment. His reflections were interrupted as the rough accompanying crew directed them towards another door in the corner of the back of the hallway that looked as though it might lead to a corridor. Before they reached it, a shrill voice ricocheted off the walls.

"Sergeant Volkov!" The voice was thin, imperious and officious in a way that sounded like a man trying to conceal his own lack of confidence. A small, wiry figure in a captain's uniform came into view around the last turn in the stairs, and Volkov's giant frame stiffened. "Where are you taking those men?"

Volkov sized the man up. "You know where." After a defiant pause he added the required, "Sir. To the pens."

"Don't take that tone with me, Volkov. I'm the chief quartermaster now, and from today the storehouse comes under my jurisdiction." Freddie sensed the man had just acquired this power and was wielding it with anxious uncertainty as he walked down the stairs.

"Savrasov only died yesterday. He's scarcely cold." Volkov's deep tone was steady and calm which gave it a menacing timbre. "I'm sure you wouldn't want to renege on the major's agreement with me."

"Yes, well, ordinarily that would be so. But these are not ordinary times. We are soon to be moved. They say we are to join the glorious armies of the Leningrad Front, so your lucrative if lurid little sideline will come to an end. It seems we all have a time limited opportunity Volkov, and must maximise our gains." He had stopped on the bottom step, in an unconscious attempt to compensate for his short stature and shifted uncomfortably in his boots as if uncertain of what to say next. "Your arena takes up half of my warehouse, so your rent is doubled."

"What!" Volkov took two bold strides towards the small, nervous frame before him, but found the captain did not shrink away. Volkov's piercing blue eyes bore down on his protagonist as he regained his composure. "I am taking these men to the pens where they will be readied for tonight. And tomorrow, you and I will discuss terms." Having delivered his judgement he began to walk away before remembering his manners and turning back. "Sir."

The captain stood his ground but did not contradict Volkov. It was clear to all that this was an ultimatum not to be defied and Freddie sensed the slight tremor in the officer's stance that destroyed the authority he sought. The prisoners were pushed through the entrance to the corridor off which sat two offices. As they were marched to the door at the end Freddie overheard Volkov's discussion with the man that appeared to be his deputy.

"We're not paying double, are we boss?"

"Do I look soft? Captain Malchikov looks depressed to me. The pressure of his new responsibility. I wouldn't be surprised if he shot himself tonight. There'll be all kinds of noise in the arena so it will be sad that no one will hear him as he blows his brains out with his own pistol."

"Are you sure?"

"Trust me, Sergei. The Colonel and the Commissar are both on side. They have too much to lose. Too many kickbacks. No one is going to ask awkward questions."

Sergei grunted approval. "Who do you want to do it?"

"I don't mind, but take six of the boys. Make sure it's done right. No other injuries."

"Six? You sure, boss? That doesn't leave many to run the show."

"The show runs itself. And you'll need to overpower him without a fight. Signs of a struggle will be difficult to ignore. Don't question me, Sergei." A threatening tone seeped into his voice.

"Sorry boss," replied Sergei hurriedly. "Of course. I'll see to it. Leave it with me." There was a pause before he asked another question. "Are we really being moved?"

Volkov grunted his confirmation. "Not Leningrad though. The Commissar tells me we are being moved to Stalingrad to join the 58th Guards Division."

"The Guards? Us?"

"They call anything a Guards Division these days, Sergei. Don't buy into that elitist crap."

"No, boss. But when are we going?"

"Monday."

"Shit! You mean..."

"This little scam ends tonight," answered Volkov.

"So why kill Malchikov?"

"Because he crossed me." Then, in irritation, Volkov barked

his orders for the dispersal of the prisoners as they were pushed through the door.

Freddie found himself in a large room with bare brick walls and a stone floor. It was some fifteen yards wide and ran away from them for at least a hundred feet. At the far end was a set of locked wooden double doors, but what struck Freddie was the ceiling that was raised to the height of two stories and the gallery of windows high up on the wall on the right that gave the place a bright, airy feel.

The space looked as though it should have served as an area for marshalling stocks and resources as they moved in or out. It was clear though that the room's function now was very different. Running along the length of both walls were solidly constructed cages, prison cells made of steel bars and open to view. On Volkov's command the ten slaves were each locked in their own individual pen.

Freddie, his wrists and ankles still shackled to prevent anything but an awkward shuffle, looked at the matchwood bed standing alone in his designated box of about ten feet square and his heart sang. This was palatial in comparison with the gulag. He had not slept in a bed for a thousand nights, and as he surveyed their new quarters the walls looked far more able to withstand the Siberian cold than the flimsy wooden shack he had come from.

The guards looked disinterested as the shackles were removed and the cells locked with large keys that clanked on a solid six inch iron ring. The prisoners murmured their approval at being able to stretch their limbs, but Freddie noticed that the six hunters all looked strangely at their beds as if recalling a past life while the four new boys lay down without a thought. The comfort of their new surroundings blinded the debutantes to the gruesome tell-tale signs of abuse. As they snuggled cheerfully into their beds, Freddie noted the faint traces of congealed blood that clung to the cracks between the stone slabs. He peered into the next cage and saw the same. The precise meaning of all this was unclear, but there was no doubt this building was a factory of death.

"Stand up you bastards!" shouted Volkov menacingly. He slowly scrutinised them before delivering his address. "You, gentlemen, are here for one purpose and one purpose only. To fight. And you will fight to the death." Freddie glanced at Bilyk whose defiant gaze slipped away as their eyes met. He knew he would triumph over any of the other men here, but his expert tutelage of his fearsome protégé would prove to be his downfall.

"You may think you can't fight," Volkov stared at the new boys, "or that you won't." His eyes bored into Bilyk. "But in front of a baying crowd I guarantee that you will." He smiled an evil rictus made the more menacing by the perfect set of bright teeth that shone from his full but regally manicured black beard. "You'll piss yourself. I've even seen men shit themselves as they stand waiting for the bell to sound. But you'll fight. The defeated die slowly." He picked up a shovel from the large wooden table that sat in the broad thoroughfare between the two rows of cells.

"I doubt you've ever seen a man quartered with one of these. A hand severed. Then the other. Then your feet. And then disembowelled with this, as the crowd cheers." He drew a large hunting knife from his belt with relish. "Then dragged back to your cell to die. It takes hours. The screams are pitiful. Personally I love it, but it turns the men's stomachs so they usually end up shoving one of these in your mouth." He brandished a sock. "Lose and you'll die in the muffled whimpers of agony. Win and you'll live to fight again."

The speech had all the hallmarks of a well rehearsed address, designed to deliver maximum horror and fear. Designed to make the men fight. For a moment Freddie considered that it was just talk, but as Volkov continued he realised this man relished the brutality he threatened and that the description of the death that awaited was all too real.

The Russian began walking slowly down the arcade of cages

with his hands clasped behind his back like a schoolmaster addressing an assembly of boys. "Tonight our paying customers will want the greatest show we have ever staged. Soon they will be leaving for the front. Many of them will die. And they want their entertainment, so make it good gentlemen, or God help me you will pay. You will fight until only one of you remains. Our champion of the day." He grinned again as his deliberate paces struck off the stone floor. "And he will have the honour of fighting the last ever bout with the greatest gladiator we have ever seen."

He was now at the far end of the room and half turned with an outstretched hand to present their nemesis. "I give you The Nomad." In the gloom of the last empty cell in the far corner Freddie made out the dark mass of a figure he had not noticed. The short but powerfully built man was sitting silently on his bed as if in a world of his own. His tangled and matted black hair and wide bovine forehead looked characteristic of the wild savages of the east. And even Freddie chilled at the prospect in his calm aura of self-sufficient strength.

Volkov marched purposefully back towards the offices. "Get your rest, ladies. And prepare to die like men!"

Freddie sat down and stared at the floor. He did not need to look at the others. Their names were a mystery to him and needed to stay that way. Conversation now might form some sort of connection. A connection that he recognised might rob him of the resolve to kill. In all their time in the camp he and Bilyk had never killed anyone from their own hut. They found that the simple act of being in the same space seemed enough to mark them as members of their tribe. Words were not needed for that bond to form. It was hard wired. The impulse to define the ingroup and the outgroup was a human instinct that he now understood more clearly than he could have imagined. To him the ingroup were humans and an extension of himself. Everyone else was foreign. Strangers. No more than animals. And it had to stay that way.

He looked up once more straight into the eyes of Bilyk. No words were exchanged but the unspoken conversation of the most profound friendship said they could not fight. With furrowed forehead and slightly pinched eyebrows Bilyk begged Freddie to kill him quickly, but the almost imperceptible down turning of his mouth and the tiniest shake of his head said he could not. Bilyk's stare intensified, imploring him, beseeching him for a quick end. Bilyk slowly cocked his head to the right exposing his left jugular and his eyes flashed down inviting the suggested coup de grace. Freddie looked away and curled up on his bed.

The wait seemed endless as Freddie struggled to put Bilyk out of his mind. He must prepare for what was to come. What weapons would they have? Shovels? Knives? Chains? Pitchforks? Hammers? Spears? Guns? No, he was sure they would not be given guns, and his mind began the grim work of calculating the optimal strategies with each combination of weapons. Could any be thrown? What other tactics might he use? Would there be sawdust or sand on the floor that he could throw into his opponent's eyes? Might that floor be slippery? Would it be covered in the gore of earlier contests? How big was the arena? Could he use his speed and agility or would his sinewy close quarter strength be needed?

He was no longer surprised at the speed and detail with which he could ponder these questions and by the time dark had descended and the noise of the excited crowd next door had risen to an expectant pitch he was ready for all eventualities. The door to the offices opened and Volkov marched in with four of his henchmen. As he issued orders for two men to be prepared for combat Freddie was aware of the sudden stench of excrement from the next cell. One of the new boys was shaking uncontrollably and had messed himself.

A guard sneered abuse as another newcomer and one of the hunters were stripped and each ordered to don a small pair of loose fitting breeches. They might have looked like two boys ready for bed were it not for the intense aggression that poured from them as taught muscles sweated in anticipation. The new boy was handed a pitchfork and a knife while the hunter was given the shovel, as Volkov exhorted them to murder. With that they were marched through a set of double doors at the office end of the prison and into the seething noise and blinding light that flooded through from the arena.

Freddie tried to catch a glimpse of the battleground to come, but it was no use. The doors closed and the crowd went silent. Volkov could be heard shouting an address to the masses, no doubt playing the role of impresario with gusto, before a bell sounded and wild cheering erupted. In the midst of the cacophony Freddie could make out the sound of a large flat piece of metal striking something solid. It could only be the shovel and it must have been striking stone. Each toll of this strange chime was greeted with a cheer, which must have meant the hunter was swinging wildly and hitting the floor. The floor was stone. Freddie recalculated. It could only be the same stone as here in the prison, which was rubbed smooth by years of use. Blood on that surface would make it extremely slippery. He noted the fact.

There was a lull in the cheers, then a groan as some interesting tactic had failed. After a pause the sound of a man in agony filled the building. But this sound had a special quality. It was controlled, self-inflicted agony, as if he were pulling a blade from his own flesh, and as he cried in triumph the crowd roared again. Freddie pictured the scene. The new boy had thrown his knife, but inflicted only a flesh wound. Now the baying rose to unprecedented heights as the shovel struck stone repeatedly. The new boy must have lost his pitchfork, for such a deluge of unguarded attacks could only be launched against a defenceless opponent. Or perhaps the hunter's wound was not superficial after all, but deep and he knew he must finish the fight soon before his haemorrhaging wound would take him.

The answer came soon enough as the unmistakable sound of the clattering of a dropped shovel rang out and the crowd gave voice to its excitement and disbelief. The hunter was felled. Freddie could imagine those brave enough to bet on the novice whooping with the delight of their high odds winnings, and the curses and mutterings of the majority who must have backed the favourite.

Then the chanting began. "Hands! Hands! Hands!" Volkov's speech earlier had obviously not just been for effect. This was a renowned ritual that the crowd loved, and now they savoured the anticipation as the shovel was hefted high in the air. One by one the sound of metal on stone rang out to ecstatic cheers. Four chimes, and the hunter's screams were drowned by the noise, as another crescendo greeted what must have been the disembowelling.

The double doors opened, and the new boy trooped back in covered in the blood of his adversary who was pulled behind on a makeshift litter. As the hunter was dragged to his cell Freddie saw the deep wound in his left thigh that was flowing with blood. His abdomen had been sliced open from sternum to pubis and his bowels flopped in a heap over his waistband topped with two carelessly tossed hands and two feet. He had lost so much blood that his cries were scarcely audible. His death was agony, but it was quick.

Volkov looked around for the next match.

And so the evening progressed; the crowd screaming its encouragement like punters at a cock fight. It was the kind of noise that can only be made by people with a stake in the outcome, especially where the end point was death and mutilation. For brutalised soldiers left in a barren wasteland it had everything to lighten their monotonous existence. Everything to assuage their frustration. That, and the kickbacks, surmised Freddie, probably explained the blind eyes turned by Volkov's superiors.

Three bouts had been staged when Volkov picked his next match. Freddie made no move. Nothing to give away his desperate desire to fight anyone but Bilyk. But maybe he tried too hard and the Russian monster who seemed to have a genius for spotting the smallest weakness picked out the remaining two new boys to fight.

"I'll leave you both to think about your fight," smiled Volkov to Freddie and Bilyk, and with an evil snigger to himself he pushed the combatants to the fourth bout.

It took much longer than the others, and Freddie sensed a growing problem. The crowd were booing loudly and the festive atmosphere at the beginning of the evening was turning suddenly ugly. Volkov could be heard shouting orders, as Freddie realised the two slaves were not fighting. Gun shots rang out, as one of the guards came running through the doors back to the office.

"Roman," he shouted to another man. "Come quickly. The crowd is turning nasty."

Roman appeared from his post. "I knew he shouldn't have sent so many of the boys to deal with Malchikov. I don't know where the hell they've got to." He checked the barrels of his revolver. "Come on then." The two disappeared back into the arena and were gone for some time. The noise did not abate, and after many more shots Freddie could hear Volkov shouting at the mass of men that seemed close to rioting. Even his presence evidently would not to settle the passion and he was greeted with fulsome jeers. The situation sounded as if it were on the verge of spiralling out of control when two single shots sounded again and the crowd cheered raucously.

It was no surprise when the bodies of both gladiators were dragged into the prison and dumped unceremoniously on the floor. Where both faces should have been there were gaping exit wounds that gave the evidence to the only spectacle that could be staged to assuage the impending riot.

Volkov was wide eyed, the full power of his dark energy

roused to action. "You two!" he snapped at Freddie and Bilyk. "Shovels!" he shouted at the panicked guards around. "No fucking nonsense, or you'll both beg for death before I'm done." There was no doubting it and they were both stripped as they stood facing each other.

"It's been an honour, Fedir," smiled Bilyk.

"It's Freddie," he smiled in reply as he took one last look at his only friend. They would both die tonight and he desperately wanted to hear Bilyk call him by his real name.

"Freddie," smiled Bilyk as he nodded. "A good Polish name. It's been an honour Freddie."

Volkov's rage overflowed as he smacked them both round the head. "Don't you dare do this love shit. Fucking fight! Do you hear me?"

Freddie stiffened and turned on Volkov with a ferocity that surprised the Russian. "Give us the shovels you fucking cunt. We'll give you a spectacle."

Volkov backed away, smiling in mock deference. "Well, ladies. It looks like we have a contest." With a flick of his head the order was given for them to be armed and marched into the colosseum.

The roar that greeted them was as stunning as the dazzling light in that cauldron and served temporarily to disorientate. The cavernous space filled the building to the roof and must have been close to fifty yards square. Erected on three sides were raised terraced wooden seats that pressed in on the central pit that was bounded by a five foot high wooden palisade. As Freddie had predicted the floor was stone, but covered in a thick bed of sawdust that now soaked up the blood and offal of four previous bouts. The pit measured about twenty yards square, and as they were marched to its centre Freddie felt how his footing moved under those patches that oozed with the fluids of the fallen.

The two gladiators faced each other in the cacophony of frenzied betting and shouting that turned the crowd once more into eager participants. Volkov raised his hands and signalled for silence.

"Gentlemen," his voice boomed in the huge space. "For tonight's final first round qualifying bout we have saved the best until last." The crowd roared its approval as hundreds of booted feet stamped on the wooden boards like drums. "The gulag's two longest survivors." A hush descended to encourage Volkov in his customary build up to the bell. His voice rose and swooped like a circus master's as he painted the picture of the conflict. "Surviving four years each, by fair means," there was a cheer, "and foul," then a theatrical boo, "the team that was the scourge of the mine." The noise rose again in anticipation and abated as Volkov waited. "I am proud to give you from Kiev, the Professor."

Volkov's hand extended towards Bilyk as half the throng erupted in encouragement. "And from Pinsk, the Beast of the Marsh." His other hand pointed at Freddie. The din that exploded was almost painful as a thousand voices packed within the walls reverberated in their cries. Volkov waited a few seconds before snapping his hands together as he retreated quickly from the arena. The bell sounded and the fight commenced.

The noise of the ringing and the deafening shouts suddenly faded to a distant melody as Freddie's mind played its usual trick and filtered out all irrelevant inputs. The cheering and jeering may as well have been a roll of thunder in far off lands as Freddie focused on Bilyk. They had both instinctively adopted a crouching pose as they began to circle each other.

Bilyk, like Freddie, was right-handed but as they prowled and sized each-other up Freddie noticed that he was holding the end of the shovel's shaft with his left hand which meant that his dominant right hand was close to the metal blade. It was the grip to take if you intended to swing the weapon like an axe. Freddie's grip was very different with his right hand holding the end of the shaft and his left hand guiding the metal head. His was the grip to use if you wanted to employ the thing as a spear.

To use the shovel like an axe was foolhardy against an uninjured opponent as the hunter had discovered in the first bout. The shovels were clearly too heavy to land a swinging blow with any accuracy, and a nimble target would always evade their blades. Bilyk swung at Freddie like a novice.

Freddie stepped aside and as Bilyk's weapon crashed into the floor he gave a half-hearted stab that caught his friend's right shoulder. A beer bottle hit him on the head as a drunken soldier a few rows back tried to aid the man he had bet on. A scuffle broke out with others who had money on Freddie.

Three more pile drivers came crashing in from Bilyk, each repulsed with meagre force from Freddie's spear. Their eyes were fixed on each other as if a continuous tunnel of light connected them to the exclusion of all around. Bilyk was inviting the strike that Freddie was still reluctant to deliver, when his hand was forced by his brother.

Bilyk smiled benignly, winked mischievously and then stood upright and dropped his weapon. His stare into Freddie's eyes remained unbroken as he cocked his head to the right offering his neck. The ire of the crowd crashed down into the pit as projectiles were hurled and fights broke out. Bilyk had invited death, and if Freddie did not deliver it quickly, Volkov would do it very slowly.

He had no choice, and in an instant he reversed the grip on his shovel and swung the axe high above his right shoulder. Still Bilyk's gaze fixed him with a look of eternal gratitude. They were both unblinking, savouring that long, last look of friendship before the edge of Freddie's blade cut into Bilyk's exposed neck. There was a cry of agonised effort from Freddie's throat as he put every ounce of force he could muster to ensure a quick, clean kill.

The years of fighting and survival had made him the strong and efficient killer he was, and that history paid its dividend as the shovel tore through muscle and vein, through artery and bone. Still it ploughed on as Bilyk's larynx popped open and shattered just as Freddie felt the resistance of the splintering vertebrae. Bilyk's body was already falling, now no more than an inanimate carcass pulled by gravity.

His lifeless form crumpled into the bloodied sawdust, his head hanging by the few remaining fibres of muscle and skin. Freddie stood over his friend, transfixed by the shock of what he had done. The grief that welled up inside made him oblivious to the seething mob that broke into angry riot. Fights coalesced into vicious battles as knives were drawn in dispute over the settling of bets. Cohorts of men with money on Bilyk protested the fixed result violently, while guns that had been smuggled past Volkov's skeleton crew were unleashed.

Bullets flew indiscriminately, killing and maiming, as Volkov's men lost all control. Freddie was vaguely aware of the huge Russian's booming voice ordering him to be bundled out of the arena as lead hissed and whined around his head. Rough hands seized his paralysed frame and he was dragged back into the prison as the doors were slammed shut and barricaded against the mob.

"Roman!" Volkov's face was bulging purple with rage. "Find Sergei! Get him back here." He spun round and unleashed the coiled power of his enormous frame as his fist crashed into Freddie's face. He had never before felt such a blow. It seemed to force his left eye from its very socket. Dazed and smashed to the floor, he was only dimly aware of being dragged to his feet and thrown over the heavy wooden table.

"Nail him!" screamed Volkov.

Freddie's muffled consciousness was skewered back into sharp relief as a nail was driven clumsily but uncompromisingly through his right hand, fixing it to the table beneath. The scream that reverberated around the prison could have been someone else's were it not for the pain it caused in Freddie's throat, and he found himself struggling in desperation against the efforts of two men holding his left hand out. Such was his arousal that it took more than a few seconds for them to plant his palm on the wood before a second nail was hammered pitilessly through his flesh.

Now he was fixed, his arms outstretched pulling his torso flat across the table as his legs just managed to reach the floor. He turned his head to the left, but could see nothing as his eye continued to close up, lost in the swelling of his face. To his right he could see the new boy who had won the first bout shaking the bars of his cage furiously. The remaining slaves were shouting and crashing against their bars like agitated monkeys, alert to the danger they faced of the mob breaking in. Even The Nomad at the far end of the room was struggling hopelessly against the solid pen that rendered him helpless.

"You!" Volkov was issuing another order to a guard behind Freddie. "If they get out of hand kill them." Then a pause before he continued in an infinitely more measured and chilling tone. "He stays alive, or you will die." The statement spoke of the torture he had planned for Freddie. As the sounds of rioting and gunfire waxed and waned Freddie took stock of his predicament. He guessed his cheek bone was shattered, and he could only hope that the eye had not been damaged by Volkov's punch. He focused on his hands. The initial pain of the nails being hammered through them had waned sufficiently for him to assess the injuries. Again, the strategist was at work divorced from emotion.

He lifted his head enough to look at the wounds and studied their positions with macabre interest. They were both positioned an inch, maybe two, down each hand from the web space between his index and middle fingers, and he wondered if the metacarpal bones were broken. He paused for a moment, knowing there was only one way to answer the question. Freddie took a deep breath and lifted the ball of his right hand.

A shooting pain like liquid fire surged up his arm as his hand collapsed back onto the table. He had his answer. One of the bones had been broken by the nail, and as the sickening pain began to subside the epicentre of its throbbing remnants was clearly below his middle finger. A fractured third metacarpal, he noted with clinical dispassion. As breaks go that would be relatively minor. He knew the other bones of the hand would splint the fracture and it should heal in time. The twin dangers in the short term were the loss of use of the hand due to pain and the risk of infection.

That damage noted, he steadied himself for the trial of his left hand. His shoulders heaved as he took a huge breath of air and closed his glottis. The pressure in his abdomen rose, sealing the larynx to prevent any audible sign of pain, and lifted the heel of his left hand. A sharp pain stabbed down through the nail, but the excruciating agony he was expecting was absent. He exhaled and looked again.

In the struggle to steady his hand and the rush to immobilise him he realised that the guards had missed the bones and driven the nail through the soft tissues. Its flat top still held him in place unyieldingly, but the bones were intact.

It seemed like an age before the unrest outside was brought under control, and Freddie was beginning to shake with the effort of supporting his weight. His legs were becoming stiff, but each time he tried to flex them to allow some rest the weight of his hind quarters dragged on his torso and sent shocks of pain through his hands. As the time ticked slowly along the fatigue in his leg muscles drove a tremor that grew. Support his weight and his legs screamed. Give in to the fatigue and the nails twisted and bit into the raw flesh and cracked bone of his hands.

This slow suffering was almost unbearable and might eventually have broken him but, the rioting subdued, Volkov could not wait to exact his revenge. A surge of adrenaline jolted Freddie as he heard his tormentor enter to the sound of something heavy being dragged across the stone floor. Volkov's heavy footsteps were unmistakable as he walked slowly to stand on Freddie's left. He could feel his presence even though his smashed and swollen eye could see nothing.

"Look at me, you scum." His deep voice was steady and measured. This was to be no frenzied attack, but an object lesson in the forensic administration of suffering. Freddie made a meagre effort to turn his head. An effort that displeased the Russian, who deliberately placed an index finger on the macerated pulp of Freddie's cheek and pushed viciously.

Freddie's head reared in response as blinding flashes of light stabbed through the darkness. Years of neglect in the gulag had left him with wild tangled hair and a matted unkempt beard through which his rasping breath now foamed frothy sputum as his good eye turned and fixed Volkov.

"I swear to God I'll kill you," muttered Freddie.

The Russian smiled malevolently. "Now that would be quite a trick. But thank you for your attention." He took his time surveying Freddie's half broken body, gleaming with the blood of combat and the sweat of the effort of holding his weight. "It really hurts doesn't it?" His tone was almost caring as he walked behind Freddie and kicked away one of his legs. Before he could respond and rebalance, his body tugged violently on his right hand, and try as he might he could not prevent himself from crying out.

Volkov collected something and walked slowly around the table to stand at the end opposite Freddie. "And so our game begins," he smiled as if they were about to play chess. One by one he laid out his tools before him, deliberately, menacingly, allowing Freddie to see and study each one in turn. He could not fail to contemplate the uses to which they could be put, fearful anticipation that was every bit a part of the torture. And in that moment Freddie learned that the most skilled sadists attack the psyche as thoroughly and meticulously as they attack the body.

The hammer was placed carefully on the bench, and just as carefully repositioned. Then the pliers. Volkov stared into Freddie's defiant eye and smiled menacingly. He lay down a pair of metal tongs. And a clamp that looked like a thumbscrew. Freddie held his gaze. Then a hand powered drill bit. A gleaming sickle whose blade looked lovingly cared for and glinted like a razor. And finally a broad hunting knife that Volkov stabbed into the wood and left standing for effect. Still the two protagonists eyeballed each other.

Volkov broke the stare and flashed a look to the men behind Freddie. It was a signal to kick away his other leg, but the warning was enough to allow an adjustment, and this time no sound rattled out of his throat. Volkov frowned and made another gesture that told the men to drag the heavy metal object into Freddie's view. It was a brazier in which glowed red hot three long wooden-handled metal pokers, and he smiled again, confident that he would break Freddie's defiance.

"How are your legs?" There was no reply. Volkov picked up the hammer and brought it down on the nail in Freddie's left hand. He screamed out as he felt it kink inside his flesh. "How are your legs?"

"Fine!" he hissed.

"Liar! I know they are screaming in agony. The only thing keeping you standing is the fear of those nails if your legs buckle. You're running on adrenaline. Pure adrenaline." He leaned forward and muttered sotto voce as if sharing a secret. "It will run out soon and then I won't have to do anything but watch your torment."

"Piss off!"

"Ah. I see you doubt me. Let me show you what I mean. Sergei. Remove those pants." A knife glided against Freddie's buttocks as the fabric fell away and he was left naked. Volkov nodded another order to the man behind Freddie who took one of the pokers and disappeared from view as his master raised a hand to signal a pause for anticipation.

Freddie could not help himself. The thought of the poker driving into his anus filled his mind and he braced himself for an agony even he could not imagine. He began to shake as more hormones flooded into his blood stream. The Russian smiled in amused contempt. One movement from his steak like hands would unleash unparalleled suffering.

His index finger stabbed the air, and the poker was thrust into Freddie's tender flesh. But the target of the searing heat was not what Freddie had feared. It was forced instead into the back of his right thigh, and in a millisecond he cycled through elation, evasion and torment.

His leg instinctively jumped forward to escape the burning metal, but as it did his hands sang out their distress. The reflex to this was to plant his foot and take his weight once more which pushed the thigh back onto the steaming iron, and so it went on. He was caught in an uncontrollable dance of searing, oscillating pain as the guards whooped with joy at his distress.

Volkov eventually signalled to Sergei to remove the poker, and looked at Freddie, his body and spirit utterly defeated. "Are you broken yet?" Freddie did not move. He could not move. Volkov ripped Freddie's head up by a fistful of hair. "Are you broken yet?" he repeated, hissing into his victim's face. "Ha!" he yelled triumphantly, slamming Freddie's head back into the bench where the crushed bones of his cheek moved again. But this time Freddie had no energy to cry out. His pain was silent.

Volkov then began his address to the cowed and mute prisoners in the cells who had witnessed the whole scene. "This, ladies, is what happens when you cross me. You may think you are strong, but I will break you. Slowly and surely you will lose everything you hold dear. Your body, your mind, your very soul. I will destroy them all piece by piece. You think this shit here is finished? That I have broken him and his suffering is at an end?" He paused for an answer he knew none of them would dare offer. "His suffering is only just beginning."

Freddie was aware of the sound of Volkov unbuckling his belt as he circled behind his prone form. Then the beating began. The thick iron clasp tore into Freddie's buttocks as each lash bit into his flesh. "You will all die, gentlemen," shouted Volkov as he poured his immense energy into the whipping. "The choice you have is how. Quickly?" Freddie relished the respite as the blows stopped. "Or like this?"

A sickening, searing pain spasmed through Freddie's bowels as Volkov forced his erection deep into him. "You can die like men." His deep thrusts forced involuntary contractions in the pit of Freddie's abdomen that intensified the ripping pain and filled the back of his throat with an overwhelming nausea. "Or you can die moaning like a fucking whore." Each thrust was driven by the purchase the Russian had on Freddie's hips and the weight of this monster tore again at his hands.

Within seconds the beast orgasmed, slamming so deep that Freddie vomited. The guards were laughing as Volkov pulled himself free.

"Jesus!" shouted Sergei. "He's got a fucking hard on." And just as Freddie drew a deep breath a heavy, military boot crashed into his exposed testicles. Every part of his body cried out for mercy, as he vomited again. And again.

When his retching had finally ended, Volkov's face was next to his. "Sleep well you little slut," he smiled. "I'm going to eat a big juicy steak, get a good night's sleep, and then tomorrow the fun really starts. I hope your friend's worth it, but I guarantee he's not."

Orders were given for the guarding of the captives, and like a man who has finished a hard but satisfying day at the office Volkov left, taking most of his henchmen with him. A sudden silence descended and the absence of Volkov's evil presence seemed to allow the room to breathe again. Freddie could feel his spirit rise. He was not broken.

He listened intently to the conversation behind him. Two young, junior guards had been left to oversee what was left of this Siberian gladiator cadre, and it was clear they had no intention of staying in this austere, depressing place all night.

"Come on, Alexei. Let's get pissed."

"We can't. Are you mad? He'll kill us. You've just seen what he does to people. You want to end up like that?"

"All right. Just a small drink. I've got some in the office."

He hesitated. "Go on then." And the prisoners were left alone.

Freddie's mind raced. He had only the smallest window of opportunity. But an opportunity he had. The nail in his left hand had bent under the hammer. Now was his chance. Might there be a weakness in the metal?

He took another deep breath and slowly drew the tips of his fingers back towards the ball of his hand so that the fingers clawed like a spider ready to pounce. Then began the awful process of pulling and manipulating the nail. Through an alternating combination of pushing into the bench with his fingers and then rocking the hand back on its heel he slowly worked away. His teeth clamped together at the sickening sensation as he worked to dislodge the metal. Intermittently he was forced to stop and breathe deeply to dissipate the pain, but no sooner would it subside than he launched himself back into the task.

"Give it up," said a flat, dejected voice that came from a cell on his left. "You're going to die. Just accept it. We're all going to die."

Freddie was about to take the hunter to task for his lack of fight when something snapped in his hand. He stopped, completely motionless. He dared not hope that the nail had yielded. It could have been one of his metacarpals snapping, but surely that would have caused pain. He took another deep breath and slowly lifted his hand. There was no resistance. His spirits soared as he slowly turned his hand over to reveal the bloodied mess and gaping hole in his palm. In the base of the crater he could just see the tortured and fractured metal and he almost cried with delight. Never before had such an ugly wound looked so beautiful.

In a moment he took control of his emotions. Nothing had yet been achieved. He must act with precision and speed. He turned his hand back over and raised it to his mouth. Gripping the head of the nail with his incisors he winced as he ripped his hand away. He spat the nail out like an orange pip before he set to work on the other hand. He had already lifted himself onto the bench and his free left hand had pulled the hunting knife from the wood. He slid the flat of the blade carefully under his palm as he prepared to use the tool as a lever to prise the nail from the bench, hand and all. He steadied himself for the expected pain when an urgent whisper stopped him.

"Huh. Friend. Wait." The Nomad stood, lifted his matchwood bed, smashed it on the floor as if it were paper and threw one leg to Freddie. The advice for Freddie to bite on the wood to prevent him crying out was unmistakeable.

He bit down hard as he levered his right hand up. The pain flooded through him, and he realised that he was close to passing out. This would be impossible. He had no idea how many times he would have to push through this pain, but it would undoubtedly defeat him.

Surprisingly, the nail slid out freely with a satisfying pop as it emerged from the wood. Freddie was left staring at the bloodied inch and a half of gleaming metal that jutted from his right palm before he pronated the hand and, discarding his wooden gag, pulled it out.

He tried his hands out for strength. The left was near perfect. The right was fine until any pressure was put on the bone and then its grip failed. He was aware of the four other prisoners imploring him to help them, to find the keys and release them, but his mind was focused on one task, and one task alone. The guards must die. Years of hunting and doing whatever it took to prevail flooded his instincts.

The sickle in his strong left hand and the hunting knife and a red hot poker fresh from the fire in his right, he kicked the brazier over and moved nimbly to crouch by the door. His lacerated and bruised buttocks hurt, and as he sat on his coiled haunches waiting for the moment to launch himself, he noticed the trickle of blood that fell from his anus and splashed on the floor. There would be time enough to reflect on that, and on the man whose seed now dripped from him. Here and now all that mattered was the dispatch of the guards.

The noise of the brazier overturning did its job as one of the guards came through the door from the corridor that led to the office. His pistol sat idly in its holster and his right hand was occupied with the glass of vodka he had poured from his cache. As the door opened he was talking over his left shoulder and joking with Alexei. There was no time to react to the feral blur that flashed in his right field of view as he turned back towards the prison room.

The point of the beautifully curved sickle blade struck him in the right eye with all the force of Freddie's pent up aggression and anger. This was a time to strike as hard and as fast as was humanly possible. The sickle followed the arc of its travel through orbit and brain and shattered back into the open through the guard's left temple, splaying the bones as it emerged. The vodka dropped to the floor as the glass smashed into a thousand pieces. The body did not collapse, but animated by a motor cortex cleft in two by the blade it flailed in a tetanic jig before crashing into the far wall and slumping to the ground.

He deftly transferred the poker to his good left hand and placed his left foot on the Russian corpse to avoid the shards of glass. As he planted himself square in the doorway Alexei stepped into the corridor. He had a look of abject horror on his face as he clawed desperately for his revolver. Freddie whipped his right arm out and flicked his wrist to send the knife on its way. His aim was off, and instead of planting deep in his target's chest it lodged firmly in the top of his left leg. Alexei screamed as the tip of the knife embedded itself deep in the recess of the joint and he started to topple. Without mercy, Freddie leapt forwards to give his victim no chance, no quarter.

Protecting his right hand from the impact, he presented his forearm that struck Alexei in the chest with his full weight, sending the young guard crashing back onto the floor with Freddie on top of him. He might have twisted and wriggled free, but for the poker that was thrust full force into the lower reaches of his exposed neck. The intense heat burned a path as the jugular vein began its slow flood of fluid over the floor before the wall of his carotid artery burned through and burst.

In that instant it was over. Any meagre coagulating effect of the poker was overwhelmed by vast volumes of blood pumped high into the air in a crimson fountain. The poker continued its journey and burned through the wall of Alexei's larynx as he drowned in his own blood. The poker came to a halt as the fountain lost its power and flickered to a standstill.

There was no time to savour his victory. Other guards could return at any time. Alexei was a similar height to Freddie, although heavier, and within seconds the white corpse drained of all essence was naked. Giving no thought or care for the blood that saturated his new clothes Freddie threw layer after layer over his frame. There was a spare uniform hanging in the office, and in a drawer two pairs of socks. His escape would be across tundra in March and caught in the open without shelter there would be a significant risk of exposure and frostbite.

Under his multiple layers he tucked both revolvers into the belt that now held up his second pair of trousers. A quick search of the drawers yielded no more ammunition, but on a large nail, as crudely hammered into the back of the door as the ones used earlier to immobilise Freddie, hung the large iron ring that bore the set of keys to the cells. He seized them, and made to return to the prison when he was drawn back. He had no idea when he would next eat and, following what was by now second nature, he pulled the knife from Alexei's hip, ripped open his abdomen and took his liver.

The prime piece of offal was slid inside his three coats, before he quickly washed his hands in a basin in the office. He paused as he considered what he knew he must now do. He held his hands out before him and looked at his palms. He took another deep breath and marched into the prison. Without allowing himself a chance to think again he took the last remaining poker that still glowed red in the coals that had been strewn around, placed his hand on the bench and applied the tip to the wound. Four times he collapsed in pain, but four times he sealed the wounds and gave himself a fighting chance against the infection that he knew would do its worst.

The two surviving hunters and the last new boy were begging him to release them, while the Nomad just stood and watched him with an intensity that reminded him of himself. He looked around to assess the situation and spoke harshly as he brought the cooling poker crashing against one of the cages to silence them in its metallic resonance.

"Shut up! All of you." His scarred and mutilated hand was held up to silence them. There was no mistaking the seriousness of the words he spoke. "If any of you makes another sound I will kill you. If you remain silent then I will free you and you will take your chance out there. Not a sound." They did not doubt him and their pleading stopped.

He approached the Nomad who stood solidly behind his bars, staring back at Freddie, watching him closely. "Thank you," nodded Freddie. The man was not as short as he had at first thought, although he was certainly powerfully built. Close up Freddie had expected to see the epicanthic folds of the eastern steppes, but they were absent.

"Prego." The softly spoken, almost cultured Italian that fell from the man's lips and the polite nod of his head stunned

Freddie as completely as anything that had happened that evening.

-oOo-

"His name was Antonio Zegarelli." It was the first time Freddie had smiled for hours. His harrowing tale had consumed the morning so completely that it felt wrong for the sun still to be shining. I looked out of the window almost in anger at its lack of sympathy with what we had just heard.

"I'm sorry Freddie. I think I need a break."

"Of course." He nodded acceptance. "I'm sorry if I have been too direct, too graphic. You are only the second person I have ever told. Even Zegarelli and I, when we finally met again could not speak of that night or that place."

"You met again?"

Freddie nodded and a warmth returned to his face. "Yes. It was a bittersweet reunion, but lovely. It was in the autumn of 1965. I had finally tracked him down through a veterans' association, and he agreed to meet. Poland and Italy were playing a World Cup qualifier in Rome, and while I was never a great fan of soccer it seemed a good excuse."

"You met in Rome?" The suffocating presence of the gulag and their Siberian banishment felt so far removed from the notion of La Dolce Vita conjured up by Rome in the 1960s that I could not really believe what he was saying. It was as if he had told me they had met later on Mars.

"Yes. He was from the north-east, but it was important for both of us to meet somewhere away from family and friends. I think we both needed to keep that chapter in our lives separate. We shared two wonderful but difficult days. He had cancer and was skin and bones. Even as we remade our acquaintance I knew we were saying goodbye. We were strangers, but strangers who knew each other's darkest recesses better than anyone. It was a most unusual meeting."

"It must have been hard."

Freddie suddenly choked up with emotion. "It was." He regained his composure by deflecting into humour. "Not as hard as it was for Poland that night. They lost 6 - 1." I laughed to allow him to regroup. "We spoke of our flight from Siberia but even then, more than twenty years later, we could not talk of that colosseum or the wretched things we did there."

My curiosity had been aroused. "But who was he? What was an Italian doing there?"

"Antonio Zegarelli was a shepherd from the Dolomites, and in his youth a boxer of some renown, or so he told me. It was natural then that he should join up with the Third Alpine Division, the proud 'Julia', when war broke out. In 1942 they were sent to join the Italian 8th Army fighting on the eastern front and were sucked into the role of defending the supply corridor that fed the German attack on Stalingrad. That was when the Russians launched operation Uranus, their counter-offensive, and the Italians cracked. Zegarelli was taken prisoner along with thousands of other Italians and Hungarians. Earmarked for the gulag, he was bought by Volkov and survived three months in the colosseum."

I got the feeling that three months was a very long time to stay alive through those gruesome competitions and said so.

"I wouldn't know Tom. I was there for only ten hours, but to survive twelve weeks in that environment I think was pretty remarkable."

"You escaped together?"

"I knew I needed someone to help me. Once I stopped and rested awhile my muscles would seize up from the beating I had taken. And in any case, a partnership will always survive better. Taras and I had proved that. I did feel guilty afterwards. He was barely cold and already I was taking another partner, but it was the logical thing to do and exactly what he would have wanted."

I nodded my agreement. Then I voiced a strong feeling I had had during Freddie's telling of events in the arena. "Don't you think that Bilyk's behaviour was selfish?"

It was as if I had spoken ill of someone newly dead, and a dark defensiveness welled up in Freddie as it would in a proud and loving father. "You wouldn't understand, Tom." For once there was an edge of a put down in his words. His smiling stoicism wavered as he defended the memory of Taras Bilyk, a man whom in a mad world he had loved very deeply. "I owed him everything. Without him I would have died that first winter. Without him I would not even have been there in that Siberian cockpit. What he asked of me in return was a trifle. There are things far more precious than your life that you can give, or that can be taken from you. And I would willingly have given him a hundred times that final reckoning."

"I'm sorry Freddie. I didn't mean to insult his memory. I was just asking."

"I know." He nodded and smiled and the intensity melted away. It was in those few isolated moments, though, that I caught a glimpse of the fearsome resolve and passion that stirred deep within. I have often wondered since how he managed to control that cauldron of emotion, how he kept a lid on the forces that surged within him. But somehow for the most part he was calm and measured, giving no hint to the volcanic forces at play inside.

"Did all five of you team up?"

"No." The answer was emphatic. "A pair is the natural bond. A hunting team, a survival team, is like a marriage. Anyway, I didn't trust the two remaining hunters. They were a pair from hut 18 and there was something about them. They were not like the other teams."

"So you chose this Zegarelli?"

Freddie turned to look at me. "God had sent him to me. Who was I to question Him? Trust your instinct, Tom. That first voice in your head is usually right." I knew he was talking of me also, and I felt a surge of pride and happiness that he would think that of me. "He and I headed back along the road to the gulag, leaving the other three to fend for themselves. I often think about the new boy, consigned to partnership with those other two. They would have carried him along until they needed a meal. That would have been the end of his journey. I wonder if I should have taken him with us, but they are the musings of a sentimental old man looking back from the comfort of his bed. I made the right decision. It's just a shame that it feels wrong."

"You can't save everyone, Freddie." His eyes were starting to slip back into that dark place they had been since breakfast, and my interjection seemed to call him back.

"No. You're right." He brushed the thought aside with a sigh, and continued. "We set the warehouse ablaze before we left, calculating that the more trouble we could create for Volkov the less likely we were to be pursued. It seemed to work, and after five days of slow progress we looked upon the railway stop that had been our arrival point so long before.

"Why did you go back to the gulag?"

"Oh, come on Tom!" His ruefulness broke into irritation at my lack of survival savvy. "Do you really think it's possible to walk out of Siberia?" My vacant expression prompted him to answer his own question. "Well, of course not. The only way out was to stow away on one of the trains taking the ore away."

"Of course." I felt embarrassed not to have thought of this point. Walking on foot, evading patrols or even just finding food and shelter, it would have been impossible to do more than five miles a day through forest and rough terrain. A year of this challenge would have done for anyone, and yet the 1500 miles covered would still leave you deep within Russia. Freddie was right. "But wasn't the train guarded?"

"We had to take our chances. As it turned out the contingent of guards was almost nil. There were no new prisoners so no need for them. The prisoner pens at the railway stayed empty. We watched as a train pulled in and I recalled the contrast with that day in 1939 when I had been herded here. In 1943 the place was deserted. Only a handful of guards drove a contingent of prisoners to load the ore onto the train, and it was easy to evade them and stow away in one of the cattle wagons."

"Why was it so empty?"

"As I said earlier, the big battle around Stalingrad and the major southern offensive that followed required every last man. It was as if the vast eastern hinterland had been drained of people."

"It must have been an almighty battle. The turning point on the Russian front. Every bit as big as D-Day."

Freddie snorted his derision and shook his head with a smile. "I love that about the English."

"What?" I had obviously said something he found hilarious, and had the feeling he was about to give me another history lesson to challenge my lazy preconceptions. He did not disappoint.

"You are a nation that conquered the world. Half the globe painted red. Your language teeming with adopted foreign words as a result. Scores of other cultures grafted onto your little Saxon island. And yet sometimes you are so prosaic." I looked back at him blankly. "In the whole of the war Britain sustained half a million dead. America. Half a million. Russia? Twenty-six million. D-Day, Alamein, Anzio? They were side shows. It might be a little churlish that the Russians call it The Great Patriotic War and conveniently forget the sacrifices made in the west, but they do have a point."

I absorbed the numbers. "So 26 out of 27 allied dead were Russian?"

"Exactly."

"Oh. I guess it's no wonder then that the place was so empty."

Freddie nodded. "Which was great news for me and Zegarelli. Of course there was the odd check here and there as the train crawled westwards, but we evaded most, and the few elderly or juvenile guards that got too close were no match for the pair of us."

"I should imagine that nobody would have been a threat to you."

Freddie nodded slowly, almost ashamed in my recognition of his position at the top of that particular food chain. He shook the thought away. "Anyway, we were soon in the sprawling mass of tracks, buildings and sidings of Moscow's central railyards. They were a city in themselves and easy enough to hide out in while we studied the movements of cargo in and out. We soon had a pretty clear idea of which warehouses and stockpiles fed the southern reaches of the empire, and Zegarelli's experiences told us that there was a major battle going on in those vast expanses between the Volga and the Don."

"So you headed south?"

"It was the obvious escape route. It was only when we finally arrived in Astrakhan that we parted company. I was aiming for Iran. If I could get myself to Tehran then I knew I would be within reach of the British. As an Italian, Zegarelli had no desire to swap a Russian prison camp for a British one, and he headed west across the Caucuses."

"But that's…"

"A very long way," nodded Freddie. "It took him months to make it through the mountains into Turkey. By the time he arrived at his embassy in Ankara Italy had surrendered and Mussolini was on the run. His homeland was nothing more than a battlefield, a playground fought over between the great powers."

"But he made it home?"

"Eventually. He spent two years in Turkey. He was lucky enough to get a menial job in the embassy until he could return to his beloved home in the mountains."

"That's quite an end to his story," I reflected, pondering on this personal account of one man's instinct to swim home against the currents of history. "And what about you?"

Godforsaken

Freddie drew a deep lungful of air through flared nostrils. "My story was really only just beginning."

VIII - Cassino Night

The morning had been traumatic for both of us. In some ways I thought the pain of recounting those unspeakable evils was offset for Freddie by the relief of laying down a burden he had carried for so long. He had mentioned that he had told only one other person, presumably someone special. Perhaps he would talk of them before we were done. But recounting his story had taken every ounce of his strength.

I was in the position of having to pick up that load and process it in some way. It had been a shock to hear the graphic account of his escape. The violence had been so gratuitous, so wanton, that it was difficult to set in any context. It left me reeling. I had guessed that Freddie's escape must have been dramatic, but I had no idea just how depraved his treatment had proved to be, or how extreme his response.

I took my leave for half an hour while he ate his lunch. He made some joke about the last meal of the condemned man and tucked voraciously into fish and chips as I went for some fresh air and a sandwich in the canteen. It was almost empty and without any conscious thought I found myself sitting in my usual place. There was something about that table and that chair that I found comforting. I laughed at myself as I noticed what I was doing, as if some insecure child within found safety in the familiarity of a particular seat.

I looked up at the table opposite and my mind conjured the ghostly image of the grey-haired old lady the day before. I saw her wiping away her tear once again and wondered why she had made such an impact on me. It was the frailty behind the strong exterior that I think had touched me so, and I found myself giving her an identity and grafting onto her an assumed back story that I knew had no justification.

For some reason the name Norah popped into my head, and

before I could stop the little fiction imp at play in my mind she had three daughters and many grandchildren, all too busy to help or even care, while Harry, her rough diamond of fifty years, succumbed slowly upstairs to lung cancer.

I shook my head in disbelief at the need we all have to project stories onto others. Perhaps it made us feel safe. Maybe a lie was preferable to nothingness, and so a story was fabricated. My job was not to make assumptions, to allow the truth to come out in its own way, and I gently chided the sprite within. I resolved to talk to Norah when I next saw her. That would burst the imp's bubble.

"You're back. Come on. Come on." Freddie was like a dog straining at the leash. The weather was cooler and the fan sat idle, but the regular whirring of the infusion machine reminded us that time was short.

"So, how did you get around the Caspian? I assume you were heading for Iraq or Iran?"

"I stowed away on a boat. I had no idea where it was going, but when you start at the north end of the Caspian everything sails south." He opened his hands to underline that it was his only option. "We had no idea what had gone on during our incarceration. Zegarelli was hardly one to keep track of international affairs even before he was packed off to the Eastern Front. And for me, Iran was little more than a kingdom in a far off place that I vaguely remembered having German sympathies."

"What? Iran?" I should have known better than to question Freddie's knowledge of geopolitics even when he admitted it was sketchy. "I thought it was a British Protectorate."

"Hah!" Another of Freddie's unguarded outbursts at my naive, rose-tinted view of British history. "I love the way you use that word. Protectorate? How you British love to justify your conquests. It became another British colony. While Taras and I were surviving the gulag, the cogs of history turned and threw Russia into the arms of the capitalist west."

"Hitler's invasion?"

"Indeed. And suddenly Britain and America needed to find a way to send arms to their new ally, the communist bear. The British already held Iraq and so even while the Panzers were driving headlong for Moscow the Russians attacked Iran from the north as Britain struck from the south."

"I didn't know that," I said meekly.

"No. Well, we all forget the wrongs we do in the name of expedience. Within a week the allies had opened up their Persian Corridor, and the guns and tanks began to flow. The Shah was deposed and replaced by his puppet son, and the needs of one war stoked the furnace of revolt that led to another."

I stumbled mentally through the line of events that Freddie was pointing me towards. "You mean the revolution? The Ayatollah?"

He nodded with a smile. "Fuelled and driven in the subjugation demanded by Stalin's need for bombs. I knew no Iranian when I arrived, but I picked it up quickly." That was no surprise. He seemed to have a gift for absorbing language like a sponge. "I was a little worried to see Russian troops in the streets, but soon learned that they shared the running of this proud cradle of ancient civilisation with the Brits. So, early on the morning of September 17th 1943 I walked into the British embassy and presented myself as a Free Pole."

"That must have been a shock for them," I laughed. "Did they arrest you, thinking you were German?"

Freddie smiled at me fondly, in the way a schoolteacher loves the class dunce for always trying. "You've been watching too many movies, Tom. All eastern Europeans sound the same to a British ear? Not at all. Tehran was very well used to Poles. Less than a year earlier a whole Polish army had passed through Iran bound for the war in the desert. Polish stragglers were commonplace."

"Really?" My puzzled expression brought a small pat of

reassurance on my hand.

"International politics is a fickle trade. As soon as Stalin needed all the friends he could get he agreed to release Poles held in the camps and formed them into a small army under the command of a surviving Polish general. Anders' Army. They fought with the Russians until late 1942 when Stalin let them join the British. They came through Iran before joining Montgomery in Egypt."

"But that can't be." I was totally lost in these revelations. A Polish army fighting with the Russians? That same army marching through Iran in an exodus to join the British in the desert? "And you. You should have been released. You were..."

"I was Ukrainian remember Tom." The irony was painfully comical. "In saving me, Lipko unknowingly condemned me to another two years in the gulag."

The door opened, and a nurse came in with a jug of juice that she set down on the table by the bed. "Are you comfortable Mr. Zamoyski?"

Freddie smiled. "Yes thank you, my dear."

"So you were sent to Egypt to join the others?"

"Eventually. I was very weak. Skin and bone. It took more than four months in a British military hospital for me to regain my full strength. While I was there the first great war council of the allied leaders took place. Churchill, Stalin and Roosevelt all in town to make their plans. But for me such things were of no interest as each day I could feel my power return as my body regenerated itself, until finally I recognised the man I had once been. I was Lieutenant Freddie Zamoyski of the 1st Mountain Brigade. I had returned from the darkest pits of the underworld."

-oOo-

Freddie sat on the bench seat in the back of the military lorry as it drove northwards, just one in a snaking line crawling its way to the front. He looked through the open rear of the tarpaulin as the dusty haze thrown into the Italian air reminded him of that fateful morning when he had watched Krakow disappear into the distance. What a journey he had endured since then as God had protected him and guided his destiny to arrive at this place. Healed, fed, strong, and recommissioned into the Polish Corp. He was back home.

His family name still resonated, but the men around him no longer looked to the past for their inspiration. Zamoyski, the Hero of Lwow, was a fading memory from a lost world incinerated in the September heat nearly five years earlier. Zamoyski, the sole survivor of the fabled Berezwecz battalion, was a hero here and now. The tigers of Wegierska Gorka, the feted hundred who had held an army at bay for three days, were the new legends. And this apparition back from the dead commanded the respect bestowed by such renown.

Like so many units, the 1st Mountain Brigade no longer existed. In their place Anders' Army, starved of supplies and guns by their grudging Russian overlords, was now reborn as the Polish 2nd Corps into the family of the British 8th Army. Here in the heart of Italy they would expunge the stain of defeat, and carry the attack to the hated Wehrmacht. And newly promoted Captain Zamoyski would inspire his men to victory.

The allied advance had stalled frustratingly on its march to Rome, held in check for four months by the ferocious defences of the Germans' Gustav Line. Three times they had attacked, and three times they had been repulsed. French, Indians, Gurkhas, New Zealanders, British and Americans had all fallen back in disarray as the ancient monastery that formed the linchpin of the defence was slowly pounded to rubble. Not a single Pole had ever before heard of the Abbey of Monte Cassino but it was a name they would never forget.

The monastery perched on an imposing bluff looking down over the coast road below as it picked its way along the plain from

Naples to Rome. Just as the Lord himself sat on high and passed judgement on our souls, this temporal throne in the sky shelled its wrath on any allied unit that was sinful enough to happen along that path. Over four months it had become an impregnable fortress of rubble and pounded rock. The protracted allied bombing had served only to create a chaotic tangle of ruins that formed a perfect defensive killing ground.

And the tenacious defenders of this moonscape were shadowy creatures summoned from the deepest bowels of Satan's inferno. The German 1st Airborne Division was hardened, vulcanised by combat, and dug so deep into the labyrinth that the mount itself seemed to breathe with them. They were feral. Demonic. An army of the undead, restless in their need to send to Hades the ranks of the wholesome mortals ranged against them.

Despite the malevolent gaze of this ghoulish barbican, detachments from some Indian divisions had managed to construct a bridge over the small stream that fluctuated with the seasons. The Rapido formed a barrier that at times of rain presented an impassable torrent and ebbed to a trickle when the heavens abated.

It was late spring and a protracted dry spell had helped the engineers in their endeavours. A wonderfully camouflaged bridge crossed the water that marked the crossing point from this place of light into the shadow world beyond. Freddie had once held a fascination for Norse mythology and as he gazed on the flimsy pontoon walkway bedecked in netting and foliage it recalled to him memories of the Gjallerbru, the wooden bridge thatched in gold that crossed the river Gjoll into the abyss of Helheim. The realm of the dead.

Freddie stared across the river into this other land hammered to destruction by the aerial onslaught, and contemplated the battle to come. Where all others had failed, they must cross into this ghost world, fight their way up the long scree and take the broken citadel, whatever the cost might be.

For five nights Anders' Army collected under the cover of darkness. The tension was unbearable. Warriors paced the ground with nervous energy. Some read, some argued. A few fought, and here or there newer men vomited. Freddie played the part of Captain Semik with ease and for his men a grim calm descended. As the other units grew fractious, Zamoyski's company grew in its quiet determination to do its job.

Freddie felt a strange detachment from reality settle on him. He was aware of the awe that he inspired in the men around him. It was is if they would follow him in any quest, pursue any goal, happy in the knowledge that his aura would protect them. Was this how Semik had felt? Where did the man end and the legend begin? He shook his head and discarded the question as irrelevant. His duty was to lead his men into battle against whatever foe might come at them, and he stood ready to deliver.

At one o'clock on the morning of May 12th the ferocious might of the restrained proud Poles crashed into battle. Freddie led his men across the Gjallerbru into the battleground like Thor invading Jotunheim. Around him the cries of battle sounded in aggression and agony. Mortars exploded randomly like ice spears thrown from the fortress of Utgard above them. Men were hurled hither and thither as death rained from the leaden night sky.

Ranks of men clashed with the dark legions as hand to hand struggles merged with canon fire, grenades, bullets and mortars. The seething chaos of combat smashed the senses to dull disorientation. Redoubts fell in blood only to be replaced by the next mound of paltry rocks to be fought over to further death. And still came the undead through the fog of battle. Ragged soulless skeletons. Endless. Unflinching.

The break of day went unnoticed as the blanket of smoke and suffering blotted out the light. On raged the fight as the piles of the dead grew. Great warriors felled by the engulfing tide of darkness. The rock ran thick with Polish blood, yet on they came. The count of the fallen seemed immeasurable, but as the black night at last closed in Freddie led the remnants of his warband to its nemesis.

The ironically named Phantom Ridge, which appeared on their military maps simply as Point 517, was the objective assigned to them by Colonel Stoczkowski whose 5th battalion was all but destroyed. The smothering blackness was so complete that the only light to guide their way in this wasteland were the explosions and flares thrown down like the vengeance of Surt the fire giant. The one who would destroy Asgard and wipe away the world of men.

The warrior code carried them forward to the summit of Phantom Ridge where a small collection of bombed out houses huddled together miserably. And that same warrior code ensured their death as they stood unyielding in the face of the dark elves' merciless counterattack. So many brave men sent to the feasting halls of Valhalla. So many brave men lost.

As the battle waned, Freddie found himself in the cellar of a ruined house. The small detachment that had carried the vanguard of the attack with him had all been killed. He was alone, while above him were the heavy footsteps of German boots on the splintered floorboards. He was trapped. There was no way out of this bolt hole other than through what sounded like half a platoon of fearsome paratroopers. What remained of his company was either dead or had finally fallen back. The attack had failed.

Freddie sat in the darkness as dust from the floorboards settled on him with each step of the bastards above. His cold, detached ego melted away and the slow fires of anger brewed in his belly. They grew and fanned into an all consuming rage. Rage at the Nazis. Rage at the Russians. Rage at Volkov. Rage at the generals who had ordered this carnage. Rage at God for allowing it. He was filled with it. It burst through his body, crackling and spitting out through his skin. It filled the cellar. It filled his world.

Revenge. He would have his revenge. It was the most unchristian emotion he had ever felt. He cared not. Revenge would be his. He would confront the Germans here and now. He would die, but like Horatio on the bridge he reasoned "how can man die better than facing fearful odds, for the ashes of his father and the temple of his gods?"

He checked the barrels of his revolver, and steadied himself for his attack. His muscles answered his call, tensing as his breathing deepened in anticipation of the frenzy of combat.

Suddenly Freddie froze. His passions were high, but enough insight pricked his red haze to understand that driving himself on to suicide with the words of a second rate English poet was folly. The icy control descended once more. He must lie low, and lie still. The attack had not failed. Poland would not be humiliated a second time. The rage that ran through him was coursing in every vein of every one of his countrymen at this very moment. The morning would come and the Germans would feel the wrath of this defiled nation as it rose in revenge and threw them from this hill.

The night was troubled. He tried to sleep, knowing he would need every ounce of energy when the sun rose and the inevitable Polish onslaught resumed. He drifted in and out of an uneasy sleep, constantly alert to the danger of being discovered by the soldiers above. Here and there the low thunder of shells in the distance was punctuated by the terrifying shriek from the nearby ground as it was ripped apart by ordnance falling close by. Each of these near explosions invoked Teutonic expletives from the men above as they were woken from their own half sleep. And in their anxious cries Freddie realised they were not demonic hosts, but men on the edge of breaking, pushed to the borders of insanity by an overwhelming foe. Freddie smiled as their frailty revealed itself, and he slept more soundly.

He woke with a start. The bowels of the earth shook as explosion followed explosion. He had no idea what time it was, but that mattered little. The floorboards above were silent. The platoon must have moved on. Slowly, cautiously, he climbed the ladder that led to the trapdoor he had bundled through the previous night to escape the German tide.

He paused before lifting it, his ears straining for any clue as to what awaited him just inches above. Sensing nothing he pushed the door a fraction. It moved with ease. He pushed a little further so he could now just see across the floorboards. There was nothing. The place was deserted. A strange light flooded in where the roof and one wall had been blown away, but he could see across what had once been a small dining room to the cracked wall opposite.

Without lifting the door any further he swivelled his head slowly taking in the scene. Mud and rubble covered the floor and to his right a kitbag had been carelessly discarded. Half its contents had spilled onto the floor. A cigarette tin, hunk of dried bread and bayonet seemed incongruous next to the open locket from which smiled the face of a beautiful woman. Freddie scanned the room, his head slowly turning. A rough blanket or tarpaulin of some description had been dumped in the far corner. It might have had something wrapped up in it, but it was difficult to tell. To his left Freddie could see out of the back of the house and across open ground which seemed quiet. The sound of action was coming from the right.

He turned back to see if there was any sign of movement, and once again gazed into the eyes of the girl in the photo. Who was she? Presumably German. Waiting in hope for her love to return, utterly oblivious to the hell that would probably take him. Of course she would have some idea of what war meant, but she could never really know what this place was, nor how it changed men. She would never see her sweetheart kill in cold blood. She would never know just what he would have to do to survive, how he would lose his humanity to make it back home. And as he drifted away on this thought he found himself questioning his own actions.

Thank God he had no girl. No one that he would ever have to

tell about the gulag or the colosseum or Wegierska Gorka. No one to reproach him. No one to judge him. No one to hold him. His inspiration was God, and He saw everything. Freddie was suddenly filled with an overwhelming loneliness. The German girl smiled back at him, her big brown eyes full of love and human understanding. For a moment he longed to be with her. To hold her. To tell her everything. To feel her tenderness. He envied the brute who had her love and who right now was probably butchering his comrades as they fought back up the hill.

An ear-splitting crack jolted Freddie back to reality. A single bullet shot. Surgical and precise. The rapier thrust of a sniper. The tarpaulin gave the slightest rustle as a rifle bolt was deftly relocated into its breach and the spent cartridge was spat to the floor. The gulag killer surged within as the sounds of battle faded behind the pulsating roar of blood flooding through Freddie's head. Adrenalin poured into his bloodstream setting every fibre on edge. He knew from long experience how to contain this overwhelming impulse to act. Every muscle and sinew craving to be released. It was almost unbearable, but the hunter knew that tethering his body's desire would make the attack all the more ferocious when he let slip the warrior.

He eyed the bayonet, judged the distance to the sniper, and breathed in the air, his nose scanning for the scent of other soldiers. The room behind the trapdoor was a dead area, blind to his sight, but probed by his other heightened senses.

In one swift movement he sprang from the cellar, scooped up the bayonet, and closed on the tarpaulin like a raptor to the kill. The sniper scarcely had time to roll to his left, caught in the folds of his camouflage, before he was skewered on his own blade. Again and again the knife plunged through the cumbersome wrapping into his trunk, slicing organs and severing arteries. Freddie's weight bore down on the man as his life force spurted and pooled inside his cocoon. The man began jerking uncontrollably in his death throes that Freddie knew so well. In a few moments he would be still.

Freddie felt the old satisfaction flood through him as he anticipated the taste of his victim. There was no other soldier in the space as he had feared. He was alone with his vanquished foe but made the huge effort of will to put his desire to one side and walk the right path.

The man was perfectly positioned for his grim job. His hiding place was nigh on impossible to find. You could have almost walked over him and still not realised he was there. He had been very unlucky that Freddie had been in the right place at exactly the right time. The crack in the wall was narrow enough to provide all the cover he would want, but wide enough to give him a full arc of fire on the advancing hordes. This was perfect. This was why he had been brought here. God had not abandoned him.

"You do work in some very mysterious ways," he smiled, as he raised his eyes to heaven.

A minute later, Freddie was lying under the tarpaulin next to the corpse. For a moment it struck him as odd that he felt no qualms about this, before shrugging his shoulders and patting the German on the back. "Thanks for the loan of the gun, Heinrich."

He settled into a comfortable repose and watched events unfold under his telescopic crosshairs. The drama was mounting on the slope below as he slowly studied the defenders' structure and operation. This was a golden opportunity that he would certainly not squander by indiscriminate shooting. His interventions must be surgical and decisive.

As he watched the brutal storm rage below he noticed two things. The defenders' method relied on a chequerboard structure that reminded him of the Roman legions. The defensive line was not flat but deliberately crenelated, which meant that if the Poles wanted to engage the entire line of defenders half of them would be exposed on both flanks. When the Germans lost a redoubt they would retreat not to the line of the posts on each side but to a point further back to maintain this fiendish crooked line.

No wonder the 5th battalion had suffered such annihilation. It was brilliant. By giving up slightly more ground each time they fell back the Germans ensured their kill rate was dramatically higher. A simple tactic invented in the heat of battle between Romans and Etruscans was being used to cull Poles on Phantom Ridge. Freddie felt a surge of respect for these soldiers who brought such artistry to their work.

The other thing he noticed was their command structure. He had read about the German command doctrine of Auftragstaktik, or mission command, while a reservist at university, but now he saw it in action, and it was effective. The principle was a simple one: any decision in battle should be taken by the lowest rank able to take it. The Polish High Command had rejected it as a comic recipe for chaos. How could an army fight if not directed by a single general, one guiding intellect? Even the ancients believed that.

The Germans had thrown that belief away. Their army would be full of decision makers all the way down to the humblest private. They would respond to what was in front of them within the clear guidance of the overall strategy. And in front of him now Freddie could see that flexibility working as each small group of men reacted to changing circumstances.

But who was guiding the overall strategy? Even under Auftragstaktik there must be a command structure. Slowly he identified the individuals who were pulling the strings, and drew up his target list. They were well covered. There would be no way that the attackers could do anything other than brute force their way through this confusing alien world.

The first target fell beneath the crosshairs as Freddie pulled on the bolt and primed the chamber. The general noise of battle was almost a melody in the background as the man shouted his orders like a character in some of the silent movies that Freddie remembered watching in awe as a child. The eyepiece gave the scene a slightly glassy hue that made it all the more other-worldly.

The man had stopped shouting his commands, and was now holding a mug to his mouth. The crosshairs were over his left eye as Freddie squeezed the trigger as gently and smoothly as he could manage.

The gun kicked Freddie in the shoulder and the crosshairs jumped slightly, but the man remained in frame. For a moment he thought he had missed. Nothing seemed to have happened other than an explosion of blood behind his target. Then the man fell. The entry site was small. The bullet had entered through the left eye socket. The exit wound was huge. As the man toppled forwards Freddie saw the whole of the lower part of the back of his head had opened up.

The bolt clicked backwards, the spent cartridge dropped to the floor and made way for the next round as the breech was closed again with a snap. Freddie left the silent movie of panicked comrades looking around for the source of the shot, and tracked his next target. The seniority of the men he was killing was uncertain. These paratroopers all wore the same heavily camouflaged battle dress and the same characteristic helmets. He wondered whether there was something in the act of throwing themselves from an aeroplane that broke down the usual hierarchy between officers and men. Something democratising in the knowledge that they were all equal in the eyes of gravity.

Target two went down.

Like a nest of ants the Germans began to respond. The first man down could have been a fluke, a ricochet. The second shot signified only one thing. A sniper. Urgent anguished shouts played out silently through his lens as Freddie culled a third. And so it went. The paratroopers command structure being steadily dissolved.

Freddie watched as two groups of men headed back up the hill. Hit squads, sent to root out the gunman. One group was heading straight for him while the other was running towards another building. He thought quickly and took down a soldier from the other team, hoping to lead them away from his lair. It was a race against time. He had thinned out the defenders and wrecked their defensive coordination. Now he was the hunted, and he would be caught. The only question was whether his countrymen would overrun the position first.

He pulled the corpse closer to him and draped it over his back. He felt for a pistol, but the man had none. All he could hear was the deafening pounding of his heart. Behind him there were shouts as the hit squad split up to search what was left of the small group of houses.

"The Poles have got a sniper in behind us, Gustav." The trooper was in the room, probably just about on the trapdoor. He was projecting his voice in Freddie's direction, his words obviously meant for the corpse that now had a name. "You seen anything?"

"No." Freddie had no idea what dialect or accent Gustav had in life, so gave him a non-description mid-Saxon semi-grunt in response.

There was a pause. A long pause. There were no footsteps. The man just stood there, before finally setting his test. "Oh, for God's sake, Gustav. You need to take more care. Your picture of Gretchen has fallen out of your bag."

This was it. The test. Was the beauty Gretchen, or was that name made up to catch him out? Was it even Gustav's bag? But she looked like a Gretchen with her beautiful, long dark hair and her big brown eyes. He hedged his bets with a non-committal grunt.

The feint failed and he heard the trooper cock his gun. It sounded just like those Schmeissers Freddie remembered so well in the barn at Wegierska Gorka. Gustav's body might absorb some impact from the bullets, but surely not all. He waited to die.

Something resonated in the trooper's mind. A doubt he could not explain. It sounded like Gustav, but he could not be sure. He knew how engrossed the man became when he was at his work, lost in a world of his own. There was no point trying to talk to him so he marched over to the tarpaulin and pulled the corner back. As he did, Gustav rose up. In a split second he saw his comrade white as snow rising like a corpse. He was a corpse! A hand, a foreign hand, came up swiftly from Gustav's armpit. Something gleamed as a rare ray of sun caught it for a moment. Then the blinding light and searing pain as his retina was torn by the blade. Then the blackness. Nothing. Oblivion.

The trooper slid off the bayonet and Freddie jumped to his feet. The Schmeisser was a far more useful weapon at close range, and the man had three stick grenades tucked into his belt. The killing machine was armed as it had never been before. Within ten minutes the German hit squad of crack troops had met their nemesis. In the open fields of a classical set piece battle perhaps they would have prevailed. Here in these close quarters no amount of training could compensate for years of gulag experience.

Having secured the half dozen or so pulverised houses at Point 517, Freddie set about announcing his presence. He knew the allied artillery would be called in, and he did not want to be their next target. An idea took root in his mind. In one building he found an old bedsheet. It was dirty, but it would do the job, and an abandoned red drape taken from an adjoining room was crudely tacked beneath with ancient nails ripped from a doorpost. Kicking the bannister off what remained of the wall of a stairwell, he hoisted his makeshift flagpole. As he wedged it against the ruined side of one of the buildings the breeze caught the sheet and it unfurled satisfyingly.

At first the assaulting Poles could not believe the sight before them, and then gave a throaty roar as the makeshift Polish flag, no more than a bedsheet and a drape, flew proudly over Phantom Ridge. The Germans were thrown into confusion, caught between this newly invigorated attack and the need to deploy more men to go back to rip down this symbol of Polish triumph.

The command structure broke, and Auftragstaktik was found wanting. Sporadic groups of paratroopers ran back towards Freddie only to be harvested by murderous fire from the Polish ranks, while the loss of men left the chequerboard strategy too thin to work efficiently. A point of no return was reached, and the whole German position collapsed.

Ten minutes later it was all over. A handful of Germans was taken prisoner. The rest refused to surrender, or had their offers of capitulation declined by the vengeful Polish wave.

-oOo-

"Phantom Ridge," sighed Freddie as a nurse checked the settings on the drip.

"There you are Mr. Zamoyski," she chirped. "That will last you the night."

"Well let's hope so, my dear." The young nurse hurried out in silence, uncertain of how she should redeem her minor faux pas. Freddie looked up at me and we exchanged a smile.

"So you avoided being killed by your own artillery. That was quick thinking."

He shrugged. "Artillery. Bombers. Who knows? It was bloody chaos. Why they kept up the bombardment I just don't know. It made it more difficult for us than the Germans."

"The flag was inspired, even so."

Freddie smiled modestly. "They seemed to think it turned the tide just as the attack was faltering. I had my doubts, but they would hear none of it. One thing is certain. Phantom Ridge was the key to the monastery. Once we took that they were doomed. They held out another couple of days, but once we had the high ground behind their position it was over."

We sat in silence for a few moments. "It is astonishing." I was almost thinking aloud as I gazed at the floor. "An army of prisoners grudgingly released by Stalin turned out to be the allies' sharpest blade."

"Anger, shame and the need for revenge. It's a potent cocktail." Something in his words hung in the air and folded itself into the silence that sprang up.

The infusion whined. Minutes went by and it whined again.

"Did they decorate you?" It was a clumsy way to break the hiatus.

Freddie flickered back into life from whatever dark place his mind had been wandering. "Oh yes." There was pride in his voice. "I was awarded the Virtuti Militari." I was struck by how important it was for him. This urbane polymath visibly grew as he told me its significance. "Very few were given. In the 2nd Corps, only General Anders and me."

"It was the highest award?" The question was unnecessary, but I had no knowledge of Polish decorations and it seemed unfair not to allow Freddie a rare, boastful moment.

"The very highest. Only the President may award it."

"The President?" A vestige of knowledge sparked in my mind, and glad of the opportunity to demonstrate even the most meagre understanding I named him. "You met General Sikorski?" Freddie's quick glance and swallowed smile told me I was wrong, and my blank look invited his correction.

He let me down lightly. "The President was a fine man called Wladyslaw Raczkiewicz. Sikorski served as Prime Minister under him." But my fall continued. "Of course, Sikorski was already dead by then. Killed in a plane crash. His replacement was called Mikolajczyk, but I received my medal from the President."

I laughed at having been doubly wrong. "I'm sorry Freddie. You must think us English all terribly ignorant."

He gave a magnanimous smile. "Not at all. Why would you know any of these characters? Churchill didn't. Nor Eden. And in any case, I knew many of them."

"Did you know this Racz..." I stumbled.

"Raczkiewicz."

"Thank you."

"Not personally. But he was another who had fought on the Lwow front."

"Of course. Everyone fought on the Lwow front." I said it tongue in cheek, and he reciprocated.

"Indeed. Anyone who was anyone." We shared a chuckle. "He knew all about me before I had even arrived in London. Of course he had known my father and seemed genuinely pleased to meet me."

"I would imagine your own exploits were every bit as celebrated by then."

He stared into space as if looking at an old Pathé news film of a man he no longer recognised. "Yes." The stare continued. "Funny. The hubris of youth. How vain we become in our own glorious reflection in the eyes of others."

"I'm sure that wasn't you Freddie."

He stumbled back to me absent-mindedly. "Hmm?"

"You're tired. I've kept you talking here all day. I should let you rest."

There was a flash of energy in his face as he gripped my forearm. "Come back early." Those eyes gave no latitude for dissent. They flicked a glance to the drip. "That stuff won't work forever." He let out a long breath and settled back into his pillows. The fire died and the mist returned.

I stood in the lift almost in tears. He was dying before my eyes. The energy fluctuated. His fuel was almost burned up, and I was filled with a dread that we may not finish. As a single salty tear trickled down my face I shook the thought from my head. But I knew that lone teardrop was not for the fear of a story unfinished. It was the first herald of my grief to come.

The doors slid open and standing before me was Norah. She flashed me a nervous glance as she waited for me to step out, but sensing my opportunity I wiped my face and blurted some nonsense about having left something on the ward. She seemed wary as she stood next to me and pressed a button. For a moment her finger hovered as if she had forgotten which floor Harry was on, before decisively pushing the big black button with a large number two embossed in white.

That was strange. I had never visited the second floor. The only ward on that level was the maternity unit. Even the sickest babies were hurried downstairs to the paediatric intensive care unit. I had been there once or twice. I hated it. There are no words of comfort or explanation that any emissary of a loving God can offer to parents holding their dead baby. I wanted to talk to Norah, but the sudden memory of dead babies robbed me of my tongue.

"Difficult day, Father?" she offered. I nodded mutely as the doors slid open and she stepped out. "I'm sure you'll find peace," she smiled with a reassuring nod, and the doors closed.

I found no peace that night.

IX - The Great Game

"Come on. Come on!" Freddie was impatient despite the early hour. The city outside was still wiping the Sunday morning sleep from its eyes as I arrived to the slightly reproachful glances of the night staff who were just about to go off shift. But he was eager to start, so start we did.

"Morning Freddie. Sleep well?"

"Not a wink." His energetic smile belied his fatigue. "I think it's this damned infernal device." He still sounded every bit the cavalry officer, and that made me smile for reasons I could not explain. His strength was back. It was brimming and fizzing. My job was to get as much of this done before his energy crashed again. "Not serving communion today?"

"I'm doing Vespers. I wanted us to have time today." Freddie gave a polite nod acknowledging my commitment and recognising the disruption to my other work that I had openly accepted as the price for supporting him. "So you made it to London," I asked by way of prompting him back to his narrative. I need hardly have bothered as he dived into his story with the same enthusiasm as if he were just beginning.

"It seems strange now to remember that first morning in London. The chauffeured car. The VIP treatment. Driving past bombed out homes to the embassy. It was all such a blur. One minute I was fighting for my life on Phantom Ridge, the next I was sharing the cold and bumpy bomb hold of a Wellington with the fabled General Anders."

"That must have been a bit of a shock."

He laughed almost to himself. "I guess so. To be honest though, nothing much shocked me by then. Bit by bit I had lost the capacity for surprise. There comes a point when you've seen it all. Or at least you think you have. And it's a sad realisation, to feel you'll never experience that childlike sensation of awe that comes with the unexpected."

"How did you get back to Britain?"

"Anders and I were flown to Tunisia and then via Gibraltar to London. It was an honour of course, but I hadn't realised why I had been chosen. And I wasn't prepared for what greeted us. Some reporter had got a photograph of the flag as it flew that decisive morning over Point 517, and suddenly the Poles were all over the front pages of the papers as the soldiers who had triumphed where all others had failed."

"And you were the embodiment of that spirit?"

Freddie's eyes narrowed a little as he looked me over. "Interesting that you should use that word." He faltered, turning over what I had said in his mind, before focusing back on his point. "Anyway, the Polish government in exile wanted to make a bit of a splash. They needed to show that they were in the club with the big boys." He thanked the student nurse as she gave him a bowl of cornflakes and carried on with his account without breaking stride. "They brought their conquering heroes back to their new home. The general who masterminded the operation and the soldier whose exploits had seared themselves into the minds of the whole English-speaking world."

"Wasn't that a bit obvious?"

He smiled a broad grin at my naivety. "Of course. But by such gestures is the great game of international power politics played. For a brief window everyone wanted to be seen with the Spirit of Phantom Ridge." He opened his hands as if presenting himself for the first time, and then recalling my words moments earlier continued. "You should become a newspaper headline writer."

I could not help but laugh. "Is that what they called you? You've certainly collected your fair share of names. The Spirit of Phantom Ridge? Wasn't that just a little flowery?"

He gave a self-deprecating snort. "Of course. One of the London papers coined the name and it stuck. The Polish leadership were delighted and flew us over immediately for the medal ceremony. It was a real coup for them, and a chance to push Poland to the forefront just before the invasion of France. It was a lure to British politicians to come to Portland Place."

"Portland Place?"

"Poland's embassy. In those days it was the seat of the Polish government in exile. The last stronghold of those Poles who managed to get out. Which seemed to be most of the leadership," he added with a heavy sprinkling of irony. "It was clumsy national self-promotion and everyone knew it. But it worked. The Brits laid on the Wellington and came in force to the ceremony."

"Wasn't it uncomfortable? The flight I mean."

"Bloody awful!" Freddie barked back, half jesting. "Not without its dangers either. It was only after we landed at Fairoaks that I was told that Sikorski had died the previous year making the exact same flight."

"You were obviously important to them."

"Expendable, would be nearer the mark." He munched into a spoonful of his cereal as he continued. "We landed in the morning after a night flight, were driven straight to the embassy and readied for the ceremony in the afternoon."

"They weren't hanging around, were they?"

"They couldn't afford to. President Raczkiewicz had already sensed that Poland might become a casualty of the manoeuvrings of the big three. Conversations were taking place and deals being made between Churchill, Stalin and Roosevelt, and Poland was likely to be a bargaining chip in those tussles. He was desperate to promote our image as a nation of noble and valiant warriors who were more committed to the British cause than the British themselves. He thought that if the British public took us to their hearts the government couldn't betray us."

I smiled as it dawned on me. "It worked." I looked at him anew. "That's exactly how we see you. The noble wronged."

"Hmm. The public maybe," he grunted. "It did us no good in the end, though. Britain and America both sold us down the river. That wasn't until a year later of course. In 1944 our star was still shining bright, and anyone who was anyone wanted to be seen with Anders and me. The men who had cracked Monte Cassino."

"I would never have thought that a medal ceremony could be so important in diplomatic circles."

He looked at me shaking his head and chuckling again. "It was not the ceremony, Tom. That was a stiff and dull affair. For Churchill it was the chance of the photo opportunity, and for the Poles it was the dinner afterwards. That's when all those vital conversations could be had. All that influence brought to bear. I was the headline act at a dinner party thrown to give the Polish leadership Churchill's ear for a few crucial hours."

"You met Churchill?"

"Briefly," he nodded.

"Now, that must have been something, even for you." I smiled, inviting him to join in the ubiquitous, almost compulsory eulogising around this totemic figure.

He just shrugged as his gaze grew distant. "I don't really remember."

"You don't remember meeting Churchill?"

"Not really." There was the slightest shake of his head and a smile of such pure happiness that I had never before seen beam from his face. "That was the day I met Lilian."

-oOo-

The presentation ceremony had been exceptionally dull. It reminded Freddie of those painful awards days at school when they would be tortured by endless speeches from masters before having to applaud the handing out of all manner of prizes that seemed to go on forever. The finale of the show was the presentation to Anders and himself before a rousing rendition of the national anthem brought proceedings to a close.

The reception was much more fun, despite the discomfort of the ill-fitting uniform they had produced for him to wear.

"Enjoying yourself, sir?" asked Olenski, the fresh faced subaltern who had been assigned to help Freddie in his preparations.

"Yes thank you, Piotr," he glanced around the room at the finery on display. "I don't know who gave you my measurements, though." He looked at the two inches of forearm that protruded from the woefully short sleeves and wriggled his shoulders very slightly as the seams bit into his skin.

"I'm sorry about that sir. It was the best guess we could come up with." Olenski returned a weak smile. "I'll go and get you another drink."

Freddie watched the young man disappear towards the door and turned back to find himself staring straight into the fierce eyes of Winston Churchill. "So you're the Spirit of Phantom Ridge." He offered his outstretched palm, "Let me shake you by the hand, sir." The powerful grip was no less than Freddie had expected. "Your country owes you a huge debt. We owe you a huge debt." His tone lowered to signify its gravity. "I owe you a huge debt."

Freddie could not imagine why Churchill owed him a personal debt, but he smiled back as press cameras flashed away and the two looked inseparable in their brotherly camaraderie. That would make good copy the next day. "I was only doing my duty."

Churchill gave him an admiring look, the gesture magnified by his heavy jowls. "I sincerely doubt it sir." His gravelly voice and the way he began a statement with something between a growl and a grunt that slipped seamlessly into the words themselves added to the gravitas. "For it was you, and only you, that raised that flag. Now Rome will fall. Italy will fall." A pause and that drop in tone. "Europe will fall."

Briefly, even Freddie was blinded by the rhetoric. For a second he believed that he had single-handedly defeated the Nazi war machine. As reality brought him back to earth Churchill was already pressing the flesh with Anders, and Freddie smiled in admiration at the ability of this man to inspire those around him.

He turned back and, without warning, the world as he had known it ended.

His mind exploded. Suddenly every fibre in his body sang in wonder and confusion. His stomach lurched. His limbs trembled. And his heart leapt into his throat, pounding in a way he had never felt before, even in the height of battle. The blinding radiance of the woman before him was a hammer blow that stunned his senses and robbed him of the power of speech.

"Captain Zamoyski, allow me to introduce Flight Officer Brown." The words of Alexander Cunningham, the stiff British major on her right were muffled and distant in the sudden light that flooded the room. She offered her hand, and as Freddie reached out to exchange the greeting electricity surged through his entire being. The discharge of energy through his frame was all consuming as her soft skin embraced his leathery, weathered palm.

The room faded to distance as she spoke. "How do you do? Captain Zamoyski." He was struck by her blinding beauty, and her warm, refined tone. He felt an emotion he had never before experienced: complete peace. So this was how life truly looked. Like God reaching out to Adam she had touched him with the spark of life. As he released her grip the room came flooding back in all its newly seen depth and colour.

"Er. Hello. Flight...." The words stumbled from his mouth, mere clumsy noises after the music of her voice.

"Flight Officer." She smiled encouragingly. "Brown." He had been in England less than eight hours, but already he was picking up different accents. Hers was smooth and rounded in a way that even without any immediate cultural cues he took to be well bred.

"Ha!" Cunningham slapped him on the shoulder. "Stunned, eh? Winston has that effect on men."

Freddie shook himself. "Yes, of course. He. Er. He is inspirational." Thank heavens Cunningham had misread events. Freddie felt acutely embarrassed at his stumbling attempts to act normally when the truth was that he suddenly felt anything but.

"Lilian here," the major threw half a glance at Brown, "works for us as an analyst." He had been introduced to Freddie before the ceremony, who had smiled at the various euphemisms that spies used to describe their work. Not that this man looked anything like a spymaster. He was showy and talked too much. There was an air of arrogance about him that Freddie thought out of place with his job. Lilian Brown was different. "She has a particular interest in central Europe, so I gather you two may have plenty in common." He leaned towards Freddie with a conspiratorial air. "Don't let her bore you to death with her incessant questions. She's like a terrier with a rat." Someone caught his eye. "Ah! Roger!" And with a cursory goodbye he was gone.

Freddie was left with Lilian. He needed to pull himself together. It would be acutely embarrassing if she had any inkling of the effect she was having on him. He regrouped. "So, Flight Officer," he began as formally as seemed appropriate. "What exactly do you analyse?"

She stood before him with her half empty glass of Chablis held delicately in both hands. Her manner was calm, but Freddie sensed an underlying impatience, an energy held in check. Beneath her relaxed exterior was her mind like his, constantly churning, always assessing, seeing everything? Of course it was. She was a spy. He shuddered at the thought of what she had already seen.

"Poland. Mainly." Her eyes shone deep blue. They immediately recalled to Freddie the hues of the Ionian Sea that had so mesmerised him as he stared into their depths from the troop ship that had carried him to Italy.

"That's a broad remit." Her skin bore no make-up and it gleamed in its own vitality. He had never seen a woman look so full of life. Unencumbered by layers of paint her whole face radiated openness and honesty. He reminded himself she was a spy. Her uniform may have been that of the Women's Auxiliary Air Force, but her job was intelligence. And intelligence about Poles too. She laughed dismissively at his comment, and smiled a warm smile back at him. He felt his being melt anew under her dazzling gaze.

"You don't need to be afraid of me Captain Zamoyski," she smiled, tilting her head to one side. "I'm one of the good guys." She retrieved a cigarette from the case in her pocket. "Would you mind?" she asked.

Freddie blushed. He could feel the colour rising in his face, and had no idea why or how to stop it. He desperately wanted to offer her a light, but had no match. "Oh. Er. I. Er." He was stumbling like a teenaged buffoon.

Lilian smiled, and holding the cigarette in her lips produced a lighter from her pocket which she offered to him. He eagerly accepted and flicked it into life as he instinctively cupped his hand around the flame. Lilian laid her hand lightly, deliberately, on his as if to steady the flame. She inhaled deeply. Her hand lingered and then retrieved the cigarette as she exhaled a stream of blue smoke towards the floor.

Freddie pulled hard on the reins. His heart was running away with him, and he needed to exert some control. "You don't look old enough to be an analyst," he remarked. It was intended as a compliment but barely had the words fallen from his lips than he recognised how patronising it sounded.

"Do you even know what an analyst does, Captain?"

"Er, well..." He was making an awful hash of this and was beginning to feel cross with himself. He knew better than this.

He took all company in his stride. He always had. What was wrong with him?

"I can assure you I'm more than old enough to know what I'm doing." Her reply, delivered in perfect, native Polish, brought him up short. A hint of a smile also played around one corner of her mouth as if teasing. Was she flirting with him? For all his aristocratic self-assurance Freddie had little experience of courting, and the few girls he had dated in Krakow had been well bred but intellectually docile. This girl was obviously the opposite when it came to brains, and her tart riposte was laced with a hint of sexual provocation. And in Polish.

A quickness of mind animated her expressive, slender face. Her accentuated cheek bones gave her a regal poise that could have been forbidding were it not for the dimples that played on each side of her glorious mouth. Her lips were wide and welcoming and Freddie felt overwhelmed by the simple child-like happiness of her manner harnessed to what felt like a deep wisdom pulsing beneath.

As she spoke he noticed her slim figure and strength of her limbs and he was consumed by desire for her. He stole glimpses of her body like a thief in the few moments he could allow himself without appearing too obvious. He had never felt emotions like this in his entire life. It disconcerted him. It troubled him. And it was glorious.

"I'm sure you are, Flight Officer Brown. I meant no disrespect. Your Polish is faultless. Where did you learn it?" Even as he was trying to extricate himself from his gaffe she smiled playfully at his attempts.

"Oh, the usual places." She waved away his question. Then she stopped playing and looked him square in the eyes. Did she know how completely he had fallen for her? He hoped to God that she did not. What was she about to ask? The pause was growing. He was beginning to feel light-headed under her intense gaze. His legs did not feel like his own.

"You want to ask me something?" he heard himself say.

"Yes." Her eyes narrowed slightly and Freddie recognised that whatever the question was she knew the answer was likely to cause her pain. "You fought at Wegierska Gorka?"

He nodded, wondering where this questioning was going. He found that he was frowning in anticipation and empathy with her and was moved to feel how her emotions spilled into him.

"You knew Tadeusz Semik?" Another nod. She swallowed hard. "Any hope?"

Feelings surged in Freddie that he did not understand. He felt her pain, but he was ashamed at the jolt of jealousy that intruded. As his mind was engulfed by that hideous last image of his hero defiled by those demonic swine he resented him for whatever bond he had shared with her.

"I'm so sorry. I saw him fall." He spared her the details.

A tear welled up in her eye and spilled onto her perfect cheek. "Thank you."

Freddie found his hand on her shoulder as she drew on her cigarette once more. "He was a remarkable man. We all looked up to him like......" He could not find the right word. "We would have followed him into hell." He paused as a tide of grief flooded through him. Now he swallowed hard. "In fact we did."

Lilian gave a thin smile as they found themselves bound together in their muted grief. She looked around, obviously careful not to be overheard. "He was my cousin." She breathed in deeply and stood more upright as if telling him this was somehow unburdening herself.

Freddie stared at her in shock. That was the last thing he expected to hear. "You certainly are an enigma, Flight Officer Brown."

She managed a small laugh at the increasingly clumsy, ongoing formality. "Please. Call me Lilian." She exhaled another lung full of smoke and looked across the room. "Were you with him? When he died, I mean." There was something deeply intimate about the way she spoke without looking at him. As if they had already reached a point where eye contact was no longer needed for them to understand each other.

Freddie relived the terrible memory of bullets carving through bodies in that barn all those years before, and he shuddered. "Yes. You know, in a way he saved my life." They stood in silence, both wanting to drive the conversation on but not sure how. Tadeusz Semik embraced them both and drew them together. They were woken from their private contemplations by the musical tinkling of a small bell. Dinner was served.

The meal was delicious. Military rations were banquets in comparison to the existence that Freddie had endured in Siberia, but they were nothing when set against the dinner that was served to them that night. Properly cooked and perfectly presented, the Poles had spared no expense in their celebration despite the fact that Churchill himself had made his apologies and left after the reception.

The diplomats and intelligence officers left behind enjoyed themselves thoroughly. A senior man from the British Foreign Office gave a warm speech veering somewhat embarrassingly between Whitehall English and broken faltering Polish. It was the message that mattered, and that was one of brotherly solidarity between the two nations. The Poles reciprocated in kind, and the night slid imperceptibly from high diplomacy into post dinner party bonhomie.

Freddie had been seated at the far end of the table from the speech makers. It was obvious that was the less important end. The end where the lower ranking of the twenty or so guests sat. He was the son of the Hero of Lwow, and now in his own right had been both a hero of Wegierska Gorka and now the Spirit of Phantom Ridge. But in this rarified company he was plain Captain Zamoyski, and he was glad of it. It put him at Lilian's end of the table.

The half dozen or so junior ranks were a strange mixture.

Alexander Cunningham spent the evening boasting about his family estate in Somerset and explaining how he could find food as good as this every night of the week. You just had to know where to look and who to ask. In short he was rich and connected and wanted people to know.

Next to Cunningham was a naval commander who spent the whole evening talking in awe about the newly evolving art of carrier warfare that was being developed and finely honed in the Pacific. To Freddie's amusement he had been visibly crushed when Lilian had asked him why he was so interested in carrier warfare when his job was coordinating intelligence in the war against Hitler's U-boats. He mumbled something before retreating from the conversation for the rest of the evening.

Next to him sat the only other Pole in their group, a diplomat who had grown up in Katowice and spoke very eloquently of the debt of gratitude owed to Britain. The saving grace was that Lilian was seated at the end of the table on Freddie's left, which gave him a perfect opportunity to monopolise the conversation with her. It was a chance that he was not going to let pass.

The most wonderful thing was that far from appearing to mind, Lilian seemed to enjoy his attention and to reciprocate it. Here and there they broke off their private conversation to engage with Cunningham or talk about the nuances of combat air patrol on a landless battleground, but the evening was increasingly theirs as the alcohol and the conversation flowed effortlessly.

Her charm and wit filled him and merged with the wine into a cocktail of happiness and relaxation. His world was becoming fuzzier at the edges and in every direction there was Lilian as far as his eyes could see.

"Where are you staying tonight?" she asked as the port was circulated a second time.

"I have a room here in the embassy." There was a brief pause before he continued. "Unless you have a better idea." The evening's familiarity and the freely consumed alcohol had lowered his inhibitions, but a deeper force was driving him now. The function was coming to a close. His dream would end and he would have no way of finding his way back to it again. Lilian would be gone and he would be bereft. Even so, he shocked himself at his audacity.

For the first time her piercing eyes betrayed what looked like disapproval. "I simply meant that as you've only arrived today what have the embassy arranged for you." He was stricken as if lanced through the chest by a rapier. "You must excuse me. I need to freshen up," she mumbled, and with a swift movement she left.

"Bad luck, old boy," scoffed Cunningham in what seemed half sympathy, half jest. "You've been working hard, I'll grant you that. But Lilian is an exceedingly tough nut to crack. It took me some time, I can tell you."

Freddie's emotions spiralled through grief to pain and on into loathing for Cunningham. His vaguely mocking tone and the implied claim that he had enjoyed Lilian's carnal affections, and said so openly before the men at the table, made his blood boil with jealousy and a feeling of protectiveness for her honour. Before he could think of a suitable response Cunningham had moved on to a conversation further up the table. The moment had passed.

The formalities were concluding and the party was breaking up. Freddie sat and played with a small pile of salt that he had poured onto the crisp white table linen. He pushed it into various shapes with a knife as he contemplated the many highs of the evening, and this crushing low. No one seemed to notice his dejected, disconsolate figure as he pondered on his behaviour.

What had he been thinking? Why could he not think straight when she was around him? What was this power she held over him? Life had ultimately been a series of triumphs, hard won to be sure, but triumphs nonetheless. He had always felt the self-assuredness to know that he would rise to any challenge placed before him. Between his resourcefulness and God's deliverance he would ride any storm. But today his powers had failed him. He could scarcely make any sense at all when he met her, and only the wine quelled his nervous anxiety.

The wine had loosened his tongue, and just as he was savouring the whole experience, wine had loosened his morals and robbed him of this woman who had so touched him. He stopped and replayed that thought. It was the wine that had loosened his morals? He had no right to blame the wine. He had brought this on himself in a moment of misguided over-excitement. What was he thinking? Was he hoping she would suggest they spent the night together? That was a ridiculous idea. The truth was that he had never been that intimate with a woman, and wondered if he would know what to do. And why on earth would she even contemplate such a thing? They had only just met. The self loathing welled up again. He stared furiously at the salt. He wanted to cry in his stupidity and in his loss.

"So, where are you staying tonight?" Lilian's voice was steady as it brought him back to reality. He had been so wrapped up in his thoughts he had not even noticed her retake her seat. The others were competitively exchanging tall stories in the loud way that alcohol encourages and were oblivious to the couple at the end of the table.

"I'm so sorry Lilian. I really don't know what I was saying. You must think me terribly vulgar." He wanted to grab her hand and press the remorse into her flesh so that she would feel its sincerity, but he restrained himself.

"It's all right Freddie. A bit of a surprise. But all right. Now, where are you staying tonight?" Her stare was as level as her voice.

"Er. Well. Er. I think they have sorted out a room here in the embassy." The startling decision she had made in the cloakroom and her iron resolve to carry it through were lost on him.

"You really are determined to make this awkward for me

aren't you?" she laughed, enjoying once more the endearingly gauche ineptitude she had witnessed several times that day. "You're not listening to me, so I want you to think very hard." Her eyes shone like iridescent blue stars. Their heat poured into him turning his core to molten desire. "Now. Where are you staying tonight?" Her fixed open-eyed stare gave him the answer.

His mind was stretched in all directions as the enormity of her rhetorical question smashed into him. It collapsed in relief like a marathon runner crossing the line at the very same time as it soared to dizzying heights and ran like a frightened child from the fear of the unknown. His stomach rolled over, he felt sick with excitement and trembled in fearful anticipation. "With you," he managed to say.

She nodded as if he had just decided on tea or coffee, and cast a glance at the others before issuing her instructions. "Give me five minutes, then leave. If anyone asks you, you are going for some fresh air. Cross the road and head west. You know which way is west?" He nodded in mild irritation at such a question. "Good. Make sure you're not followed and turn left into Harley Street. Walk 50 yards, then stop and wait. Got that?"

Freddie was mesmerised by the sudden change in her. From delightful dinner party company to brutally logical field commander, the switch was flicked in an instant. "Yes, ma'am," he replied with a smile.

"Don't mess this up Freddie." The dinner party smile returned as she bid the others goodnight, remarking on a headache that forced her early departure.

"That'll break Zamoyski's heart," joked Cunningham, just loud enough for Freddie to hear. "The poor chap's distraught about what he said. Now he won't have a chance to make it up to you."

"He'll get over it," replied Lilian, coldly. And then she left. It was as simple as that. A brief conversation, a set of instructions, and Freddie watched Aphrodite as her slender, shapely hips swayed away from him and down the stairs in the full knowledge that she was to be his. She was to be his!

He did as instructed and ten minutes later a small car with understated military markings pulled up in front of him as he stood on the pavement. "Get in," said Lilian as she pushed the door open. The journey was not far, although driving in a city under a black out was not easy even if they were just about the only traffic.

After a short drive, Lilian parked in a quiet side street somewhere in the dense forest of imposing four story brick terraces that melted into one, and led Freddie through a large door and up three flights of stairs. When they reached what seemed to be the attic she flicked a key into the lock and smiled over her shoulder at him. "It may not be much, and it may not be mine, but for now this is my home."

The small sitting room was sparsely furnished, but a few homely touches defined it as Lilian's personal space. Freddie looked upon the small sofa, the neat writing desk and the few smiling photographs as if he were being allowed into the Holy of Holies. He could feel his heart pounding in his chest, still worried that this was some sort of dream that might evaporate if he lost concentration and woke up.

She turned to look at him with a gentle smile and for the first time he sensed her apprehension too. "Are you afraid?" she asked almost in a whisper.

"Yes," he nodded.

"So am I." She reached up and softly placed her palms on his cheeks. As she guided his face towards hers, she lifted her eyes to his. Slowly, instinctively, they misted and closed as her head tilted and his lips brushed the warm fullness of the mouth that had so hypnotised him.

He exhaled as the most wondrous calm descended on him. The pounding in his head stopped, the shaking of his hands drained away and he stood in tranquility as their lips touched again. His rough hands, his killer's hands, gently came to rest on her shoulders as they stood as one in the lightest of embraces, breathing each other's breath, inhaling each other's scent, sharing each other's soul.

He had no idea how long they stayed there, as their lips caressed and the world receded. As his fingers played through her hair he thought he had never felt such happiness. Not even on the night that Anna had come back to him. For this was real. Lilian was real. She was here. She was with him, and she wanted him as much as he desired her.

His body crackled as her mouth opened and the tip of her tongue slid across his lip. As it finished its slow, sensuous sweep and fell away he was aware of his involuntary movement that followed, as if asking it to come back. His mouth pushed imperceptibly into hers. She did not pull away. They were one.

Her tongue joined with his and for what seemed like an age he could not breathe such was his rapture. Hers was becoming deeper and more urgent. He could feel her arousal, just as he was aware of his own. His muscles were tensing and his hands no longer held her in a delicate embrace.

They drank deeply of each other as her hand held his head firmly while the other pulled his waist towards her in a powerful hold. They lost themselves as his lips ran down her exposed neck and her perfume filled every corner of his mind. Her rasping breath was hot on his neck as she writhed in delight at his touch, her rhythmic movements fomenting his caged arousal that announced itself uncompromisingly against her thigh.

There was a blur of frenetic movement as their inner passions were unleashed. Their languorous tenderness erupted into a fumbling frenzy that revealed their naked forms in all their shared glory.

He was suddenly conscious, as if burned, of the wet heat of her desire on his leg as she pushed against him. She let out an involuntary whimper as her body shuddered slightly. His right arm tightened its hold pulling her ever more forcefully against him and he felt more suppressed spasms in her delight. Her firm breasts pushed into his rib cage as his hand slipped into the tightly defined valley between the muscles of her lower back. His palm touched her buttock, finding its way to that most feminine recess as it met her thigh. His hand tightened involuntarily as she gave another breathless gasp.

The tension in his own body grew beyond reckoning as four perfectly manicured nails drew themselves slowly up his inner left thigh. He was aware of making some sort of noise as they brushed delicately over his scrotum which contracted electrifyingly in response. After that he had no sense of anything other than the slow deliberate ecstasy as she took him in her hand.

"Come with me," she whispered in his ear as she led him through the door behind her.

The bedroom was small but welcoming as she held his hand and lay back on the freshly starched sheets, inviting him to her. As he carefully leaned forward taking his weight on his arms she slipped her leg outside his knees and caught him in a gaze of profound longing as her hand guided him.

She had often dreamed of this moment. In her younger mind it had always been a nervous vision, the culmination of a white wedding in an idyllic country village, away from the smoke and grime of her upbringing. Her husband, her saviour from the constraints of her poverty, as inept and faltering as herself. But the war had changed everything. Her mythical liberator had disappeared in the cauldron of conflict that had blurred all the boundaries, as unworthy suitors had come and gone, all rebuffed. And now, here she was in a moment of crystal clarity, as she chose this foreign stranger. This enigma with whom she felt the deepest connection.

"Gently," she breathed in his ear. Why she had finally chosen him above all others was beyond any reason. It was driven by a deep intuition that had struck her the moment their hands had touched. She had read his file, she knew his background. And yet this cold-hearted warrior, so skilled in the arts of war had appeared to her so vulnerable, so in need of protection.

Even his crass, fumbling attempt at sexual suggestion had a child-like sweetness to it. She had sensed immediately his attraction to her. His stumbling words and awkward replies were at complete odds with the poise she had observed from afar. But nevertheless, his blurted words at dinner had taken her by surprise and sent her scurrying to the bathroom where she had taken stock. This was no time to hesitate. There would be no second chance. And in that moment she had looked at herself in the mirror and reassured the woman who stared back at her that it was time to follow her instinct. This was a man she could trust. Finally, here was a man she could love. And given that either of them could die tomorrow there could be no half measure. She must seize the day. And seize it she did, with both hands.

Her fingers ran across his shoulders, the muscles rippling like waves in their erotic power and sending her desire beyond control. He was poised over her, straining to contain his own ferocious energy. She had never experienced such electrifying force. She felt sure that if she had touched a light bulb to his skin it would have shone, such was the power that radiated from him.

She could feel his desire to thrust deep and hard as she lay back and spread her arms on the sheets in welcoming sacrifice. An anxious fear drove through her mind. Did he understand? Did he realise this was her first time? She made a conscious effort to reject the thought and relax every fibre in her body, to savour this unique moment.

Freddie was overwhelmed by the sensations flooding through his being. She had told him to be gentle, and he must obey, he must resist the primeval urge to drive into her. He could feel his engorgement straining as it had never strained before as it slid slowly into the body of his goddess. But the profound sense that filled him was of the connection with her eyes, with her heart.

He had been elevated far beyond his lowly station to be at this place at this time with this divine woman. He pushed again as her eyes widened and she let out a small cry. Still their gaze did not break. Her face was a furnace of emotion as the smallest of his movements elicited ecstatic whimpers. Still their eyes were locked. For a moment he thought she was fading away, as if she might faint, but as he nudged again her intense life force welled in those deepest hues and blinded him.

In a moment she moved from hesitant debutante to high priestess as he passed her threshold. Her soul opened wide again, but this time in pure desire as she roughly brought both hands down on his loins and pulled him deep inside. As she did so she let out a long, deep, throaty groan that reverberated around the room. It was vulgar and irresistible.

She did not care. She was consumed by the overwhelming physicality of his body. His immense weight was now fully on her, pinning her to the bed with an uncompromising pressure that was surpassed only by the force of his hardness deep inside her, filling, stretching every part of her. She blanked out for the briefest moment as another orgasm flooded through her without warning. She had never in her wildest dreams believed this experience could be so profound. Yet another spasm engulfed her.

Still their gaze was locked, her beauty magnified a hundred fold in her supreme arousal as Freddie found himself thrusting rhythmically into her depths. Her taste, her smell, her gaze, her skin, her breasts, her groans, her beauty, her sweat, her soul, her wetness, her heat, her desire, her eyes, her eyes, her soul, her eyes.

Freddie spasmed. For just a moment he lost himself utterly. Lilian let out a deep throated roar. Or was it him? Or was it both of them? Then he convulsed again. This time the groan was his. A blinding light seared through him, yet above all shone two deep blue eyes, always connected, always one.

After what seemed like an age both of their bodies gave up. He collapsed onto her as she kissed him over and over again as they slipped into a light sleep. Glorious visions of her flooded through his restless driftings. But he was far too awake to slumber. Too alive to dream. But something was slowing him down. A cloak of calmness, free from pain, wrapped itself around him. His world was warm and feathered and safe. And at its centre was his beloved Lilian whose skin fused with his under the sheets.

"Are you asleep Freddie?" Her voice was soft and happy and echoed his joy.

"No." His reply was dream-like as their soft focus blurred the edges.

"I feel wonderfully weird."

"I know. Do you think this is what opium is like?"

"No. You have to come down from opium. This will last forever. Maybe this is heaven."

Freddie rolled onto his side so that he was facing her. "Lilian. I think I..." He hesitated in his anxiety not to spoil the moment by going too far.

She drew her mouth into a broad smile. "Shhhh. I know. I feel the same." She was lying on her back, her eyes closed, savouring the bliss. Her profile looked resplendent in her repose as her ribs slowly rose and fell. The white sheet slid back and forth over her perfect breasts still flushed from her orgasms. Her stillness radiated light and heat and transcended her mortal form bathing Freddie in its protective glow. He wanted to tell her everything.

"That was my first time," he said awkwardly.

She turned her head dreamily. "Me too." The fire in her eyes had faded to pale blue embers. His face betrayed his thoughts. "What? You thought it wasn't?"

He was not sure if there was a hint of reproach in her voice. "I just... I mean, Cunningham said..."

She let out a gentle laugh. "You shouldn't listen to his bravado, Freddie darling." The word skewered him deliciously.

He was her darling. "He's full of nonsense, but don't let his manner fool you into thinking he's stupid. He's not. He's very good at what he does." She lifted her arm and stroked his cheek with the back of her hand. "He's tried it on with me. Many times. But I know how to handle Alex Cunningham, so you needn't worry."

"I'm sorry Lilian. I didn't mean...."

She smiled at him again and shook her head slightly. "Don't worry. We're here now. You and me. That's all that matters."

"Why did you... I mean, how did..." He had no idea how to phrase his question without sounding either dreadfully conceited or excruciatingly prissy.

"Why did I say yes to you? Why, after knowing you for only four hours did I decide to bring you back here where no man has ever been and then offer you my virginity on a plate?" As the words came out they sounded utterly preposterous to Freddie. How could that have possibly happened? All he could manage was a sheepish nod of the head.

Lilian let out a long sigh. "Do you want to do this? Do it properly, I mean?" The mist had cleared and her eyes had turned a darker shade as the intensity stoked once more. He nodded again, trying to speak, but there was no need. The deal had been sealed. "Okay then. But here's how it has to be. This wretched war could take either one of us at any time. There's no room for playing games. I don't want to be left with a telegram telling me you're dead and regretting all those things I wish I had said but hadn't. We have to tell each other everything. No matter how scary. No matter how dull. No matter how dark." The passion in her gaze was a raging fire.

"I understand." His voice was steady. His commitment was plain.

"Good. So why you?" Her face melted into a warm grin. "Because you are wonderful." His uncertain look made him the more lovely. He was completely unaware of how fine he was to her. "When they told me I was going to the ceremony I checked your file. I realised you had been at Wegierska Gorka, so you must have known Tadeusz. I made a beeline for you because I wanted to talk about him, but when I saw you I went weak."

"Really?"

"Yes. And then when you touched me. I can't describe it. It was like I had always known you. I'm sorry if my hand lingered a little too long on yours when you lit my cigarette."

"Tried to light it more like." Freddie gave a self-deprecating laugh. "What a mess I made of that. I felt sure you must have thought me a complete idiot."

She grinned in her memory of the moment. "Yes, you were a bit all over the place. It was very sweet though. To think all those battles you have fought, and yet put a girl in front of you and you go to pieces."

"Not any girl. Any girl would have been fine. It was you. I couldn't breathe let alone think. I was terrified that you would see through me. See just what an effect you had."

She giggled. "I did. Straight away. You wouldn't make a very good spy Freddie Zamoyski. I was just pleased that you couldn't see that you were having the same effect on me."

"I can't believe that."

"Scout's honour," she laughed lifting her left hand and pinning her little finger down with her thumb. Freddie looked perplexed at the gesture which made her laugh more. "It's the truth, darling. It means it's the truth." There was that word again.

"I'm so sorry about that awful, suggestive comment." Lines furrowed his forehead.

"That's still bothering you, isn't it?"

"Yes."

"Well, don't let it. Without that we might not be here now. After all, it did rather crystallise everything."

He laughed. She might actually have been right. "So what's your connection with Poland?" As he asked the question his hand strayed to her breast and began lightly caressing the warm, soft skin.

Lilian drew a sharp breath, as it tingled deliciously and her nipple immediately hardened once more. "My father," she answered through broken breathing. Freddie suddenly felt embarrassed at his presumption and pulled away, but Lilian immediately took his hand and placed it back onto her flushed, rounded form. "Keep doing that and I'll tell you everything," she purred. She explained that her father had been Polish and his sister had been Tadeusz Semik's mother. He had come to London before the Great War for reasons that seemed to have been lost over time. There, he met and married Lilian's mother and settled, changing his name.

"It was much easier to find work as a Brown than as a Bronowski," she commented, as the circular motions of Freddie's hand brushed her nipple, making it more engorged and sensitive than she had ever known it.

In 1918 he had returned to Poland to fight for his homeland's independence, and never returned. He was killed at the Battle of the Wistula. Lilian had been three years old at the time. In the mid thirties, as soon as she was old enough, she had travelled to Poland to meet her father's family and had immediately forged a bond with Semik whom she loved as a brother. She spent two years living in and around Krakow where her Polish became fluent and she picked up a working knowledge of German, Czech and Hungarian.

"I must have left Krakow at around the time you arrived," she smiled. "It's funny to think that we could have passed each other in the street and not given a second look."

"I don't think that would be likely," replied Freddie, recalling his first sight of her earlier that day.

"Perhaps not. But you know what I mean." Her abdominal muscles contracted as Freddie lightly twisted her nipple between his thumb and forefinger.

"And then you came back to Britain and joined the Air Force?"

"Yes, and you know the rest." Her rushed speech and lightly closed eyelids betrayed her sudden disinterest in any further talk. Without shame she slid her hand down to his groin and on finding him handsomely ready pulled him onto her aching frame.

And that was how the night passed. Between talking and enjoying each other in the most glorious exploration they filled the all too brief hours before the sun flooded in through the window to discover their secret cocoon and break the spell.

Freddie floated back to the embassy where he received something of a dressing down for having gone missing. But no one really quite seemed to know who had the authority to discipline him, and given his celebrity status and the fact that there was some dispute as to whether or not he was on leave, he escaped with a mild ticking off. In any case, President Raczkiewicz and the other top brass had decided that Freddie had made enough of an impression to be of some use in their dealings with British Intelligence. He protested at his lack of experience or training in the field, but was forced to concede when it was pointed out that the limited human resources available to the Poles must often be deployed wherever they might happen to find themselves. "Beggars can't be choosers," pronounced one colonel tartly, and the matter was decided.

And so it was that his transfer was confirmed and he became the military attaché to the British. It came with a promotion to major, and a remit that allowed him the freedom to come and go as he pleased. He briefed the Polish High Command, such as it was, on the various developments their hosts deemed fit for him to know while providing them in return with valuable insights into the likely political manoeuvrings in occupied central Europe. But as the weeks unfolded his greatest contribution came in the form of a new sort of warfare, to combat a new weapon. It involved the warfare of the mind, and he proved himself a skilled player.

The invasion of France pushed their work into a higher gear as they rose to meet the German response to the attack. Almost as soon as the landings started the Nazis began firing their new wonder weapon at London. They called it the V1, but the crude signature note of its revolutionary pulse jet engine earned it the nickname doodlebug. And it was feared across London. When the fuel ran dry the coarse drone stopped and there was an agonising silence as the bomb fell to earth in the blind lottery of death.

It was a masterpiece of destructive weaponry but worse still it sapped the morale of the population. It had one weakness. To hit London the engineers at the launch sites in France needed to set the gyroscopes accurately, and that required feedback on the location of each ground strike. This became Freddie's new work, and he was very good at it. The Germans relied on their network of spies to tell them where their bombs were falling, and that was the allies' point of attack.

Most German spies had been turned, and with his language skills and his fierce intellect, Freddie was given increasing control of more of these double agents in a game of bluff and double bluff. He coordinated a progressive programme of increasingly divergent reports to be sent back to his spymaster counterparts in the Wehrmacht. Over three weeks he orchestrated the drift of V1 launch vectors so that many now fell harmlessly in the fields of Surrey, saving thousands of lives. It was tricky work. At the time he had no idea who his adversary was, but the name of his German opponent in this mind game that transcended the gambits of chess was Oberst Max Wachtel.

And Freddie knew that Max was onto him. Increasing numbers of doodlebug wreckages were found to have radio transmitters on board, and the allies realised that these were being used by the Germans to confirm their ground reports of their aim. By mid August Freddie was sure that his faceless opponent was poring over radio data telling him his bombs were missing the mark and comparing it with Freddie's lies that told him he was spot on target.

Through Freddie's skill, intuition and, crucially, his instinct to know when to tell the truth, Wachtel decided that his radio transmitters were the ones at fault and carried on firing his death machines at farms. How many thousands of lives he saved with this work would never be known, but his renown within this secret world grew. More than once he was requested to attend briefings at the War Rooms where Churchill specifically asked him by name for his assessment. His rise was meteoric.

Every spare moment he could find he spent with Lilian as their love blossomed beyond his wildest dreams. True to their word, they shared everything. Their hopes, loves, fears and secrets. She was truly divine. Not just her physical form that aroused Freddie more and more every day he knew her better, but also her soul that exuded such kindness. She was no empty-headed beauty. Her mind was sharp, her insight complete. She was disarmingly direct, but always with a gentleness that softened even the harshest perspective. She saw him for everything that he was, and loved him the more for it. In return he was utterly lost in her. She was his life.

The night he told her of the gulag and the colosseum she wept for him while cradling him in her arms. Perhaps he did not tell her every last detail in the way he confessed to me, but there was no judgement from Lilian, just love and understanding as she kissed the knotted stigmata on his hands. A month earlier he could never have dreamed of telling anyone of the things he had done to survive. To have told a girl and risk the rejection that would come from the vacuum of understanding would have been unthinkable. But she was not just any girl. She was not just his girl. She was the fulcrum on which his world turned. She completed him, and as their bodies, minds and spirits fused into one being he could not imagine keeping his story from her.

"My poor love," she whispered as she kissed his hair. If there was any space at all between them it evaporated that night in the act of redemptive love they made. Now she knew every part of him. He was hers for life.

Three months after the invasion life turned again. He had never been happier. His professional skills were attracting admiration from his superiors and the British alike, and Lilian was bound to him in a way he could still not believe. After two months of hard fighting the battle in Normandy had concluded as the Americans broke out into the open countryside to the south and on towards the valley of the Loire, while the jaws of the allied pincers had locked shut around the Falaise pocket. The Germans had poured men and equipment into the conflict in a last despairing attempt to keep the allies locked against the coast. They knew that failure would cost them everything, but in this game of poker in the west they continued to match the Americans division for division as they raised the bidding to painful levels. At the end of August their gamble ran its measure and their whole position collapsed as the allies swept through France with alarming speed.

And Lilian had finally decided that it was time for Freddie to meet her family. He was nervous and excited, keen to make a good impression, but was aware that she seemed troubled. For the first time he sensed her holding something back. He asked, but she brushed his questions aside with her usual charm. He would have to wait.

The pounded city held a grim beauty, bathed in the bright September sunshine of this Sunday afternoon. Piles of rubble decorated their route where once had stood homes. The random destruction that had rained upon this defiant people in their darkest hours was everywhere. No longer did the waves of the Luftwaffe sweep across the skies like angels of death, but instead Wachtel's blindly murderous automata terrorised the capital.

Freddie looked at the new craters and heaps of pulverised

masonry as they drove and wondered if he should push harder in his game of intrigue. As he looked on those destroyed houses the impact of his intervention was brought home to him. In some sense he held the gift of life and death for these poor people, and while he could not choose where the bombs fell, maybe he should lure more away from these packed streets. But that would risk being discovered and an even worse death toll, and the utilitarian voice in his head steadied his ruminations.

Lilian was uncharacteristically tense as they drew up outside the humble dwelling in a half bombed-out street in the city's east end. "Don't be surprised if my accent changes a little, darling," she warned as she squeezed his hand as much, he thought, for her own reassurance as for his. In the short time he had been in London he had noticed the range of dialects that appeared to mark social standing to an extent he had not seen anywhere else. He had not asked, but had wondered if the tones and vocabulary that she used had been learned. Her story was of a working class girl who had used her wit and intellect to climb both the social and professional ladders. Now he would see her roots, and it made her anxious.

"Don't be afraid," he whispered earnestly as he enveloped her in his broad arms. "I love you. I love every part of you. I love your present and I love your past. It has made you what you are." She kissed him deeply in response, smiled, and knocked on the door.

Lilian's mother was a thin, welcoming woman whose grey hair and slight stoop spoke of the hardships she had endured to raise her two daughters alone. She embraced Lilian with unconditional love before pulling away and holding her shoulders steady like a photographer composing a shot.

"Let me look at you Lil." Her accent was so heavy, her English so vernacular, that even Freddie struggled for a few minutes to tune in to her meaning. "You've changed, girl." Her keen gaze scrutinised her daughter, seeing all. A smile grew to a grin as she passed a look at Freddie and back. "You're in love. Oh my God girl, I never thought I'd see it." She turned to Freddie. "You must be quite a fella. Melting this one's heart. No one else ever managed it. What's your name again?"

He stiffened slightly in respect and offered his hand. "Major Freddie Zamoyski, ma'am."

She shook it hesitatingly. "Well, Major Freddie Zosky. Just you look out for my Lil here. She's special, she is."

"Ma." Lilian was trying to interject.

Her mother pressed on regardless. "She's never fallen. Never allowed no one in. So you treat her right. You understand?" She was ageing, but the delicate beauty that shone from Lilian was still there, if a little fading. Freddie could see where his love got her looks as well as her direct manner. Of course she wrapped it in a softer package, while for her mother it just flowed straight from the heart.

"Mum! Stop it!"

Freddie smiled warmly, ignoring her attempt to protect him from the full force of this matriarch. "No, mum. Don't stop it. Keep fighting her corner. As I always will." They were still holding hands which added to the weight of his words. "I love your daughter with a passion and a depth I never thought possible. She lights my life and makes me whole. There is nothing I would not do for her. You have nothing to fear, Mrs. Brown."

For a brief moment she looked slightly stunned, before glancing at Lilian. "Poetic bugger ain't he?" She turned back and staged her final rearguard action. "All right Major Zosky. Just you see you do." She withdrew her hand, and the trial was complete. She wandered away as she called over her shoulder. "Sit yourselves down then. I'll put the kettle on."

"Sorry," she offered as they sat together.

"Don't be. She's wonderful."

"She likes you. And that's no mean feat. She doesn't suffer fools."

"I can see that," he smiled and rested his hand on hers.

"So. You going to bugger off back to Poland too?" The accusation came unexpectedly from Freddie's blind side. He turned quickly to see a plain woman standing in the doorway to the hall. He opened his mouth, preparing to respond. "'Cos if you are then do it now before you break her heart."

"Maggie!" Lilian flashed an angry look at her sister.

"Don't you 'Maggie' me," came the sharp reply. "Why is he any different to dad? Pissing off back to his 'beloved Poland' and leaving mum in the shit."

"I'm sorry, Freddie. This is my sister Maggie."

There was no time for him to stand. Maggie was in full flow. "Don't you apologise for me, you stuck up tart. What's wrong? We ain't good enough for your posh friends?"

Lilian was on her feet in an instant and battle was joined. "You're more than good enough you silly cow." Her polished vowels were discarded as the east end girl flooded out. "But he ain't like dad. Not like that. You've got him wrong."

"Have I?" She turned on Freddie and issued her challenge. "Have I really?" She was a little taller than Lilian with dark, limp hair. Freddie opened his mouth again, but too slow to stop the whirlwind. "What's the matter? Cat got your tongue, has it?"

"Maggie! Stop it!"

"Stop it? Stop it? I'm looking out for you, you silly moo. The bloody war'll be over by Christmas, and you won't see him for dust. And who do you think will pick up the pieces?" She threw her arms around her sister's neck and hugged her so close she could have suffocated. "I couldn't bear that. I couldn't bear to see you suffer what mum did."

"Margaret Brown. Sit down!" Their mother's stern voice called an end to her children's fracas. "Please accept our apologies, Major Zosky," she offered with an authority that defied challenge.

"Of course, Mrs. Brown. There really is nothing to apologise for." He was doing his best to defuse the confrontation that had erupted between these powerful women whose free flowing verbal aggression and honesty was breath taking. His experience was of sedate family life, cosmopolitan society and the deep privations of war. This open passion born of true love was new to him and it explained so much. Lilian applied a sophisticated veneer, but not far beneath the surface raged this torrent of emotion. And here she was fighting his corner, protecting him like a wild cat with her cub.

"Yes there is. You know better than to speak like that to a guest, Maggie." She turned her forensic gaze on him. "And for what it's worth, I believe Major Zosky here when he says he loves our Lil. He won't run off, will you Major Zosky?"

It was clearly more of an instruction than a question, but he answered anyway. "No ma'am."

There was a brief silence that was broken by Lilian's correction. "It's Zamoyski, mum."

"Don't you get clever with me, Miss Hoity Toity." Her eyes flashed, before she turned back. "Tea, Major Zosky?"

"Yes, thank you, ma'am. And please, call me Freddie."

"All right Freddie. One honest east end cuppa coming up."

The rest of the afternoon went well. The sisters had got most of the fight out of their system, although there were a few milder flashpoints. Maggie had said what she needed to say. Her delivery perhaps lacked some finesse, but her motives were genuine and heartfelt. It was clear that they both loved Lilian with a depth that they could express only at tangents, translating it to sarcasm, humour or aggression as the moment required.

"So, Lil tells me you knew my nephew," questioned Mrs. Brown as the conversation lulled.

"Yes ma'am." He paused for a moment as the significance of the day welled up within him and he steadied his emotions. "It was five years ago to this very day that he died by my side." For once all three women were silent, absorbing the meaning of his words. "Forty of us were rounded up by the Germans, herded into a barn and machine-gunned. Captain Semik fell onto me. It was his body that shielded me. I owe him my life."

As the day grew longer Maggie warmed a little, but she was difficult to read. She was as shrouded in defences as Lilian was open, but Freddie sensed that deep inside she was softer and less resilient than her older sister. Just as he seemed to be making ground and forming a connection she would slam the door in his face with some brutal comment that elicited a protective snarl from Lilian. It was like taking tea with a pride of lionesses, as Freddie saw clearly the source of Lilian's passion.

"Well, that was an experience," he smiled as they lay back naked in each other's arms. Their love making was flowering to dizzying heights. As their spirits fused, their physical union was beyond imagining and made that first night seem like a gentle stroll in the foothills of the Olympian peaks on which they now strode.

"You did so well, darling. I was worried how they would be with you." The sophisticated vowels and precise pronunciation had returned.

"They are only looking out for you. I understand their concern."

She cast him a look of doubt. "Are they right to be?"

"No. Never." His stern stare dispelled any question. "Maggie's quite a force, isn't she?"

"You mean she's rude."

"No. I didn't..."

"Well, she is. She was very rude to you. She's always pretty prickly, but today she was extra defensive. She was terrified of letting you in, but I could see her almost unable to help herself." She stared meaningfully at him. "You know, I think she was just a bit smitten by you."

"Don't be silly," he frowned.

"You were a bit uncomfortable with our honesty, weren't

215

you?"

"No. Not uncomfortable. But it's an acquired art, and I'm still learning the ropes. I'm still working out the boundaries."

"There are no boundaries for you and me, Major Zosky," she smiled teasingly.

He paused, staring at her. As so often, she had presented him with a choice. Brush aside the profound and focus on her mother's groping attempt at his name, or discard the trivial and talk of the bottomless abyss of their love. "No boundaries." The late summer sun was glancing through the window and caught her hair that shone like a lantern in the growing gloom of the room. This feeling was so good it almost hurt. It could not get better.

"What did Maggie mean with that phrase?" He replayed it in his head to form the words. "When she was comparing me to your father? She said something about you being left like your mother. I think she said 'Up the duff.'" His head shook in mild puzzlement. "I have not heard that phrase before. What's the duff?"

She took a deep breath and exhaled. "Pregnant, my darling." His body fizzed again at that word, made even better by being used in its possessive form. "It means pregnant."

"Ah." He smiled, recognising the context in which it had been used. "That would explain your mother's reaction. Well I can understand that. I'm sure she would have made it much harder for me if you were." He snuggled into the crook of her arm as his mind floated away still wrapped in the after-glow of their passion.

"I am," she said softly.

The words struck him like a bolt of lightning. His world lurched, as it cracked and ripped in the face of this earthquake. His open-mouthed stare grew in stages through a smile to a grin to an uncontrollable rictus. She was pregnant. Images of their future together flooded through his mind, of the children they would have, the happiness they would experience, and the old age they would share. There was the smallest tear in her eye, as he scooped her in his arms and kissed her deeper and longer than ever before.

"You're not angry?" she whispered.

"Angry?" He pulled away so that he could look her full in her beautiful face. "Angry? I am ecstatic. We are going to have a baby!"

She nodded as tears of joy rolled down her face. "Yes. We are."

"Marry me Lilian." The words came out plain and clear, from a place deep within his being. The idea had not been thought through. There was no decision to be made. It was a simple statement of how the world should be, of everything that he desired.

Tears poured down her face, her lips quivered and the broadest beam lit up her wet face. She was completely dishevelled and had never looked more stunning.

-oOo-

"We were married in late September," smiled Freddie in the warm embers of the memory. "It was a small affair in Whitechapel. But it was the happiest day of my life."

"She sounds wonderful," I reflected.

"That doesn't even begin to describe her." He held out an unsteady arm and fumbled with the bedside cabinet. With a little help from me he found his wallet and carefully pulled out a photograph. The woman who stared at me was uniquely beautiful. I could have looked for hours on her mesmerising face projected across the decades.

"Gosh."

"Hmmm. Gosh indeed," agreed Freddie.

The door opened with a cursory knock and a young doctor entered. She was slim and blonde and full of life as she asked

217

Freddie how he was feeling. He was tired, but otherwise felt no different. She checked the machine and looked intently at the observation chart clipped to the end of his bed.

"I'm going to increase your drip a little," she explained. "Just some fine tuning."

"You mean I need even more of this stuff to keep me going a little longer," he said without any hint of irony.

She sighed and took a long look at him, before gliding around the end of his bed and sitting by his feet. "I think we both know what is happening Mr. Zamoyski."

"Please. Call me Freddie."

She nodded with a warm smile. The sort a grown woman secure in her vitality might give to an ageing and crumbling grandfather. "Freddie," she agreed in a sympathetic tone. There was kindness in the way she broached this most painful thing. "What's that?" she asked pointing at the photo still clutched in Freddie's hand. It was a transparent attempt to move the conversation away from his imminent death, but he was happy to share Lilian with the world.

"It is my wife," he said with sweet tenderness.

"She's beautiful," remarked the doctor, staring in genuine admiration at the slightly fading image.

"She is." There was a silence as we both looked at his calm face. "I know now that she is waiting for me. And I am ready to go to her."

The thought of losing Freddie was terrible, and in my private space I had pleaded with the God I had rediscovered to let him live. But in that moment I saw that to die would be the release he sought, and in a strange way his simple heart-rending statement brought me peace.

"You remind me of her," he smiled at the doctor. "She was very beautiful and very kind. And you have her dimples." In any other context it would have sounded inappropriate, but somehow Freddie made it seem natural.

She smiled self-deprecatingly and brushed off his compliment. "You're very kind Freddie." Then she turned to me. "You're not tiring him now, are you Father?"

I rather suspected that I was, but Freddie came to my rescue. "Of course he isn't, doctor. He is my very dear friend." As he said those words he fixed me with a profound stare that told me he was talking straight to me. "And I think he needs some lunch."

"Yes. Me too," she replied. "These weekend shifts are killers."

"When did you last sleep, you poor thing? You look tired." As I looked again I saw he was right. She fizzed with life, but when her concentration waned it left a drawn expression on her delicate features.

"Thursday night," she reflected wearily. "I'll sleep well tomorrow. Now." She held her index finger out to issue her orders. "You rest. And you," she turned to me. "Not too late." Freddie smirked and glanced at me as if we were two naughty boys being admonished for staying up past our bedtimes.

"Yes doctor," he nodded, still with a smile. Once she had left he turned to me as if taking me into his confidence. "She really does remind me of her, you know." He smiled, and his gaze drifted to the door as if Lilian's essence still hung there. "Bah! See what this stuff does to you?" He glanced back at the machine. "By the time I die I'll be having all kinds of hallucinations." He shook his head and smiled. "You'd better get something to eat, Tom. Apparently the canteen runs short on Sundays."

As the words passed his lips the door opened again as an orderly brought his lunch in. It was my sign to depart, so off I wandered to the lifts. I leaned against the wall waiting for its arrival, when the doors opened and out stepped Norah.

"Hello again," I smiled.

"Hello Father," she replied, casting me a nervous glance.

"I hope you don't mind me intruding, but you seem troubled. If there is anything I can do to help then please let me know." Still she looked hesitant. "Is your husband on the ward?"

She paused before answering. "A very dear friend, Father."

"I'm sure God is looking over him," I offered with renewed confidence that it was so.

"I hope so," she mumbled with a distant look. "I hope he finds Him before the end." She turned and walked off deep in her thoughts.

X - Liberation

"Are you sure you want to carry on with this today, Freddie?" The break for lunch had allowed me time to think about what the doctor had said. Perhaps I was pushing him too hard.

"Tom," he smiled at me. "It is time to finish. We both know that."

He was right, of course. He was always right. And so he picked up his story whose trajectory seemed inexorably tied to the fortunes of war. He told me how his position as attaché to the British was compromised by his marriage, and the solution decided on by his masters.

"I think Cunningham knew something was going on," he smiled. "It turned out that he was not as insufferable as he at first appeared, and he had a genuine fondness for Lilian. She said that he had changed since I was around. That he recognised that I was the better man for her. But she was always saying kind things like that. She always saw the best in people."

"Well, the cat would have been well and truly out of the bag with the wedding," I said, stating the obvious.

"Exactly. And that's when things started to go awry at the embassy. The Brits were giving me less and less information, and eventually I had to accept the fact that Poland was being slowly squeezed out of the picture."

"And your bosses blamed it on your marriage to Lilian?"

"It was not an unreasonable assumption at the time, although it soon proved that relationships between the governments were cooling rapidly and it was really nothing to do with me. Stalin was making rapid advances in Eastern Europe and it was looking increasingly likely that he would take Berlin well before the Americans and the British got there. That meant that Poland would be hundreds of miles behind the Russian front."

"The iron curtain," I offered.

"In a manner of speaking." He let my ignorance down gently again. "That came a little later, but it was soon clear that Stalin wanted Poland to be run by the Polish communists as a puppet state. And for Britain to get its way in other countries like Austria and Greece it had to compromise."

"It's weird isn't it?" I reflected, frowning. "The war that started with France and Britain making a stand for Polish freedom ended with us trading them like chips in the game of international politics."

"That is how the world works, Tom. But we're ahead of ourselves again. Lilian and I moved into what they called married quarters." He smiled mischievously at me. "It was just her old flat redesignated."

"That must have been quite a change for you. Married life. And in such turbulent times."

"I suppose. But it was perfect." He looked wistfully into space. "Life seemed so simple. So certain. I had survived the gulag, we had found each other and when the war was over we would live the life of the British middle class with our perfect children." He came back from his dream. "You have enough tapes?"

"Yes," I nodded. "Don't worry about that. Keep going."

-oOo-

Freddie was living a dream that he could hardly believe. God had delivered him from certain death, and given him the gift of Lilian's love. His years of belief and faith had been repaid a thousand fold as they made their plans for the future and for the April child that would seal their union.

Cunningham was sorting out the paperwork for Freddie to stay in Britain after the war was over, and it puzzled them both that he seemed so focused on what they assumed would be nothing more than a formality. It was only later that they realised he must have suspected that the British government were considering the almost forced repatriation of many of their Polish guests to placate Stalin.

Even Maggie had finally accepted Freddie into the family. She was fiercely loyal to her mother and sister, but that intense protectiveness now draped itself over him too. She was quite unlike Lilian. Dark haired, plain and stolid, she would never attain the same heights, but her unswerving loyalty marked her as special. She could see how happy Freddie made her sister and she loved him for that.

November had wrapped its foggy shroud around the city, robbing the light of its glint and the sound of its resonance, as Freddie reported for his weekly meeting with the policy makers at Portland Place. It was a brief affair that did nothing to lift the strained expressions on the faces around him.

"There's nothing in your report, Major, that we couldn't get from the pages of The Times." General Gano was the kind of shrewd calculating man ideally suited to his role as the nation's spymaster. It was whispered that he had coordinated the recent uprising in Warsaw, that miscarriage of defiance that had ended so calamitously. The government in exile had gambled on the advancing Russians being shamed into helping the insurgents, only to watch as Stalin's icy indifference allowed their slaughter. They were losing their influence as the wheels of statecraft turned irresistibly against them.

"I can only pass on what I am told, sir."

"Yes, but why is that drying up?" Gano's eyes peered out from his urbane face. His countenance had always been unreadable, but as the old alliances melted in the flux of destiny Freddie sensed his desperation. "This girl?" he continued with uncharacteristic directness.

"You mean my wife," retorted Freddie with a sharpness that surprised even himself.

Gano shrugged and gave a grunt of ambivalence. "You're

losing your touch. And now these flying bombs have stopped it seems our hosts find you of limited use."

"I really don't think that..."

"No. I'm sure you don't, Major Zamoyski." Gano had decided on his course of action, and it was clear that he would not be deflected. The other men sat impassively, watching the inevitable unfold before them. One shifted uneasily in his seat, embarrassed that Freddie should be chosen as the sacrificial offering, but no one sprang to his defence. "I'm redeploying you, Zamoyski."

Faced with this bluff resolve, Freddie accepted his fate with the same stoical bearing he had so often seen in his father. "Yes sir."

"How's your French?"

"Fluent sir, though with an accent."

"And your German?"

"Clean." His answers were clipped and formal, but inside his mind was racing. What did this puppet master have planned for him? Six months earlier the notion of being dropped behind enemy lines would have caused him no anxiety, but now he had something to live for. How much longer could he ride his luck? What would he do trapped inside the chaos of a disintegrating fascist empire with Lilian hundreds of miles away?

"Good. And your Russian?" Freddie looked bemused. "Hmmm. Yes. I imagine that's clean too."

"It is sir," he frowned. "For what purpose would I need these languages?"

Gano picked up the pipe that sat on the table before him and began filling the bowl with a generous charge of loose tobacco. "I'm sending you to France."

France. Not Germany. Freddie's poker face did nothing to betray the relief that he would not be assigned some crazy mission concocted by this desperate man. He had heard of men being dropped behind German lines with little training, but perhaps that was not to be his fate.

"The British are terrible linguists and have an appalling shortage of interpreters." Linguists? Was he to be sent out as some sort of liaison officer with the armies advancing through Holland? "But the Americans are even worse. Some people question whether they can even speak English." There was a ripple of polite laughter. "So I'm sending you to join their Third Army." He lit a match and drew the flame through the pipe.

"Yes sir." After his experiences of close quarter combat Freddie found himself relieved at the thought of being attached to the general staff of a field army. For a fleeting moment a voice in his head accused him of cowardice, but it was quickly answered by the reasonable retort that bravery is defined by how adversity is met and not in recklessly seeking it out.

"Patton is about to cross into Germany and is short of intelligence and signals officers fluent in German. There is also reliable information that installations in southern Germany are full of Polish, Czech, Russian and Ukrainian forced labour. Your skills could be vital when it comes to liberating them." Plumes of thick purple smoke billowed up.

"I understand sir, but the work I'm doing at the moment..."

"Is done Major. The rocket sites have been overrun. The threat has gone. You're needed elsewhere." There was no arguing. "I'm promoting you to Lieutenant Colonel." Gano's decision was made. The promotion was a sweetener to move him on. "You leave next week."

And so it was that Freddie's time in London came to a close. An overnight propaganda visit had turned into the most significant six months of his life, and he reflected on how abuse and violence might dictate a man's path but in God's tender care only love can define his destiny.

Lilian took the news with the strength Freddie expected, although they were both stunned at the thought of their imminent separation. Their love affair had been so total, so embracing, that they had never for one moment considered how it would actually feel to be parted despite the knowledge that it was an ever present threat.

Their last few days together were the closest Freddie could imagine being to another human. They became one in every sense he could describe as he felt her presence light up all the corners of his soul. The night before he left, Cunningham came to their flat to give Freddie the papers that guaranteed his right to stay in Britain.

"Keep them safe," he said grimly.

"You think they will be that important?" asked Freddie as Lilian busied herself in the small kitchen making them all a cup of tea.

He nodded gravely. "Yes."

What he knew of the diplomatic manoeuvrings Freddie dared not ask, but understood the risk his friend feared was growing for the Poles here in Britain. "Thank you Alex. You are a true friend."

Cunningham smiled. "I know you thought I was a cad. But I hope you see now that's just a front. People underestimate you if they think you are superficial."

"I know that," he smiled in return before glancing over his shoulder to check that Lilian was still out of the room. He turned back with a look that told Cunningham something of deep significance was coming. "If I die I want you to take care of Lilian."

"Don't be silly, old boy." He refused to consider the scenario. "You won't die. You'll return."

"Promise me."

Eventually he gave a small nod of capitulation. "Of course, Freddie. You know I will."

"What are you boys planning?" chirped Lilian as she floated back into the room that was still heavy with conspiracy.

Freddie laughed and thought quickly. "Nothing, darling. I

was asking Alex to promise to use the intelligence network to let me know as soon as you've delivered."

"That's right," confirmed Cunningham. "Letters can take weeks to get to the front, so a suitable intelligence message wired to the field staff of the Third Army would be just the trick. Delivery of tanks for a boy, and artillery for a girl."

Lilian beamed. "What a wonderful idea. Thank you Alex." Then her smile broke and she raised a more serious question. "Now, I need to ask you a favour. It's about.... Well, it's....."

"Your pregnancy?" he offered, to spare her embarrassment at trying to find a delicate way of expressing her concern. "Don't worry, Lilian. Baker Street has a way of getting what it wants. I've already put in the paperwork."

Again, he had proven himself to be a man of foresight and a very great friend. Lilian's pregnancy was becoming hard to conceal, and yet she knew that WAAF regulations dictated that she should be removed from duty. She loved her work and wanted to continue. Eastern Europe was again in the melting pot and the next few months could dictate the shape of the world for decades to come. She was desperate to carry on the work she had been so good at, and his assurance that the shadowy influence of the Special Operations Executive would ensure this was welcome.

"Thank you Alex," she smiled.

"That's my pleasure." He flashed a theatrical look around the flat. "It means you get to stay here too," he added, before finishing his tea and bidding them farewell.

They held each other so close that night that the line between them blurred to nothingness. Their hearts beat as one. Their minds wrapped themselves into a single tangle of consciousness. And their souls melted to a soft unity. As they lay together in their rapture Freddie felt a small kick against his stomach and his ecstasy was complete in the union of three.

Morning came with the pain of the wrench of separation. As Freddie collected the last few items for his kit bag it felt as if a limb had been torn off. Lilian stood before him, her flowering womb neatly perfecting her feminine vitality, and he gazed on her naked form one last time. The emotion of the moment robbed him of the words to express himself, but none were needed in that unspoken farewell. His mind painted the portrait of that moment that would forever hang in the gallery of his memory. A moment he would have given anything to hold forever.

But time marches to its own pace, oblivious and uncaring to the desires of men, and soon enough they stood facing each other on the platform of Waterloo station. Beside them in the smoke of the cavernous lair stood the carriages in their forlorn shabby livery of the Southern Railway, once resplendent in malachite green with vivid yellow lettering.

She took his hands in hers as the sound of slamming carriage doors cut through the steam that swirled around them like dragons' breath. She wore her uniform with her hair drawn up under her cap and Freddie was stunned anew as he gazed upon that very same beauty that had ended his old life that night in Portland Place. It was as if they had come full circle together. But gone was the inquisitive, coquettish gaze. Adoration poured from her eyes as if to smother him in a protective cocoon that no threat could penetrate.

"You listen to me Freddie Zamoyski," she ordered. "You stay alive." Her grip tightened. "You do whatever you have to do." Her eyes burned. "You hear me? Anything. I know you. And I love you for everything that you are. Everything that you've done." Her grip was crushing his hands with a power that startled him. "If you have to do that again then you do it. But you come home to me. You hear me? You come home!"

She released his hands and they held each other one last lingering time. Her scent filled his head as the softness of her mouth filled his being before the long, shrill cry of a whistle ended their embrace. His heart was torn from his chest as their hands slid over each other until the last brush of their fingertips was broken and the train pulled away.

He leaned out of the carriage looking back at her motionless form that stood proud and resolute. A tear slowly ran down her cheek like a raindrop on a windowpane as she receded into the mist. The carriage rattled and shook as the details of her face faded and Freddie was left with nothing more than a solitary nondescript shape in the gloom that was everything he held dear in the world.

The weather in the channel in late November was grim. Despite their rapid advances across France the allies had failed to take any of the deep water ports on the coast and the whole invasion was still being supplied through Cherbourg, the only facility that could handle the traffic. Antwerp had finally fallen a week or two earlier, but the harbour entrance was a mass of mines and scuttled wrecks that would prevent serious supply for weeks to come.

The crossing from Portsmouth to Normandy was rough, but the stench of vomit from a thousand men hardly registered as Freddie gazed back in his mind at that last sight of Lilian. Cherbourg was a seething mass of activity straining every sinew to deliver the means of conquest to the rapiers of the advanced columns hundreds of miles away. The mix of salt spray and diesel was powerfully evocative and took Freddie to the memory of that first landing in Italy when he craved the chance to confront the German war machine. Lilian would be forever with him, but the old warrior instinct stirred. He would do whatever he must to survive.

It was on the first day of Advent that Freddie climbed out of the truck into the teeth of the worst Lorraine winter for years. Étain was normally a sleepy settlement nestling in the rolling and fertile countryside of eastern France, but its location only fifteen miles from Verdun meant that it had seen more than its fair share of war, trapped as it was in the cockpit of a millennium of European conflict. And the soldiers were back again. The

Americans had set up their headquarters here as they had planned and executed the slow destruction of the German defenders of Metz to the east. That city now lay in ruins, pounded to dust in the clash of titanic wills as the armies fought to a standstill, both starved of supplies.

As he planted his feet firmly on the soil of this new battlefield Freddie was greeted by the tall, wiry figure of an American officer bearing the insignia of a major, and an unusually patrician demeanour. "Colonel Zamoyski?" The man raised his salute which Freddie returned.

"Major Pfann?"

"Got me in one," smiled the ageing staff officer, "But please call me George. Let me show you to your quarters."

The general staff had take up residence in a small chateau outside the town that bore some scars of the recent fighting but had been relatively spared by the Third Army's rapid advance that had given the defenders little time to prepare any effective defence. Freddie's room was basic but comfortable and had a sort of classic rustic charm, snuggling under the eaves of the building.

"Dump your kit bag and I'll give you the tour," smiled Pfann, evidently keen to strike up a relationship with this new and rather exotic import. "I'm the secretary to the general staff here, so if you have any problems then I'm your man."

"Thank you," smiled Freddie, slightly bemused by the major's informality. "With whom will I be working? I believe the designation of your signals adjutant is G6?" His skill with languages was enough that even as the sentence passed his lips he sensed it grating in this strangely different yet disconcertingly familiar setting. The town was a hive of intense military activity, yet the soldiers moved in a natural, fluid way as if they were walking to the grocery store. Even their salutes lacked structure and Freddie had his first inkling of the vastly different national culture from which these men sprang.

"G6? Well, yes. Signals would normally be handled by our

G6, but he was shot last week. The general believes in the staff here being in close contact with the brigades so we are regularly out at the front." He paused and looked at the floor. "John was a good friend. Damned sniper." He drew a sharp breath and resumed the tour. "His duties have been taken over temporarily by our G2, Oscar Koch."

The army's senior general staff were referred to in this generic manner which made it easier for men to orientate themselves if they needed to move between units. G6 was the standard designation of the signals officer, and in his absence his work was being done by the G2, the head of intelligence.

Colonel Koch was a shrewd man with a canny eye for character. His balding head, wire rimmed glasses and precise manner gave him the appearance of a high school teacher of mathematics and within moments of his introduction Freddie could feel him calculating his worth, extrapolating his value.

"Your file makes for exceptionally interesting reading Colonel Zamoyski." Freddie could not read his expression and replied with an equally bland nod of his own. "Your work with the buzz bombs is particularly fascinating." That was significant. In the whole of his file the piece that was worthy of note was his game of chess with Wachtel, and Freddie saw his first glimpses of the grandmaster he would come to admire in Koch.

"Thank you." The men looked at each other, their faces giving nothing away.

"It says here you speak both German and Russian fluently."

"That's right."

The stare continued until finally the corner of Koch's mouth turned up and he pulled the glasses from his face, discarding them onto the papers before him. "I'm acting G6 here Zamoyski, as if I don't have enough on my plate already running our intelligence. You'd think with a name like Koch," he used the usual Milwaukee pronunciation with a soft "ch" like cochineal before giving it its true German root, "or should I say Koch, that I'd have a working knowledge of Kraut. The truth is I could just about ask directions to the town hall, though I doubt I'd understand the answer. And now I'm supposed to make sense of the stuff we pick up from these bastards."

"You're picking up German communications?"

"Half their men are raw and most of them have given up using that Enigma crap. The prisoners we've taken say they're so short of equipment that most of their combat units don't even have the encrypting machines they need."

"So you're getting everything?"

"Well, we would, but the language they use is so idiomatic that we can't make head nor tail of it. You think you can?"

"I'll do my best."

"Good. That's decided then. You'll be acting G6, but you report to me. Understand?"

"Yes Colonel," smiled Freddie.

"There's not much going on in this sector right now. They have no men and we have no fuel so you should have time to get used to it all. Get Pfann to show you the signals centre."

It was a five minute walk from the headquarters to the farmhouse that had been taken over to serve as the army's link to the outside world and the command structure above. After introducing him to the men that staffed it Pfann went on his way. The half dozen or so staff seemed more than competent in the technology of their craft as they explained to Freddie how their operation worked, but he had the distinct impression that they viewed him as a novelty. His square cap and traditional Polish uniform looked like a nineteenth century throwback in the midst of the paraphernalia of this modern force.

There were piles of paper with unintelligible messages in rough German that they had given up on, neatly stacked on a table in the corner of the dining room that now served as their coordination centre.

"Are these in chronological order?" asked Freddie of the

corporal whose thick Brooklyn accent was a little difficult to follow.

"Sure are, sir."

Freddie took a generous sheaf from the top of the pile. "We'd better get started then."

He took over a room on the upper floor and got to work. He had not been going long when the corporal came in and placed a mug on his desk.

"Thank you," smiled Freddie as he was struck by the distant memory of a so familiar smell. "Coffee?"

"Yes sir. Courtesy of Uncle Sam. We may be low on gas, but we have plenty of this." He beamed proudly.

"What's your name, Corporal?"

"Bruce, sir. Tony Bruce."

"That's very kind, Tony. It's a shame we can't get Shermans to run on arabica." The joke was lost on the man.

His next four days were occupied with working through the backlog. He had a large operational map of their sector hung on the wall and correlated each message to presumed locations of enemy units as he developed a referencing system to make sense of the snippets of disparate chatter.

A picture was building of a starved, demoralised enemy digging in sullenly to the Palatinate, that parcel of land between the Rhine and the French border, as the promised food and ammunition failed to materialise. Time and again resentful references were made to "The Watch" that seemed to be stripping them of their resources, and a vague thought whirled tantalisingly around Freddie's mind. It was something important and yet it eluded him. The more he strained to hear the faint nagging voice in his head the less he could find its frequency in the wavebands of his thoughts.

On the fifth day he came upon a phrase that nudged the tuning dial the fraction that was needed for the signal in his head to spark into definition. He froze in terror at the message it delivered. Buried deep in a missive bemoaning the lack of leave and rest for his men a major on the Siegfried Line mentioned "Der Wacht Am Rhein". The Watch On The Rhine.

"So?" questioned Koch abrasively as Freddie breathlessly blurted this finding. "The Watch On The Rhine. We've been aware of that for weeks. It's the Germans' code name for their defence of the Saarland. That sector was virtually undefended and we'd have swept through it weeks ago if we'd had the supplies. They're just papering over the cracks."

"No," retorted Freddie. "They're planning an offensive."

"Don't be ridiculous. The war is over. Once we open Antwerp and resupply, this thing will be done before the spring."

Freddie steadied himself and laid out his fears. "The Germans can't win in the conventional sense. But they are developing a new generation of weapons that will make tanks and infantry as obsolete as the bow and arrow. The V1s were a child's toy compared to what is to come."

"You mean these V2s?"

"Yes, but much worse. When I was in London we heard of secret installations developing some sort of super weapon. A bomb that can obliterate a whole city."

"That's impossible."

"No. It isn't! The scientists say it is possible, and the Germans are ten years ahead of us. It could be only months before they can put one of these bombs on a V2."

"They don't have months," snapped Koch, sticking to his position.

"No, they don't. Unless they keep us rooted here, which means taking Antwerp and preventing our diesel from getting through. That would buy them another six months, and if they get their bomb to work then the war is over. We lose."

Koch took a deep breath and scowled as he saw the logic. "All right. But The Watch On The Rhine. It's a defensive operation."

"You'd think so wouldn't you?"

"You think different?"

"When I was a cadet I won a competition with a dissertation on von Moltke the Elder."

"That's nice." The reference to the great Prussian general who masterminded the breathtaking defeat of France in 1871 needed no explanation. "But your point is?"

"The Prussian columns that smashed the French in humiliating defeat marched to the unofficial nationalist anthem 'Der Wacht Am Rhein'." His words echoed in the silence. "The Watch On The Rhine is a German call to arms to smash the French into the sea."

Koch's mouth fell open as his gaze fell to the map on the table. Was this Pole delusional, or had he stumbled upon a threat that could change utterly the fortunes of the whole war? "All right. Let's play make believe. Let's say they're close to having this super-weapon you believe in. Let's say they could scrape together ten divisions with enough fuel and ammunition for a limited campaign." He perused the chart. "The thrust would have to be quick. Quicker than they could manage through Holland with its interminable canals and waterways."

"Exactly." He had the American's attention. "They would need to attack through Belgium from here," he indicated the area around Bitburg, "towards Liege and on to Antwerp."

"Jesus," exclaimed Koch. "That sector is covered by Hodges, and his army is in bits." His eyes darted across the map assessing the threat. "Did you find anything else?"

"Only that the German defences have been stripped of all their heavy and mobile equipment. And they must be using it somewhere. I tell you, there's an armoured onslaught about to come through the Ardennes. All they need is a week or two of bad weather to keep our planes out of the sky."

"So Antwerp falls."

"And we're stuck here while they perfect their bomb."

Koch was anxious but unconvinced. To raise this possibility

among the general staff could make him a laughing stock. The High Command had known about Operation Watch On The Rhine for over a month and had dismissed it as a minor defensive exercise designed to slow their advance into the industrialised heart of the Reich. But if this Zamoyski was right then he had to act.

The strange Pole was clearly smart. He had been with the Third Army for only a week and yet already his stiff English accent was loosening into something that sounded like passable American. He was a quick learner, but could Koch risk his career on these recollections of a schoolboy project?

Despite Freddie's protestations he pondered and reflected on the situation for a whole week, before finally deciding to put the matter to Patton himself.

"I'm taking one hell of a gamble on this, Freddie," he said as they were shown in to the general's private office. It was the first time he had used his first name.

"Your faith will be repaid, Oscar."

Patton was a man whose reputation went far before him. He was brash and aggressive, but there was a depth to his uncouth manner that suggested it was a calculated means to an end. His questions and challenges to Koch's analysis came thick and fast as he assessed the situation. It was clear from the outset that he understood the threat.

"I don't know about this bomb theory, General," accepted Koch, "but if there is anything in it then Colonel Zamoyski might have seen a strategy that we've missed."

"Bomb theory?" boomed Patton as his electrifying energy filled the room. "Hell! We're building one of our own." The revelation visibly shook Koch as Patton turned on Freddie. "You seem pretty well informed Zamsky. And you came up with this all by yourself?"

"Yes sir."

"So how come my G6 didn't see this before?"

"A lot of the intercepts are in dense German, sir. With a lot of allegory and cultural references."

"Allegory?" scoffed Patton. "You expect me to dispose a whole army on the basis of allegory? Where did you learn your German, Colonel?"

"I'm a linguist, sir."

"Jesus Christ, Oscar," he shouted, turning back to Koch. "You come in here with this horse manure story and expect me to roll the dice? If they'd given me the gas I would have been in Berlin already. Ike gives all our supplies to that a-hole Montgomery and now you want me to look like an even bigger a-hole. Hell, we outnumber them five to one. You think they're stupid enough to attack?"

"Armed forces abroad are of little value unless there is prudent counsel at home, sir," interjected Freddie.

Koch's eyes opened wide in fear of the mauling he was about to witness. Patton lifted himself up in his seat and stared icily at Freddie. His anger steadied as he studied the presumptuous foreigner that dared to counter his thoughts. "It's a long time since anyone has quoted Cicero at me, Colonel." Freddie's self assured gaze was unflinching. Somehow he knew this brash good ol' boy exterior masked a student of the classics.

"General, I'm sure he..."

"Shut up, Oscar," barked Patton without breaking eye contact. The silence grew as he searched for uncertainty in Freddie's face.

"If you were von Rundstedt and you had fifteen divisions what would you do with them?" He knew exactly what Patton would do, and the general reluctantly answered.

"I'd smash Hodges and drive the hell to Antwerp."

"Singing Der Wacht Am Rhein all the way to the sea."

Patton's tense frame relaxed as he broke his ocular wrestling match and gazed out of the window in reflection. He gave a long sigh and looked intently at the map. After minutes of deep thought that felt like hours he finally spoke. "We can pull three divisions out of the front and position them ready to drive north. That would cut the neck of the Krauts' advance." He thought some more. "And if you're wrong Zamsky?"

"If I'm wrong and they are defending in depth then all you'll lose is the few days to put them back in the line, sir."

A troubled look crossed Patton's face. "Thank you gentlemen. That will be all." He stood and walked to the window, staring across the fields of eastern France.

Three days later he gave the order to disengage three divisions from the front and assemble a combat force ready to strike north through Luxembourg. It was a gamble, but ultimately a limited one and given the stakes if the Germans were to attack he decided that it was a risk worth taking. His men and tanks were still assembling as the weather closed in on the 15th of December, grounding their planes in conditions that were forecast to last at least a week. If Zamsky was right then the Germans would launch their attack within 48 hours. If he was wrong then Patton would look like a fool.

The morning came with a blizzard of frenzied communications as units of Hodges' First Army reeled under the onslaught of a new German blitzkrieg. Across a thirty mile front fearsome Tiger tanks and their agile but deadly Panther supports carved through makeshift defences as Hitler launched his devastating offensive that had been so well concealed. By the eighteenth it was clear that the allies were facing a major campaign that had caught them completely unaware as their forces rested and refitted.

The following day Eisenhower, the Supreme Allied Commander, called an emergency meeting of his generals at his command centre in Verdun. The situation was critical, as the threat to Antwerp and their supply lifeline became only too obvious. But Eisenhower was determined to remain positive.

"We can destroy the German forces much more easily when

they are on the offensive and out in the open," he told the array of grim-faced warriors seated in the room. "The present situation is to be regarded as one of opportunity for us and not of disaster. There will be only cheerful faces at this table."

As the generals glanced uncertainly at each other Patton offered his characteristically wry take on things. "Hell, let's have the guts to let the bastards go all the way to Paris. Then we'll really cut them off and chew them up!"

"Oh, really!" replied an exasperated Montgomery whose contempt for Patton was undisguised. "We're in full scale retreat. Antwerp is threatened. All our armoured columns are in forward positions and it will take a fortnight for us to be able to mount any significant counter offensive. They could be at the coast by then and my battle group will be cut off."

Eisenhower disliked the self-serving British commander, but knew that he was making a fair point. Nevertheless, he needed to soften the message to prevent further rancour among his senior officers. "Let them go to Paris? I'm not quite that optimistic, George," he smiled. "Your forces will be well placed to threaten their supply lines, but how long will it take you to pull some divisions out of the line and attack north? When do you think you'll be ready to go?"

Patton's reply was immediate. "As soon as you're through with me!"

Disbelief erupted around the room as even the Americans acknowledged the hubris in their comrade's claims. A logistical genius might manage the job in a week. "Don't be fatuous, George." Eisenhower faced the gravest crisis of his career and his subordinate's bluster was sorely trying his patience. "If you try to go now your divisions won't be ready and you'll go piecemeal. It will be a disaster."

"This is just typical," complained Montgomery, relishing the opportunity to embarrass his rival. "The man's not fit to command."

Hodges, whose First Army was being destroyed as they spoke, sprung to Patton's defence. "Hold on now, Bernard. We're professionals together. My boys are being murdered out there, so let's hear what George has to say."

"Very well," replied Montgomery sardonically. "Let's hear how George has stolen a march on Jerry shall we? Come on George. How did you do it?" He expected Patton to squirm in his inability to deliver on his rash promise. Instead, his aggression was channelled to straight talking as he rose to address the gathering.

"This defensive 'Watch On The Rhine' crap is just a load of damn horse manure. Always has been. Which you would know, General," he spat the word as an insult at the preening moustached Briton, "if you read your history. The Watch On The Rhine was the battle song of von Moltke's columns. Hell, it's their version of 'When We Were Marching Through Georgia.' I saw this coming a mile off, while you were still licking your wounds over that Market Garden crap." His reference to Montgomery's disastrous operation at Arnhem was deliberate and stung. "Now, I have 30,000 men with full armoured support ready to go." He turned to Eisenhower with a nod and a smile. "You just say the word Ike. My boys are ready."

Three days later the Third Army struck north and carved into the exposed flank of the German advance. The weather was clearing enough to allow allied planes to harry the Germans, and the narrow forested roads of the Ardennes had slowed their advance. But it was Patton's assault that sealed their fate. By the end of January what remained of the enemy either ran in disarray or were captured.

"Hell Freddie, that was some stroke of genius," beamed Patton as the general staff celebrated their success. "The look on the face of that son of a bitch Monty was sweet."

"Thank you, sir." He hated the brash overconfidence that so often came with Patton's ways, but he could hardly deny him his moment of smugness. He had taken an enormous gamble in listening to Freddie and Koch and it was a mark of his leadership that despite external appearances he was willing to heed their advice. Now he was taking the accolades he had earned.

"Not that he's admitting he was wrong. He's telling anyone who will listen that he saved the day. That's bad faith Freddie. And I can't abide bad faith." That he was calling Freddie by his first name was a rare mark of respect afforded to few on his staff. His star was shining bright once again.

February came with a revitalised allied attack. Fuel poured in through Antwerp and the armies that had been stuck frustratingly on Germany's threshold for three months began to advance once more.

They were good days. Letters arrived from Lilian with reassuring frequency. She was in fine health and had heard of Patton's success in what they were calling at home The Battle Of The Bulge. She had even started going to church, encouraged by Maggie, but most of all she was safe. Freddie replied at every opportunity and their love seared itself into the pages they shared.

Patton's impatience to attack the enemy at every opportunity was a constant source of tension among the generals of the High Command. As G6, Freddie read every one of the irritated dispatches aimed at curtailing the exuberance of this arch advocate of armoured warfare. Patton's replies were no less pointed, but he had a way of making Freddie laugh that showed the many sides to this deceptively bright man.

On the second of March they drove headlong into the strategic city of Trier just as Freddie received instructions from Eisenhower's headquarters. The Americans had cleared the city and Patton was standing in the main square relishing the moment of victory when Freddie handed him the order. "Bypass Trier. Estimate four divisions needed to take."

The general gave one of his rare, open laughs and surveyed the prize he had taken as if contemplating his next move. "Give me a pencil," he ordered. He took the paper that bore the order and laying it on the bonnet of his jeep, wrote a response on the back. He shoved the paper into Freddie's hands with a mischievous smile. "Send that back."

As he drove off to direct his continued advance Freddie looked down at his scrawl and laughed openly. "Have taken Trier with two divisions. Do you want me to give it back?"

His contempt for Montgomery was highlighted at the end of March as he ordered the crossing of the Rhine. He had no authority to take this step and kept his movements secret from his immediate superior, Omar Bradley. On the night of 22nd March elements of the Third Army crossed the river in boats and established a bridgehead with engineers rapidly laying down a pontoon bridge.

"That's one in the eye for the Brits," he chuckled, as Montgomery belatedly crossed the river far to the north the next day. And in another moment of pure theatre he lifted his troops again as he crossed the pontoon. He ordered his driver to stop on the west bank so that he could walk across the Rhine. His men cheered wildly as he stopped half way across and urinated into the river.

It was another example of his crass coarseness that puzzled Freddie and intrigued him. "Why do you do it?" he asked later.

"Okay Freddie. You asked, so I'll tell you." He spoke like a father teaching his son the secret of the perfect curved ball. "In any war, on any day, a commander, no matter what his rank, has to send to sure death a certain number of men. Some are his personal friends. He is responsible for them as his troops and to their families. Any man with a heart would sit down and bawl like a baby. But he can't. So he sticks out his jaw, and swaggers and swears. I wish some of those pious sons of bitches at home could understand something as basic as that." Then he smiled philosophically. "And as for the kind of remarks I make. Why sometimes I just, by God, get carried away with my own eloquence!"

As April bloomed into life the Third army was driving deep into the heart of Germany. Frankfurt and Wurzburg fell as the sudden shock of flowers reminded Freddie of Lilian and her imminent delivery. The excitement of the advance was beginning to fade as the German defenders increasingly offered little resistance, many of them gladly laying down their arms. As they pressed on towards Weimar, the seat of the old discredited republic assembly swept aside by the Nazis, Patton's main headache was the challenge posed by the 400,000 prisoners his men had taken as they swallowed enemy armies whole.

But a new energy seized him as one by one his men came upon labour camps the like of which they could never have imagined. It was becoming clear to Koch that what remained of the fanatical SS brigades still at large were exterminating prisoners with alacrity. With their dreams of supremacy in tatters and their country collapsing, the only remaining value held by these subhumans was murder.

On April 4th the army overran Ohrdruf concentration camp. Patton was visibly shaken as he returned to his headquarters after visiting the site with his commanding officers, Bradley and Eisenhower. That evening was the only time Freddie ever saw the general drunk.

"What those bastards have done is sick. Sick beyond belief." He poured another large glass of bourbon. "You can't imagine it, Freddie." He stared into the flickering fire as the sap from the freshly felled spring trees cracked and spat.

"But I can, sir." The dancing flames played in his eyes that could see only the gulag. "I was held like that four years."

"I'm not talking of prison. It's unspeakable. Words fail me."

"Corpses piled up like lumber? Others lying where they have fallen? Quicklime scattered on mounds of humanity to quell the stench?" Patton stared at him in shock. "Oh, I've seen it. I've seen it all. Men worked to death. Starved to death. Beaten to death."

"Jesus! You were in a German camp?"

"No." The general had never seen this intensity in his protégé he now considered a friend. "The Russians. Hitler. Stalin. It's all the same."

"Hell. Four years? How did you survive?"

"In the same way that you would survive." His gaze turned on his commander as he echoed his own words. "In the way that none of those sons of bitches could ever understand." And Patton saw the steel that ran through his enigmatic signals officer.

"You a God-fearing man, Freddie?"

He nodded slowly in reply. "I was about to join the priesthood when the war started."

"You think God has a plan for us? A purpose?"

"Yes. I do."

"Hell. You're right." He drained his glass and grimaced as the liquid burned. "That's why we're here. To save those poor bastards."

The next morning Freddie's head hurt and his senses were dulled. His men were still bringing their full equipment forward from Mannheim and he was temporarily operating from the back of a converted half track as he scanned the airwaves. By noon his mind was clearing, as he slowly adjusted the tuning knob listening for traffic. The static was punctuated by two blips before the white noise closed in again.

Freddie stopped and slowly turned the knob back. The morse sounded once more as his mind tuned to its structure. Three dashes. Then three more. "SS". His ears pricked as he grabbed a pen. The world around him disappeared as he strained every neurone on the wobbling signal.

There was a pause. Had he lost it? His heart pounded in his head as he implored God to give him another chance. The code started again.

"To the allies. To the army of General Patton. This is Buchenwald concentration camp. SOS. We request help. They want to evacuate us. The SS wants to destroy us."

His mind exploded into life, his hangover suddenly irrelevant. As the message ended he flicked the switch to transmit and began tapping his reply. "KZ Bu. Hold out. rushing to your aid. Staff of Third Army." He was acting way beyond his authority, but was sure that Patton would order the mission.

"Harkins!" boomed Patton at his Deputy Chief of Staff. "What do we have ready to go?"

Harkins was a slick operator with an encyclopaedic knowledge of the army's units and dispositions. "There's the 9th, sir," he answered referring to the battalion of armoured infantry that was resupplying at Wittlich. "But they've lost their CO. Fred Keffer is acting up"

"Keffer? That crazy bastard that relieved Bastogne?"

"That's him sir."

"Okay Zamsky," he smiled, now knowing perfectly well that he was mispronouncing his name. "Go with them. It's time for you to do some more of that Phantom Ridge crap!" He had never mentioned that before, and in the heat of the moment Freddie saw just how well he knew his men.

The 500 men of the 9th battalion drove headlong for Buchenwald, sweeping aside what feeble resistance they met until at 3.15pm on April 11th they entered the camp unopposed. It was a Wednesday. Unbelievably, some of the inmates had stormed the watchtowers with weapons they had kept concealed, and held out for the Americans' arrival.

Some liberators were lifted onto the shoulders of the emaciated skeletons who were barely able to stand. Others vomited at the sight that greeted them. Freddie surveyed the scene in revulsion as his eyes settled on the wrought iron lettering set into the camp's main gate. "Jedem Das Seine."

"What does that mean?" asked Keffer, stunned by the scene around him.

"Everyone gets what he deserves."

They stood in silent rage at the inscription that dared to present this calculated mass murder as a morally self-conscious post-Christian philosophy. Behind them came the sound of shouting and hissing as the small army of grey wraiths jeered and cheered. They turned to see a tall, blonde man with SS insignia on his collar being dragged by four soldiers into the open ground in front of a row of huts.

"We should stop this," said Freddie with no conviction. Keffer gave a small nod and looked on.

"You fucking bastard!" shouted the swarthy sergeant who led the group as he pulled out a revolver and held it to the man's temple. The crowd whooped and bayed for his death, as he in return raised his head and sneered.

"Untermenschen!" he shouted defiantly.

The sergeant could not contain his hatred. "A bullet's too good for you, you son of a bitch." He threw the gun away and kicked his furious might into the man's stomach. The others joined in with boots and rifle butts as blood flew into the air. "Wait!" ordered the sergeant. The beating stopped as he dragged the man back onto his knees. Blood streamed from his jaw that had already ballooned around its fracture and his left arm hung uselessly, its fingers soaking in the wet mud. Still he looked up defiantly. He tried to say something, but blood just bubbled from his lips.

The sergeant moved to the crowd and beckoned forward a tiny scrap of bones held together by only the skin that clung like paper to what was left of her body. Still Freddie and Keffer looked on, unable or unwilling to intervene, as the sergeant handed her a bayonet. They assumed it was a woman from her tiny size, probably less than five feet. They could not tell her age, such were the ravages of the deprivations that had turned her into one of the undead.

She stepped forward and looked at the guard with a chilling malevolence that even Freddie had never before seen. The crowd had fallen silent in anticipation. The only sound in this desolate landscape were the harbinger calls from the black crows watching from their treetops.

The blade rose slowly as if it took all of her effort to lift it. It stopped in front of his stomach as she stared into his eyes. His black soul stared back, and in that moment she acted. With the strength of pure hate she lifted the knife and pushed it slowly but firmly into his neck. Blood spurted as his body writhed in its death dance and the crowd cheered limply. His body fell into the mud as silence descended once again. In the void were only the mocking cries of the ravens. A void that no measure of revenge could fill.

The next day journalists arrived to report on the horror. They were experienced news men, used to the travails of war. There was nothing that they had not seen. Nothing that could shock them. What they saw left them traumatised and numb.

Stinking pits full of rotting bodies heaped in careless piles filled the air with a cloying stench. The features of the poor nameless masses were burned and blistered by the lime sprinkled by their tormentors lest the smell affronted their nostrils and reminded them of their demonic barbarity.

In a pathetic attempt to conceal their crimes, some guards had dug up a mass of buried bodies and piled them on a large wooden griddle made of railway sleepers. Covering the corpses with pitch they had lit the fire and now, in the embers of the pyre, the haphazard, cracked bones jostled with charred remains of smoking flesh as a gardener would dispose of the detritus of unwanted cuttings.

Behind the ovens, stacked in neat rows five deep, was the substrate of a more ordered disposal process. Sunken faces of white skin stretched over diseased bone stared unblinking at the world that had allowed this nightmare. The slaves that laid out the bottom rows were the very same who succumbed and in their turn were laid in the rows above. Each face a cherished mother, wife, husband or son in this self-assembled wall of death.

Inside the buildings it was worse. In blockhouses built for cattle, bodies were crammed onto communal wooden bunks stacked high, the living crammed in with the dead. The reek of filth and decomposing bodies mixed in a putrid vapour that was beyond description. A veteran reporter, Ed Murrow, whom Freddie was escorting could take no more. He broke down in tears at the sight of two elderly shadows crawling towards the latrine, no longer with the strength to stand. His broadcast on CBS in the evening told just a little of the evil he saw there that day. Just one day in twelve years of indescribable misery.

Here and there Freddie noted the few inmates whose frames were sturdier than the others, and in their furtive glances he saw the reflection of the gulag survivor he knew so well. The man who had done whatever it took to live. He hated them. He hated himself.

XI - Judgement

The day was growing old as the sun completed its languid descent towards the horizon. Freddie was looking pale as he craned his neck to see the last sliver of gold dip from sight. His gaze lingered as if in final farewell to this constant friend.

"Freddie, I should go," I said. His condition was deteriorating rapidly. Even I could notice that his breathing had become shallower and more laboured in just the past few hours.

"No!" He was emphatic.

"But the strain. You're not well. I should let you rest. We'll finish tomorrow."

His hand grasped my forearm with a force that startled me. "Stay. I need to finish this. And then it will be done." The light in his eyes grew dim, but the embers of his passion burned hot.

The door opened and the ward sister looked in. "Oh, I'm sorry Father. I wasn't sure if you were still here."

"We won't be much longer. Half an hour," said Freddie, although his voice was already weaker.

"Right," replied the sister. "Well in that case I'll just, er..."

"Yes," he replied. "Please do."

The door closed as I frowned at him, the cogs turning slowly in my head. "Is somebody waiting to see you Freddie?"

"No." He shook his head, but some sense told me otherwise. In a moment of lucidity I saw the link. Norah was waiting. All this time I had her talking to her Harry. But outside she was waiting for me to stop. Yearning for time with him while I selfishly used up the last few precious moments he had left. I pulled myself away and ran onto the ward looking anxiously for the grey haired lady. There was no one. I ran to the corridor, to the lift, and checked the stairwell. Nothing. I was so wrapped up in this story of decades past that I was beginning to lose my perspective on the present. With some embarrassment I returned to his bedside.

"I'm sorry Freddie. I thought... Oh, I don't know what I thought."

He gave a weary smile. "You're a good man, Tom." He took my hand in his. "A very good man." I looked down at the gnarled scar in the centre of the back of his hand that spoke of his suffering. "You have guided me back to God."

"I don't believe you ever left him." I looked at his fading body. How I wished I could reverse whatever process was taking him from us. From me. "Whatever you did. You never really turned away. He was always there, and He still is. He is waiting for you." The words resonated through my soul and chimed true. In all honesty it was Freddie that had brought me back.

-oOo-

"Hell Freddie, they might just as well chop my arm off," fumed Patton. "You're the best goddam G6 in the service."

"Thank you sir."

"And cut the 'sir' crap. You're leaving tomorrow. Call me George. You know it's strange. You give everything for your country. Lead it through the blood of half a continent, and it turns out the man you trust the most is a goddam foreigner."

They both laughed. "Thank you George."

He took a gulp of bourbon. "Ah, who knows? Maybe it's for the best. You ain't been the same since Buchenwald. I should have known that. After what you told me of that business in the gulag. I shouldn't have sent you."

Freddie's reply was immediate: "I'm glad you did. It forced me to look back at the man I once was."

He nodded his understanding. "Anyway, you don't want to come with me on this horse manure wild goose chase Ike is sending me on into Bavaria." Patton deeply resented his new orders to move south east. "We should be charging to Berlin. We could still beat the Ruskies, Freddie."

"The way you charge, George, I don't doubt it." Silence settled on them as they shared their final moments. Two warriors together, soon to be like Alexander, with no one left to fight.

"You know they're sending you over to Hodges so you can make sure his boys don't get into a dust up with those damn communists?"

"You think?"

"I know. They'll link up in days, and we're short of men who can speak English, German and Russian. Someone has to interpret or they'll be shooting each other."

"Well. Here's to the Russians. Brothers in arms." He lifted his glass.

They both drank. "You heard yet from your girl?"

Patton had done it again. Just when you thought his mind was filled only with war, he had this knack of showing how he saw so much more.

"I didn't know you knew."

"Hell Freddie. Just 'cos I don't wear my heart on my sleeve doesn't mean I don't have one." He winked. The mannerism was so incongruous and at the same time so natural it made Freddie laugh as he dropped his head.

"No. No word yet."

"You got a name?"

"Anna. After my sister."

Patton almost dared not ask, but that was not his way. "She still in Poland?"

"No." He shook his head. "I buried her in 1939 with my parents."

"I'm sorry. War is a hell of a thing." They sat in silence again. "And if it's a boy?"

"George," he smiled. Patton's eyes narrowed in mock suspicion. "After my father."

"Ha!" It was his turn to lift his glass. "To George!"

Two days later Freddie was travelling with the 69th infantry division as they closed on the Elbe, the last remaining river barrier between them and the Russians advancing from the east. Just as Patton had predicted he had been reassigned to the First Army. He was to act as the senior interpreter and liaison officer at the first point of contact between the two armies who were allies in name, but fast becoming rivals.

All sense of civil order had broken down and the countryside was full of roving bands of desperate German troops, petty looters, and a patchwork of allied units of different nationalities. It was a dangerous time, and imperative that the official meeting at the Elbe ran smoothly.

The Americans occupied the small town of Torgau nestling on the river's west bank on 26th April and anticipated the meeting ahead. As a senior officer from army headquarters sent on attachment to the divisional staff he was afforded whatever luxury could be bestowed. In this devastated land this meant a room of his own in what had been a thriving guest house, but little else.

As he pulled his boots off and stretched out on the surprisingly comfortable bed there was a knock at the door. A young soldier from the divisional communications team entered on his order and handed him an envelope as he saluted. "Private Thackray, sir. A message for you from headquarters."

"Thank you, Thackray." It was marked for his personal attention which surely meant that it was from Cunningham, given that he had only just arrived and most of the world thought he was still with the Third Army marauding through Bavaria. His heart flipped as he contemplated the message it held.

For a second he hesitated. What if the news was bad? Childbirth could still be a dangerous time. Either mother or baby could fall foul of nature's ways. He took a deep breath and opened it.

"To US 69th Infantry from British Intelligence. Artillery

delivered. Combat strength full."

Freddie's mind spun in ecstasy. He yearned to be in London with Lilian. God, how he missed her. How he longed to hold her. He closed his eyes and gazed on the picture of her that hung in his mind's gallery. A girl. A baby girl. He was a father. And they were safe.

Emotion welled up inside him. It fizzed and crackled. He wanted to hug someone, to tell someone, but outside the men of the 69th were strangers to him. It was the weirdest feeling, and never in all his life had he wanted to be somewhere else as much as he did then. All those years of desperation to be free of the gulag were as nothing to the price he would have paid to be transported to his angel's bedside.

He took a grip of himself and remembered his duty. To the fresh faced combatant before him he was a renowned fixer, the expert brought in to ensure the smooth link up with the Russians. His professional facade could not crack. He wrote a hasty reply for the radio team to send back to England and handed it to the young runner with clear instructions.

He slept fitfully, and the sun rose to find him dressed and ready. The crackling of gunfire on the eastern bank had died away before midnight, and the assembling group of soldiers in the town square contemplated their meeting with the Red Army. At 9am the message came from observers in the tower that overlooked the river to say that Russian tanks and men were on the opposite bank. It was time for Freddie to go to work.

Holding a white flag, and ever mindful of the danger that some German sniper might still be lurking in an attic room or foxhole he began his slow walk over the bridge. The mass of troops behind him waited like children for Christmas morning as his strides paced out the length of the crossing. As he did so a similar figure in ceremonial Russian uniform walked the reciprocal path from the east.

They stopped a few yards short of each other as the mature

Russian, bearing the insignia of a major, frowned. "Polish?"

"Colonel Zamoyski, attached to the US 69th infantry division."

A broad smile grew over the Russian's face as he took the last few strides. Freddie went to offer his hand in friendship, but was engulfed in a firm Slavonic hug before being kissed on both cheeks. The Russian pulled away. "The Americans. They have no Russian speakers?" He laughed heartily.

"It's doubtful they have any English speakers," joked Freddie in perfect Russian, and the concord was sealed.

Major Alexei Zhukov introduced himself as a battalion commander of the 58th Guards Division, and made a suggestion. "Our people have waited a very long time for this moment. Finally, we have triumphed in The Great Patriotic War, and banished the fascist pigs. We must get photographs as our troops meet. We will shake hands?"

"Certainly."

"Good. Good. We have some ordinary soldiers. Glorious workers in arms. Your generals will not be insulted?"

Freddie smiled at the assumption. "The Americans will send ordinary soldiers too."

"Really?" Zhukov looked puzzled. There was a pause before he shrugged. "Good. Good." He glanced at his watch. "Shall we say 10 o'clock?"

Freddie nodded. "Ten men?"

Zhukov pondered for a second. "Six. Plus photographers."

They both beamed their agreement, hugged again and returned to their respective camps. The photographs of ordinary soldiers meeting spontaneously on the bridge at Torgau, ecstatic in their brotherhood, made the front page of every newspaper across the world. The detail that Freddie and Zhukov had engineered the spontaneity was naturally glossed over. The allies had finally embraced after each fighting through half a continent and the days of the Third Reich were over.

As the Russians poured over the bridge into the town a party atmosphere grew. The High Commands of both sides need not have feared the clash of cultures that so worried them. It seemed that their simple front line troops knew more about trust and friendship than the theorists and intellectuals back in their bunkers fretting over the ensuing new world order. That day in Torgau the torment of years melted away as whiskey was exchanged for vodka and back-slapping fraternal good will poured forth. The residents hid, fearful of the way this party atmosphere between two foreign armies, intoxicated by victory, might develop.

In the midst of this happiness a strange splinter pricked in Freddie's mind. He could not place it, and just as four months earlier he had tried to force the lost memory of "Der Wacht Am Rhein" from his psyche, there was something nagging that he could not grasp. Something that Zhukov had said. He decided to let it go. It would come to him soon enough.

It was mid afternoon when Zhukov came running up in a state of child-like excitement. "Freddie," he exclaimed. "We have a great idea." After a couple of shots of spirits, Freddie was ready to listen to any suggestion, particularly from this exuberant man who was so easy to like. "We liberated a camp yesterday, and one of the prisoners is an opera singer."

"That's nice." He was bemused as to where the conversation might be heading.

"She's here now. And our boys have the most fantastic orchestra."

"What! An orchestra? Don't be ridiculous."

Zhukov smiled and shrugged. "Okay. A band. You capitalists are so status conscious." He laughed loud and long. "But," he suddenly held a finger up, "let's put on a concert. Here. Tonight. In the square. She sings like an angel. It will be wonderful."

"Don't be daft Alexei. We can't stage a concert in five hours time. Where would we get the instruments? Where would we get the drink?"

"We have instruments. And as for drink." Zhukov looked around in mock conspiracy. "I have a solution to that." He pulled Freddie to one side and dropped his tone. "We have a man. A fixer. A bit of a rough diamond from the 415th, but he can get all the drink we need. He knows of a place in Wurzen. Contacts." He tapped his nose to indicate the less than official nature of the plan.

"Wurzen? But that's on this side of the Elbe." The wheels in Freddie's mind were suddenly turning at lightning pace, and he could not believe what they were telling him. Could this be true? The splinter that had troubled his mind now erupted into view. The 415th battalion? A fixer? In the breadth and span of an entire continent could this be possible? In an instant of overwhelming temptation he made his decision, and put it into action.

"We can't let one of your boys loose east of the river. There's a good chance he'll be shot if he runs into one of our patrols. There are units everywhere, and they don't all know what's happened here."

"Exactly," exclaimed Zhukov. "So you must go with him." He beckoned Freddie down a side street. "Come with me. We have a truck ready to go."

Freddie's heart was pounding in disbelief as Zhukov opened the passenger door of the truck whose engine was running. "Now you're sure you can get this stuff?" he shouted into the cab.

"Don't be a cock, Zhukov," came the insubordinate reply from the driver. The voice was like a knife through Freddie's soul. It was him. He could not believe it. It was him! Vengeful hatred gushed through his body.

"Good. Good. This is Colonel Zamoyski. He's with the Americans. Be nice to him, Volkov. He's the man who will stop you being shot by them."

As Freddie climbed into the seat and closed the door it felt like he was engulfed in a shower of electric sparks. The vast bulk of Volkov exuded the same malevolent energy that Freddie remembered so vividly, as he forced the truck into gear and pulled away.

The truck left the town behind as Volkov looked again at Freddie. For a moment he thought he saw the flickering of recognition. "So what's a Polack doing with the Americans?" His surly timbre and choice of insulting label radiated the same defiance of civilised behaviour that had made him so successful.

"Military intelligence."

Volkov grunted and fixed his gaze back onto the road. "How did you get out?"

Freddie's heart leapt into his mouth. He had recognised him? No. That was impossible. He bore no resemblance to the wild man that had been bought to fight. To Volkov he had been just one of a whole flow of victims, and while he had probably presented more of a problem than most he had been in Volkov's company for just a few hours. He held his voice steady. "What?"

"Of Poland? How did you get out?"

His internal sigh of relief was almost audible. "Through Rumania." The road dropped into dense forest as Freddie kicked at a pile of tools cramping the space for his feet. He noticed a hammer lying in the foot well by his right boot. Without warning the memory of his abuse forced its way into his mind. For a moment he could feel Volkov's erection thrusting inside him again and his rage grew.

"One of the lucky ones, eh?"

"You could say that. Oh damn! My shoelace." He reeled himself in as the exclamation almost took on a theatrical tone.

Volkov glanced at him in disgust. "Fucking officers." The bottom of the hill was approaching as a left hand bend presaged the climb on the other side. A small house sat off the road to the right. As he slowed to navigate the junction Volkov was acutely aware that this would be a good place for an ambush by German stragglers. His senses were focused on the woods as something glinted in his right eye.

-oOo-

"The house in the woods was empty," explained Freddie. "I dragged Volkov's unconscious frame inside and tied him to a bed. Then I drove the lorry on a few miles and crashed it into a ditch. I fired some rounds into the cab to make it look as though we had been ambushed and walked back to the house."

"You hit him with the hammer?"

Freddie nodded with the guilt of ages on his shoulders. "The worst thing was that I was worried I had killed him."

"But that wouldn't have been a bad thing," I suggested.

Freddie's dark stare told me different. "I wanted him alive so that he could suffer. Death would have been easy for him. A cheat."

"Did he really not know who you were?"

"Not in the lorry. Why would he? The man he knew was skin and bones. Feral. Wild. And Ukrainian. The man he picked up in Torgau was a refined Polish Colonel. He found out soon enough when I spelled it out to him."

"You killed him?"

Freddie nodded, tears welling in his eyes. "It was like I was suddenly possessed by a demon."

"Yes, but what he did to you. I mean, anyone would have snapped."

"Perhaps." The tears splashed over his eyelids and trickled down his cheeks. "But God had brought me through the war. The number of times He had saved me. It was for a higher purpose, and I turned my back on him."

"But..." I tried to protest, but Freddie was certain.

"I went back to the house. I was filled to bursting with a rage that I could not control. Back in London my baby girl was opening her eyes for the first time, but here in Germany I turned my back on my new life and lost myself in the vengeance of my past."

"Did you tell him who you were?"

Freddie looked taken aback by the question. "But of course. I wanted, I needed him to know who I was and which of his lifetime's terrible sins had finally caught up with him." He was staring at the bed sheets with a distant gaze far away from our room. "He did not believe it at first, but then I described in great detail how Taras had dropped his guard and I had all but scythed his head from his body with a shovel." Freddie's eyes rose to meet mine. "He believed it then."

I could not speak. There was a mixture of abject remorse and steely determinism that swirled into an indefinable brew in the depths of his eyes. "How did you kill him?" I managed to utter. At one level it seemed like a trivial question, but I sensed it was important for Freddie's closure to tell me how the act was committed.

He shook his head as if he was not entirely sure himself of the order of events. "There was an axe outside the house. I can't remember how it came to be in my hand, but as Volkov spat his defiance back at me in my grief it was flashing through the air." He looked at me and prepared to rid himself of decades of guilt. "I attacked him the same way I had killed Taras. The axe buried itself in the crook of his neck. But it was blunt. Taras had been felled in a single coup de grace. Volkov?" He sighed as he let go of his burden. "God help me, but his screams stopped after the sixth or seventh blow." The tears poured freely. "I was lost to God."

"No."

"Yes!" His eyes were aflame. "When I trudged back to Torgau the next day and told them of the ambush and my escape they were full of sympathy." His head dropped in grief as he cried like a child. Through his tears he continued. "It was then that they told me the news of Lilian."

I think I had been expecting this turn, but had somehow

hoped it would not be so. "Lilian?"

"While I was in that house in the woods losing my soul, God took her."

I stared back, almost not daring to ask. "How?"

For a moment he was lost in his own world of grief before he answered my question. "The official version is that no one knows."

"And the unofficial version?"

He took a deep breath, bracing himself to talk of his love's end. "Anna was only two or three days old. Apparently Lilian wanted to get out for some fresh air so Maggie went to the flat to baby sit. She was gone for less than ten minutes when without any warning there was a massive explosion in the next street. A policeman had just passed Lilian, so the inquest was sure she was there, along with the other 20 people killed in the blast."

"A V2?" I asked, assuming that this would have been the only explanation for a sudden and unexpected explosion in London in April 1945.

"Officially," he sighed, "no. The armies in Europe had advanced far enough that the rocket launch sites were out of range of London. Officially, the last V2 landed on Orpington at the end of March."

"But you think different?"

"I know different." A darkness had descended on him. "Cunningham confided in me after the war. We became good friends, and one night after too many brandies he told me what had almost certainly really happened. The Germans called the V2 rocket the A4. It had a range of about 200 miles, so once Monty had driven through Holland, London was safe. Or so we thought."

I was puzzled. "Did they find a way of launching them from submarines?"

Freddie managed a small laugh. "You really have been watching too much James Bond, Tom." He paused for a while before explaining what had killed Lilian. "When the allies overran some of the manufacturing sites they found a small number of larger rockets. They were the same basic design, but had a greater fuel load so longer range. The intelligence services called them A4Bs, and they could just reach London. Their existence was kept classified for fear of the effect on morale."

"I suppose if you had just removed the threat of the V2s the idea that their big brother was back would have dented spirits."

"Exactly. And it seems there was just a handful of them anyway, so the cover up continued. It was known to so few that the story of the A4Bs seems to have been lost to history. And none of the governments were interested in raking over the coals too deeply. They wanted the captured scientists to build rockets for them, so were keen to keep the spotlight off Hitler's rocket programme, and the atrocities it inflicted."

I reflected on this snippet of secret information that changed things a little. "But that's not an act of God, Freddie."

"You think not? Without warning, death arrives from the heavens ten times faster than a speeding bullet. You don't even hear it. Tons of explosives. One minute you are walking down a quiet street in London, the next moment you are dead. Killed by a weapon that is officially out of range. You think that's not an act of God?" I sat silently, reflecting on his words. Perhaps he was right. "God took her from me because of my sin."

"I don't think that's The Lord's way Freddie."

The anguish on his face was heart breaking, as he began to nod. "I see that now. But in my grief I hated him. I turned my back on him. I failed him." There was nothing I could say to ease his suffering. He coughed with difficulty in a bubbling, wheezing rasp. His breath was shortening, and I knew his time was near. "Receive me back into his love, Tom," he gasped.

I took his frail hands in mine and said the incantations he longed for through my spluttering tears as the room grew dim. As my words came to an end a look of serenity took him as he settled back on his pillow, but the pain that left his soul flooded into mine as if my hands had sucked up his grief. The recorder rattled and clicked loudly as the tape reached its end.

He laid his hand gently on mine and his eyes flickered open. "Tell Karol," he whispered. "Use the tapes. Help him understand. He was always the one."

My thoughts were a confusion of grief and pain. He was rambling as he slipped from me. "I'll stay with you."

He smiled, and the love that cascaded over me heightened my impotence. "You have been my great friend, Tom. My strength. My guide. My saviour. But now it's time for you to go."

I hesitated. My soul cried out to stay, to be with him. But his wishes were clear. I kissed him gently, lovingly on his forehead as he squeezed my hand with what remaining strength he had left. "Goodbye Freddie," I whispered. "Godspeed."

My world disintegrated as I left his room. The clear view of creation we all take so much for granted collapsed into a mosaic of ill-fitting fragments that left me lost in my grief. I needed to hold myself together at least until I reached the car. I took a deep breath and strode out into the ward, walking purposefully for the stairs. Was that Norah sitting at the nurses' station? I think it was. She was crying. Or was my pain playing tricks on me?

I kept walking, and drove away. I needed to be alone. I knew he would die that night. He knew he would die that night. I would not see him again. His remarkable life would come to an end and the world would lose a little of its glow.

XII - Revelations

The night was torture. I could not help recalling the way Freddie said he felt that night in Torgau. How he yearned to be somewhere else. I felt the same overpowering emotion that robbed me of my sleep. As I tossed and turned in my bed those last few hours played themselves over and over.

Had he been rambling? Was it the drip talking? Or was there something profound in his last words? Karol. Karol? The name echoed in my head as I replayed his story. The only Karol he had mentioned was the impressionable youth in Krakow, planning his life with his beloved Ginka. Could that be who he meant? It seemed unlikely, and how would I find him? How many displaced men with that name were scattered like dried autumn leaves across the continents by the chill winter of war?

I looked at the clock. The luminous hands told me it was 4am. I yawned with fatigue, but it was no use. I knew that sleep would evade me. I turned on my bedside light and stared at the ceiling. I looked through the wall, as if it were transparent, to the hospital a couple of miles away. How I wished I could be there.

My eyes focused back into the room onto the cross on the wall. Its simple wooden form was adorned with a carving of the suffering Christ who looked down benevolently at me. Drips of red decorated his hands so that even this simple effigy of my Lord took my mind back to Freddie. How I hated the thought of him dying alone.

I looked up from the cross into the smiling eyes of Pope John-Paul that shone from his portrait. The warm serenity that emanated from his genial face always lightened the world for me. It was as if somehow his soul was so pure, so bright, that even his image could bring hope.

My mind floated away on a tangent. What hardships, what sacrifices had he made on his journey of ultimate grace? Those same sacrifices to which I was now committed. What worldly comforts had he foregone? What solace in the union with another human had he missed? Had he ever doubted his path, as I had doubted mine? Had there ever been a sweetheart left behind as he followed his calling?

Even his name was discarded as he ascended the Holy See. His culture, his history, his secular self. And yet like a butterfly undergoing its ordained metamorphosis, his sacrifices had transcended suffering and brought joy and peace to millions.

"You've come a very long way, Karol Wojtyla," I said to his smiling face. I smiled back. As I did I was struck with the force of a thousand hammers. My eyes opened wide as the rest of my body froze in complete paralysis. This was not possible.

I took a grip of myself and cleared the tornado of images, thoughts and connections that swirled chaotically inside my mind. I ran downstairs to the bookshelves I rather laughingly called my library. Somewhere among these heavily thumbed volumes was his biography. Another beaming smile looked out at me from its cover as I frantically searched the index. There was no entry for "Ginka", but as I devoured the text of his early life everything fell into place.

He had been a student in Krakow at the outbreak of the war, and had shown a great interest in dramatics. Something seemed to have happened around the time of the German invasion that set him on a path to the priesthood. I played the tape from a few days earlier and listened again to Freddie's recollections of the meeting in the cafe. The reference to the play. "Twardowski's Magic."

I scoured the pages for that specific reference. It had to be there. I searched and searched, but nowhere was the production mentioned. His time as a student seemed of minor interest to the author who began writing copious amounts of inconsequential detail only after this Karol was ordained in 1946.

Karol was a common name. How many must there have been

in that city back then? How many Toms were there in London? Surely I was seeing connections where none existed. But still the nagging doubt remained. Why had Freddie asked me to tape his confession? There must have been a purpose. It was as if in speaking to me he perhaps was also speaking to someone else. Someone who would hear his words and understand. Someone dear. Someone special.

I closed the book and pondered on how I could investigate this further. As I stared at the sides of its dense pages sandwiched between the flimsy covers I noticed the thin layer of brilliant white glossed leaves that bore the mandatory collection of photographs every publisher hated because of the cost. I opened the book again and looked through them. The first face had three images of his early childhood with tiny lettering to give some context.

I turned the page to see a group of young men in what looked like fancy dress. Beneath the faded image was the explanation. "Karol Wojtyla with the cast of 'Twardowski's Magic' performed in summer 1939."

My mind emptied and I sat in silence. For me the world had just changed beyond recognition. I had spent the last few days in a personal audience with the man who had inspired the greatest pope in 500 years. It was as undeniable as it was impossible. My fugue was rudely ended by the harsh tone of the telephone, and in that moment I knew a burning light in this dark existence had gone out. Freddie was finally with Lilian once more.

The sun was scarcely a cool bronze rim peeping over the horizon as my car found its own way to the hospital, but somehow it already seemed hotter as if ordered to compensate for the loss of light beneath heaven. I almost ran to the ward as something deep inside felt angry with the world for its lack of respect. Everything was just as it normally was. The porters trudging here and there, the delivery men, all the paraphernalia of a busy city waking from its slumber carried on as if nothing had happened.

Was it the same two millennia ago that black Friday on calvary? When that light had gone from the world had Jerusalem continued its inconsequential daily rituals, blind to its profound loss?

The ward sister gave me the sympathetically pained expression I had seen her deliver a hundred times. It was not insincere, but the formulaic offering of a professional who would have lost her sanity years earlier had she not confined her empathy within safe boundaries. It was the kind of look I myself often gave and it was strange to see my own coping mechanisms reflected in her smile.

I went to the door as she gave her warning. "She's in there father."

I looked back at her and as I paused all the pieces of the puzzle fell into place. I nodded and taking a deep breath I knocked gently. There was no reply so I carefully turned the handle and went in.

Freddie lay serenely on the bed, finally resting in his eternal sleep. Death had taken away the frailty from his wise features. His arms sat softly on the covers as Norah held his hand and wept.

"Maggie?" I asked in hushed whisper as my face trembled on the brink of breaking.

She lifted her eyes in quiet grief. "Father," she replied.

There were no words to offer. Nothing that could have expressed my feelings or assuaged her suffering. I simply knelt beside her and held her hands in mine as she held Freddie's in hers. Five hands lovingly bound by the patterns of history. By the grace of The Lord.

We said nothing as the silence drew us together in our love for this man. It was difficult to comprehend that he had finally gone. In life he was so vital, so full of spirit, that the body that remained was nothing but the echo of a glorious song.

After an age she turned to me with a look of gratitude that I felt I did not deserve. "You saved him Father. He is at peace for the first time in decades."

"I'm sorry Maggie." I paused, suddenly questioning my familiarity with this woman I felt I knew. "I mean Margaret."

She smiled. "Maggie," she answered as she turned to Freddie. "Only he called me Margaret. Always so formal. Always so proper. Always so Polish."

"Maggie," I confirmed. "I'm sorry that I took so much of his last days. I didn't know."

"Don't," she said. "He needed you. He needed that time. He was tortured, and you gave him release."

"Thank you. But he should have spent all of the little time he had left with his wife."

"I wasn't his wife." Her flat voice gave nothing away as she continued to look at his face so I could not see her expression.

"I'm sorry. I didn't mean to suggest..... It's just that I've seen you around the hospital so much."

"Oh, we lived together, Father." She regained her composure and turned to look me in the eye.

"I see." I was not sure that I did see. So much of Freddie's life was cloaked in mystery.

"It wasn't like that," she stiffened in defence. I replayed my words and realised that she had thought my assumption was of sinful living. In fact it was nothing more than an absent minded conversation filler as I grappled with what was happening.

"I'm sorry Maggie. I really didn't mean to imply..."

"We'll you did imply," came the sharp rebuke.

"We didn't talk of any of this Maggie. He only told me of the war."

It was difficult to hold a conversation with a complete stranger whom I knew so well, especially being in the dark as to how much of the story he told me was known to her. In Freddie's restful aura she told me of their life together. Of how he had descended into a deep depression after his return from the war. Maggie had always thought it was more than grief. She was rough and uncultured, raw and genuine. Freddie's description of her had been perfect. What you saw was exactly what you got. She had such a disarming honesty in her delivery that it was impossible not to warm to her.

"He seemed completely lost when he came back. He had always been so energetic. Confident." She half snorted. "Even cocky."

"I don't think he was, really."

"No. But that's how he sometimes came over back then. But then he came home from the war and he was just a shell of a man. It was more than grief. For years I couldn't place it. He stopped going to church." Her eyes suddenly burned into mine with a ferocity I had not seen and it took me aback. "Don't think badly of him, Father. Something happened. I don't know what. He never told me. But something happened. I know it did. It was as if he carried a guilt with him. Like he blamed himself for Lil's death."

"Well, some people do."

"We'll that's bloody ridiculous." Her retort snapped so quickly it surprised us both. "I'm sorry, Father." She looked a little embarrassed. "I sometimes speak without thinking."

I told her not to worry, and she went on, filling in the 45 year gap that was a mystery to me. She told me how she had cared for Anna after Lilian's death, and how she had been given a council house in Walthamstow after her own had been condemned. Her mother had crumpled after her daughter died, and even the delight of a grandchild had not stopped her from turning her face to the wall.

By early 1946 Maggie was alone in a strange part of London, removed from her few friends. She was adrift in the world when everything she had ever known had revolved around her mother and sister. Freddie finally returned as the warriors came home and a victorious but exhausted and dislocated society began the task of rebuilding itself as the old certainties were swept away.

"Churchill sent most of them back you know," she explained. "Freddie stayed on in Germany because he was British. I only met Cunningham once." Her eyes narrowed and her voice dropped as if sharing a state secret. "I thought he was a proper idiot, but he had done all right by Freddie, so I forgave him all that poncing around." I smiled as I recognised how her summing up matched perfectly with the man from Freddie's words.

As the rank and file of Polish defiance was sent home to the uncertain mercy of Stalin's empire, Freddie washed up at Maggie's. He had no other family and his daughter had already bonded with this woman who could never be his lost Lilian, but who constantly reminded him of her.

"He moved in as my lodger," reflected Maggie. "He paid me rent and everything. He found himself a job as an interpreter. It wasn't well paid, but it was regular. I looked after Anna, and he supported us."

"So you were like a family?"

Maggie's look of distant ambivalence was unconvincing as she explained. "Not really. That would mean a couple sharing all of the things a couple should share." The bitter edge in her voice was softened by her unerring love for the man that had brought us together.

She told me of the overwhelming love that Freddie poured into Anna. An all consuming passion that saw his love for Lilian projected into this earthly echo of her memory.

"To start with it was all very well. What little girl doesn't want to be the centre of her father's world. But then as she grew older his endless love began to smother her. She was just like Lil, she was. Independent and headstrong, and his constant watching over her drove a real wedge between them."

"It must have been difficult."

"I'll say. It wasn't much to begin with, but then when boys started getting involved it grew into a chasm. She was a pretty thing. Beautiful. Just like Lil. Boys were always coming round chancing their luck. Freddie would have none of it, and then of course she fell for one of them and all hell broke loose. A real battle of wills. That was when she left. Ran off she did. One day she was there. The next she had gone."

"What? Just gone?"

She nodded in pain. "My baby just left. We never saw her again." Her face hardened in a failed attempt to hide the vulnerability of pain as she swallowed her urge to cry.

"I'm so sorry. Do you know what happened?"

A small tear trickled down her cheek. "They found her a few years later. In a flat in Whitechapel. She had overdosed on heroin. The police said it was an accident."

The silence that hung in the air spoke her doubts. "You think she took her own life?"

"I have no idea." She closed off. "What I do know is that it hit Freddie harder than I could ever have imagined." She gazed back down to him, and the tear grew to a stream and then a torrent as the dam that contained her grief finally burst.

The next few days were a blur worthy of Gauss himself. The mundane fused with the remarkable and the profound with the prosaic. Maggie's acerbic wit was her constant defence when the pain of Freddie's loss threatened to intrude, but there was an unconstrained warmth in her personality that radiated hope. In many ways she was more of a comfort to me than I was to her as we both began the long and painful process of coming to terms with his passing.

There was a pervasive sadness that for over four decades she had lived with and loved a man as fully as any wife, and yet had always been in the shadow of her sister. The ghost with whom she could never compete. And yet in the half light of that limbo it began to dawn on me that it was Maggie, not Lilian, who in many ways had been the love of his life. She may not have experienced the intensity of his passion or the depths of his desires, but for forty-five years she had been his constant partner.

His land lady, surrogate mother to his daughter, but in the end his one source of strength.

If love is what is left when passion has burned itself to ash, then Maggie was the true one, and as this idea grew in my head I felt the need to give voice to the thought. Maggie's response was uncompromising and direct.

"You really are a bloody priest, ain't you?" I must admit to having been quite taken aback by the ferocity of her riposte to what I had hoped would have been a comforting thought for her. "Do you have any idea what it feels like to love a man so much it hurts. To yearn for him to touch you just once the way you know he is capable of? The way he touched her. To have something right in front of you but always just out of reach?"

"I'm sorry Maggie," I stumbled.

"You don't know nothing. It was Lil. It was always Lil."

I retreated, and did not mention the subject again, but still I clung to the belief that in private she might have reflected on my words and hoped they might dilute the weltschmerz that threatened to drag her into a vortex of despair.

And as we talked and planned Freddie's funeral, other events unfolded. To the casual observer these might have seemed a remarkable and profound contrast to the mundane process of arranging a remembrance. To me they were a sideshow, irrelevant against the need to give Freddie the passing he deserved. And yet this sideshow was important.

With trepidation I copied the tapes and bundled them together in a parcel marked for the Vatican. The very notion of a junior priest daring to send a personal communication to His Holiness was outrageous. As I handed it over to the woman in the post office I knew it was as ridiculous as it was futile. The package would be opened by some underling and vetted by the Swiss Guard. Surely no one would disturb the Pope with the suggestion that he should listen to some random tapes sent to him from a minor outpost in his empire from a country that had fallen from the true path and embraced Luther's heresy?

The letter I sent with the tapes was brief but to the point. Whoever was going to read it would not get past the first couple of sentences so they were crafted and re-crafted a dozen times in order to get them right.

The Polish diaspora in London presented a different challenge. It seemed utterly bizarre, but the government in exile had continued to do its business ever since the war had ended. As Stalin installed a puppet regime and the west gave in to his pressure, the embassy was handed to the communist government in Warsaw. This left the small band of émigrés to conduct their government of nothing from the private residence of President Raczkiewicz at 43 Eaton Place. And so they continued down the decades, nothing but a symbolic shell. A government with no land. An administration with no people. A court with no friends.

Somehow they had maintained diplomatic missions with an ever dwindling clutch of countries, until finally in 1979 the last handful of allies, Ireland, Spain and the Vatican withdrew their recognition. Yet still they carried on. When I managed to contact them I was greeted with polite coolness.

"I understand," said the young secretary without any hint of an accent. Was she second generation, or was she simply an employee? "I will pass your message on to President Kaczorowski. There is a cabinet meeting tomorrow when I am sure they will discuss your news."

A cabinet meeting? To discuss what? Devaluing the Zloty? Concluding a trade agreement with Chile? Was this the unswerving dedication of a group in exile carrying the cultural torch of a nation overrun once again by foreigners? Or had it become a folie a plusieurs? A self-perpetuating, deluded psychosis running through this tiny enclosed population?

I thanked the girl, who sounded as if the closest she had been to Warsaw was Southend, and continued scripting my eulogy. Maggie kept me well supplied with tea and biscuits, although a more than sneaking suspicion grew that this was just an excuse for her to keep an eye on what I was writing.

The service was planned for the following Monday. A whole week to wait, but time I thought that was necessary. It was like living in a strange mist where the normal landmarks and waypoints in life suddenly disappeared. I lost track of the days as I found myself wondering if anyone at all would come. I placed notifications in the national press announcing the final passing of the "Spirit of Phantom Ridge". A sub-editor at The Times even asked me for a short obituary which I gladly produced, even as I suspected the request was a lazy means of filling his page without any personal effort.

Nothing came back. Why should it? It was like shouting into a vast void, and strain as I might I could hear no echo.

The Church of Our Lady and Saint George was tucked away in a quiet back street protected from the cut and thrust of the world. The limited parking seemed ample enough as the dawn broke and I stood on the tarmac breathing in the warm morning air and contemplating the day ahead. Giving a service to a coffin and one old lady was something I was used to, even if it always seemed so futile. Today, though, it was anything but meaningless. It had all the point any service could possibly hold. Today I would ask God, my God, Freddie's God, to accept him back into His love, and keep him safe forever. Nothing that I had ever done or would ever do could be more important than to help this rare and extraordinary man find his way home.

I was not prepared for what the day would bring. The service was scheduled for 11 o'clock but as much as an hour before, the roads around the small church were becoming snarled up. Shernhall Street was at a standstill, a fact not helped by the increasing number of cars that were simply being abandoned as mourners gave up their quest for a legal parking space. Cars were backing up into the roads around, but it was only when the silt of traffic dropped out of the side streets to foul the main thoroughfare of Lea Bridge Road that the police became anxious.

But there was nothing to be done, and so Walthamstow ground to a halt that Monday morning as it felt the weight of respect heaped upon its forgotten scion. The church could hold two hundred comfortably, but most services echoed around a brave core of a couple of dozen. That day we could have filled the place five times over. It seems strange to me now, in a world surrounded by electronic gadgets of all flavours, but that was the first day that I was struck by the impact of the mobile phone. Many people in the church stood with their phones held aloft to carry my words across the bandwidths to friends who could not squeeze within the walls. I pictured groups of people outside huddling around a phone here or there to listen, and it brought a smile to my face as I recalled how Freddie had described the men in the Cafe Sobieski gathered around the wireless set waiting for news that fateful week five decades earlier.

I was humbled by the outpouring of grief for my friend. The service over, we began the difficult business of getting the cortege moving. The gridlock had been almost total, and now that Freddie was placed in his hearse the jockeying to be at the front of the funeral procession was almost comical. My eulogy had gone by in a blur, and I smiled wistfully as I pondered on why those most precious moments in our life so often evade our memory. Even when we try our hardest to remember every breath, every heartbeat, every word.

The police did what they could to help our progress along Oxford Road to the cemetery. President Kaczorowski was assured a place near the front of the line as two bodyguards used their imposing presence. Like members of a security service that existed only in their own minds, they protected their leader and afforded him the respect his office demanded. But he was not the only dignitary with a personal bodyguard, as the entourages of half a dozen self-made men jostled for their employers' places in the ex-patriate pecking order.

While the crowd watched these antics as they bumped along their uncertain way to Freddie's final resting place, a small group of discreet men in neat Armani suits headed down Maynard Road that had been supposedly closed off by workmen the night before. They were lucky the work had not started, unless of course they had planned the ruse, and their fortune or guile allowed them to beat everyone to the cemetery.

The crowd was of the like I had never seen before as I said the last rites over Freddie's final resting place. I was aware of a slight rustling in the throng to my left as I reached the end of my address and began to throw dirt onto the solid lid of the coffin. Cloaks were thrown back as five men in full Polish Army uniform hoisted rifles that were no doubt illegal, and fired three volleys on the orders of an granite-faced man who commanded the retinue. The few police that had attended in a last minute vain attempt to marshal the crowd immediately recognised the futility of any attempt to apprehend these men and let the military show pass without further incident.

It was only then, as that final act was concluded, that my mind sprang back to the personal. I had played a role, a part on the stage. I had been the priest that conducted the funeral of the Spirit of Phantom Ridge. Now I could set that aside and be myself as I stared at my friend's coffin. It was strange. Distant. It was not Freddie. I could not even picture his body inside that wooden box.

Freddie was not in there. He was in my heart. He was in me. A tear trickled down my face as I tried my hardest to hold the emotions back. I was still on show, and a priest should not be seen to cry at a funeral. I looked up, straight into the reddened and salt soaked eyes of Maggie. She attempted a smile through quivering lips and nodded her approval of my work. I felt torn in half as the man inside wanted nothing more than to cry uncontrollably while the priest demanded discipline.

I stood over the grave for longer than I dare to guess. The

crowd had abated, making their way to the wake in the pub on the High Street that would undoubtedly fail to cope with the unexpected hundreds that would descend. Even Maggie had walked away, leaving me alone over Freddie. Alone in the cemetery, save for the small Armani huddle sheltering in the shade of a tree.

My eyes lost their focus once more as I stared at the grave, seeing only the Freddie I knew from those hours by his bed.

"He was truly remarkable." The soothing, lyrical voice on my right could only be an expression of personal experience. I turned to comfort the old man standing slightly hunched in his perfect suit, but his wise features in profile and radiant complexion bathed me in such peace that no words were needed.

"Karol?" I asked softly, forgetting my place in our shared personal moment.

He turned his head slowly and my pain melted away in the humanity of his tranquil gaze. He nodded and placed his hand on mine. He saw deep into my soul that felt safer under his gaze than I could have ever thought possible. "It takes a great love to see someone for who they really are. That is a gift that few possess. I will be forever in your debt that you were there for him when he most needed you."

I felt a fleeting urge to express modesty, but his calm loving eyes shining brightly with God's grace told me such platitudes were unnecessary. "He saved me."

Karol nodded, seeing all. "He saved many. But in the end it was you who saved him."

I turned to the Holy Father, and with my head bowed cried as I had not cried since I was a child. He placed a hand on my cheek that flowed with the river of my grief. It was only as I cleared my eyes of the tears that distorted my sight that I saw the trickles of his own pain etched on his face.

We needed no words as we stood together in Freddie's love.

THE END